Savage Apocalypse Book Three: The Roar Of The Dead

By Scott Dokey

This book is dedicated to my beautiful daughter, Kaylee, whose smile and laughter brighten my world every day and give me a reason to push forward.

Chapter 1

As Silas floated in the silent void of space, the only sounds were the faint hum of the ship's systems and his own breath echoing in his ears. Below, the mysterious planet loomed like a globe drenched in swirling blue and white, its cloud formations twisting in chaotic dances. It was beautiful, even mesmerizing. Yet, there was also something wrong about it.

For all the wonders this planet might hold, Silas couldn't shake the gnawing question clawing at the back of his mind: *Will they think I'm a monster?* It was a question born from experience. In every corner of the universe, one truth had remained constant—fear. Fear of the unknown, fear of the other. Civilizations didn't need a reason to destroy what they didn't understand. And if this planet's inhabitants saw him, saw any of them, as a threat…

His mind conjured up an array of scenarios too terrible to dwell on.

Jeron's voice broke the silence. "That's a lot of blue down there."

Silas blinked, shaking off the dark thoughts that were threatening to consume him. He'd been so lost in his own head that he barely registered the others. He glanced at Jeron, then back at the planet. "I'd say about seventy-five percent of it is water."

Ridley's reaction was immediate. Her wide eyes darted to the viewport, her breath catching in her throat. Then a full-body shudder rolled through her. She staggered back, one hand pressing against the cold wall of the ship as though the floor had suddenly dropped beneath her.

Her heartbeat hammered in her ears. *Not again. Please, not again.*

The planet stared back at her, an unbroken abyss of water, stretching endlessly beneath the clouds. *So much water!*

Her throat tightened. She couldn't breathe.

She was seven years old again, at the edge of the lake on Terran, her mother laughing as she waded into the shallows. "Come on, Ridley, just a little further!" Her voice was gentle. Safe. Encouraging.

Then the lake bottom gave way to nothingness, and suddenly, she was sinking, her tiny arms flailing, water closing over her head like the jaws of a beast. Cold, suffocating darkness swallowed her, pressing into her nose, her mouth, her lungs.

She thrashed around desperately, but the more she struggled, the deeper she sank.

Her mother's voice became distant, warped by the depths.

This is it, she had thought. *I'm going to die.*

Then, air followed a violent wrenching motion, water spewing from her mouth, her mother's arms pulling her back into the world of the living.

After a long moment of darkness, the memory shattered like glass.

Back in the present, Ridley sucked in a sharp, desperate breath, her vision cloudy and her body trembling.

Aldin grabbed her. "Hey, hey, you're okay," she whispered, holding her close. "You're here. You're safe."

Ridley shook her head, her fingers digging into Aldin's arms. "No. No, we can't go down there. It's everywhere."

Her voice was barely audible and filled with fear.

Aldin stroked her hair, grounding her. "It's just water, Rid. It's just a planet."

Ridley knew that. But logic didn't matter when the fear was wrapped around her like unseen hands, dragging her down into the murky depths of despair, drowning her all over again.

Silas turned from the viewport, concern flickering in his usually unreadable eyes. "Ridley, just breathe. You're giving in to your fears."

She tried. She really tried. But the ocean below wasn't just water. It was the unknown. The depths. The silence. The drowning.

Jeron, oblivious to the tension, was busy at the console. "I'm tying into their comm system," he muttered. "Should be able to pull something—"

A sharp burst of static filled the cabin before a horrific screech blasted through the ship.

The cabin shook as a wave of static crackled through the speakers.

Then the voices began.

At first, it was nothing but distorted whispers. But as Jeron adjusted the frequency, the sound warped.

"Mom?"

Ridley's stomach plummeted.

The voice was her mother's.

"It's so dark—"

The ship's lights flickered.

"They're still burning!" a man shrieked.

Silas's breath caught in his throat. He knew that voice.

Then came the others.

Hundreds. Thousands. Millions

The sounds of dying people, calling from across the abyss, carried on a signal from a world that no longer existed.

"No, no, don't let them in —"

"Oh God, oh God, my son — please —"

"—HELP ME!"

Mishka clawed at her ears, her voice ragged with horror. "That's Hessa!" Her sister's name tore from her throat. "I—I watched her die! I saw her body!"

"Why is it still screaming?"

Jeron's hands froze over the controls.

Because now, the voices weren't just coming from the speakers.

They were inside the ship.

The walls hummed with them. The metal creaked, as if something was pressing against it from the outside.

And then, one voice cut through the storm.

"WHY DID YOU LEAVE US?"

The lights died completely.

In the darkness, the air felt thicker, heavier.

Silas could feel them. The dead. The weight of a billion lost souls, pressing against the hull, pulling at them through the void.

"COME BACK."

Then a deep, wet gurgling sound slithered through the speakers.

A sound that wasn't human.

Jeron slammed the console, ripping the power feed from the comms.

For a long, stretched moment, no one moved as the ship became deathly silent.

Then, the ship's emergency lights flickered back on, faint red glows bathing the cabin.

No one spoke.

No one could.

Everyone was trembling, their bodies rigid with terror.

Silas turned back to the viewport.

The planet below stared back. Its swirling waters deep, endless, waiting.

But that wasn't what scared him.

What scared him was the knowledge that their world had followed them.

Across an entire galaxy, through the impossible void of space, the screams of the dead had chased them down.

And in his mind, they were still screaming.

***

For a long time, silence hung over the group like a death shroud, until Mishka's voice cut through the moment. "What's the plan?"

Ahead of them, the meteors that had shared their journey through the cosmos now drifted lazily in the planet's orbit. Their jagged, blackened shapes seemed almost peaceful, suspended in the void. But then, slowly, they began to shift. The planet's gravity was pulling them in.

Silas exhaled slowly. "We'll monitor the situation. It's not just the meteors I'm worried about." He hesitated, then voiced the fear that had been gnawing at him since they left their world behind. "The organism… it might have survived. And if it gets loose down there…"

Aldin's face went pale. "You think it could survive in space?"

Silas nodded grimly. "It's possible. We don't know enough

to be sure. If one meteor makes it through the atmosphere… we'll need to be ready."

Mishka scoffed, her sharp eyes narrowing. "Why? What do we care? We don't owe them anything."

Silas paused, his heart heavy with the weight of a billion lost souls. "If one of those meteors breaks through, it could trigger a cataclysm. Whatever life is down there, they might not survive."

"So what?" Mishka's voice was cold and distant. "Our world didn't survive. Why should theirs?"

Her words hung in the air, thick and suffocating. She was right. Their entire world was gone, wiped clean by something unimaginable. And here they were, drifting through space like the last remnants of a broken dream. How could they care about anything anymore?

Silas clenched his jaw, feeling the weight of those lost souls relentlessly pressing down on him. His gaze swept over the others, their faces etched with grief and despair. They had all lost everything. Except for Jeron. He was the only one who didn't seem to care, didn't seem touched by the sorrow that draped over each of them like a thick shroud. A heavy silence followed. The possibility of facing another savage apocalypse on a foreign world was suffocating.

Aldin lowered her head, her shoulders trembling. *Not again!* her mind screamed. Not another world lost because of me. She couldn't bear it, couldn't endure the thought of watching it all happen again—the death, the destruction. She had already carried one apocalypse on her shoulders. She wouldn't survive another.

"Let's just hope none of them get through," Ridley said, her voice barely a whisper.

Silas nodded, though he knew hope wasn't enough.

* * *

***

Jeron's eyes glowed in the dim light of the cabin, the eerie blue hue from the screen reflecting off his face. His fingers danced over the controls, but his mind was elsewhere. He glanced around the ship, his head turning just enough to catch the soft rise and fall of the others' chests as they slept. Quiet, rhythmic snores interrupted the stillness, a comforting lullaby for the exhausted. They were oblivious. Trusting.

He smiled. *Good.*

He returning his gaze to the monitor. Outside, the meteors drifted silently against the backdrop of space, dark shadows against the glittering stars, just as they had for hours now. Slowly, steadily, they moved toward the planet below, their erratic course becoming more deliberate as they felt the invisible pull of gravity drawing them closer. Jeron's heart pounded with growing excitement. His pulse quickened, fingers tightening on the edge of the console as if by sheer force of will he could guide the rocks himself.

The ship's system displayed the data in cold, clinical figures, but Jeron's eyes flicked past the numbers, focusing instead on the spectacle unfolding before him. The meteors gathered speed as they neared the planet's atmosphere, like wild animals converging on prey, hungry and relentless.

Then, just as quickly, flames licked at their jagged surfaces, and one by one, they began to burn up. Fiery streaks lit up the thermosphere, each meteor a brilliant burst of light before disintegrating into nothing. Jeron clenched his jaw, a flicker of frustration creeping in as he watched them die off, consumed by the planet's atmosphere.

But not all of them.

His heart skipped a beat when he saw it. One meteor, larger than the rest, blazing through the firestorm and

7

punching through the barrier, undeterred. The air around it screamed as it tore downward, descending faster and faster toward the surface of the world below. For a brief moment, Jeron's breath caught in his throat. Then, a smile tugged at the corner of his lips—a cold, predatory smile.

It had made it. *Yes!*

His gaze narrowed as the meteor streaked toward its destination, vanishing beyond the horizon and out of view. He didn't need to see it hit. He felt it—deep in his gut—a tremor that reverberated through the quiet of space, through him.

A few seconds later, a dull thud registered on the monitor from the impact. The screen flashed as the planet reacted to the sudden intrusion. Jeron's smile grew wider, more sinister.

"It has begun, Uncle," he whispered under his breath.

He leaned back in his chair, eyes lingering on the now-empty void beyond the ship's viewport, the meteors gone, their purpose fulfilled. The others wouldn't know, not yet. They had no idea what had just been unleashed below, what his actual mission was. They thought they were survivors, trying to find a new home, clinging to hope after the destruction of their own world. But Jeron knew better.

He had other plans.

The words of his uncle echoed in his mind, *"You know what to do, Jeron. It's on your shoulders now."*

He turned back to the sleeping crew. Silas, Ridley, Mishka, Aldin—they had no clue. They thought they were all in this together. How wrong they were.

Jeron chuckled softly. He had waited for this moment, the anticipation gnawing at him since they'd first launched. And now, as the pieces fell into place, that gnawing hunger transformed into something darker, something far more dangerous.

He leaned closer to the monitor, zooming in on the surface of the planet below. The meteor had landed in a remote area, but he knew it wouldn't stay contained for long. Soon, the organism—the one they thought they had left behind—would spread. Relentless. Insatiable.

The crew wouldn't suspect his true purpose, not until it was too late. And by then, the world below would be nothing but a husk.

Chapter 2

As time passed, Silas shifted in his seat, causing Jeron's heart to skip a beat. Without missing a second, he slumped his head to the side and let his eyes flutter shut, feigning the deep, undisturbed sleep of someone lost in exhaustion. He had perfected this act over years of playing both sides, a talent that had always served him well.

Silas's voice broke the silence a moment later. "Anything happen while I was asleep?"

Jeron held his breath, keeping his eyes closed to sell the act to perfection. He didn't stir until he felt Silas vigorously shaking his arm.

Jeron cracked his eyes open with a slow, practiced grogginess. He stretched, exaggerating the motion, his arms wide and yawning, putting on a show as though waking from a restful slumber. "What's going on?" he asked, trying to sound dazed.

"You fell asleep," Silas stated flatly.

"I'm sorry," Jeron replied, feigning embarrassment. "I guess I was exhausted."

The disappointment was evident in Silas's voice, "You should've woken me up. Now we have a big problem."

Jeron kept his face neutral, forcing a mask of mild confusion. "Why? What happened?"

Silas's eyes narrowed as he gestured toward the screen. "The meteor cluster is gone."

A spark of satisfaction flickered deep within Jeron, but he kept his face carefully composed. He leaned closer, peering at the monitor. "Are you sure? They were on the radar earlier. Maybe they pulled away from the planet's orbit and floated on?"

Silas shook his head. "Highly unlikely. It's more probable that they fell from their orbit and descended toward the surface."

Jeron forced himself to swallow the smile threatening to creep up. "Let's hope none of them made it through, then."

Without responding, Silas began typing commands into the instrument panel as Jeron watched him out of the corner of his eye, trying to maintain his nonchalance. Silas muttered to himself, "Maybe I can rewind the radar and satellite feeds enough to see what happened."

A tense minute passed as Silas's commands locked onto the trajectory of the meteors. One by one, the meteors blinked on the screen, their paths traced as they approached the atmosphere. Jeron's heart pounded in his chest, but he kept still, watching eagerly as he relived the event he had witnessed earlier with sinister satisfaction.

Each one vanished, consumed by the atmosphere's wrath, until there was one. The last meteor, undeterred, streaked through the planet's protective shield and plunged toward the surface below.

Silas leaned back in his seat, with a frown covering his face and concern filling his eyes.

"Well, that's not good," Jeron said, barely able to disguise his genuine excitement.

Footsteps approached from behind, and Jeron didn't need to turn to know who it was. "What's not good?" Mishka asked.

Jeron flicked his eyes toward her, maintaining his outward calm. "One of the meteors crashed into the planet."

Mishka's brows furrowed. "So?"

"So," Silas said in a low voice, "now we have to go down there and find out what the damage was."

A moment later, the others gathered around the console. Aldin's voice then broke the tension. "You mean, to see if the organism was present?"

"Yes," Silas replied flatly.

"I don't like the idea of going down there," Ridley said nervously. "Can't we just try to find another suitable planet to live on? This doesn't feel right."

Silas's voice hardened. "My earlier analysis indicated there aren't any other such worlds in this galaxy. Plus, if we start skipping from galaxy to galaxy, we'll eventually run out of fuel. Unfortunately, we don't have the luxury of options right now, Ridley."

As the weight of the situation pressed down on them, the ship's console emitted a soft beep. A satellite image of the planet's surface flickered onto the screen, displaying the meteor's impact site. A jagged, smoking crater marred the lush landscape below, steam rising from the smoldering earth.

"What's that?" Mishka asked, her eyes widening as she took in the image.

"It's the location where the meteor crashed," Silas said grimly. "Unfortunately, it's on the other side of the planet."

"How long will it take to get there?" Aldin asked, her voice hushed.

"Not long," Silas replied. "But we'll need to find a

secluded place near the crash site to land the ship undetected. This isn't going to be a simple scouting mission."

Jeron leaned in, tapping a few keys on the console. "I can help with that. I'll run an algorithm that generates an energy field around the ship that will cloak us from their systems. It'll keep us hidden from whatever's down there."

Silas glanced at him with a hint of surprise in his eyes. "You've certainly picked up a few tricks since I saw you last."

Jeron shrugged, his smile just a little too forced. "I've always been interested in quantum mechanics and nano-science. Just never had the motivation to pursue it further until recently."

"When did the meteor crash?" Aldin asked nervously.

"A little over a cycle ago," Silas replied. "We'll need to move quickly to assess the situation, figure out if the organism survived entry, and if it did, how much damage it's capable of doing."

An eerie silence fell over the group. The organism, the thing that had wiped out their home, was now possibly on another world, wreaking the same devastation that had led to their planet's destruction.

Silas watched the image of the smoking crater intently. "You three," he finally said, addressing Aldin, Ridley, and Mishka, "go check out the storage containers and see what kind of gear we have available. We need to be prepared for anything."

Jeron leaned back in his chair, watching them shuffle out of the cockpit. His mind, however, was already far away—focused on the surface below. His heart raced as a sinister smile crept up his lips, hidden from view.

If the organism had indeed survived the cruelty of space, there would be no stopping it now.

* * *

***

As the women sifted through the cargo hold, their hands running over the cold metal of containers stacked tightly against one another, Ridley's mind was elsewhere. She was silent for a moment longer, but a gnawing suspicion was clawing at her insides, a feeling she couldn't shake. Her eyes darted to Mishka, then to Aldin, before she finally whispered, "I don't trust Jeron."

Mishka paused mid-search, her fingers grazing over the sleek surface of a medical kit, and looked up. "What do you mean?" she asked curiously.

Ridley's lips pursed into a thin line. "You didn't see him back on Terran, before we escaped from the lab. He was… off. Creepy, even. And the way he smirks when he mentions his uncle…" Her voice dropped lower. "It tells me he's hiding something. I think his uncle was Jensen."

The name hit Aldin like a gut punch. Her breath caught in her throat, her lips trembling. Jensen—the man who had ruined everything, whose shadow still hung over them like a curse even after his death.

"That's a stretch," Mishka replied, though her voice was laced with uncertainty. "His uncle could've been anyone."

Ridley's eyes hardened. "Think about it," she pressed. "It makes perfect sense. Jensen was a control freak. He would've had someone on the inside at the ancillary lab, someone to keep him informed of any developments, someone to warn him of threats to his work. Jeron was there, wasn't he? And now, he's here, right when we're at our most vulnerable."

Aldin closed her eyes, trying to steady her nerves. The idea sent chills down her spine, but she wasn't ready to accept it. "Okay, say Jensen was his uncle," she said in a shaky voice. "What do we do?"

Ridley's hand slid to the grip of her blaster, her fingers tightening around it. "For now, we keep a close eye on him," she said, her voice cold and resolute. "And if he does anything radical… I'll take care of him."

Mishka snorted, rolling her eyes. "That's a little dramatic, don't you think?"

"Jensen fooled us before," Ridley hissed. "I'm not going to let his crazy nephew fool us, too. Not again."

Mishka shook her head, a smirk tugging at her lips. "You're being paranoid." But there was a flicker of doubt in her eyes, a shadow of unease that hadn't been there before.

She moved to the next container, prying it open with a groan of metal. Her breath caught as her eyes widened in delight. She reached inside and slowly pulled out a sleek, black blaster rifle, cradling it like a lover long lost to the void. Her fingers traced its contours, her smile stretching wide, full of a dark satisfaction.

"Now that's more like it," she said excitedly.

Aldin and Ridley exchanged a glance as they watched Mishka's strange reverence for the weapon. Mishka laid the rifle gently at her feet before diving back into the container, pulling out more gear, her excitement growing with every item.

Ridley crouched beside her and helped dig through the contents. In no time, they had a small cache of weapons laid out before them—blaster rifles, tactical gear, and sleek, dark uniforms that looked too ominous to be standard issue.

Aldin glanced nervously at the door. "We should hurry."

Before they could check the last few containers, Silas's voice rang through the ship's intercom. "We're above the descension point. It might get a little rocky for a few seconds before we hit the lower atmosphere, then it'll smooth out."

Ridley and Mishka exchanged tense glances. There was no

such thing as a *smooth* descent—only varying degrees of controlled chaos.

The ship groaned, its metallic frame shuddering as it plunged downward. A deep vibration coursed through the walls, growing from a low hum into a violent tremor. The lights flickered erratically, casting disjointed shadows that danced across the cabin. The sensation was like being swallowed whole by a violent storm, helpless against its raging forces.

Ridley's grip tightened on the edge of a crate, her knuckles turning bone-white. "I hate this," she muttered under her breath, but no one was listening.

Then the ship lurched, a sudden, stomach-dropping motion that sent Mishka stumbling forward, slamming into the side of a console.

A deafening boom reverberated through the hull, and suddenly, everything tilted.

The ship was spinning.

Alarms blared, shrill and frantic. A deep metallic screech echoed through the cabin as the hull fought against forces threatening to tear it apart. Ridley barely had time to brace herself before another violent jolt ripped the floor out from under her, sending her sprawling. Mishka crashed down beside her, gasping as a cargo container broke free, smashing into the wall in front of them with a force that dented the metal.

The instruments blinked wildly, systems failing one by one as the ship's engines sputtered and howled. The floor beneath them vibrated in unnatural pulses, as if something within the ship had come loose.

Ridley's stomach clenched. They had hit something.

"I think we clipped something in the atmosphere!" Mishka shouted over the chaos, gripping onto a nearby railing. Her dark eyes darted toward the cockpit. "That or—"

She didn't finish.

Because Ridley was already thinking it.

What if this wasn't turbulence?

A sickening realization settled deep in her gut. Jeron was up front with Silas—the same Jeron who had already proven he couldn't be trusted. Had he done something?

The ship pitched sideways, sending loose equipment hurtling through the air. A med-kit clipped Mishka in the shoulder, knocking her sideways. Sparks rained down from an exposed panel as the ship twisted violently, gravity shifting unpredictably.

Ridley gritted her teeth. If Jeron had sabotaged them, there was no telling what else he had planned.

She tried to push herself up, but the moment she did, another violent tremor rocked the ship. Her vision blurred as she was thrown sideways, barely catching hold of a railing before she could be flung across the hold.

Then there was a deep, sickening *crack!* The ship lurched so hard that for a split second, gravity seemed to vanish entirely. The artificial stabilizers were failing.

Aldin's voice was filled with panic. "We're losing altitude too fast! If Silas doesn't..."

Another *impact.*

Another scream of metal as something massive tore through the underbelly of the ship.

Ridley's breath caught in her throat. *This is it,* she thought somberly. *After everything we've gone through, this is the last moment of our lives.*

This was the moment they either regained control or died burning through the atmosphere.

Chapter 3

The city was burning.

Rodrigo's boots pounded against the pavement as he sprinted down East Palm Canyon Drive, weaving through the chaos. Cathedral City had turned into a war zone—screaming people, overturned cars, glass exploding from storefronts as looters smashed their way inside. The air stank of burning rubber, gunpowder, and something else—something foul and rotten, like roadkill baking under the desert sun.

They hadn't planned for this.

The night had started like any other—racing through the streets, taunting cops, looking for easy scores. But once the screaming started, the gunfire followed. Then the monsters came.

Rodrigo dove behind a wrecked sedan, barely dodging a pickup truck speeding in reverse, its tires screeching as the driver panicked. Through the smoke and flashing lights, he saw what the man was running from.

Dogs! At least a dozen of them, but they weren't normal. Their fur hung in rotten patches, their eyes burned red with something unnatural, and their jaws were stretched too wide, gaping like broken bear traps, lips torn back to expose rows of jagged, yellowed teeth.

One leaped onto the pickup's hood, claws scraping deep into the metal. The driver screamed as another beast lunged through the open window, and the truck veered off, slamming into a fire hydrant. A geyser of water erupted into the night as the man's screams turned into choking gurgles.

Rodrigo swallowed hard. "We gotta move. Now!"

"Rodri, move your ass, homie!" Hector shouted from behind, firing wildly into the street.

A black-feathered blur screeched overhead. Rodrigo ducked as a massive raven slammed into the car beside him, its talons ripping deep into the frame. It let out a guttural, unnatural caw, wings flapping as if trying to shake off the rot eating through its body.

"Fuck this," Rodrigo spat, raising his shotgun. He fired once, the blast tearing through the bird's torso. The raven reeled back, but it didn't drop. It didn't die.

It kept coming.

Lobo staggered past, clutching a wound on his arm. "Rodri, we gotta get the fuck outta here, man!"

Rodrigo turned toward the alley where their ride was parked, but the street had turned into pure hell. Packs of infected coyotes and feral cats tore into the crowds. A group of rioters—looters, mostly—tried to fight back, but the animals didn't stop. A coyote, half of its face missing, clamped onto a man's leg, dragging him to the pavement. He screamed as the rest of the pack pounced, ripping into him like raw meat.

Hector fired another round into the horde, but the undead animals barely reacted.

"Get to the garage!" Rodrigo barked, shoving Lobo forward.

They sprinted toward the parking structure up ahead. More people were running now—cops, civilians, gangbangers—all scrambling for safety.

But then, the birds came.

Hundreds of them descended from the sky like a black storm, shrieking as they dove at anything that moved. Rodrigo saw one man go down, his face vanishing under a mass of pecking, ripping beaks. His muffled screams curdled into a wet gurgle.

"Go!" Hector shouted.

They barreled up the parking ramp, shoving past a group of terrified teenagers. The second floor was mostly empty—except for the wrecked police cruiser near the far end.

Then Rodrigo saw them.

A pack of undead German Shepherds slinking between the parked cars, eyes glowing like embers.

Police dogs.

"Shit," Lobo breathed.

One of the Shepherds tilted its head, like it was listening. Then, all at once, the pack charged.

Rodrigo fired, the shotgun blast tearing into the closest one's chest. It should've died. Instead, the dog stumbled, then snarled—jaws unhinging too wide—before lunging again.

"Second floor! Move!" Rodrigo roared, sprinting toward the stairwell.

Lobo and Hector scrambled after him, but the pack was too fast. One of the dogs lunged at Lobo, its jaws snapping around his arm. He screamed, slamming it into a wall, but it wouldn't let go.

Rodrigo aimed and quickly pulled the trigger. The Shepherd's head snapped back. The thing slumped, finally still.

Lobo gasped for air, staring at the deep, oozing bite

wound.

"Fuck, man," he muttered. "I don't… I don't feel right."

Rodrigo yanked him up, ignoring the burning dread clawing at his gut. "Come on."

They burst onto the second level just as the Shepherds howled behind them.

Rodrigo turned, his eyes full of desperation as he raised his shotgun.

Chapter 4

The streets of Cathedral City were drowning in blood.

Rodrigo's tires screeched as he swerved through the chaos, barely missing an overturned vehicle. His pulse pounded in his ears, almost louder than the gunfire erupting all around them. Hector leaned halfway out of the passenger window, unloading rounds at the creatures swarming the streets— dogs with rotting flesh hanging off their bones, birds diving like kamikaze pilots, twisted things that were virtually unrecognizable for what they once were—lurching forward with hunger in their dead, glossy eyes.

From the back seat, Lobo groaned, pressing a blood-soaked rag against his leg. "Rodri, we gotta find cover, man! I ain't dyin' in this goddamn car!" Rodrigo's knuckles went white on the wheel. "We keep moving until we find somewhere secure!"

Ahead, an explosion rocked the pavement as something crashed through the window of a gas station. Flames shot up, illuminating the nightmare unfolding around them.

Rodrigo clenched his teeth and spotted a parking structure up ahead. "There!" he shouted, yanking the wheel hard. The car fishtailed, tires screeching as they barreled through the entrance. The metal gate crunched under the impact, and Rodrigo slammed the brakes, bringing them to a skidding halt inside the dimly lit garage.

"Out, out, out!" Hector was already dragging Lobo from the backseat, his gun still raised.

"They're right behind us!" Rodrigo grabbed his shotgun and sprinted for the nearest stairwell, but then a sound ripped through the night.

It was a screech, high-pitched and unnatural, vibrating in Rodrigo's chest like a tuning fork against his ribs. Every single infected thing in the area stopped, their heads twitching as if caught in some invisible force. The birds dropped from the sky mid-flight, their bodies hitting the pavement like sacks of meat. The dogs whimpered, convulsing before going completely still. The unrecognizable things spasmed violently, limbs jerking in broken, unnatural movements—then collapsed.

For several agonizing seconds, nothing moved. Then, silence. Rodrigo barely realized he was holding his breath.

Hector broke the silence first. "What the hell…?" His voice was barely above a whisper.

Lobo, still leaning against the car, stared at the corpses. "Did we win? Is it over?"

Rodrigo's heart was still hammering. He didn't trust this. Didn't trust that things just stopped like that. He took a few cautious steps forward, nudging one of the fallen creatures with the tip of his boot. It didn't move.

For the first time in hours, the night was still. The city, once alive with screams and gunfire, had gone completely silent.

Rodrigo looked up toward the sky. Smoke still curled from burning buildings. The bodies littering the streets weren't getting up anymore. It was over. And yet, as he looked at his crew, battered and bloodied, something in his gut told him they weren't safe. Not really.

Hector shifted, checking his ammo. "So… what now?"

Rodrigo was silent for a long moment. They had lost so many of their own tonight. Those things had torn through their people like they were nothing. And no one was coming to save them. The city was theirs to rot in.

Lobo spat onto the pavement. "We stick together."

Rodrigo looked at him. Lobo met his stare, unwavering. "Ain't nobody left to watch our backs. No gangs, no cops, no government. Just us. And you know what? I ain't dyin' like the rest of them. We play this smart, we make it through whatever's next."

Hector scoffed. "And what the hell's next, huh?"

Rodrigo didn't have an answer. But as they stood there, surrounded by the twisted bodies of dead things, he knew one thing for sure—this world had changed. And if they wanted to survive it, they would have to change too. He took a deep breath and slung his shotgun over his shoulder. "We get off the streets. We find somewhere secure. And we don't trust anyone but each other."

The others nodded, knowing they were all that was left.

***

The scent of burned rubber and gunpowder lingered in the air, thick as the smoke curling from the wreckage around them. Luis's BMW sat wedged between an overturned delivery truck and a burned-out sedan, its once-polished black exterior now streaked with blood and dust.

It had started as a little bit of simple fun, trying to outrun the Marines, make them eat dust as they tore through the streets in their sleek ride. But then the world turned inside out, and now they weren't racing soldiers anymore. They were running for their lives.

The city had gone to hell.

Luis wiped a hand down his face, smearing dirt and sweat across his cheek. His pulse still thundered from the chase—first against the Marines, then against something worse. The creatures had come out of nowhere, tearing through the streets like rabid animals from a nightmare. And now… now they were just gone.

Benny sat slumped in the backseat, his shirt torn, a gash running along his arm. "What the fuck *was* that?" His voice trembled, his usual cocky edge stripped away.

Rico stood a few feet away, staring at the road like he was expecting something to crawl out of the darkness. "They just dropped, man. Like someone hit a switch."

Luis exhaled sharply, gripping the top of the car door to steady himself. His knuckles were raw, scraped from the frantic nightmare they'd barely survived. He had seen things tonight that didn't belong in the world—things with twisted, mangled bodies that shouldn't have been able to move, let alone hunt.

And then… silence.

Chuy let out a ragged laugh, tipping what remained of the tequila bottle into his mouth. His gold teeth flashed in the dim streetlight. "Guess that means we won, huh?" He wiped his mouth and spat. "Told y'all we were untouchable."

Benny shot him a look. "Won? Are you fuckin' serious? We lost half our boys tonight. Tavo, Malo, Spider—" He shook his head, his voice cracking. "We were supposed to be out messin' with the cops, racing through Cathedral, not… this."

Luis clenched his jaw. He hadn't processed it yet—the fact that half their crew was dead. Torn apart, screaming, their bodies ripped open like old trash bags. And the worst part? He couldn't even remember running. It was just chaos. A blur of blood and fire.

And then the sound.

That screech. That unnatural, piercing thing that had split the night wide open.

It wasn't human.

Rico was the first to speak the thought they were all avoiding. "This ain't over."

The words sent a chill through Luis's spine. He looked at the others—Benny clutching his wounded arm, Chuy trying to laugh off the fear, Rico standing stiff, every muscle locked like he was waiting for something to come back.

And maybe it would.

"Alright," Luis said finally, his voice low, steady. "No one's coming to save us. Cops are dead, Marines gone. We're on our own." He kicked at a severed hand near the curb, the fingers curled like they had died trying to grasp something. He didn't flinch.

Benny let out a bitter chuckle. "Yeah? And what the hell do we do now, Luis? Hide? Pray?"

Luis shook his head. "Nah. We own this city now."

Rico turned to him, eyes narrowing. "You think we can just go back to business after what happened?"

Luis leaned against the BMW, crossing his arms. "I think we got two choices, homie. We either end up like the ones that didn't make it tonight, or we make sure that never happens to us again." He looked at each of them, letting the weight of his words settle. "We stick together. No more dumb shit, no more petty beefs. We're in this for survival now."

Benny ran a hand over his shaved head, exhaling through his nose. Chuy, for once, didn't have a joke.

Rico was the last to speak, his voice quieter than usual. "Yeah. We survive."

For now, the streets were quiet. But Luis knew better than

to believe it would stay that way.

And when the next nightmare came knocking, they'd be ready.

Chapter 5

The parking garage was a tomb of echoes. The stench of gasoline, blood, and sweat clung to the air, thick as the smoke curling from the wreckage outside. Rodrigo and his crew pushed deeper into the structure, weapons drawn, their movements sharp, tense. Outside, the city was still smoldering, but the silence that followed the apocalypse was worse than the chaos before it.

Rodrigo motioned for them to slow down, keeping his shotgun raised. "Stay sharp. I don't trust this quiet."

"Shit, man," Hector muttered, glancing over his shoulder. "Feels like we just walked into our own grave."

From the far end of the parking structure, footsteps scraped against concrete.

Rodrigo's stomach twisted. They weren't alone.

A shadow moved between the dimly lit cars, then another. The unmistakable silhouette of figures armed and dangerous.

"Yo, you see that?" Lobo whispered, his grip tightening on his pistol.

Rodrigo held up a hand, signaling them to hold their ground. "Whoever the fuck's out there, you better step out real slow."

A chuckle echoed through the structure, low and taunting. Then, from behind a dented BMW, Luis and his crew emerged.

Rodrigo's jaw clenched. Luis.

Luis smirked, resting a bat on his shoulder. Chuy stood beside him, still clutching the near-empty bottle of tequila, while Benny and Rico flanked them, guns ready.

"Well, well," Luis spat. "Ain't this a bitch? Thought all you motherfuckers got wiped out."

Rodrigo sneered. "Wish I could say the same about you."

Hector took a step forward, gun half-raised. "We got bigger problems than old beef, man."

Luis laughed, shaking his head. "Nah, see, that's where you're wrong. Doesn't matter if the world's ending—some things don't change. And where I'm standing? You're still the same little punks that thought they could run shit."

Rodrigo's grip on his shotgun tightened. The tension crackled like static in the air.

"You wanna do this now?" Rodrigo hissed. "Right here, surrounded by all this death?" He gestured at the city beyond the open garage entrance, at the bodies littering the streets, the ruins of their former lives. "That shit out there don't scare you?"

Luis's smirk faltered for a second, but he covered it up with a shrug. "It ain't about fear, homie. It's about respect. And I don't see no reason why I should let you walk outta here alive."

Chuy chuckled darkly. "You should've stayed dead with the rest of your crew."

Rodrigo's eyes burned with rage. "Say that again, motherfucker!"

Chuy barely had time to blink before Rodrigo's fist connected with his jaw. The tequila bottle shattered against the pavement as Chuy staggered back, spitting blood and laughter.

Then everything exploded.

Hector tackled Benny, their bodies slamming into the hood of a wrecked sedan. Lobo and Rico swung at each other, fists flying, grunts and curses filling the air. Luis barely had time to react before Rodrigo drove a knee into his ribs, sending him stumbling back.

"You dumb motherfucker!" Luis roared, swinging his bat. Rodrigo ducked, but the wood grazed his shoulder, sending a sharp jolt of pain down his arm.

Gunfire erupted—wild, reckless shots aimed at the ceiling as one of them lost control of their trigger finger. The sound reverberated through the structure, deafening, chaotic.

Rodrigo grabbed Luis by the collar and slammed him into a support pillar. "I should kill you right now," he growled through gritted teeth.

Luis coughed, grinning through bloody teeth. "Then do it."

Rodrigo's grip tightened—

And then the ground moved. It was a deep, violent shake, like the city itself was trying to shake them off its back.

The parking garage groaned, concrete shifting as the tremor intensified.

"Earthquake!" Hector shouted, scrambling off Benny.

A second later, a deafening CRACK split the air as part of the ceiling caved in near the entrance, sending dust and debris raining down. A parked SUV tumbled onto its side, its alarm wailing pathetically before dying out.

Rodrigo and Luis staggered apart, both instinctively looking up, watching as another chunk of concrete broke loose and crashed to the floor.

"Shit—outside, now!" Luis barked.

Forgetting their fight, both groups bolted.

They sprinted through the trembling structure, dodging falling debris, their boots pounding against cracked concrete. By the time they reached the open street, the worst of the quake had passed, but the damage was done. Behind them, the garage groaned one last time before settling into eerie silence.

For several moments, no one spoke.

They just stood there, panting, bruised, and bloodied, but alive.

Rodrigo wiped sweat from his brow, looking at Luis. "That's twice tonight something tried to kill us."

Luis, still breathing hard, let out a short laugh. "Guess we got unfinished business with Death."

Hector exhaled sharply. "Look, we can beat the shit outta each other all night, or we can get smart."

Luis wiped blood from his mouth, considering it. "And what's smart?"

Rodrigo sighed. "We stick together. For now."

Luis smirked, shaking his head. "Ain't that some shit?"

Rodrigo extended a hand.

After a brief hesitation, Luis took it.

Their grip was tight. Not in friendship. Not in trust.

But in survival.

Chapter 6

The force from the crash hurled the three women across the metal floor, their bodies colliding with the walls of the ship as if they were playthings caught in a storm. Aldin barely had time to brace before she slammed into a storage crate, her breath ripped from her lungs. Mishka hit the wall hard, a sharp crack echoing through the cabin as her shoulder connected with unforgiving metal. Ridley rolled across the floor, her head narrowly missing the edge of a console.

Alarms blared, flashing red strobes slicing through the suffocating dimness. The ship's frame groaned, metal twisting and buckling as if being torn apart by unseen hands. Sparks rained from an overhead panel, the acrid scent of burning wires filling the cabin.

Silas fought against the ship's controls, his knuckles white, jaw clenched. *"Come on, come on—"*

Outside, the viewport was a blur of fire and speed. The planet's atmosphere ripped against the hull, the friction igniting a sheath of plasma around them. Violent turbulence rocked the ship, sending it into a stomach-churning spin.

"We're losing altitude too fast!" Jeron shouted from the cockpit, his voice edged with something between fear and exhilaration.

"No kidding!" Silas barked. His hands flew over the controls, struggling to stabilize the vessel, but the thrusters were unresponsive.

Then, the real terror began.

A loud bang echoed through the ship, followed by a jarring lurch as something ripped away from the hull. A sickening drop hit them next, as though gravity itself had momentarily let go before snapping back with brutal force.

"We lost part of the landing apparatus!" Jeron shouted, scanning the readouts.

Ridley struggled to pull herself up, her vision swimming. "Can we still land this thing?"

Silas gritted his teeth, wrestling against the violent pull of gravity. "Landing isn't the problem—surviving the landing is."

The ship spiraled lower, plummeting toward the surface at breakneck speed. Through the fractured viewport, jagged mountain peaks rose up like a wall of spears. If they hit those…

Silas forced the thrusters into emergency override, his muscles burning with the effort. The ship responded sluggishly, its damaged systems groaning in protest, but the spin slowed.

"Brace for impact!"

The first hit sent a shudder through the ship as they clipped a rock formation, shearing off another chunk of the hull. A deafening screech of metal against stone filled the cabin, and for a moment, Aldin was convinced the ship was about to tear in half.

Then—impact.

The ship slammed into the rocky terrain, bouncing once, twice—each collision rattling their bones. A side panel ruptured, venting steam and debris into the cabin. A shower of sparks rained down as a console exploded. Mishka barely managed to roll out of the way before a loose crate smashed into the spot where she had been.

They weren't stopping.

The ship skidded, carving a deep scar into the earth as it barreled forward, shedding pieces of itself along the way. The screech of metal on stone was near-deafening, shaking the very air around them.

A final, violent jolt threw them forward.

Silas pulled back on the failing controls with every ounce of strength he had left. The nose of the ship tipped up just enough to avoid an outright catastrophe as they plowed into a mountainside ravine.

For a moment, everything was eerily quiet, save for the distant hiss of steam and the crackling of fires smoldering inside the ship.

Silas slumped forward, chest rising and falling, his hands still gripping the controls in a death lock.

Aldin coughed, groaning as she pushed herself up, her entire body screaming in protest. A sharp pain stabbed through her ribs, but she was alive.

Mishka groaned from nearby, cradling her shoulder. "That… sucked."

Ridley let out a sharp breath, trying to steady her shaking hands. "Tell me we're not dead."

Jeron, who had managed to stay in his seat, gave a low chuckle. "If we were, I'd expect the afterlife to be less on fire."

Silas exhaled, finally releasing the controls. He surveyed the flickering monitors, eyes scanning for any sign of movement outside.

They had landed.

Barely.

The ship, now a battered wreck, was nestled at the base of the mountain range, hidden in the shadows of towering cliffs. The terrain outside was jagged and uneven, scattered with debris from their violent descent.

Jeron rushed to check the spectrum inhibitor, his fingers flying over the controls. Relief washed over his face as the device blinked, indicating that it was still functional. Their location remained cloaked for now. "What the hell was that, Silas?" he groaned.

Silas shook his head. "No clue. Nothing showed up on the scanner. But we hit something that was most likely too small to register."

"It felt like multiple something's," Mishka stated flatly.

Silas ignored her and turned to Jeron, "Get the communication system back up and see what you can find out. Focus on local frequencies in lower bandwidths. See if you can pick up anything about an alien presence. And if you do, hopefully, it's not about us."

"What are you going to do?" Jeron asked as he watched Silas get up from his seat.

"I need a drink," he replied.

Silas immediately went to the row of lockers and began to open them, one by one, as if he were searching for something specific. They were each filled with personal items, apparently the property of those lost souls who were originally scheduled to depart on this ship. Finally, the fourth locker revealed what he had been looking so earnestly for: a bottle of Kandrake venom.

He closed his eyes and said a silent prayer for all those that had been recently lost before downing a shot. Immediately, he felt the fire circling through his veins, hoping it would take the pain and heartache away. Although it helped to ease the tension, he knew nothing would ever erase the loss from his mind. He sighed and took another shot before placing the bottle in the pocket of his robe.

"Hey guys, I found something," Jeron suddenly called out.

The rest of the group shuffled to the front of the cabin and watched tensely as a video feed materialized onto the screen. "This time I was able to hack in without any of that creepy stuff we heard earlier," he said.

A few tense minutes passed before the cabin was filled with the crackle of static. Then, slowly, voices began filtering in—strange and fragmented. Jeron worked quickly, shifting through frequencies until a video feed flickered to life on the main screen. They all watched in stunned silence.

"They look… like us," Jeron said, his voice barely containing his surprise. He glanced at Silas and smirked. "Well, maybe not you, big guy."

On the screen, uniformed men poured out of a large transport vehicle marked with the letters S.W.A.T. They were dressed for battle, guns drawn, advancing on a crumbling structure. Moments later, gunfire exploded across the screen. Bodies fell, blood spraying in thick red arcs.

Silas's stomach churned.

Jeron quickly switched the feed, pulling up another scene —a competition of some kind. The combatants were once again clad in armor, engaging in brutal hand-to-hand combat over some strangely shaped object. The violence was measurable.

One more time, Jeron changed the frequency. This time, the feed showed two people sitting behind a desk, calmly relaying the world's news. But even then, the images that followed were more of the same—war, conflict, destruction.

"So much violence," Aldin murmured. "How are we supposed to survive in a world like this?"

"By sticking together," Silas replied, though even he could

hear the uncertainty in his own voice. "And praying that what we see isn't an accurate reflection of their world."

The video suddenly changed to a broadcast concerning recent events, with the letters, KESQ in large letters at the bottom. A woman dressed in business attire was addressing her invisible audience through an audio device she held in her hand: "Authorities have confirmed that the violent animal threat is now over, though experts remain unsure about the cause of the virus that ravaged the Valley's wildlife. In total, nearly three hundred and fifty people have been confirmed dead, including Captain Gerald Henderson of the La Quinta Police Department, along with a significant number of his officers. Our thoughts and prayers go out to the victims' families."

The feed switched to another topic and Jeron promptly switched it off, leaving everyone speechless.

Finally, Mishka said, "Well, I guess that answers the question about whether the organism found its way here."

"I'm surprised they could stop it," Jeron said, "given how primitive their society seems."

"Maybe that's exactly why they could beat it?" Silas offered. "For all our advances in science and technology, the organism itself was raw and savage, and it took something just like it to defeat it."

"And we're supposed to live here?" Aldin said.

"It might not be all that bad?" Ridley said with little conviction in her voice.

"I still want to check out the crash site just to make sure the threat is indeed over," Silas said.

"How far is it from here?" Mishka asked.

"Our incident a few minutes ago—"

"You mean our near-death experience?" Ridley interjected.

Silas raised an eyebrow and continued, "However you'd

like to call it, the episode took us away from the site a little bit."

"Just how far?" Aldin asked.

"Not a lot, but we'll need to be extra cautious to avoid unnecessary interaction with local inhabitants. We should also wait until it's dark, just in case."

"Well, I'm excited!" Mishka said sarcastically. "Who else is excited?"

She looked around at each one, failing to get the response she had hoped for. Then she noticed that someone was missing. "Um, where's Jeron?"

Before anyone could respond, Jeron snuck up behind them, emerging from the rear of the ship with a big smile on his face, "Hey, guys! Come see what I found."

"What are you wearing?" Mishka asked with a cold stare after she recovered from being startled.

Jeron twirled around in front of the group, showing off a long, black robe similar to the one Silas wore. "I found this in one of the lockers in the back." He walked over and stood next to Silas, "We're practically twins now, big guy. What do you think?"

Silas eyed Jeron and merely grunted.

Mishka snickered, "You are nothing like Silas."

Jeron scowled at her for a second before saying, "Anyway, this isn't what I wanted to show you. Come on. I think you'll be pleased."

As the group followed him toward the back, Ridley grabbed Aldin's hand and squeezed it gently once more, nodding toward the quick flash of a blaster rifle that peeked out from inside Jeron's robe when he turned to walk toward the rear of the ship.

Ridley made a mental note of the weapons cache that was now scattered all over the floor of the ship. *I wonder what else he has hidden up his sleeve?*

Jeron brought them to the very back of the ship directly in line with the rear compartment hatch, and pressed a button on the side of the large storage container there that spanned nearly the whole width of the ship. He proudly held his arms out wide as the walls of the container disappeared into the floor to reveal a trio of gyro-cycles flanking a small personal transport.

Ridley squealed as she rushed over to the nearest cycle, while Silas approached the transport like it was a long-lost friend he was reuniting with after a lifetime apart.

"These should help get us where we need to go," Jeron said with a smile.

"But won't they be noticeable if someone spots us?" Aldin asked.

"I can attach a spectrum modifier to each one and link it to a personal transceiver," he suggested. "That'll effectively make us invisible to those outside the immediate area while allowing us to maintain communication between each other."

"Before we can go anywhere, we need to make sure the air outside is safe for us to breathe," Aldin said.

Silas replied, "I ran atmospheric diagnostics as we were descending and everything checks out. Aside from the higher levels of greenhouse gases than we're used to, the air is very similar to what Terran's was."

Aldin cringed inside at the last part of that statement. *I don't think I'll ever be able to quiet these demons*, she thought bitterly.

Ridley asked, "How long before we're ready to go?"

"Are you that eager to jump into the unknown?" Mishka said.

Ridley replied, "No, but the sooner we get out there and check out the site, the sooner we can get back here where we know it's safe."

Mishka replied, "You do realize that we won't be able to stay in this ship forever? Eventually, we're going to have to venture outside and try to fit in with whatever kind of hole we've found ourselves in."

"Maybe so, but we don't have to rush right into it."

"I'll get everything ready as fast as I can so we can get out there and back quickly," Jeron interrupted. "Then everyone will be happy."

Jeron left both of them pouting for a moment and then returned a few minutes later carrying a bunch of electronic components in his arms.

"That was quick," Ridley stated.

"I helped load the cargo onto this ship," Jeron explained. "Luckily, I still remembered where some of it was."

He handed a thin silver neck strap to each one and promptly placed one around his neck. "These will help us stay in contact with each other. Once you press the button on the back, they'll sync with your biometrics. They'll also enhance your vision so we can see where we're going, as well as allow us to see the modified vehicles, since someone here suggested we venture out at night." He turned to Silas with an accusatory look in his eyes.

Silas just stood there silent, with a hard look on his face.

Each one placed their device around their necks and pressed the button, the strap glowed a soft blue for a brief second before it changed color to blend seamlessly into their skin, making it basically invisible.

Jeron then went to the nearest gyro-cycle and placed a small round disk on the side of it. After tapping on the disk, a swirl of energy spun around the cycle. A second later, the cycle was gone. Jeron stepped into the energy field and sat on the seat of the cycle, disappearing as well.

He reappeared a moment later, after he had tapped the disk once more to deactivate the spectrum modifier. "What do you think? Pretty cool, huh?"

Ridley stood there with her arms crossed and a flat expression on her face. "I guess it'll work," she said.

"I'll send the location coordinates to each of the vehicles," Silas said. Then he looked around at everyone, "Are we ready to do this?"

A nervous murmur rippled through the group. Only Jeron seemed excited about the prospect of venturing outside into this strange new world—a world they would now have to call home.

A few minutes later, the rear hatch of the ship opened up and Silas led them out in his new transport. Jeron and Mishka followed him in their gyro-cycles, while Aldin sat behind Ridley on the third cycle, holding tightly onto her waist.

They sat there for a long moment, taking in the landscape. Even at night, the sweltering heat reminded them of the Sandscapes on Terran, although the terrain here was far less barren.

"Everyone, stay close and go slow," Silas said. "We can't afford to draw attention."

Before they even got started on their clandestine journey a loud howl rose through the air nearby.

Chapter 7

Ashton hadn't heard from Clause in hours, and that gnawing sense of unease had evolved into something far worse. Something had gone terribly wrong. He could feel it. As the minutes ticked by, his agitation grew. He stared at his phone again, his finger hovering over the call button. If Clause was in trouble, he needed to know.

He hit dial, the phone ringing once, twice, three times, before finally, the call connected.

"It's about time you answered the damn phone!" Ashton barked.

But it wasn't Clause that answered.

William's voice was low and menacing, "Ashton Brown, I presume? I'm sorry to tell you that your boy Clause is dead. And we're coming for you next."

A chill ran through Ashton, coiling itself around his spine. His mouth went dry as he gripped the phone tighter. "Who is this?"

"I'm the man who put a couple of holes in his chest before the Marines finished him off," William growled.

Ashton's heart thundered in his chest. *Clause… dead?*

He immediately ended the call, his mind spinning in rapid

calculation. He knew what was coming. They wouldn't be far behind. He had no time to waste!

He bolted from the office, his heart racing. When he reached the lab, his voice was sharp and urgent. "Drop everything. Follow me. Now."

Kafka and Vogel looked up in confusion. Kafka raised a skeptical eyebrow, while Vogel nervously exchanged glances with her, unsure whether to follow. But there was something in Ashton's eyes—something dark and full of panic—that spurred them to their feet.

They followed him down the corridor, their footsteps echoing ominously in the dim light. At the far end of the hallway, near the elevator, Ashton stopped outside a plain, unremarkable wall sconce. The two scientists exchanged uneasy glances again. "What's going on?" Kafka asked.

Ashton didn't reply, instead reaching for a hidden switch embedded in the fixture. With a soft click, the wall opposite them hissed and groaned, sliding open to reveal a secret door they had never seen before.

"What the hell?" Vogel muttered, his voice barely a whisper.

After a few taps on a keypad near the door, Ashton then inserted a key into a slot before he stepped through the opening without answering. The two scientists followed reluctantly, the air growing colder and heavier. The lights flickered on as they entered a long hallway. The smell hit them first—a faint, metallic odor, like blood or something far worse.

Ashton turned to face them, his grin unnerving. "This is where we can work. Without oversight. Without interference. Here, we are free to explore… the limits."

Kafka and Vogel watched with dawning horror as the hallway opened into a large chamber, where glass containment tubes lined the large room, stretching from floor to ceiling. Suspended inside each tube were bodies floating in some viscous, yellowish liquid, their faces distorted in agonizing screams and their limbs bent at grotesque angles.

Instantly, they realized that the secret lab was a tomb of nightmares.

"What is this place?" Kafka asked, her voice trembling.

"It's our future," Ashton replied coldly. "And now, it's our only chance."

Vogel's stomach churned. The truth settled over him like a shroud. He and Kafka had become expendable the moment they entered this place. If they didn't cooperate, they would end up like those floating in the tanks—suspended in some half-death, secrets locked inside their corpses forever.

"We need to move fast!" Ashton said urgently. "Get everything from the other lab. Samples, equipment— everything. Move it here before the authorities come sniffing around."

There was no argument, no resistance. They worked feverishly, the fear of what might happen if they didn't, propelling them onward, through the grueling task of transporting every aspect of Ashton's unholy work.

By the time they finished, hours had passed, and their nerves were frayed. The scientists slumped to the floor, exhausted.

Kafka's voice was hoarse when she finally spoke. "What now?"

Ashton handed them each a small key. Although tiny in size, it was heavy with the weight of the secrets it unlocked.

"You'll come and go as I need you," Ashton said flatly. "No one knows you've seen this place. No one can. If anyone asks, I was here one minute, gone the next. Sick. Vanished. Understood?"

Both of them nodded, though the dread was plain in their eyes. The keys felt more like shackles than privileges, but they had no choice. They were in too deep now. Too far to turn back.

As they sat in silence, Vogel's hand trembled as he turned the key over and over in his palm. His eyes wandered to the containment tubes again, the bodies swaying slightly as though something unseen moved within the liquid. He blinked, his breath catching in his throat. Was it his imagination, or had the eyes of one of the suspended figures just opened?

And then, just as quickly, they were closed again.

He felt something cold crawl up his spine. He wanted to say something, to tell Kafka, but the words wouldn't come. All he could do was stare in frozen horror, wondering if whatever was in those tubes was waiting for the right moment to wake.

Ashton's voice broke through the thick tension in the room, his expression unreadable. "Guard your keys with your lives," he said, his voice low, almost a growl. "Because if anyone else finds out about this place… you'll end up just like them."

He nodded toward the tubes, where something—someone—shifted ever so slightly.

Chapter 8

The rhythmic slap of running shoes against pavement echoed faintly through the night, blending with the distant hum of the desert wind. Two young women moved at a steady pace along the deserted sidewalk, their breathing controlled but slightly uneven. Though they exchanged casual conversation, their eyes flickered toward every shifting shadow, every rustle in the dry brush.

"I can't believe we're doing this," Mara said, her voice light but tight with underlying tension. She tucked a loose strand of hair behind her ear, trying to suppress the shiver crawling up her spine. "Night jogging? After everything that's happened? We must be out of our minds."

"No, we're reclaiming normal," Elena replied with forced confidence, her ponytail swaying with each step. She shot Mara a playful smirk, though her fingers clenched a little too tightly around the small flashlight in her hand. "The world's not ending anymore, remember? No more rabid coyotes, no more dive-bombing birds. We have to stop jumping at every little noise."

Mara exhaled sharply, glancing toward the darkened horizon. The Coachella Valley felt different now. The stars still glowed in the vast, open sky. The warm desert air still wrapped around them like a familiar embrace. But the silence was heavier, tinged with memories of the horrors that had plagued the region only days before.

"Easy for you to say," Mara muttered. "You weren't the one trapped in a gas station while a pack of zombified dogs tried to claw their way in."

Elena faltered slightly, the reminder dimming her bravado. "Yeah… I know." She swallowed, shaking her head as if to dismiss the creeping unease. "But that's behind us. We can't live in fear forever."

Mara let out a humorless chuckle. "Tell that to my brain."

A sudden rustling from the bushes just off the path made both women flinch instinctively. Mara grabbed Elena's arm, halting their jog. They held their breath, their bodies tensed. The flashlight beam swept toward the movement, illuminating the dry, brittle branches as they quivered ever so slightly.

Nothing emerged.

Elena released a slow breath. "It's probably just a rabbit," she whispered, but the doubt in her voice betrayed her.

Mara's grip tightened. "Or something else."

They stood frozen, straining their ears against the night.

Then—laughter.

Soft, distant, carried on the wind. But not their laughter.

Mara turned sharply. "Did you hear that?"

Elena nodded slowly, her bravado now completely gone.

They scanned the area, finding nothing but darkened houses, empty streets, and the vague outline of the hills beyond the town's edge.

"Okay," Elena admitted, forcing a smile that didn't reach her eyes, "maybe we've had enough 'reclaiming normal' for one night."

Mara didn't argue. Together, they turned, jogging a little faster now, not speaking, not daring to look back.

Further down the ravine, concealed within the shadows, the figures watching them remained perfectly still.

***

Aldin tensed, gripping Ridley tightly as the eerie howl echoed through the night. "That sounded close," she whispered, her voice quivering.

Ridley kept her gaze steady ahead. "Just hang on, we'll be alright," she reassured. "We don't know anything about this place yet. Whatever it was, might be like the Dengo's back on Terran—all noise, no danger."

Aldin's voice was grim. "Except the last one I saw… was a nightmare come to life."

Ridley sighed. "Try not to think about that. I'm here. I'll protect you."

Aldin nestled closer, her tension easing ever so slightly. "I know. You always do."

With a brief, tender stroke of Aldin's arm, Ridley returned her hand to the cycle's controls, urging it forward to keep pace with the group. They navigated cautiously, weaving through a dry ravine, eyes scanning every shadow for movement. A flickering red light on their screens blinked as their destination neared. Silas, leading the way, halted suddenly.

"Hold position," he ordered in a low voice.

"What's going on?" Jeron asked, straining to see ahead.

"Two figures approaching. Stay silent until they pass."

Everyone froze, barely daring to breathe as two young women jogged by, their conversation hanging in the air. They wore a mixture of running apparel and summer clothing.

"Were they just… running for fun?" Mishka muttered in disbelief.

Silas nodded, bemused. "It appears that way."

"And in the dark?" Jeron added, incredulous.

"Maybe they're not as primitive as we thought," Silas remarked.

Mishka shook her head. "They're not very smart, though."

"Let's not judge too quickly," Aldin said softly. "This world may share some similarities with Terran, but it's bound to have its own rules, and its own dangers."

"She's right," Silas agreed. "If we want to survive, we'll have to adapt."

He started moving forward again, continuing down the ravine. As it started to curve South, they noticed some homes a short distance away, sitting in a row, some with lights twinkling in the night, others completely dark. Each one had a distinct color, giving it its own personality.

"These look like personal dwelling structures," Aldin said as she looked at each one in wonder. "I've never seen so many together in one place before."

"Like I said," Silas stated, "we have a lot to learn."

A sudden gust of wind whipped up, swirling sand and debris around them in all directions. As the force howled against the base of the nearby mountain, it sounded as if it were a wild animal gathering itself for the hunt.

"Put your visor shields up!" Jeron said as he was pelted with sand, causing his eyes to sting and burn.

Each one pressed a button on the small console in front of them and a curved panel of glass materialized in front of them, shielding them from damage. It couldn't protect them from the smell, though. The stench of death and decay rode the air currents like an invisible wraith, stinging their nostrils and burning the back of their throats, making it even harder to breathe.

The wind came at them periodically for a time, hitting them forcefully in short bursts and then dying down for a while as it built its strength back up to attack once again. Finally, as they came to the end of the ravine, the wind all but disappeared, relegated to just tiny wisps here and there.

A long stretch of road lay ahead, their first foray through an inhabited section of this world. Small, personal dwellings lined both sides of the road, with numerous vehicles parked in front of them. Most of the dwellings were dark and silent, but a couple of them had lights filtering through fabric coverings on the windows.

"Stay close and follow in single file," Silas said through the communicator as he led them slowly down the road.

A pair of light beams suddenly rounded the corner up ahead, coming directly toward them. They waited anxiously as the vehicle came into view. Similar to Silas' transport, this one was tall, with gigantic wheels and an open rear compartment. The driver, a young man with dark skin, passed them without notice, moving at a fast speed. A loud, disjointed arrangement of music sprang from a device inside the man's vehicle, creating a low reverberation that shook everything nearby.

Silas cringed as the driver sped past them. "What a horrible sound," he stated through his communicator.

Mishka replied, "I kind of liked it. You said they were raw and savage. Their music seems appropriate."

Silas grunted and just said, "Let's keep going."

As they entered a more populated area, the smell grew even stronger. When they came to a bend in the road, they saw why. A large mound of charred, dead animals stood off to the side of the road in a small, barren field, an attempt to clear the stain of their scourge from the earth.

"That's disturbing," Mishka stated as they drove past the still smoldering pyre.

"At least they're dead," Jeron said.

"And we need to make sure they stay that way," Silas replied. "We should be at the crash site soon.

"What are we looking for?" Ridley asked.

Aldin replied, "Anything that we can run bio-scans on, like animal tissue and soil samples, electromagnetic readings, radiation levels."

"So, science stuff?" Ridley quipped.

Aldin chuckled and hugged her a little tighter, "Yeah science stuff."

As they rounded a corner onto a small road that led to the entrance to the park, the darkness started to lift, announcing dawn's arrival. "We won't have a lot of time," Silas said. "We need to gather as much as we can, as quickly as possible."

They crept toward the park entrance, the silence heavy as their eyes scanned the ground. Tire tracks, crisscrossing wildly, told the story of panic, as if whoever had been here had driven in a frenzy, desperate to escape whatever nightmare they had faced. Dark patches of blood soaked the earth in erratic splashes, leaving ugly crimson stains that seemed to pulse under the dim light.

Just off to the side, the carcass of a massive animal lay severed clean in two, its innards spilling out in grotesque, tangled loops. Around it, the bodies of smaller creatures lay scattered like discarded playthings, each one a mangled heap of fur and gore.

The group halted their vehicles and dismounted, stepping out from the cloaking field that had kept them hidden in this new world. For the first time, they were exposed and vulnerable. Ridley's fingers tightened on the handle of her blaster, her eyes darting over the desolate landscape.

While the rest of the group moved with purpose, their shoulders tight and their movements stiff, Jeron, in contrast, seemed far too eager, his hands diving into the entrails of a mutilated beast with unsettling enthusiasm, pulling apart the brain and intestines as if savoring the grisly task.

The sudden snap of a branch jerked them all to attention, their hearts thundering in their chests. A small, black-and-white spotted dog limped out from the brush, its uneven gait casting a shadow of terror over the group. There was nothing overtly monstrous about it—no signs of decay, no twisted limbs or bloodshot eyes—but something about the way it moved, stuttering and hesitant, made them all pause. The air grew colder, and for a moment, the world held its breath.

Then the dog collapsed in front of them with a soft whimper, its small body trembling. Aldin slowly kneeled down beside it. "Oh no," she murmured, creeping toward the creature. "It's hurt."

"Be careful," Ridley said firmly. "We have no idea what these animals are capable of."

Aldin's hand hovered over the dog cautiously. The dog flinched but didn't flee. Slowly, carefully, she reached for its leg, where a large thorn was embedded deep in its paw. The dog whined and whimpered with fear, but it didn't resist as Aldin braced herself and pulled.

The dog let out a short, high-pitched yelp, but almost instantly, its fear transformed into a joyful bark. It pounced on Aldin, its small body vibrating with excitement as it licked her hands and face. Aldin laughed, a sound so genuine and pure it momentarily cut through the grimness of their mission. For the briefest second, the horrors of this world faded away.

"We don't have time for this, Aldin," Ridley said, watching with a mixture of exasperation and distaste.

"I think she likes me," Aldin said, her face glowing. "Or is it a he? How do you even tell?"

Jeron, still wrist-deep in entrails, glanced up. "I think they call it a dog. Saw one on the surveillance feed earlier. People here keep them as pets."

Aldin's eyes sparkled, and she shot Ridley a pleading look.

"No," Ridley said firmly.

"But it's alone out here!" Aldin protested, scratching behind the dog's ears as its tail wagged so fast it was a blur.

Silas, who had been silently observing, chimed in. "Ridley's right. We have more pressing matters. We can't afford distractions."

Aldin's face fell, her eyes misting over. This small, helpless creature had somehow wormed its way into her heart in mere moments. Still, she knew they were right. With a heavy sigh, she set the dog down. "Go on," she whispered sadly. "Go back to where you came from."

But as she moved back to the cycle, the dog didn't leave. Once Aldin had disappeared under the cloaking shield, it followed her, sitting obediently by the vehicle, tail wagging and eyes fixed on her. "It can see us!" Aldin exclaimed in surprise.

Ridley sighed deeply. "Silas?"

Silas rubbed his forehead. "Fine. Aldin, bring your friend. It can stay with us until we're done here. Then we'll figure out what to do."

Aldin's face lit up. She gave Ridley a quick kiss on the cheek before scooping the dog up and climbing into Silas's transport. The dog wasted no time in resuming its slobbery assault, licking her face as if making up for lost time. She laughed, her nose brushing against the dog's. "I think I'll call it Izzit."

"Izzit?" Silas raised an eyebrow.

"Short for 'who is it?'"

Silas sighed. "What have we gotten ourselves into?"

The road curved ahead, and as they neared the bend, Ridley stiffened. There, in the distance, was a large body of water. It wasn't the vast Seascape from her nightmares, but it was enough to stir the old fear deep within her. She longed for Aldin's arms around her, a slight comfort in this desolate place. But before the dread could consume her, the road curved away into the woods, where the towering trees swallowed them whole.

Moments later, they reached the edge of a massive crater. The ground was scorched black, with puddles of thick, oily ooze dotting the landscape like malignant sores. Dead animals, grotesquely deformed, lay scattered at odd angles, their bodies twisted as if they'd been frozen mid-scream.

"Spread out," Silas ordered. "Same drill. Gather whatever we can analyze."

Aldin climbed out, leaving Izzit in the transport. The dog let out a low, uneasy growl, but Aldin was already too far to hear.

Then the earth beneath their feet trembled. The tremor was brief but potent, rippling through the ground like the echo of a far-off nightmare. Each of them exchanged glances, eyes wide with growing fear.

"Let's make this quick," Silas muttered, his voice tight with urgency.

As they fanned out, the oppressive weight of the place settled over them like a heavy, suffocating fog. This wasn't just a crash site. It was a graveyard, and they all had the feeling that something—whether living or dead—was watching.

***

* * *

Jeron edged closer to the center of the crater, moving with a deliberate slowness that belied the growing excitement thrumming beneath his skin. The others were still scattered along the perimeter, focused on collecting data from the less volatile outskirts, but Jeron's eyes were fixed on the meteor's impact point—the jagged heart of the crater. His breath caught when he spotted the faintest flicker of movement in a nearby puddle. It was almost imperceptible, a ripple that barely disturbed the slick, oily surface, but it was there. Alive.

His heart raced, but he fought to keep his expression neutral. His fingers moved deftly as he crouched, scooping a small amount of the strange liquid into a glass vial. The viscous substance clung to the sides of the vial, shimmering with an unnatural, otherworldly sheen. He should have stashed it in his kit—protocol demanded as much—but instead, his hand slipped the vial into the deep pocket of his robe. The glass felt cool and secret against his flesh, a treasure that he alone understood.

Jeron straightened and moved on, pretending to collect a few meaningless samples from the surrounding debris. His mind, however, was already racing ahead, plotting. He wouldn't share this discovery with just anyone. No, this would be something special. He would reveal it only when the moment was right, and only to someone who truly deserved to witness its power.

Silas's voice crackled through the comms. "We're done here. Time to go."

Jeron practically leaped into motion, his legs twitching with anticipation. He was so eager to leave the scene that he nearly collided with Mishka, who shot him a sharp look.

"Watch where you're going!" she snapped, rubbing her shoulder where he'd clipped her.

"Sorry," Jeron said, barely able to suppress the grin stretching across his face. "Just… eager to get out of here."

The sly smile deepened as he hurried back to his gyrocycle. His mind raced with possibilities, the dark thrill of discovery coursing through his veins. Whatever secrets this world held, he was determined to be the one who unlocked them. And when he did, no one would be able to stop him.

***

"Lay all the specimens on top of one of the containers," Silas instructed. "We'll use it as a makeshift workstation."

The group carefully unpacked their samples and spread them out in the dim light of the ship's hold. Initially, Izzit sat on the floor at Aldin's feet, watching her eagerly. After a few minutes, a sharp, playful bark erupted from her, forcing Aldin to divide her attention between the dog and the task at hand.

"Aldin, you're in charge of repurposing whatever resources from the ship you might need to accommodate the necessary research equipment," Silas continued. "And make sure that your friend there doesn't get into trouble."

Jeron interrupted, "There should be a couple of portable workstations onboard, if I remember the inventory correctly, along with a number of handheld scanners."

The group searched through the remaining contents of the ship that had been strewn about during their descension until they located two large rectangle cases, one of which was severely damaged. When they opened them up, they found that only of them was operable. "Well, I guess one is better than none?" Jeron suggested.

Minutes later, the lab was alive with the hum of scanners and the low chatter of exhausted voices. Silas was hunched over the main console, scrolling through data with a look of grim concentration, while Mishka sorted the samples, occasionally muttering curses when an instrument beeped at her in protest. Aldin carefully placed a meteor fragment into a containment chamber, watching the blue glow pulse around it like a heartbeat.

Meanwhile, Izzit sat near the workstation, ears perked, tail flicking in quiet anticipation. She was small, unassuming—just a little black-and-white animal with big eyes that could melt hearts. But there was something calculating in the way she watched them, like she was taking it all in, deciding when to strike.

Near the far side of the lab, Jeron stood apart from the others, arms crossed, watching with mild disinterest as they cataloged their samples. His face was unreadable, but the way his eyes flicked to each specimen showed he was taking mental inventory of everything they'd brought back.

"Careful with that," he said as Mishka set down a sealed container. "You drop it, we might all die."

Mishka didn't reply, instead just shooting him a threatening glare.

Silas barely looked up. "If you're not going to help, Jeron, at least don't be a distraction."

Jeron smirked. "Oh, I am helping. I'm supervising."

Mishka rolled her eyes, turning back to the workstation. Aldin, meanwhile, was too busy making sure none of the more delicate samples had been compromised during their rough trip back.

That was when Izzit made her move. Her nose twitched. Her tail gave a little flick.

She moved slow, quiet, creeping toward the workstation. On the table, near the edge, sat a small sample container holding a substance that shimmered under the overhead lights, just sitting there, unattended. With a sudden hop, Izzit leaped onto a low storage crate and then onto a chair.

Jeron's eyes narrowed as he noticed the dog edging closer. "Uh… does anyone see what the little creature there is doing?"

No one looked up.

Silas was focused on the scanner, Aldin was adjusting containment settings, Mishka was swearing at a sensor malfunction.

Jeron sighed, rubbing the bridge of his nose. "Fine. Don't listen to me."

And that was when Izzit snatched the container between her tiny jaws and bolted.

"Izzit!" Aldin shouted, lunging for her.

Too late. The little dog was a blur.

Mishka turned just in time to see Izzit tearing across the lab, container clenched between her teeth, paws skidding against the smooth floor. "Oh, you little—GET BACK HERE!"

Jeron snorted. "Well, this should be entertaining."

Ridley moved fast, cutting Izzit off near the supply cabinets. "Alright, creature. Game over. Hand it over."

Izzit skittered left, then right—faking them out. She darted under the workstation, tail wagging, eyes glinting with pure mischief.

Aldin made a grab for her, but Izzit was too quick. She twisted out of reach with a sound that was somewhere between a growl and a giggle.

Mishka, however, had the patience of a predator. She stood still, watching, waiting.

Izzit hesitated. Just for a second.

That was all Mishka needed.

With one swift motion, she snatched the little beast up, holding her at arm's length. "Gotcha, troublemaker."

Izzit wriggled, but refused to let go of the container.

Aldin pried it free, heart hammering as she inspected it for cracks. By some miracle, it was still intact.

She turned to the dog, still dangling from Mishka's grasp. "You can't just steal things, Izzit!"

Izzit, entirely unbothered, stretched out her tiny pink tongue and licked Aldin's nose.

Ridley snorted. "Well. At least she's settling in."

Jeron crossed his arms, watching the entire debacle with a smirk. "You know, if you guys can't even keep a dog under control, I'm really questioning how you plan to stop an apocalypse if it shows up again."

Silas shot him a look.

Jeron held up his hands. "Just saying."

Mishka set Izzit down, and she immediately trotted back to the workstation as if nothing had happened. She plopped down beside them, ears perked, watching. Waiting for her next opportunity.

As Silas turned and headed toward the front of the ship, Aldin called after him. "What are you going to do?"

"I'm going to see if I can patch into a local data source and figure out if that tremor we felt earlier is anything to worry about."

"They appear to run everything on a basic binary system," Jeron suggested matter-of-factly. "If you adjust the bandwidth on the receiver, you should be able to hack into their systems with little trouble."

Silas paused, glancing over his shoulder. For a moment, Silas considered how far the man had come, his once-raw potential now honed to a razor's edge. A flicker of unease rippled through Silas's chest, an icy whisper in the back of his mind urging him to watch Jeron more closely.

He turned back to the console, his fingers working swiftly

to tie into the planet's information network. Within moments, data began to stream in, a tangled web of communications unfurling before him. As he sifted through the noise, his shoulders relaxed—nothing catastrophic. It turned out that the tremor was part of a series of mild seismic disturbances, common in this region. He let out a slow breath, leaning back in his chair as the tension in his body unwound.

Silas closed his eyes, allowing himself a brief rest. His mind drifted, thoughts of the strange samples they had gathered fading into the background as exhaustion took over. He didn't dream. The kind of sleep that found him now was deep, almost suffocating in its intensity.

Chapter 9

Jeron stood at the edge of the ship's hold, his gaze flickering back toward the group as they worked on cataloging the strange specimens. He had felt the weight of Silas's eyes on him earlier, a brief moment of suspicion that was cause for concern. But now, they were all preoccupied, too focused on the tasks at hand. It was the perfect opportunity.

He kneeled by one of the specimen containers, careful not to draw attention as he slid the vial from his pocket. The liquid inside shimmered, almost alive, as though the substance had its own sentient awareness. He hadn't told anyone what he'd seen in the crater—the slight ripple in the puddle, the way it seemed to respond to his presence. There was something in that black ooze, something powerful. And Jeron knew, deep in his gut, that it was meant for him.

Jeron watched the others from the corner of the ship, his eyes flicking between them as they slowly drifted off, one by one. Mishka was first, her head resting on a bundle of supplies, breath slow and even, followed a short time later by Ridley. Aldin lingered the longest, working with the same exhaustive intensity that had caused the disaster on their home world—just as Jensen had foreseen. Jeron could see her lips moving, silently talking to Izzit, who lay curled at her feet.

The ship's hum softened, and a heavy quiet settled over the crew, like a blanket of stillness draped over their weary bodies. It was the moment Jeron had been waiting for.

He had been patient. Too patient. Ever since he had pocketed the vial from the crater, it felt like time had stretched and slowed, each second dragging painfully as he waited for his chance to leave. The small container of black ooze in his pocket had become an unbearable weight, its energy pulsing through him, urging him to act. But he knew better than to rush. He needed the others sound asleep, completely oblivious to what he was about to do.

As Aldin finally dozed off, her head tipping to the side, Izzit stirred, but remained still at her feet. Jeron's heart quickened.

Moving slowly, he rose from his corner, careful not to make any sound that might wake them. He took a step toward the door and paused, waiting for any signs of movement. Mishka mumbled something in her sleep but didn't stir. Aldin shifted, Izzit's ears twitching briefly, but the dog remained silent.

Jeron moved again, crossing the room lightly, his hands shaking as he approached Izzit. The dog opened one eye, glancing up at him with mild curiosity. Jeron crouched, running his hand over the dog's soft fur.

"Come on, girl," he whispered, glancing back at the others, his pulse pounding in his ears. Izzit gave a low whimper, but got to her feet, stretching and shaking out her fur before padding silently toward Jeron.

Jeron hesitated for a moment, his hand hovering over the dog's head. He hadn't planned on taking Izzit with him, but when a sudden inspiration struck him, he knew he needed to act on it.

He reached the ship's main hatch and stopped, his hand hovering over the control panel. His heart hammered in his chest as he glanced over his shoulder one last time. The others were still deep asleep, unaware of the betrayal about to unfold. A slight wave of guilt washed over him, but it was fleeting, overshadowed by the thrill of what was waiting for him outside.

With a quiet hiss, the hatch slid open, letting in a breath of cool night air. Jeron hesitated for a moment, feeling a wave of anxiety pressing down on him. But the vial in his pocket promised him a future far more exciting than the fear of the unknown at the moment. Crouching low, he exited the ship, closing the hatch behind him quickly before the others woke.

Stepping out into the darkness, Jeron felt a strange sense of liberation as he silently pushed one of the gyro cycles across the threshold. The alien world spread out before him, vast and unforgiving, yet alive with possibilities. Izzit followed at his side, her tail wagging gently as they moved beyond the ship's cloaking field.

For a moment, Jeron simply stood there, breathing in the night air, savoring the freedom. He glanced down at Izzit, who sat obediently beside him, head tilted as if waiting for Jeron's next move.

Jeron took a deep breath, steeling himself for what lay ahead, and picked up Izzit, cradling her in his lap as he started driving the cycle down the dried ravine. The trees loomed in the distance, dark and foreboding, but they also beckoned to him with a promise of something greater. Something dangerous.

As he and Izzit approached the tree line, a shiver ran down Jeron's spine. The night was unnervingly quiet, the air thick with tension, as though the world itself was holding its breath. Jeron's mind raced with a thousand thoughts, but he kept pushing forward, deeper into the unknown.

A faint rustling in the underbrush ahead froze him in place. His pulse quickened as he strained to see what lurked beyond the trees. Izzit let out a low growl, pressing close to Jeron's chest, eyes locked on something in the shadows.

Against his better judgement, Jeron stepped from the cycle, holding Izzit close to him, and approached the trees cautiously. Every fiber of his being screamed for him to back away from the hidden danger, to flee until he knew more about this strange world he had been thrown into. But if he had learned anything from his uncle, it was to pursue the advancement of science with a sense of purpose mingled with a bit of reckless abandon.

From the darkness, a pair of glowing eyes appeared, staring directly at them.

Jeron's breath caught in his throat and his body tensed as he readied himself to run. But then, something strange happened. The vial in his pocket pulsed, sending a wave of heat through his body, and Jeron realized that the creature wasn't interested in him. It was fixated on the organism.

Whatever the organism had become—however it had mutated back on Terran—it was more than just a simple, mindless thing that maddened the creatures it came in contact with. It had power. And now, so did Jeron.

He took a cautious step back, his hand tightening around the vial. The creature stayed where it was, still watching, but not advancing. Jeron's heart thundered in his chest, and he knew this was his moment.

Jeron pulled the vial from his pocket, the liquid inside glowing faintly in the moonlight. He stared at it for a long moment, marveling at its beauty. With each passing second the organism within began to move a little more, as if waking from a deep slumber.

Jeron looked down at Izzit, the dog staring up at him with wide, trusting eyes. A pang of guilt twisted in his gut, but he shook it off. There was no going back.

"Come on," he whispered to Izzit as he walked back toward the gyro cycle. "We've got work to do."

And with that, he disappeared deeper into the forest, the vial glowing faintly in his hand, the night swallowing them both whole.

***

As the dim interior of the ship filled with the dull hum of systems rebooting, Silas stirred from his sleep. The weight of his exhaustion still clung to him, but something wasn't right. He felt it in the pit of his stomach. His eyes darted around the dimly lit space, his senses gradually sharpening.

"Where's Jeron?" Silas growled as he sat up, scanning the small compartment before shuffling toward the back of the ship.

Aldin, still half-asleep, rubbed her eyes and groaned softly. "What's going on?" But as she blinked into the low light, she froze. Her heart skipped a beat. Izzit, who had been curled up at her feet, was gone!

"Ridley," Aldin whispered urgently, nudging her awake. "Ridley, something's wrong."

Ridley jolted upright. Her hand instinctively brushed the weapon holstered at her side as she scanned the room.

"Where is Jeron?" she snapped.

Mishka joined the others. "He's gone... and so is the animal," she said as she looked between Aldin and Ridley.

Silas stormed toward the ship's interface. His fingers flew over the controls as he called up the external camera feeds, prompting the system to rewind the feed to the moment the rear hatch had opened. Static flickered on the screen, followed a moment later by the outline of the barren landscape outside. And there, in the distance, a figure moved swiftly, disappearing into the shadow of the ravine.

"He took Izzit with him!" Aldin cried, her voice cracking as her eyes misted over.

Ridley grabbed a tactical belt from the weapons cache and fastened it tight, checking her weapon. "He's not going far," she growled.

"Wait," Silas said sternly. "We don't know what he's after. If he took something dangerous from the crash site, it could be catastrophic."

Aldin's mind raced, approaching the edge of panic. "He wouldn't—would he?"

Mishka's voice cut through the tension like a blade. "He's been acting strange ever since the crash. What if he—"

"Enough!" Ridley said sharply. "We'll find him. If he's been playing us this whole time, we'll handle it. Got it?"

"He's armed himself, too," Silas added bitterly, glancing toward the weapons locker where they had stored their cache. The door hung open, and the emptiness inside told the rest of the story. "Half our blasters are gone."

As they moved toward the exit, Aldin's heart hammered in her chest. She couldn't shake the image of Jeron with Izzit. What was he planning?

Ridley looked back at Aldin, her voice softening just for a second. "We'll get her back, Aldin. I promise."

The group emerged into the sharp, biting wind, the desert air swirling with dust around their feet. Silas's eyes narrowed as he scanned the clearing where their cycles had been parked. His heart sank. Only two gyro cycles remained, their sleek frames dimly illuminated by the ship's external glow.

The third was gone.

Ridley followed his gaze, her expression darkening. "He took one of the cycles," she growled, her jaw clenched.

Aldin's stomach lurched as she shifted her focus to the remaining transport. Her eyes widened. "It's not just the cycle. Look."

The group rushed forward, and Silas hissed as he kneeled by the transport's exposed panel. Wiring lay in a mangled heap, circuits frayed and connectors severed. The drive stabilizer had been torn out completely, leaving a hollow cavity in its place.

"He sabotaged the transport," Silas muttered grimly, his fingers tracing the jagged cuts in the cables. "We won't be going anywhere in this."

Ridley kneeled beside him, examining the damage. "He's more thorough than I gave him credit for."

"That's not all." Mishka had moved to inspect the remaining cycles. She let out a sharp curse, shaking her head. "He rigged these too. The power cells are fried—one bad ignition, and they'll burn out."

Aldin's hands clenched into fists, frustration coursing through her. "He planned this," she whispered. "He didn't just steal a cycle to get away. He crippled us."

Mishka's lips pressed into a thin line. "He's buying himself a head start. Now we're stuck without a way to follow him."

Ridley inhaled slowly, eyes hardening as a plan began to form. "We're not stuck. We have parts on the ship. We'll strip whatever we need to repair the cycles and the transport."

Silas gave her a sharp look. "You want to cannibalize our own systems?"

"If we don't, he gets away," Ridley snapped, rising to her feet. "We're not leaving him out there with Izzit and whatever horror he found at the crash site."

Driven by urgency and desperation, they immediately sprang into action. Ridley dropped to her knees beside the ship's lower hull, her tools already in hand. She yanked open a sleek access panel, revealing a complex matrix of interconnected circuits glowing faintly with residual energy. Thin filaments of violet wiring snaked through the compartment, their pulse-like rhythm indicating active power flows.

She twisted her wrist and activated her vibro-driver, the tool emitting a low hum as its rotating tip resonated at high frequencies. Sparks danced as she deftly unscrewed micro-bolts securing the thermal regulator to its housing. A cooling module hissed as it depressurized, releasing a plume of chilled vapor into the air. She set it aside carefully—it would be needed for the transport's overclocked fuel exchanger.

"Careful with that thermal inducer," Silas muttered as he joined her, a bundle of carbon-conduit cabling slung over one shoulder. His hands moved with methodical precision, prying out a pulse regulator node from the life-support grid. The cylindrical component emitted a sharp, whining pitch as he disconnected it, its glow fading as he severed its quantum-lock tether. "This stabilizer's meant for oxygen flow, not propulsion. We'll need to recalibrate the resonance field."

"Understood," Ridley said. She extracted a crystalline capacitor, its prismatic surface refracting the dim light into a kaleidoscope of colors. The capacitor hummed with stored energy—a volatile but necessary component for retrofitting the cycles' damaged power cells.

Meanwhile, Mishka kneeled beside the gyro cycles, her fingers a blur of motion. She pried open a fused power coupling, its internal circuitry scorched and charred from Jeron's sabotage. She unclipped her diagnostic scanner from her belt, its holographic interface springing to life in front of her. Lines of cascading data scrolled across the translucent display as she traced the damage. Her gaze narrowed.

"Power flow's been rerouted through a redundant node," she muttered, selecting a bypass module from her repair kit. The small, metallic device clicked into place with a satisfying snap. Mishka toggled a sequence of holographic switches, and a surge of violet light coursed through the cycle's energy conduits, illuminating the fractured frame with a steady glow. "That should hold for now."

Minutes bled into hours, each second a bitter struggle against the relentless passage of time. Sweat dripped from Silas's brow as he spliced delicate fiber-optic relays, his hands steady despite the tremor of fatigue threatening to creep in. Aldin hauled an electromagnetic pulse inhibitor from the ship's navigation system and soldered it directly into the transport's stabilizer core, her gloves sparking with each connection.

At last, she fitted the final conduit into place with a sharp twist, securing it with a magnetic clamp. The connections glowed a fierce amber, indicating a stable circuit. She flexed her blistered fingers, exhaling a ragged breath. "Done," she said in a low and exhausted voice.

Silas slowly climbed into the transport. He toggled the ignition. For a tense heartbeat, nothing happened. Then, with a sputter that quickly steadied, the engine roared to life. A ripple of relief swept through the group as the vehicle thrummed beneath him, its systems humming in reluctant cohesion.

"It'll hold," he said, a tight smile pulling at the corners of his mouth. "For now."

"Then let's move," Ridley said, swinging onto one of the cycles. "We've already lost too much time."

Aldin's heart pounded in her chest as she thought about

Jeron out there with Izzit—armed, moving fast, and possibly with something dangerous in his possession. She couldn't wrap her head around it. This was Jeron, the same guy who had escaped alongside them, joked with them, and now… he was a threat. Maybe worse.

"We've got to figure out why he did this," Aldin said, her voice shaky. "He wouldn't just turn on us like this unless…"

"Unless he's been planning this for a while," Silas interrupted, his voice cold, the realization sinking in. "This wasn't some spur-of-the-moment decision."

Ridley mounted the first gyro-cycle. "Whatever his reasons, they don't matter right now." Her eyes cut to Aldin. "We're not letting him get far."

Mishka moved beside her, placing a hand on her shoulder. "We'll find them, Aldin. But we've got to move fast."

"The ravine curves about two miles ahead," Silas said. "If we're lucky, we'll catch up to him before he gets too deep into the terrain."

Ridley locked eyes with Aldin for a moment before revving her own cycle, her voice hard but steady. "He's not getting away with this. Not on my watch."

Aldin nodded as her eyes began to tear.

Ridley's sharp gaze locked on the faint tracks left by Jeron's cycle in the dirt. "Let's move," she said.

While her eyes were filled with determination, Ridley's heart ached to see Aldin so upset over the loss of her furry friend. Even though she had been against it at first, the only real thing that ever mattered was for Aldin to be happy. And for that, she would brave the very edges of this new world and face whatever hidden dangers it presented.

They mounted their rides, the hum of the engines cutting through the desert night, a trail of dust rising behind them as they raced toward the unknown, the wind whipping against their faces, the dark landscape around them looming with shadows that threatened to engulf them at every turn.

Whatever sinister plan you have in mind, Jeron, Silas thought, *I pray you have enough compassion left inside you to end it now.*

Chapter 10

The team tore across the desert, their vehicles kicking up clouds of sand as they raced through the barren, rocky terrain. The sun was just beginning to set over the horizon, casting a deep orange glow over the rugged landscape. Ridley sped forward, her eyes locked ahead, scanning the horizon for any trace of Jeron. She felt the tension in the air, the way the wind seemed to carry an edge of warning. Behind her, Mishka kept pace, her sharp gaze flicking from one cactus-studded ridge to the next, searching for signs of disturbance.

A broken creosote bush caught Mishka's attention—a branch snapped clean off and pointing northwest, where the trail veered suddenly. "Over here! He's heading toward the rocks, at the base of something called the Arial Tramway," she called through the comms.

They turned sharply, weaving through boulders and gnarled trees as they followed the faint signs of Jeron's passage. The valley was alive with the distant calls of desert animals and the dry hiss of the wind scraping over the cracked earth. Above, the sky suddenly darkened as thick clouds rolled in, casting eerie shadows that shifted over the landscape like specters.

"Ridley, run a thermal scan," Silas ordered over the comm.

Ridley toggled her wrist console, her visor lighting up with a heat map. "Got him," she said. "West, moving fast. He's making for the rock formations along the ridge."

Silas clenched his teeth. If Jeron made it to the ridge, he'd have high ground and cover in the twisted rocks—an advantage they couldn't let him reach.

They gunned their engines, their vehicles roaring as they sped through clusters of large rocks, the sun's fading rays painting the desert floor in ominous shadows. Jeron's path was erratic, zigzagging through ravines and shallow canyons, but they managed to keep the faint trail in sight. And then, abruptly, it disappeared.

Silas's voice crackled over the comm, "Hold up. He's gone off-course."

They dismounted, fanning out and scanning the quiet landscape, every sound amplified in the desert's stillness. Aldin kneeled, examining a patch of sand where faint tracks led away from the road.

"He's on foot now," she murmured. "And Izzit's still with him."

Mishka's brow furrowed as she examined the broken shrubs around them. "It's almost like he's leading us," she said slowly. "But to what?"

Ridley's gaze narrowed. "He wants us close, but why?"

They moved cautiously, tracking Jeron's path as it wound up a rocky slope. As they climbed, the terrain became steeper, scattered with jagged stones and creosote bushes clinging to the dry soil. The path finally ended at the edge of a cliff, overlooking a wide, desolate valley below. And there, standing silhouetted against the stormy sky, was Jeron with his gyro cycle perched beside him. In his arms, Izzit trembled and whined, her wide eyes beckoning to Aldin with a look of pure terror.

He must have installed an anti-gravity dampener on the cycle at some point, Silas thought grimly, again confirming that he had been planning this for some time.

"Izzit!" Aldin cried, causing the dog to squirm and fight to free herself from Jeron's grasp. But Jeron held firm.

"Jeron!" Silas called, his voice echoing off the mountain. "Stand down and come with us. Whatever you're planning, we can work this out."

Jeron simply smiled, a wild gleam in his eyes. His hand rested lightly on the grip of the blaster at his side, but his fingers remained steady. "Work it out? You think this is just a misunderstanding?" he laughed, a bitter, hollow sound. "You have no idea what the future has in store for this new world. If you thought the destruction of Terran was catastrophic, wait until the savage apocalypse is released on this planet! Its transformation will be a thing of beauty."

"And let me guess," Silas said, "You're going to be its king?"

Jeron's smile grew wider. "Something like that."

Ridley stepped forward, her tone calm but commanding. "We've heard this nonsense before, Jeron. It was the same egomaniacal talk that spouted from your uncle Jensen's mouth. It won't end the way you want it to. Look at what happened to Jensen in the end, destroyed by his own abomination."

Jeron's laughter died away, replaced by a stiff smile. "I see you've put the pieces together." He shook his head. "His tragic downfall was certainly devastating. Maybe if he had been surrounded by a more competent group—who understood his genius—he'd still be alive to see the full beauty of his work realized." He pulled out a small, portable tablet and held it up, "But I do have the benefit of his previous research, all locked away in here."

He slipped the tablet back into his robe. "And now I have something else that gives me the power," he continued as he held up the small vial, its contents swirling darkly even in the fading light.

Silas's jaw tightened as he recognized it for what was—the same organism that destroyed their world in the blink of an eye. "Jeron, don't," he warned. "You've seen what that can do."

"Oh, I know exactly what it can do." Jeron's smile grew reckless, triumphant. "And I don't need your permission to use it."

Jeron quickly hoisted Izzit up and onto his cycle, revving the engine in a roar that echoed down the valley. Ridley lunged forward, her fingertips just brushing his robe before he wrenched himself out of reach. He sped forward, his cycle darting dangerously close to the cliff's edge before it shot down a steep, narrow path leading deeper into the valley.

"Back to our vehicles!" Silas shouted.

As the group rushed back down the hill, they moved fast, scrambling over rocks and skirting around desert foliage. Ridley was almost to the cycles when her foot caught on a jagged rock hidden in the sand. She stumbled forward, her ankle twisting hard as she tried to regain her balance. She let out a sharp cry, clutching her leg as she went down. Aldin and Mishka rushed to her side and helped her up.

Ridley grimaced, testing her weight on the injured ankle. "I'm fine," she bit out through clenched teeth. "We don't have time for this."

Aldin frowned and shook her head. "You can barely stand. Let me take your cycle and you ride with Silas."

Ridley hesitated, torn between her own rising fury and the

throbbing pain shooting up her leg. Finally, she nodded. "Fine, but you stay on him. Do not let him out of your sight."

They helped Ridley into the transport, securing her ankle as best they could. She gripped the doorframe tight as they eased her in. "Keep the comms open," she ordered, her voice steady despite the pain. "If you spot anything unusual, call it in immediately. This whole thing feels like a trap."

Aldin nodded and climbed onto her cycle, silently wishing she had trained with the vehicle in the past. Looking back now, there were a lot of things she regretted not experiencing —little moments in time that had passed her by—things she'd never get the chance to do anymore, the opportunities lost with the destruction of her world.

"Let's move," Silas said, glancing at Aldin and Mishka. "We're not letting him get away."

The cycles kicked up a spray of sand and dust as they roared off into the desert, following Jeron's trail. The path wound treacherously between rocky outcrops and steep ridges, every bump and turn making Ridley wince, but she kept her teeth clenched against the pain.

The sky was growing darker by the minute, and the valley around them seemed to close in, shadows stretching over the landscape as if the desert itself were swallowing the light. Mishka took the lead, her gaze scanning the terrain as she watched for any sign of Jeron's path. The faint glow of his cycle shimmered in the distance, just barely visible.

"There!" Mishka's voice crackled over the comm. "I see his signature moving along the eastern ridge."

"Stay close!" Silas urged, pushing his transport harder to keep up.

They sped forward, their cycles humming as they gained ground. The terrain became rockier, the path narrowing until it was barely wide enough for one vehicle at a time. The wind picked up, howling through the mountains, carrying with it the scent of dry earth and something faintly metallic.

Suddenly, a deep rumbling echoed from the cliffs above. Silas barely had time to react before an avalanche of rocks came crashing down, pelting the ground around them. Aldin swerved to avoid the debris, but a large boulder smashed into the ground just inches from her cycle, sending a spray of gravel and dust into the air.

"It's an ambush!" Ridley's voice crackled over the comm.

Silas's grip tightened on the steering console as he strained to keep the transport under control.

The canyon walls loomed closer as they sped forward, maneuvering around the falling rocks, their path narrowing into a tight corridor with sheer rock faces on either side. The air was thick with dust, choking the air from their lungs and making it hard to see.

Finally, they broke through the last of the narrow passage, emerging into an open area where the cliffs sloped down into a wide, sandy basin. Jeron's cycle gleamed in the distance, cutting across the basin at a breakneck speed. He looked back, and even from a distance, Silas could see the wild gleam in his eyes as he revved his cycle harder, urging them to follow.

"Let's finish this," Silas muttered, his eyes locked on Jeron's shrinking figure.

"Box him in!" Mishka shouted, veering left to cut him off from the open desert, while Aldin veered right.

Silas nodded, pushing his speed to match hers as they tightened the gap. They closed in, steering him toward a narrow pass that would bottleneck his escape. But just as they thought they had him cornered, Jeron let out a manic laugh. His hand moved to a lever on the side of his cycle, and suddenly the vehicle jerked, catapulting him and Izzit clear over the side of the cliff.

Silas's heart sank as he watched them plummet toward a ledge far below. Just as they were about to hit the ground, a pair of wings erupted from the sides of Jeron's cycle, transforming it into an aerial glider. With one last taunting look, he shot off, disappearing into the darkening clouds above.

As the group skidded to a halt at the cliff's edge, they could do nothing but watch as Jeron and Izzit vanished into the storm. A heavy silence settled over them, the kind that only the desert knows—a silence as ancient and relentless as the mountains themselves, waiting for whatever came next.

Chapter 11

The desert night was unnervingly silent, the kind of quiet that pressed against Hector's ears and made his heart beat a little harder. The stillness wasn't natural—it felt hollow, like something had stolen all the sound from the world and left only his own heartbeat pounding in his chest.

The moon hung high, casting twisted, jagged shadows across the craggy terrain. The ridge ahead jutted into the night like the broken spine of some long-dead beast. Hector adjusted his grip on the rusted rifle slung over his back, his boots crunching softly against the loose gravel as he climbed higher.

He needed space.

Rodrigo and the others had been on edge ever since Cathedral City fell. Hell, Hector was too, though he'd never admit it. Surviving something like that—watching the streets swarm with things that shouldn't exist, seeing friends torn savagely apart in the dark—it did something to a man. It made the world feel thinner, more fragile. Like at any second, reality could split open again and spit out something worse.

And Hector was sure something worse was coming.

He exhaled, forcing himself to breathe steady. It's just the wind. Just the quiet. He told himself that, but deep down, he knew better.

Then he heard it.

A low whine, barely audible over the wind. Faint, ghostly. Engines. Moving fast.

Hector froze. His gut instinct kicked in before his mind caught up, and he ducked low, pressing himself against the cold rock. His fingers curled around the rifle's stock as his eyes flicked down into the valley below.

At first, all he saw was the vast emptiness of the desert, stretching endlessly into the black. Then, a streak of movement.

A single figure, hunched over a sleek, glowing cycle, tore through the desert below. The vehicle barely seemed to touch the ground, skimming the desert floor like a ghost, kicking up a shimmering dust cloud in its wake. Too smooth. Too quiet. Too fast.

Hector's stomach twisted.

The rider's robe billowed behind him like a tattered flag, and his arm was wrapped tightly around something struggling.

Hector squinted. The creature—a small, black and white dog, with its ears pinned back in terror—writhed against the man's grip, not attacking, just scared.

Then, three more vehicles emerged from the shadows, silent as wraiths. Their drivers moved with unnatural precision, weaving through the rugged terrain without hesitation, without the struggle of tires against sand and stone.

Hector's breath caught.

That ain't normal, he thought. But then again, what was normal anymore?

There was no bouncing, no rattling, no resistance even, as

the wheels barely touched the ground.

The cold, gnawing dread that had been sitting in Hector's gut since Cathedral City lurched violently once more.

Then the lone rider, with the dog held tightly against his chest, did something impossible.

He angled his bike straight up the mountainside and gunned it.

Hector's mouth went dry. No machine could make a climb like that. The incline was too steep, the terrain too unstable. It should've stalled and flipped, sending the rider tumbling to his death.

But it didn't.

The cycle glided upward, hugging the rock like it was magnetized to the stone itself, moving with an eerie, effortless grace.

The vehicles of the three pursuers, however, weren't equipped with the same gravity-defying technology as their quarry, forcing them to abandon their transports and start climbing.

Hector's skin crawled as he watched them climb.

They weren't moving like normal people. While three of the adversaries scaled the mountainside like hunters, their bodies flowing over the jagged rock smoothly, the fourth one moved a little more deliberately. But even then, the effort was clearly otherworldly.

The chase ended at the very edge of the ridge, just before the drop-off into an abyss below.

Hector's fingers tightened around his rifle, watching.

The four figures stood there, still as statues, locked in some kind of argument. The tension between them was thick, even from this distance. Their body language said it all—anger, defiance, something *worse*.

Then, the lone rider smiled.

It wasn't a grin of amusement. It was something else.

Something colder.

He reached for the controls on his cycle, preparing to drive straight off the cliff.

But then, he hesitated.

For a fraction of a second, his head tilted slightly. His gaze flicked sideways, toward the ridge.

Toward Hector.

Hector's breath caught in his throat.

It was too fast, too subtle to be certain. Maybe it was just a trick of the moonlight, and his mind was playing games with him.

But in that brief moment, Hector could've sworn that the man saw him.

Not just spotted him. Acknowledged him.

Like he'd known Hector was there all along.

Then, he was gone.

The cycle plummeted over the cliff, only to rise a moment later, wings unfurling like a metal beast taking flight.

Hector sat frozen, his heart hammering in his chest.

The rider and his dog vanished into the dark, swallowed by the night, leaving the other figures standing at the ridge.

And for a long, stretched-out moment, they didn't move.

Then, one of them slammed their fist against a boulder hard enough to crack the stone.

Hector's pulse quickened. *Normal people don't do that.*

Holding his breath, Hector slowly backed away from the ridge, taking each step carefully, silently. But his mind raced, replaying that single glance.

It had only lasted a second, but Hector knew what he saw. The lone figure had looked right at him.

And there had been something in his eyes—not surprise, not alarm. Just recognition.

Like a player in a game who had just discovered a new piece on the board.

A chill spread through Hector's veins.

He tore himself away, moving faster down the slope, his breath coming in quick, shallow gasps.

He needed to tell Rodrigo.

Because whoever these people were... they knew he was here.

And that meant they might come looking.

Chapter 12

The desert night stretched wide and endless, a vast sea of black beneath a canopy of cold stars. Jeron hunched low over the steering column of his gyro cycle, the wind whipping at his face, carrying with it the scent of dry earth and distant rot. He barely glanced back, though instinct screamed that he should. He knew they were out there, somewhere behind him—maybe close, maybe miles away. It didn't matter. He needed distance. He needed cover. He needed a place to think.

Nestled in the crook of his arm, Izzit trembled, her tiny body curled into itself. She didn't make a sound. Smart dog. Somehow, she knew the weight of the moment, sensed the urgency in the way Jeron clenched the throttle like a lifeline.

Then, out of the darkness, something took shape. A massive, hulking shadow against the barren skyline. An old warehouse, skeletal and forgotten, standing like a grave marker in the middle of nowhere. The windows were shattered, gaping like the empty eye sockets of a long-dead thing, while rusted metal groaned in the wind.

Jeron veered toward it, cutting the engine as he rolled up to what had once been a loading dock. He dismounted in a single fluid motion, activating his cloaking device with a soft click. Instantly, he vanished, a phantom slipping into the abyss. He cast a quick glance over his shoulder when he thought he saw a flash of light in the distance, and for a brief moment he thought they might still be on his trail, until the light faded, and silence crept back.

He crept forward, boots crunching softly over loose gravel. A side door hung half open, yawning into the darkness beyond. He nudged it with the muzzle of his blaster, and it swung inward with a loud screech. Jeron winced, slipped inside, and pulled the door shut behind him.

The air was thick with mildew and decay, the stench of old rot hanging heavy in his nostrils, and the echo of his own footsteps seemed to chase him down every corridor. The place had been abandoned for decades—shattered glass littered the floor like scattered bones, and forgotten crates slumped against the walls, their labels worn away by time. Something skittered in the rafters, unseen but present. Every shadow seemed alive, shifting as his invisible form disturbed the dust in the air.

Jeron moved deeper, his footfalls whisper-quiet. The emptiness felt unnatural, like the warehouse itself was holding its breath.

He found a small office in the back corner and crouched down. As he settled, he unshielded himself, sinking into visibility with Izzit by his side. The dog whimpered softly, her eyes darting around nervously at every slight sound.

"Shhh, it's alright," Jeron whispered.

He reached into his pocket and pulled out the vial of writhing black liquid, his "prize." He watched it twist and writhe within the glass, a sinister, hypnotic dance that almost seemed to respond to his fear. While Izzit buried her face into his lap, his eyes lingered on the substance, mesmerized, until a sudden noise jolted him.

Footsteps echoed down the hallway outside the room. Jeron's heart raced as he held his breath, his fingers tightening around the vial. He couldn't risk being discovered, so he shrouded himself and Izzit once more, pressing himself against the damp, crumbling wall.

The footsteps paused just outside the door. He could hear shallow breathing just beyond the threshold, as if someone was listening for him. A dim light flickered under the door.

Jeron held his breath.

A shadow stretched across the doorway, long and distorted by the dim flicker of a dying light bulb somewhere in the distance. Whoever was standing there wasn't moving.

Then, without warning, the shadow shifted—and the door creaked open.

Jeron quickly spun away, melting into the darkness. A dim flashlight beam cut through the black, sweeping over the walls, the floor, the empty crates. Jeron pressed himself against the damp, crumbling wall, forcing his breath to steady.

The man moved further in. He was bundled in ragged layers, his movements cautious. A vagrant, maybe. Or something else. The flashlight trembled slightly in his grip.

"I told you," the man muttered under his breath. "This place ain't right…"

Another voice, gruff and irritated, called from the hall. "Shut up, Mike. Grab what we need and let's get the hell outta here."

"I'm tellin' ya, Reg, I heard something in here."

Jeron's grip tightened on his blaster.

After a long moment of rummaging through piles of debris, the man stumbling from the room with an armful of rotted wood and broken boards. As he joined the other man outside the room, Jeron let out a soft sigh of relief.

Finally, he heard their footsteps growing faint as they moved down the hallway, heading toward another part of the warehouse. Jeron exhaled, easing his grip on Izzit, who whimpered again, a small, pitiful sound that almost gave him away.

When he was sure the coast was clear, he slipped out of the office, moving silently down a different hallway, looking for an exit. The shadows seemed to tighten around him, and he felt eyes on his back, though he knew he was invisible. Every step through the warehouse felt like he was traversing a labyrinth of shifting shadows and lurking horrors.

As Jeron reached a side door, a flicker of light appeared just outside, coming closer, casting shadows through the grime-coated windows. He instantly froze. Whoever had come in earlier wasn't alone anymore. There were voices now, low murmurs and occasional chuckles. Silently, he edged toward the exit, doing his best to keep Izzit quiet.

Jeron waited nervously as the voices drew nearer. He inched back down the corridor, stepping lightly, letting his invisibility cloak them.

The voices were rough and grizzly. Peering around the corner, Jeron spotted three men bundled in ragged jackets, each with wrinkled, leathery skin. He realized then that they were merely vagrants gathered around a makeshift fire, oblivious to his presence. Empty cans of food and dirty blankets lay strewn around them, the scent of smoke mixing with the sourness of their unwashed bodies.

One of them, a wiry figure with hollow cheeks, began to speak, his voice slurred. "I told ya, Reg, this place is haunted. You hear things…see shadows. Makes me feel like we're being watched."

"Shut it, Mike!" snapped a large man with a scar winding

down his cheek. "Ain't nobody out here but us. Ain't nobody stupid enough to come out here."

Jeron felt a flash of irritation at the assumption. He had a mission, one that couldn't risk the prying eyes of these wanderers. Silently, he reached for the blaster holstered at his side. The metallic grip felt reassuring in his hand as he steadied his breath, timing his movements with the crackling of the fire.

With a swift, silent step, he advanced, raising the blaster and firing a bolt that struck the wiry man first. He crumpled instantly, the smell of burned fabric and flesh filling the air.

The others whipped around, their eyes wide with horror, but Jeron moved quickly, turning his blaster on the scarred man. The derelict tried to shout, but the sound was choked off as another bolt hit him square in the chest. He fell back, toppling into the flickering fire, embers scattering as his body thudded against the concrete.

The last man stumbled backward. He turned to run, but Jeron ran after him, his invisible footsteps echoing in the empty warehouse. The man's desperate panting grew louder as he looked frantically around, unable to see the shadow following him.

Jeron uncloaked just long enough for the man to see him, terror widening his eyes as he stumbled back. Before he could scream, Jeron fired, and the man fell, his body crumpling in a lifeless heap.

Quickly, Jeron dragged each body one by one into a darkened corner of the warehouse. He covered them with broken crates and metal debris, concealing their forms in the shadows. He couldn't afford any traces, no matter how unlikely it was that anyone would stumble across them here. He glanced over his handiwork one last time, ensuring no evidence of their presence remained.

Satisfied, he turned toward the exit, wiping the sweat from his brow. He felt the weight of the vial in his pocket, its presence like a living thing against his skin.

He pushed the door open just enough to squeeze through, and inched toward his gyro cycle parked in the shadows. He slid onto the seat with Izzit nestled in his lap as he twisted the throttle and peeled off into the night, leaving the warehouse behind. *This will do nicely,* he thought.

It was quiet. Forgotten. A perfect place to begin again.

Chapter 13

Hector ran.

Loose gravel slid under his boots as he stumbled down the ridge, his pulse hammering in his ears. Every breath burned, the desert air slicing into his lungs as he sprinted toward the gas station below—their makeshift hideout, their only refuge. His mind was still reeling from what he'd seen.

It didn't make sense. And yet, it was real. All of it.

By the time he reached the cracked pavement of the parking lot, his legs felt like they would give out beneath him. The station's shattered windows loomed ahead, the rusted skeleton of its once-bright signage flickering weakly, bathing the ground in an eerie glow.

Inside, Luis's crew had settled in as if they owned the place, lounging on upturned crates and passing around a stolen bottle of tequila. The two gangs had been working together for days now, but the tension still lingered. Old habits, old rivalries—old grudges.

Rodrigo sat on the counter near the register, flipping a knife between his fingers, his boot tapping against the cracked tiles. Luis leaned against a wall, arms crossed, eyes half-closed in boredom.

Benny took a swig from the bottle, laughing at something Chuy said, but the second Hector stormed through the door, panting and wild-eyed, the mood in the room shifted.

Rodrigo narrowed his eyes. "Damn, man. You look like you just saw La Llorona." He smirked, passing the knife from hand to hand. "Or you just that excited to see me?"

Hector didn't stop to catch his breath. He slammed his hands on the counter. "You're not far off."

Rodrigo raised an eyebrow.

Luis let out a lazy chuckle from across the room. "Shit, what now? More nightmares?"

"I just saw something," Hector said, voice sharp, urgent. "Out in the mountains."

Rodrigo groaned, rubbing his face. "Let me guess. The aliens came down to bless you with a prophecy?"

Hector shot him a glare. "Listen to me, cabrón. I don't care if you believe it or not, but something's out there."

The others exchanged glances.

Rodrigo sighed. "All right. What the hell did you see?"

Hector's stomach clenched as he recounted it all, every single bizarre detail, slowing down several times to catch his breath and quiet his building nerves.

By the time he was done, the room was deathly silent.

Then Luis let out a slow whistle, shaking his head. "Man… you've lost your goddamn mind."

Hector gritted his teeth. "I know what I saw."

Rodrigo scoffed. "So what, we're in a fucking sci-fi movie now? That's what you're tellin' me?"

Oscar snorted. "Dude's been in the desert too long. Brain's fried."

Hector clenched his fists. He knew how it sounded. Hell, if someone else had told him this, he wouldn't believe it either.

"But what if he's right?" Rico spoke up for the first time,

his voice calm, measured. "We've seen some crazy shit, man. Animals turning into monsters, insect swarms from Hell."

Rodrigo exhaled, rubbing the bridge of his nose. "Look, whatever you think you saw, it ain't our problem." He gestured to the room. "We got real shit to worry about. Keeping this crew together. Finding supplies. Figuring out what the hell comes next."

Hector scowled. "And what happens when they show up here? Because they will."

Rodrigo rolled his eyes. "Yeah, whatever you say, man."

Hector exhaled sharply, shaking his head. *Fine.* If they weren't going to listen, then fuck them. He turned toward the exit and threw the door open, only to stop dead in his tracks.

A figure stood at the edge of the lot, partially illuminated by the soft glow of the moon overhead.

The man, clad in a dark robe, was holding something bundled in his arms. Instantly Hector realized it was the same man he had seen in the mountains.

His blood turned to ice.

Rodrigo's voice floated in from behind him. "Hector, what the hell are you doing?"

Hector swallowed hard. "We have a problem."

Rodrigo stepped up beside him and froze.

The man took a step forward, out of the shadow of the station's eroding marquee, and the moonlight finally hit his face. He was younger than Hector had thought, and his eyes held something cruel and otherworldly in them. A smirk tugged at the corners of his mouth, like he knew something they didn't.

The bundle in his arms moved and a soft whimper escaped from the small black-and-white dog nestled there.

Rodrigo's eyes grew wide. "The fuck?"

Before anyone could move, the man raised his arm and

pointed a strange-looking gun in their direction. A blast of crackling energy surged forward, slamming into the sign that hung above the center of the building. The explosion sent sparks and debris flying in all directions.

Hector and Rodrigo dove to the ground as the others rushed outside with their weapons drawn.

The man lowered his blaster and looked at the group through calculating eyes. "Now that I have your attention."

Hector's ears were ringing, his heart hammering against his ribs.

Rodrigo groaned, pushing himself up. "Who the fuck are you?!"

The man tilted his head. "The only person who can keep you alive."

Rodrigo and Hector exchanged a wary glance.

Luis sneered, stepping forward. "Yeah? You just shot at us, motherfucker."

The stranger chuckled. "If I wanted you dead, you'd be dead." His sharp gaze swept over the group. "I need people. You need protection. We can help each other."

Rodrigo narrowed his eyes. "Help you do what, exactly?"

The man smiled, slow and cold. "Change the world."

Hector swallowed hard. *I don't like the sound of that.*

Rodrigo, though, looked intrigued.

Luis scowled when he saw Rodrigo's interest in the stranger's proposal. "You serious, Rod?"

Rodrigo dusted himself off. "He's got tech we ain't ever seen. What he just did? That's power."

Luis shook his head. "Man, you don't make deals with crazy. You put a bullet in it."

The stranger sighed, looking almost bored. "If that's your answer..." His hand twitched toward his side.

Rodrigo reacted first. "Wait."

The stranger stopped, raising an eyebrow.

Rodrigo exhaled, his mind racing. He hated this. Every instinct screamed this was a bad idea. But instincts wouldn't keep them alive. Power would.

He looked at Hector. At Luis. At the battered, bloodied men around him.

Then he looked back at the stranger.

"Let's talk. But first, I want a name."

The stranger smiled at Rodrigo, his expression a mixture of genius and lunacy. "The name is Jeron."

Chapter 14

The Coachella Valley lay sprawled beneath the scorching sun, a dust-laden desert scape peppered with silent, jagged rock formations that loomed like ancient sentinels. Silas narrowed his eyes against the glare, the reflection of the mountains casting shadows that played tricks on the mind. The place was hauntingly silent, but every creak and whisper of wind through the sagebrush felt like it was hiding something. After hours on the hunt, patience was wearing thin.

"Why are we still here?" muttered Mishka, her eyes scanning the horizon in frustration. "We've been combing the same rock piles all day."

"Because it appears that Jeron is exceptionally good at hiding," Silas replied. "And we have no idea what kind of tricks he has up his sleeve. Keep your eyes sharp."

The desert stretched out before them like an endless graveyard of cracked earth and sun-bleached rock, a desolate wasteland where the only movement came from the lazy sway of heat rising off the sand. Silas sat at the helm of his transport, its engine humming beneath him, his eyes scanning the barren landscape ahead. The mountains loomed in the distance, jagged teeth silhouetted against the dying light. It was beautiful in a way—if you ignored the sense of isolation clawing at the edges of your mind.

Ridley rode beside him, her gaze fixed ahead, lips set in a thin line, with Aldin holding tight against her. Mishka followed close behind, checking her scanner every few seconds, frustration creeping into her features.

They had been at this for hours, tracking every faint heat signature, following footprints that led to nothing, chasing ghosts. They quickly realized that the desert was a cruel mistress, erasing signs of life in a matter of minutes.

The drone hovered above them, its whirring blades a constant companion. Every so often, Mishka's handheld screen flared with a potential hit, only for them to arrive and find subtle signs that Jeron had been there, but he was always one step ahead.

Mishka growled. "Well, if he's out here, he's not making it easy."

Silas didn't respond immediately. He adjusted his visor, tapping into the drone's thermal imaging. The scanner flickered with bursts of red and yellow, mapping out the valley's heat signatures, but none of them matched the one they were looking for.

"He's hiding," Silas finally said. "And if we don't find him before nightfall, we're at a disadvantage."

That was the truth. The valley still held remnants of things they didn't fully understand. Though the immediate threat had been dealt with, something about this place felt... wrong. The air was too still, the silence too heavy. Even the creatures that should have been stirring at dusk seemed absent, as if the desert itself had learned fear.

Silas glanced at Mishka's scanner again, watching the display shift and flicker as the drone completed another pass. He was about to suggest doubling back when a new heat signature flared on the screen. One that he recognized.

Silas stiffened. "There."

Mishka zoomed in, enhancing the image. The signature pulsed near an old gas station, half-buried in sand and decay, on the edge of the valley.

"That's him," she confirmed.

Without another word, Silas revved his transport and took off, the others following close behind. They wove through scattered Joshua trees and the skeletal remains of long-abandoned structures, the scent of dry rot and sunbaked asphalt growing stronger as they neared the station.

It had once been a bustling pit stop, a place where weary travelers refueled, grabbed a quick meal, and continued on their way. Now, it was just another corpse in the desert, leaning slightly to one side, as if too tired to keep standing. The roof had caved in on one section, exposing rusted beams and shattered glass. The gas pumps stood like headstones, their paint peeled away in jagged scars. Graffiti layered every remaining inch of the walls, overlapping in chaotic colors, some of it fresh, others faded, remnants of different groups that had claimed this place over time.

But it wasn't just the decay that set Silas on edge—it was the signs of recent occupation.

The skeletal remains of a bonfire sat in the cracked pavement out front, surrounded by empty cans and discarded bottles. He could see tread marks in the dirt of various vehicles, evidence that multiple people had left in a hurry. The front of the station bore scorch marks, the twisted remains of a shattered neon sign clearly burned by a blaster rifle. Bullet holes pockmarked the walls, and the old, rusted No Trespassing sign dangled uselessly from a single broken chain.

They dismounted silently, spreading out as they neared

the entrance. The air was thick with dust, tinged with the stale scent of sweat and motor oil. Whatever gang had holed up here, they hadn't been gone long.

Inside, the station was dark, its floor littered with broken glass, discarded food containers, and scraps of paper that crunched underfoot. Shelves stood in various states of collapse, their contents long since scavenged. Against one wall, empty crates had been stacked into makeshift barricades, and a few upturned chairs suggested a hasty retreat.

A soft creak echoed from deeper inside the station.

Silas and Ridley exchanged a glance. No words were needed.

Mishka and Ridley flanked out, covering the side rooms, with Aldin covering the rear, while Silas moved straight ahead. He stepped carefully, his boots brushing aside spent shell casings. A dark stain on the ground caught his eye—blood, dried and cracked like rust against the dirty floor.

In the far corner, an old portable device blinked faintly. Silas crouched, scanning the space.

"He's been here," he said. "And not long ago."

"Think he'll be back?" Ridley whispered.

Silas shook his head. "I doubt it. But he left something behind."

He reached for the device, the screen flickering as his fingers brushed against it. Whatever Jeron had been planning, this place had been part of it. And now, it was up to them to figure out what came next.

"We'll analyze this when we get back to the ship," Silas said, handing the device to Mishka, who slipped it into a secure pouch. He stood and gestured for the team to continue moving. "He's leading us somewhere, and we're going to find out where."

A sudden beep from Silas's comm device startled the silence. "There's an update from the drone," he muttered, checking the screen. Jeron's heat signature had appeared again, tracking southeast, toward the distant hills. Jeron was heading toward the desolate foothills of the Salton Sea, a place known only for its deadly quiet and eerie, decaying structures.

They piled back onto their vehicles and sped off, kicking up clouds of dust in their wake. The landscape around them transformed as they approached the Salton Sea, twisted and abandoned, the sun casting ominous shadows over broken-down buildings and rusted-out cars. The eerie stillness seemed to suck the air from the valley, and the team fell into tense silence as they moved through the empty streets.

The terrain had changed. Silas could feel it in the way the ground softened beneath the transport's tires, how the air thickened with something unseen but oppressive. The land here had been dead for a long time. The sky stretched out in endless, colorless expanse, and before them lay what Mishka's map referred to as the *Salton Sea.*

But it was no sea.

The water, if it could be called that, sat heavy and still, like a massive, infected wound across the land. The air carried an acrid, sour scent that burned the nose, a mix of decay, stagnant salt, and something chemical. Along the shore, skeletal remains of creatures long since perished curled in the dirt—bleached bones of strange, finned animals, their empty eye sockets reflecting the last remnants of daylight.

"This place is cursed," Aldin murmured, frowning as she looked out at the vast body of lifeless water. "Death hangs heavy here."

Ridley adjusted her grip on the cycle's controls, fighting to keep back the inner terror that the sea brought forward in her mind. "It does not belong," she agreed. "And neither do we."

Silas kept his gaze on the scanner, his fingers tightening around the device. Jeron's heat signature was here. Flickering. Pulsing.

They advanced cautiously, their vehicles kicking up loose earth as they maneuvered toward the location marked on the map. The skeletal remains of structures dotted the shore—abandoned dwellings and rusted-out machines that once moved across the land but had long since succumbed to time. Everything here felt unnatural.

Mishka checked her screen again, narrowing her eyes. "His signal is fluctuating."

Silas frowned. "Explain."

She tapped at the display. "It's erratic. There's some kind of interference—possibly artificial."

Jeron's unmistakable heat signature pulsed near the remains of a rotting pier. But something wasn't right.

"It's too still," he said.

They spread out, circling the area cautiously, weapons raised. The only sound was the lapping of the toxic water against the shore, accompanied by the distant groan of metal as the wind pushed through the skeletal remains of old buildings. As they approached the decayed pier, something flickered on Mishka's scanner.

"I don't like this," she whispered. "It's like he's just... waiting."

Ridley kept her rifle focused straight ahead. "Since when does Jeron just wait for us?"

Then, as if answering her question, a figure stepped into view beneath the pier, half-shrouded in the encroaching darkness.

Silas tensed.

The figure didn't move. It just stood there, motionless, like it was waiting for something.

"Step out where we can see you," Silas ordered, keeping his weapon trained.

Nothing. The shape remained frozen, its silhouette barely distinguishable against the shifting hues of the dead sea.

Mishka took a slow step forward. "Silas... something's wrong."

And then, the air shifted. The shape flickered.

The device Mishka had found back at the station beeped loudly from her pack, its display suddenly flashing erratic data streams. The team jolted as the figure under the pier disintegrated into nothing but light—a mirage, a projected heat signature.

Mishka hissed. "It's a decoy!"

A blast of static crackled through their comms. The faintest, mocking laugh echoed before the feed cut to dead air.

Silas's eyes darkened. "He played us."

They'd been tracking a ghost, a programmed misdirection leading them straight into nothing. The realization sank in like a weight in his gut. Jeron had known they were coming and had led them here deliberately.

But why?

Then, before anyone could answer that unspoken question, the Salton Sea answered for them.

The lake *moved*. Not in waves. Not in ripples. It *boiled*.

Thick, sulfurous bubbles erupted from beneath the surface, breaking through the oily sheen of the water with sluggish, oozing bursts. The stench that followed was overwhelming— a putrid mix of rotting fish, ammonia, and something chemical.

Ridley recoiled, coughing into her sleeve. "What *is* that?"

Aldin checked her scanner, then grimaced. "Methane,

hydrogen sulfide, and in high concentrations. The water here is decaying from the inside."

The bubbles expanded, and the first wave of dead things hit the shore.

Fish. Hundreds, thousands of them. Some half-dissolved, others grotesquely bloated, their scales peeling away in patches. Their mouths hung open, frozen in silent screams, their sunken eyes staring at nothing.

Then came the birds.

Gulls, pelicans, blackbirds—falling from the sky in twisted, convulsing heaps, their wings spasming before going still. Some had already begun to rot mid-air, their feathers slick with something tar-like, as if the air itself had poisoned them.

Ridley's hand went to her weapon instinctively. "This place is dying *again*."

Silas remained still, scanning the lake. The heat signature was gone. The only thing left was death.

"We were never following him," he said finally. "This was a decoy."

Mishka cursed under her breath. "Jeron created a false marker to lead us away from him and into this death trap."

The realization hit hard. They had wasted time chasing a ghost, while the real Jeron was somewhere else, unseen, unbothered.

Ridley wiped the back of her hand across her mouth, her face pale. "We should *not* be here."

"No," Silas agreed. "We should not."

Then the ground trembled.

A deep, *sick* vibration beneath their feet, like the planet itself was exhaling. Silas steadied himself as cracks slithered across the dirt, fissures splitting open, releasing more of the foul-smelling gas.

Then, the *hissing* started.

It came from beneath them, from the cracked land itself. The sound of something being released. Something *escaping.*

Aldin gasped as a sudden burst of heat struck her face. Not fire. Not air. Something unseen, but dense, like stepping into a cloud of invisible smoke. She stumbled back, her breathing shallow. "We have to *go,*" she choked.

An instant later, Mishka collapsed.

Her body jerked, limbs locking up as if she'd been electrocuted. Her fingers clawed at the air, her mouth opened in a silent scream. Then, just as suddenly, she went still.

Ridley was at her side in an instant, pressing two fingers to Mishka's throat. "She's alive," she said, voice tight. "But her pulse—it's erratic."

Silas didn't hesitate. He slung Mishka's limp body over his shoulder, his grip firm but careful. "Get to the transports. *Now.*"

Ridley and Aldin scrambled forward as the hissing grew louder, rising from the cracked earth in unnatural *whispers.* The shadows around them lengthened, bending at impossible angles, reaching like skeletal fingers toward their retreating forms.

Aldin stumbled as another wave of invisible heat rolled over them, thick as a wall pressing against her chest. Her vision blurred at the edges, the distant hills distorting into something stretched and unnatural. She barely managed to stay on her feet, dragging herself toward Mishka's gyro cycle.

Ridley wasn't far behind, her breath coming in short, sharp bursts. She glanced at Aldin, eyes searching, making sure she was still standing. "Are you good?"

Aldin nodded, though her fingers trembled as she gripped the steering console of her transport. "I'm fine."

Ridley mounted her cycle, steadying herself, then shot Aldin a look. "Be *sure.*"

Aldin forced herself to breathe, to focus, to shake off the lingering haze. "I will be if you are."

Ridley let out a short, breathless chuckle. "You always worry too much."

"You don't worry *enough*."

A second passed—long enough for their eyes to meet, long enough for the words left unsaid to settle between them. Then Ridley reached over, gripping Aldin's wrist for just a moment. "Don't fall behind."

Aldin squeezed back, her own pulse steadying at the contact. "You either."

Then, without another word, they both revved their cycles and shot forward, desperate to leave the unnatural *hissing* behind them.

Silas had already secured Mishka onto the back of his transport, her unconscious form slumped against him as he pushed the machine to its limit. The toxic gas geysers behind them erupted in force, spewing foul-smelling plumes into the air.

The crater they left behind deepened, widening, a wound splitting open in the earth, as if something had been buried beneath the Salton Sea and had been woken up.

Chapter 15

William was running.

The ground beneath him was soft and wet, sucking at his boots with each desperate step. Around him, the world twisted in grotesque shapes—trees that bled red sap, rocks that pulsed like beating hearts. The air reeked of decay, a stench so thick it burned his nostrils. The buzzing was everywhere, a relentless hum that crawled inside his skull and echoed through his bones.

He turned a corner, his lungs burning and his chest heaving as he gasped for breath. Ahead, a little girl stood in a clearing, with her back to him. Her yellow dress was torn and splattered with blood. Her curls bounced as she swayed from side to side.

"Don't move, little girl!" he called out desperately.

She didn't turn around.

Then the buzzing grew louder. His heart pounded even harder as a dark cloud gathered in front of her, a living, writhing storm of wings and legs, with mandibles clicking like bone on stone. The swarm rolled closer, devouring everything in its path—trees stripped to splinters, the ground turned to rot.

"Run!" William shouted.

Slowly, she faced him, and what he saw shook him to his core, making his skin crawl and his blood run cold.

Her eyes were hollow. Insects poured from her mouth, writhing black things that scuttled over her chin and into her ears. She reached for him, fingers twitching, nails crusted with blood.

"Help me!"

William raised his gun. The trigger was heavy, a huge weight that pulled at his soul.

"Please…" Her voice broke into a whisper as more insects surged from her throat, filling her scream.

The swarm lunged forward and he fired.

The blast echoed through the night like thunder.

A second later, she dropped to the ground. Her body twitched for a brief moment then went still.

The ground shuddered. From her stomach, something moved. The insects boiled up, seething from her broken flesh, their eyes glittering with a horrible, wicked light. They twisted together, a black mass writhing to form a shape, then into a face.

A face he knew. Clause's face.

It grinned. "You'll never save them all," he screeched.

The swarm exploded toward him, a million deadly mandibles snapping hungrily.

***

William woke with a gasp, his body jerking violently upright.

Cold sweat slicked his skin. His heart slammed against his ribs, and the sound of his own ragged breathing filled his ears.

Buzzing.

For a split second, it was still there—an echo of the nightmare—but then he blinked, and it was gone.

He pressed the heels of his hands against his eyes. *It's just a dream. Just a dream.*

The bedroom was dark, except for the thin slivers of moonlight that snaked through the blinds and slashed pale stripes across the floor. The quiet hum of the ceiling fan did nothing to still the storm in William's mind.

He sat at the edge of the bed, elbows on his knees, head bowed as if weighed down by the memories that clung to him like a second skin. Sweat trickled down the back of his neck, cold against his heated skin. His bare feet rested flat on the wooden floor, but it felt as if the ground beneath him was shifting, like quicksand threatening to pull him under.

He clenched his fists, the tendons in his hands stretching tight as cables. His breath came shallow and uneven. *Don't look back. Don't let it in.* But it was already there, crawling behind his eyes, slithering into the corners of his mind.

The sounds came first.

Buzzing. A thousand wings drumming in unison.

Then the screams.

They rose from somewhere deep in his memory, cutting through his defenses like a scalpel. He squeezed his eyes shut, but it only made the visions sharper. Blood sprayed across pavement. A girl's wide, terrified eyes pleaded with him for salvation he couldn't give. Insects writhed in her mouth, spilling into her throat. Her body contorted, spasms wracking her frame as he raised the gun.

He shuddered, his fingers digging into his scalp as if he could claw the images out.

"William?"

He flinched at the sound of Melinda's sudden voice.

Her voice was soft, still laced with sleep, but it cut through the darkness. She stirred beside him, her hand brushing lightly over his arm. "What's wrong?"

He didn't answer right away. He kept his head bowed, his body rigid. "Go back to sleep."

"I'm not going to sleep while you're sitting there like this." She shifted, rising onto one elbow. "Talk to me."

"I'm fine."

"You're not fine." She touched his back gently. His skin was clammy beneath her fingers. "You haven't been fine for a long time."

His breath caught in his throat. "I can still see her."

Her hand stilled. "Who?"

He didn't answer immediately. When he spoke again, his voice was raw and shaky. "All of them. The ones I couldn't save. The ones I—" He swallowed hard. "I see their faces. Every time I close my eyes."

Melinda moved closer, wrapping her arms around him from behind, her embrace firm, grounding. "It wasn't your fault."

"It doesn't matter." His voice cracked. "I killed her. I had to. But it doesn't matter—she's dead because of me."

"You did what you had to do," she whispered.

"I pulled the trigger."

She tightened her arms around him, resting her cheek against his shoulder. "You saved so many lives."

He clenched his jaw. "It wasn't enough."

Her breath warmed his skin, her voice steady. "It was more than anyone else could've done."

He sat there, silent and still, her warmth seeping into him, pushing back the cold shadows that refused to let him go. For a moment, he allowed himself to believe her. But deep down, he felt the weight of something unfinished.

And he knew, even as she held him, that the storm was far

from over.

Chapter 16

The hospital smelled of antiseptic and fading hope. William had come to know it well in the long weeks since Andrea had been admitted. He moved through the quiet halls with practiced ease, past the nurses who barely looked up anymore, so used to his presence they hardly registered him. Room 417, third door on the left—he could find it in his sleep. And in a way, he had.

Every night, he sat in that hard plastic chair, staring at Andrea's still form, hoping for a twitch of a finger, a flicker of an eyelid—anything. But the machines did all the work, keeping her alive when her body refused to do it on its own.

Today was no different. He eased into the chair beside her bed, rubbing a hand over his face, exhaustion weighing him down like an anchor. The heart monitor beeped in its steady, cruel rhythm, a sound that had become a kind of white noise in his world. He leaned forward, elbows on his knees, studying her face. Pale, thinner than he remembered, but still Andrea. The woman who had survived the apocalypse, who had fought through hell and come out swinging. The woman who had taken a bullet because she refused to back down.

"Evening, Doc," he muttered, voice hoarse from disuse. He

reached out, brushing a strand of dark hair from her forehead.

He exhaled, shaking his head. Talking to her like this was starting to feel more like talking to himself. But if he stopped, the silence would be unbearable.

"Guerera says hi. She wanted to come by, but, you know, Marine stuff. Ashley said for you to get better. And Melinda —well, she's trying to make me sleep more, but you know how that goes. Tommy and Kate are doing okay, considering."

A small, sad chuckle.

"And Samuel… well, he'd be here too, if he could."

His throat tightened. He never said it outright. Never let himself voice it in the quiet of this room. Because if Andrea woke up and he hadn't spoken the words, maybe there was still a sliver of time where it wasn't real.

The chair creaked as he leaned back, tilting his head against the wall, staring at the ceiling, willing time to shift forward or backward, just not remain in this goddamn limbo.

And then, it happened.

A sound—not the steady beeping of the machines, not the hum of the ventilator—something small, almost imperceptible. A rustle. A breath.

William shot forward, eyes locking onto Andrea's face just as her eyelids fluttered, the faintest crease forming between her brows. He held his breath, heart pounding.

"Come on, Andrea," he whispered, gripping the side of the bed.

Her fingers twitched.

Then, with an agonized slowness, her eyes cracked open, pupils dilating against the harsh fluorescent light. She blinked sluggishly, confusion washing over her as she tried to focus.

William swallowed hard. "Andrea?"

Her lips parted, dry and cracked. She tried to speak, but no sound came. Her throat bobbed as she swallowed. Her brow furrowed, and when she finally found her voice, it was barely a whisper.

"Where...?"

"You're in the hospital," he said gently. "You got shot. But you're safe now."

She swallowed thickly, and for the first time, genuine fear flashed in her dark eyes. "How long?"

"Almost three weeks," William replied softly, watching as her mind struggled to catch up, the weight of lost time crashing down on her.

She exhaled sharply, turning her head slightly, scanning the room as if searching for someone. Her lips parted again, forming a name he already knew was coming.

"Samuel?"

William's heart clenched like a fist in his chest. The moment he had been dreading, the moment he had spent every visit wishing he could delay just a little longer, was here.

She turned her head fully to him, eyes locking onto his, pleading for an answer she wasn't ready for.

He opened his mouth, then closed it. His fingers curled into his palms. There was no way to soften this. No way to make it hurt any less.

"He's gone, Andrea," William said, his voice barely more than a breath.

The room went deathly still.

Andrea's gaze remained fixed on him, her breathing shallow, her chest rising and falling in rapid succession. Her fingers twitched against the sheets, as if trying to grasp something that had already slipped away. Her face crumpled, the realization slamming into her like a physical blow. A ragged sob tore from her throat, her body shaking beneath the thin hospital blankets. She turned her head away, her tears pooling onto the pillow, silent but endless.

William reached out, hesitating before resting a hand gently over hers. "I wish I could tell you it wasn't true," he said softly. "I wish—" His voice caught, and he looked away, blinking hard.

For a long while, neither of them spoke. Just the sound of the machines, the rhythmic beep of the monitor, the quiet weeping of a woman who had already lost too much.

Finally, Andrea inhaled sharply, struggling to steady herself. She turned back to him, eyes red and raw, but filled with something new. Determination.

"Tell me you got the bastard?"

William met her gaze, and in that moment, he knew that Andrea Melborne, despite the tears on her face, despite the weakness in her limbs, was still very much the same woman he had fought beside before.

"Yes," William replied somberly. "He can't hurt anyone anymore."

Her breathing was still uneven, her body trembling from the weight of William's words. The heart monitor beside her beeped steadily, each sound drilling into the silence that followed. The tears had slowed, but her eyes remained wet, dark pools of grief and something colder, harder—resolve.

Clause was dead. But Ashton wasn't. And Andrea was going to make damn sure he paid for it.

She turned her head toward him again, swallowing past the lump in her throat. "Tell me..." she rasped, her voice raw. "Tell me we're going after them."

William exhaled slowly, rubbing his hands together, staring at the floor as if the answer were written in the sterile white tiles. He had been expecting this question. Hell, he had been asking it himself ever since the first signs of the savage apocalypse had surfaced.

"I am," he finally said, his voice steady but weighted with something else. Something she couldn't quite name yet. "I rejoined the force."

Andrea blinked, confusion flickering across her face before narrowing into suspicion. "You—what?"

"I'm going back to the police department," he repeated. "I'm getting my badge back in a couple weeks."

Andrea let out a short, humorless laugh that turned into a weak cough. "You're going back after everything that's happened?"

William shrugged, leaning back in his chair, arms folded across his chest. "Funny thing about near-apocalyptic disasters. They make people rethink who they want in charge when things go to hell. The department needs someone who knows what's really out there. And I need resources. If I have a badge, I can pull files, request surveillance, track movement. I can get access to information I wouldn't have otherwise."

Andrea studied him carefully. "And Ashton?"

William's jaw tightened, his fingers curling into fists in his lap. "I'll find him."

A shadow crossed Andrea's face, her exhaustion momentarily forgotten as she pushed herself up slightly, wincing.

"The bastard went underground, but no matter how deep he goes, I'll get him. For you. For us. For Samuel."

Andrea stared at him for a long moment, then let out a slow breath. "You're going to need help."

"You're in no shape to be running around chasing ghosts," William said firmly. "You just woke up from a coma. You need time to recover."

Her fingers tightened around the sheets. "Screw that."

William shook his head. "Andrea—"

"No." Her voice was stronger now, anger fueling her words. "You don't get to do this alone, William. We lost too much because of him. I need to be there when we bring him down."

William let out a slow sigh, rubbing the back of his neck. He had expected this too. Andrea wasn't the kind of person to sit on the sidelines. She never had been.

"Let's start with me finding out where he is," he said finally.

Andrea nodded, though he could tell it wasn't enough for her. It wouldn't be until she was out of that bed and back on her feet, back in the fight where she belonged.

A long silence stretched between them. Then, quietly, she asked, "Does Guerera know?"

William hesitated, then nodded. "Yeah. She wasn't thrilled."

Andrea huffed a small, tired laugh. "I can imagine." She let her head rest against the pillow, staring at the ceiling. "And Melinda?"

William swallowed, the thought of his wife's worried face flashing in his mind. "She just wants me to be careful."

Andrea closed her eyes for a moment, then opened them again. "Then don't get yourself killed."

William smirked. "I'll do my best."

Andrea let out a slow breath, her eyelids heavy. "Wake me up when you've got a lead."

William nodded, watching as her exhaustion finally took hold, pulling her back into sleep. He stayed in his chair a little while longer, staring at the quiet hum of the machines.

Soon, he'd be back in uniform. Back on the hunt.

And if Ashton Brown was still out there, William Patterson was damn sure going to find him.

Chapter 17

The smell of fresh pastries and dark roast coffee wafted invitingly throughout the bustling small coffee shop on the corner. Melinda sat at a corner table with Guerera, a loose stack of papers scattered between them. One of the pages was a crude sketch of the police precinct featuring stick-figure officers holding balloons and a poorly drawn banner.

Melinda tapped her pen against the page. "The cake goes here," she said, circling a spot near the breakroom door. "I'm picking it up in the morning. It'll say 'Welcome Back, Hero'—Tommy insisted on the wording."

Guerera smirked and rolled her eyes as she bit into a muffin. "He'll love that. And I've got decorations handled. Streamers, confetti, and…" She pulled a small box from her jacket pocket, eyes sparkling mischievously. "A little something for flair."

Melinda leaned in. "No. That better not be—"

"A portable air horn," Guerera confirmed with a wicked grin. "One blast when he walks in, and he'll jump out of his skin."

Melinda covered her mouth to stifle a laugh. "You can't blast that in a police station."

"Why not? He survived the fucking apocalypse. I think he can handle a little noise."

The door chimed, and Melinda's laughter died in her throat as William unexpectedly walked into the shop. The moment instantly froze.

"Act natural," Melinda whispered, shoving the papers under her napkin.

"I am natural," Guerera hissed, fumbling to cover the drawing with her notebook.

William approached the table, his gaze bouncing between them. "Hey, you two. I didn't expect to see you here. What are you guys up to?"

"Nothing," they each said quickly.

William raised an eyebrow. "Really? Then why are you cramming paper under a muffin?" He pointed toward the suspicious bulge under Guerera's napkin.

Guerera thought fast. "We're planning your birthday party. Top secret."

He narrowed his eyes. "My birthday isn't for six months."

Melinda cleared her throat. "Exactly. She's obsessed with getting ahead. Over-prepared. It's her thing."

William didn't seem convinced. "Right." He gestured at the cluttered table. "And why are you meeting at *this* coffee shop instead of the one near home?"

Melinda blinked, scrambling for a reason. "Uh... free refills."

"And muffins," Guerera added, biting into one.

William folded his arms. "And what's under the napkin?"

Melinda swallowed. "Another muffin."

He gave a long, suspicious look before sighing. "You two are terrible liars."

Guerera grinned. "It's charming, though, right?"

"Charming's not the word I'd use." He rubbed the back of

his neck. "I was just making a quick stop on my way to pick up supplies for the back patio. I'll be at the hardware store if you need me."

As he walked toward the counter, Guerera leaned over, smirking. "You think he bought it?"

Melinda frowned. "Not for a second. We'll have to be more careful."

Guerera rolled her eyes but smiled. "This party's going to be legendary... and loud," she added with a mischievous wink.

***

Jeron slipped into the dim, cavernous space of the abandoned warehouse, its cracked concrete floor strewn with discarded scraps of wire and broken machinery. A shaft of sunlight cut through a jagged hole in the roof, illuminating the dust that swirled in the stale air. He smiled grimly. It was a sanctuary of forgotten things—perfect for his work.

He moved quickly, unloading a duffel filled with scavenged tools. A standard cordless drill, a soldering iron, and a bundle of wiring were transformed into precision instruments under his deft hands. A cracked flat-screen television, salvaged from a nearby dumpster, became the central interface of his makeshift control hub. He dismantled a pile of old smartphones, extracting cameras, processors, and batteries, reshaping them with alien ingenuity. In minutes, he crafted micro-surveillance drones disguised as ordinary insects—small flies with reflective, mechanical wings.

Next, he wired a set of motion detectors from a store-bought home security kit into a sophisticated sensor grid, capable of picking up fluctuations in temperature and electromagnetic fields. A simple baby monitor was rewired, its range extended, becoming a directional audio amplifier sensitive enough to capture whispered conversations through walls. Jeron laughed softly as he mounted it to a tripod made from repurposed curtain rods.

The generator hummed to life, powering his crude command station. Holographic projections sprang into being as he linked his devices to an alien data core he had embedded inside a refurbished game console. The screens displayed street maps, citizen registries, and surveillance feeds from public cameras.

Jeron leaned forward, his fingers dancing over a touch interface as he brought up archived footage of the first outbreak. Grainy clips of feral creatures tearing through streets, bloodied claw marks on glass, and terrified screams filled the screen. He absorbed every detail, his eyes narrowing as he traced patterns of infection and response times. Each keystroke brought him closer to understanding how the humans had contained the threat.

"Ah, here we are..." he murmured, pulling up the personnel records linked to the incident. A series of names scrolled past: Dr. Patrick Leonard, Kelvin Knepler, Guerera, and finally William Patterson. He tapped the last name, a sly smile curving his lips as a picture of the former police officer appeared.

"William," Jeron mused, studying the face of the man who had stood against the first wave. "You've already danced with death once. Let's see how you fare when it comes knocking again."

His eyes darkened as he tracked William's movements through public records and surveillance data. Scenes unfolded of William with his wife, Melinda, and their children. He stopped on an image of them at a grocery store

—an ordinary moment, filled with laughter that Jeron found particularly distasteful.

He whispered to himself, "So much to lose."

He paused as he pulled up a live image of William Patterson. The feed showed William stepping out of his home, a weary smile on his face as he waved to his wife and children. Jeron's eyes narrowed as he noted the limp in William's stride and the tension in his jaw. He keyed in a command, setting automated alerts to flag any unusual activity involving William or his known associates.

"Let's see how vigilant you really are, hero," Jeron muttered, his voice dripping with scorn.

He installed modified insect-drones in strategic locations—one inside a potted plant near William's front porch, another hidden within a light fixture at the police precinct. Their miniature cameras transmitted sharp, fisheye views directly to his makeshift lab. Each subtle movement of William and those around him would now be Jeron's to observe.

As the sun dipped below the horizon, he leaned back, surveying his newly established web of surveillance. The warehouse now buzzed with the hum of technology disguised as relics of a discarded world. His tools were crude by Terran standards, but they would suffice.

Jeron clenched his fist, the vial of dormant alien organism still safely locked away in his pack. He wasn't ready to release it—yet. Timing was everything. First, he would watch. Learn. Stalk the prey until the perfect moment to strike. This time, there would be no salvation. Only chaos.

Jeron whispered, "The game begins, William Patterson."

Chapter 18

Jeron crouched in the darkness, high above the facility, perched on a steel support beam that overlooked The Ames Research Facility stretching out beneath him, a sprawling maze of laboratories and restricted corridors. But his interest lay in the secret buried deep in its lower levels. Ashton Brown.

A small, sadistic smile crept across Jeron's lips as he activated his cloaking field, his form shimmering before vanishing into the night.

He moved like a shadow, slipping past the outer perimeter undetected. Cameras tracked the empty corridors, motion sensors swept the paths leading toward the lower levels, but Jeron wasn't bound by the limitations of human security. With a flick of his wrist, a thin, neural interface flickered to life along his forearm, displaying a pulsating grid of security nodes. He reached out with his mind, tapping into the facility's encrypted systems, rewriting its rules as easily as one might rearrange letters in a child's puzzle.

A *click*. A pause.

The cameras looped. The alarms disarmed. The doors—

Hiss.

—unlocked.

Jeron moved swiftly through the darkened halls, descending deeper into the restricted sectors of Ames. The air grew colder the further he went, the usual hum of a bustling facility giving way to an eerie, clinical silence. It reeked of chemicals, sterilized surfaces, and something… older.

Something rotting.

The corridors narrowed, twisting into a labyrinth of secured chambers and laboratories that the outside world would never know existed. He passed several rooms where things floated in thick, amber-colored liquid—unborn experiments, human tissue spliced with something unnatural. One chamber held a row of steel tables, each occupied by something once human, its body stretched, misshapen, wires snaking in and out of its flesh like a grotesque marionette.

Jeron exhaled slowly, amused.

He had been right about Ashton.

This was not just a man of science. This was a man of vision.

Then, he found him.

Ashton moved like a man possessed, his hands working feverishly at a console while rows of monitors flickered with schematics, data streams, and biological scans. The room itself was unnerving, a surgical theater fused with a madman's workshop. Tubes of viscous, glowing liquid lined the walls, each containing some grotesque specimen—hybridized organs, severed limbs, partially formed human faces frozen in twisted expressions. The air was thick with the scent of disinfectant, scorched metal, and something else—something rotten.

Jeron's lips curled into a smirk.

This was not just a man of science. This was a man

unshackled by morality.

The overhead lights cast long, skeletal shadows as Ashton moved between workstations, pausing occasionally to murmur notes into a recorder. His voice was clinical, detached, filled with the kind of arrogance Jeron had come to expect from men who saw themselves as gods.

"Subject 47's cellular decay is accelerating beyond projected rates. Increasing electrical stimulation has only prolonged viability by twelve percent. Will require further modification."

Jeron tilted his head.

On one of the monitors, an emaciated human figure twitched violently, strapped to a table in a soundproofed chamber. Its body was riddled with pulsating tubes, wires snaking into its flesh. Jeron recognized the readings instantly—forced reanimation experiments. Ashton was toying with the limits of death itself.

Another screen displayed a blueprint for a new project, something labeled ANDROMEDA INITIATIVE. The schematics were too fragmented to make full sense of, but Jeron's keen eyes caught words that sent a thrill through him: "viral restructuring," "adaptive mutation," "human integration."

Ashton stood alone in the dimly lit chamber, hunched over a large, circular console, his fingers twitching against the keys. The lab around him pulsed with a quiet hum— monitors flickered, data streams rolling endlessly across the screens.

At the center of it all stood a series of containment chambers, their glass walls fogged from within. The dim glow of the interface displayed vitals, pulses, numbers that Jeron recognized immediately. Suspended inside one of the largest pods, bathed in eerie blue light, was Ashton himself—

or at least, another version of him.

A clone? A backup?

Jeron smirked.

Ashton must have felt him before he saw him. He stiffened slightly, his fingers hovering over the console before turning slowly, his expression unreadable.

Jeron deactivated his cloaking, stepping forward with deliberate slowness, like a predator making itself known to its prey.

Ashton barely reacted. If anything, he looked... intrigued.

"Well," Ashton murmured, tilting his head, "that was unexpected."

Jeron's gaze flicked to the containment pods. "Insurance policy?"

Ashton followed his line of sight, a sly grin forming. "You can't be the architect of the future without preparing for your own."

Jeron took another step forward. "I've been watching you, Ashton."

"I assumed as much."

"You understand things most of your kind never will," Jeron continued, his voice barely above a whisper. "Life is not sacred. Evolution is violence. And the future must be engineered."

Ashton's grin widened, his eyes glinting like a man who had just found religion. "Go on."

Jeron reached into his coat, withdrawing a small, reinforced vial filled with a writhing black substance. The liquid shifted unnaturally, as if it had a mind of its own. Then, with his other hand, he pulled out a sleek, dark tablet and extended both toward Ashton.

"Consider this a gift," Jeron said. "A legacy of knowledge, left behind by a brilliant mind. One that I suspect you may appreciate."

Ashton hesitated only for a moment before reaching for the tablet, his fingers skimming across its cool surface. The screen flashed to life, revealing intricate genetic sequences, formulas, notes scrawled in a language that should have been impossible to decipher—but Ashton's brow furrowed in intrigue rather than confusion.

"This is…" Ashton murmured, his voice nearly reverent.

Jeron's grin widened. "My uncle's work. A mind greater than most, and yet, unfinished. He dreamed of perfection, of rebuilding the world in his own image. And now, I give that dream to you."

Ashton finally reached for the vial, holding it up to the sterile light above. The inky substance curled toward the glass, stretching like it sensed its new master.

"And what, exactly, do you expect in return?"

Jeron stepped closer, lowering his voice to a near whisper. "I expect the future. A future where we are not bound by weakness or the failures of lesser men. Where death is nothing more than an inconvenience. Where the true potential of evolution is realized."

Ashton turned the vial slowly, watching the substance shift. A hunger flickered in his expression.

Jeron stepped back, re-engaging his cloaking field, the faint shimmer of his form disappearing into the dim light.

"Use it wisely, Dr. Brown," Jeron's voice echoed through the lab. "Your new world begins now."

And with that, he was gone.

Instantly, Ashton felt a newfound sharpness cut through his fatigue as he focused on the alien vial, rushing toward the nearest workstation and placing it beneath the microscope. As he peered into the eyepiece, the tiny organism came into focus, undulating like a macabre dancer, tendrils swirling and expanding with haunting grace. It was exquisite, a primordial creature that seemed both delicate and lethal, something that held the weight of ancient secrets in its microscopic twists and turns.

"Hello there, my little queen," Ashton murmured, a crooked grin curling his lips. He could almost hear the organism hum back at him, as if it, too, recognized the potential of their dark partnership.

Without wasting a second, he hit the button on his desk's intercom, summoning Kafka and Vogel to the lab. When they arrived, he showed them the tablet and the specimen with an almost feverish gleam in his eye, his voice hushed but alive with a fierce intensity.

"Time to get to work," he said, his gaze drifting toward the lab's front chamber. Clause lay in there, cold and lifeless—a wasted vessel. But Ashton's mind was already spinning with possibilities, calculations, ideas far more ambitious than mere research.

"Kafka, Vogel," he said, glancing at each of them with a solemn gravity, "we're going to unlock every secret this specimen has to offer. And I know exactly where we'll begin."

Chapter 19

William jolted awake and sat up in bed, his breath coming in ragged gasps. His face was drenched in sweat, a product of the nightmares that tormented his sleep nightly. Sometimes they were of monsters—the dead things that had destroyed their world not so long ago—but mostly they were of Clause, the first man he had killed in nearly ten years.

Glancing down at Melinda, who grew restless for a brief second before settling back to sleep, he carefully got out of bed, threw on his robe, and left the room.

The sun was just beginning to peek its head above the mountains to the East, sending a warm orange glow through the kitchen window as William sat down at the kitchen table, waiting for the coffee to brew.

As he gazed out at the approaching day, he thought back to that day. He knew he shouldn't dwell on the past like he did, let it drag him down into that dark place in his soul, but he couldn't help it. He didn't want to be known as a killer again. That was a part of him that he had buried long ago; a part he had hoped would never be resurrected. But Fate had other plans.

* * *

***

In a flash, the shots rang out, sending both of the scientists crashing to the floor. Instantly, William dropped to the ground and whipped his gun around just as a bullet flew past. As he rolled to his left he fired at Clause, hitting him twice in the chest.

Clause immediately fell to his knees with an incredulous look on his face, like he couldn't believe someone had actually shot him. The Marines then riddled his body with bullets, finally putting an end to his madness.

***

William sat at the kitchen table, his hands wrapped around a mug of coffee that he couldn't remember making. The house was too quiet, like a held breath. The room seemed to stretch and twist in strange angles, shadows lengthening, bending into dark shapes that weren't there before. He sipped the coffee, though it was cold as ice, and shivered. Somewhere, in the silence, he thought he heard a scream—Ashley's scream. It started low, barely audible, then rose, slicing through the quiet like a blade.

"Are you okay, hun?" The voice came from across the table. He looked up, startled, and there was Melinda, watching him with a gaze that was too intense, too still.

"Yeah," he mumbled, his words heavy and sluggish. "Just… couldn't sleep anymore."

She smiled, but there was something wrong with it, something stretched and brittle. Her eyes glinted, catching a strange light, and the corners of her mouth twitched as though struggling to hold their shape. "You shouldn't beat yourself up, William. None of it was your fault."

He glanced down, struggling to shake the sense of wrongness. But her words felt hollow, echoing inside him like a distant, empty chant. "I could have done something… should have done something," he murmured, trying to hold on to the thread of his thoughts as they started to fray.

Melinda's face shifted as he spoke, her eyes darkening, her skin pulling tight over her bones until it seemed to stretch too thin. Her fingers twisted together, growing longer, her knuckles knobby and sharp. She leaned forward, her voice barely a whisper, "You were never strong enough, were you?"

He blinked, his heart starting to pound in his chest. Her hands—he couldn't look away from them, those twisted, skeletal fingers reaching across the table. A shiver ran down his spine as her face began to shift, her eyes sinking deeper, mouth stretching wider, until the smile warped into a wide, toothy grin, her teeth glinting in the dim light, too sharp, too many.

"William," she hissed, her voice a rasp that seemed to come from everywhere and nowhere. "You're weak. You always have been."

And then she lunged. Her hands clawed across the table, fingers elongated and inhuman, nails like talons. William stumbled back, the chair screeching as it toppled over, her hands grasping at his shoulders, her nails piercing his skin. He tried to scream, but no sound came out. She held him down, her mouth stretching wider, impossibly wide, as her teeth gleamed, closing in—

"William!"

He jerked awake, gasping, his heart pounding so hard it felt like it might burst. The kitchen was quiet again, the real kitchen, warm and still, lit by the soft light of early dawn. He looked around, disoriented, his hands trembling as he gripped the edge of the table.

Footsteps approached, and Melinda stepped into the room. "Are you okay?" she asked softly.

For a moment, he couldn't find his words, his heart still racing from the lingering grip of the nightmare. She placed a gentle hand on his shoulder, her touch grounding him and pulling him back to reality. He let out a shaky breath, nodding as he finally met her eyes, the last traces of the nightmare slipping away, though a strange, lingering dread remained, whispering that the darkness he feared might not be so easily left behind.

As he looked into her eyes, he saw her unending love and remembered just how much she had changed him from a monster into a man. He got up and kissed her lightly on the forehead.

***

The large bare patch in the middle of the yard was a sad reminder of what they had lost not so long ago when the world had gone crazy. He said a silent 'Goodbye' to King as he walked to his truck, still feeling the emptiness that his death had left. They had all lost a tiny piece of themselves that day, creating a hole that would never be filled.

As he drove toward the precinct, he could still see evidence scattered here and there of the nightmare that had ripped through the valley at a fevered pace. Most of the damage had been repaired, but not all. The wreckage that remained served as notice to cherish every second, because life could be violently ripped away at a moment's notice.

Even when he pulled into the station, it was there. The glass had been replaced, the parking lot re-surfaced, the lights repaired, the walls painted, but he could see it—little patches here and there that were darker than the others where the blood had still managed to seep through the thick coats of paint and primer.

He didn't know what to expect as he prepared himself to enter the building. There were so many memories that surfaced immediately, both good and bad, threatening to undermine his good intentions and reconsider his un-retirement. William took a deep breath as he grabbed the handle and opened the door.

As soon as he entered the precinct, a chorus of claps and cheers rose from the officers gathered there, mixed with the loud wail of an air horn. Some of them he knew, some he didn't, a byproduct of both his time away from the force and the need to transfer officers in from other precincts to fill the empty spots left by those who had recently perished.

After a flurry of handshakes and congratulations, William was surprised to see Guerera standing on the other side of the room, holding Ashley in her arms. Melinda stood next to her with a proud smile on her face. He rushed over and gave them both a big hug. "I knew you guys were up to something at the coffee shop last week!"

"It was all your wife's idea," Guerera said as she looked at Melinda. "She told me today was your big day, so we thought we'd make it a little special for you."

"I can't take all the credit," Melinda said. "I seem to remember that you were quite eager to help."

Guerera smiled and held up the air horn, giving it one more quick blast.

William laughed, "Thank you. I'm glad you did."

"I'll give you two a minute while I get the cake ready," Melinda said before she excused herself and walked toward the opposite end of the precinct.

William's eyes lit up. "There's cake?"

"I wouldn't figure you to have a sweet tooth?" Guerera stated.

"It's my one vice."

"Only one?"

William went silent for a second, and Guerera felt immediately that she had hit a nerve. "How are you holding up?" she asked.

"About as well as can be expected." He glanced around the room at the streamers and balloons that dotted the ceiling, "I'm not big on the fanfare stuff, though."

Guerera chuckled. "Yeah, I know what you mean."

"What about you? What are you planning on doing?"

"With everything that's happened, when my term was up, I decided not to re-enlist. I have an aunt that lives in Indio that said we can stay with her."

"Well, if you need a job, I could use a strong person like you around here."

Guerera laughed, "Me? A cop?"

"What's so funny? You'd make an excellent police officer."

When Guerera realized he was serious, she changed her tone, "I guess crazier things have happened. I'll think about it."

"How are Fisher and Jackson holding up?"

Her eyes misted over, "They're okay. We had a large memorial service last week. It hit everybody pretty hard."

"Yeah, I know what you mean."

As Guerera wiped her eyes with the back of her hand, she crouched down toward Ashley, "Why don't you see if one of these nice officers will get you a balloon to play with?"

Ashley's eyes lit up, "Sure thing, G!"

As Ashley rushed off to the nearest officer, William smile at Guerera, "G?"

Guerera chuckled, "She has a hard time pronouncing my

name, and I don't really like my first name, so we came up with that as a nickname."

William laughed, "Sounds more like a rapper name. Suits you, though."

"Hey, I've been known to throw down a beat or two."

"I'm sure you have. And what's so horrible about Jazmine?"

"Jazmine's always been too girly for me."

Her tone changed suddenly, "Have you talked to Andrea recently? How's she doing?"

"She's okay. It's going to take her a while to get back to normal."

"Does she know anything else about the guy who sent Clause?"

"Ashton Brown?"

"Yeah. Has he been found yet?"

William looked at her sternly, "Not yet. We're still working on it. But you need to let this go. Clause is dead. It's over now for you. Let me take care of this."

Guerera's lips started quivering, "But it's all my fault Samuel is dead."

"That's ridiculous. Clause was a madman, pure and simple. There's no way you could've known what he'd do."

As soon as those words had left his mouth, he heard Melinda's voice in his head saying the same thing to him. A soft chuckle escaped his lips.

"What's so funny?" Guerera quipped.

"I just realized my wife's been saying those same words to me every day now since this whole thing happened."

"We both know the 'if onlys' that run through our heads, They're like a goddamn barrage, " Guerera said.

William quickly changed the subject, "We were talking about taking the kids to Disneyland in a couple of weeks. You and Ashley should come too."

Guerera hesitated, "I don't know? I don't enjoy large crowds. People tend to irritate me."

William chuckled, "It'll help get us back to some sort of normalcy. Plus, I think Ashley and Kate will hit it off big time."

Just as Guerera was about to answer, William stiffened. Gazing over the precinct, his eyes suddenly stopped on a strange man standing in the corner, watching him intently. Something about him seemed off. He was thin and tall, with a jaunt face, and was wearing a brown robe. But it was his eyes that were disturbing. They were larger than normal and had an eerie quality to them.

Guerera sensed the change in his demeanor and asked, "What's wrong?"

"I'm not sure," William said. "Wait here."

As soon as he started walking forward, the guy turned and walked quickly toward the exit. William rushed to follow him, but when he got outside, the man was nowhere to be found. As he looked around, he thought he heard a slight hum nearby before it faded to silence.

Chapter 20

Jeron activated the video feed on his main system with a wicked smile stretched across his face. He watched with a barely restrained excitement as Ashton Brown's face appeared on screen, his eyes widening at the specimen Jeron had left for him. The scientist's expression told Jeron everything he needed to know—Ashton was hungry for this knowledge, ravenous even, and in that moment, Jeron knew he'd chosen the perfect pawn. This man would do more than continue his uncle's work; he'd elevate it, weaponize it. Ashton would be the scalpel to Jeron's vision, the clean, clinical edge cutting through this primitive world's defenses.

He slipped away, blending into the shadows of the city with a spring in his step, his heart pounding with anticipation. His next destination lay closer to ground zero— the epicenter of the chaos he would reignite, only this time with no one left to extinguish the blaze. He moved carefully, his eyes flicking around as he took in the dense, labyrinthine alleys and intersections, every step calculated. If any of the others were out there tracking him, he'd see them long before they saw him.

Tracking down William Patterson had been laughably

easy. Jeron marveled at how primitive these networks were, how carelessly connected, like veins throbbing with exposed lifeblood. The man's address was right there, waiting to be plucked. He had been pivotal in ending the first wave of attacks—an error Jeron had every intention of correcting. This time, William Patterson would be front and center, a twisted participant in the destruction he once tried to stop.

Jeron followed him silently through the streets, his gyro-cycle cloaked and noiseless. The pulse of his engines and the hum of its spectral shield made him almost invisible as he tailed William's car. When William finally stopped at a brick building with a grim-looking sign that read 'La Quinta Police Department,' Jeron felt a flare of satisfaction. His mouth twitched into a grim smile as he watched the man vanish inside.

He parked his cycle around the corner, hidden from view, and walked toward the entrance, his hand brushing the cold metal of his spectrum-modifier necklace. It had enough charge to keep him invisible in brief bursts, but energy was becoming a problem. The primitive technology of this world offered no quantum magnifiers, thus, no easy recharges. He had to conserve, to use every second wisely.

Inside, he scanned the building, every detail heightened, every sound stretched and sharp. The officers moved with an easy, unearned confidence, oblivious to the threat lingering in their midst. Jeron stayed back, observing, analyzing. These officers wouldn't simply let him wander in. He needed perfect timing.

The precinct door swung open, and in a single, practiced motion, he tapped his necklace and slid invisibly through the threshold, his movements smooth and unhesitating. On the other side, he hit the button again, slipping back into the visible spectrum, before hiding in the shadows.

It took mere seconds to locate Patterson, who was in the main office, surrounded by a crowd of cheering officers. Jeron's eyes narrowed at the sight, his mind working at breakneck speed. Among the officers, he spotted a woman and a young girl approaching Patterson, each step deliberate, each word exchanged foreign and yet unmistakably significant. This was no ordinary reunion; it was charged, intense. And Jeron's eyes glittered with a new, wicked idea. If he could catch them both...he imagined Ashton's face when he delivered such a twisted prize.

He activated the amplifier on his neck, straining to listen as the ambient noise filled his ears, giving way to fragments of conversation. One word cut through the haze: Melborne. Another scientist. Jeron's lips curved into a slow, sinister grin. He had plans for her too.

But then, Patterson turned, his gaze locking directly on Jeron. His eyes were sharp, piercing—a cold instinct that sent a ripple of unease through Jeron's chest. He spun on his heel, slipping back out of the building and tapping his necklace to vanish as he strode back to his cycle, every step echoing louder, his heart pounding.

Sitting on the cycle, he watched William from the shadows, hands clenched. Patterson was sharper than expected; this might not be as simple as he'd hoped. But Jeron's eyes were lit with the fervor of a man possessed, a man with a mission. If Patterson posed a threat, then Ashton would need to invent something truly monstrous, something that would rip the strength right out of William Patterson's veins.

And he would be right there to watch.

***

Jeron slid through the dim streets until the abandoned

warehouse loomed before him, a hulking skeleton wrapped in the rotten breath of mildew and decay. Its charred walls and gaping wounds, remnants of some long-ago inferno, whispered a chilling welcome as he glided his gyro-cycle through the jagged hole in the crumbling wall. Shadows stretched and pooled in the dark space as his cycle settled, its faint hum fading like a dying heartbeat. The warehouse was a tomb, a den of forgotten violence, cloaked in damp darkness —and Jeron relished every murky inch of it. This was a sanctuary of secrets, a place for those who knew the language of the shadows.

Beyond the scent of burnt wood and wet rot, the place held an eerie silence, the kind that warned the sane to stay clear. Only the foolish or the utterly desperate would dare set foot here. But for Jeron, it was the ideal fortress, a hidden vantage from which to execute his scheme. He'd scavenged the scorched remains, salvaging a pair of warped solar panels and a defunct satellite dish, enough to hijack just a trickle of this world's weak energy—enough to tether him to the grid, to communicate with Ashton Brown in whispers only they could hear.

He dismounted and reached into his bag, withdrawing the purloined iPad Pro. It had once belonged to some coffee shop regular whose complacency he'd capitalized on, lifting the device and gutting its pathetic factory specs. He'd jury-rigged the thing, planting a sliver of quantum energy into its fragile processor, bending it to his will, outfitting it with just enough power to give him a foothold in this primitive tech ecosystem.

The device flickered to life, the screen's cold glow a harsh contrast in the darkness. Jeron's fingers glided across it, running a code so complex it blurred, tapping into the energy, and moments later, he stood back, his form captured in the frame, like a dark, otherworldly figure summoned into view.

"Ashton," he murmured, his voice a low growl, thick with satisfaction.

***

Dr. Kafka stared down at Clause's corpse, her face twisted in unease. He lay sprawled on the metal slab, his chest and abdomen cratered with bullet wounds, each scar a brutal testament to his last moments. His lifeless eyes seemed to bore into the darkness, unseeing, his mouth set in a grim, unnatural line. He looked more like a broken mannequin than the cousin she'd once known, a hollow shell emptied of life and humanity.

"This... doesn't feel right," she murmured, her gaze lingering on his expressionless face.

Ashton barely glanced at her, his hands already occupied wheeling another table next to Clause's. Upon it lay a sedated gorilla, massive and muscular, its broad chest rising and falling under the weight of the drugs coursing through its veins.

"It couldn't be more right," Ashton replied, his tone as clinical as the steel instruments glinting under the overhead lights.

Kafka swallowed, feeling a cold sweat prickling the back of her neck. "But we're playing God, Ashton."

Ashton's face split into a thin smile, sharp and mocking. "Playing God? Isn't that the essence of science itself, the very pursuit of knowledge that shapes us into something more than we are?" His eyes flicked to Vogel, who stood silent in the shadows, impassive as ever. "Religion, science—they're two paths leading to the same summit, except science has a tangible road."

Kafka glanced toward Vogel, hoping to catch some glimpse of agreement or dissent, but his face was as unreadable as always. She clenched her fists. "Clause was family, Ashton."

"A family member who was betrayed and murdered," Ashton replied coldly. "And now, he'll be useful."

The tense silence shattered as a faint hum filled the air, and a hologram shimmered into existence beside them, coalescing into a tall figure with eyes that seemed to glow with an inner fire. Kafka froze, her breath catching as the figure solidified. Vogel even took a step back, his gaze fixed in shock.

Ashton, however, grinned like a child who'd just unwrapped his first gift under the twinkling lights of a Christmas tree. "Jeron," he said, voice trembling with excitement.

The hologram gave a thin smile, sharp as glass. "Dr. Brown."

Jeron's gaze shifted to the tables, lingering on the gorilla's drugged, slumbering form. "I see you didn't waste any time applying my uncle's research. That creature—such strength. We had a similar beast on Terran, the Pentu. Your selection is… wise."

Ashton's face lit up, eyes nearly feverish with delight. "It's as close to human intelligence as anything I could find, and its genetic composition should integrate smoothly. It lacks our reasoning, yes, but it has strength, agility—attributes perfectly suited to what I have in mind. Its genome is… ideal."

Jeron's smile twisted with dark approval. "If everything goes as planned, you'll have your creation soon enough. And there's no better test than to set it loose on those who wronged you." He paused, letting his words sink in. "Two weeks from now, William Patterson and the soldier Guerera will be… occupied at a place called Disneyland."

Ashton's face contorted into a grin, a feral light shining in his eyes. "Perfect."

Chapter 21

The lab was too cold, the kind of sterile chill that seeped into the skin and settled in the bones. It wasn't just the temperature—something about the place felt fundamentally wrong. The overhead surgical lights buzzed faintly, flickering at uneven intervals, their pale blue glow casting long, angular shadows across the steel surfaces.

Dr. Kafka stood motionless, her arms crossed tightly over her chest, staring down at the mangled corpse of Clause. He lay lifeless on the surgical slab, his chest a ruin of shredded tissue and splintered bone, bullet wounds leaving deep, gaping cavities where his body had been torn apart. His arms were still rigid, locked in death's final grasp, and his mouth hung slightly open, as if caught mid-scream.

She had seen plenty of corpses in her career. Too many. But this?

This was something else entirely.

Ashton, on the other hand, looked positively delighted, adjusting the angle of the laser scalpel in his gloved hands. His movements were methodical, precise, as if he were fine-tuning a masterpiece rather than preparing to carve into the remains of a man. His glasses reflected the overhead lights, concealing his eyes behind a pale glare, but the eagerness in his body language was unmistakable.

Behind them, suspended in the restraints of a reinforced steel medical frame, was the beast.

The gorilla was enormous—nearly 500 pounds of dense, primal muscle. A thick mane of dark fur covered its shoulders and back, but patches of skin had already been shaved away, revealing exposed tissue marked with pre-surgical incisions. The powerful animal was sedated, its breaths coming slow and deep, a faint tremor in its fingers the only sign that it was still alive. Thick restraints held it in place, metal cuffs reinforced with titanium plating, designed specifically for creatures far stronger than humans.

Kafka exhaled slowly, the acidic taste of bile creeping up her throat. "This… doesn't feel right."

Ashton didn't look up, simply adjusting the settings on the neural interface module attached to Clause's skull.

"Feelings are irrelevant, Doctor," he said flatly. "What matters is progress."

She clenched her jaw. "Clause was family."

Ashton's fingers paused, just for a second, before he resumed working.

"We've had this discussion already, doctor. In the end, he failed," he corrected coldly. "But I refuse to let his potential go to waste."

Without another word, he pressed the laser scalpel to Clause's throat. The blade hummed, glowing with a blue-white intensity, and the smell of burning flesh filled the air as he began to saw through the lifeless tissue.

Wet.

Peeling.

The sound of separating tendons was sickeningly crisp, like cutting through a thick slab of raw meat. Blood pooled across the steel slab, sluggish and dark, and Clause's head rolled free, landing with a dull, wet thud against the tray below.

Kafka whipped her head away, squeezing her eyes shut, her fingers pressing into her palms so hard her nails nearly broke the skin.

"Don't look away," Ashton scolded, amusement lacing his voice. "This is history in the making."

She forced herself to turn back.

Ashton lifted Clause's severed head, cradling it with eerie gentleness, and carried it to the second surgical slab where the gorilla lay restrained. The autonomic response machine beeped steadily beside the beast, registering stable vitals.

"All right," Ashton murmured, mostly to himself. "Let's begin."

Kafka watched, her breath coming slow and measured, as Ashton secured Clause's head into a metal frame, suspending it over the gorilla's open chest cavity. The machine adjusted, lowering the severed head into position, aligning the base of Clause's spinal cord with the surgically prepared vertebrae of the gorilla.

Vogel stepped forward, silent as ever, carrying the biomechanical fusion device—a thick, cylindrical tool covered in cable-like appendages tipped with surgical-grade nanoblades. He positioned it at the exposed spinal connection, his movements practiced, eerily precise.

The fusion device whirred to life, the nanoblades whirling as they latched onto the severed nerve endings. A series of micro-pulses surged through the tissue, forcing the organic material to stitch itself together. Clause's head jerked, muscles spasming as the connections bridged. The biometric monitor spiked, heart rate accelerating as the nervous system re-established itself.

Kafka swallowed hard as Clause's mouth twitched.

The body was rejecting the foreign connection, struggling to reconcile the human brain with the primal physique of the gorilla. Ashton calmly reached for the neurological stabilizer, a thick, needle-like device filled with a specially synthesized neural suppressant compound.

He drove it directly into Clause's brainstem.

The monitor flatlined for three seconds.

Then—

THUMP.

The gorilla's heart slammed back to life, harder, faster.

Clause's eyes snapped open.

In the corner of the room, a massive containment cylinder hissed open, releasing a cloud of cryogenic mist. Suspended in the liquid were eight writhing, pulsating tentacles, their sucker-lined surfaces flexing in anticipation.

Each one had been genetically modified, spliced from a deep-sea cephalopod, reinforced with synthetic muscle fibers to allow for increased strength and dexterity.

Kafka took a step back as the tentacles uncoiled, the tips twitching like hungry, searching mouths.

Ashton was already working, his hands steady as he positioned the first appendage over the exposed shoulder cavity of the gorilla's body. The bio-surgical clamps latched on, adhering the alien limbs to the open tissue.

The fusion process began.

Tendons merged.

Nerves synched.

Blood vessels rewired themselves.

Clause's new body bucked violently, the tentacles convulsing, slamming against the walls, sending metal trays crashing to the floor. His human mouth twisted into a sneer, his gorilla lips curling back in a snarl.

His voice, guttural and uneven, rumbled through the lab.

"…Guerera."

Kafka's eyes grew wide as her stomach plummeted and her skin crawled. The thing that had just spoken was no longer her cousin. It was an abomination, pure and simple.

Ashton simply grinned, his eyes gleaming with satisfaction.

"Welcome back, Clause."

The tentacles curled inward, then lashed outward, snapping one of the overhead lights in half, sending sparks raining to the floor.

Clause laughed, a deep, wet sound.

His new limbs flexed, testing their strength.

Ashton stepped forward, placing a steady hand on the abomination's heaving chest.

"You'll have your revenge soon enough," he murmured.

Clause stilled as he considered the future.

Then, slowly, a monstrous grin stretched across both his faces.

Chapter 22

The desert night stretched on, endless and suffocating, as if time itself had slowed to mock their desperation. Silas crouched low at the edge of a dry ravine, sweeping the terrain intently with his scanner. The soft hum of its sensor grid pulsed faintly, detecting heat signatures and electromagnetic fluctuations. But each flicker of movement proved false. He exhaled slowly, his patience wearing thinner with every second.

Behind him, Mishka leaned against her gyro-cycle, her eyes glinting with simmering frustration. "It's a waste of time," she muttered, snapping a small twig between her fingers. "We've been combing this cursed valley for days. He's not here."

"He's out there somewhere," Silas said quietly, not turning.

"Great," she snorted. "And where's 'there' exactly? Because it's not *here*."

Meanwhile, Ridley paced back and forth across the rocky outcrop. Her hand rested on her blaster, her fingers tapping an irritated rhythm against the metal. "We're chasing ghosts," she muttered. "He's always a step ahead of us—because we let him be."

"Stop," Silas warned, his tone flat but edged with steel.

"Stop what?" Ridley's eyes narrowed. "Telling the truth? We've been running in circles since he left the ship. Every lead dies out. Every trail goes cold. Maybe if someone—"

"Enough!" Silas snapped, his eyes flashing as he turned on her. The rare sharpness of his voice cut through the night like a blade.

Ridley stiffened, her jaw tightening.

Aldin knelt nearby, examining a cluster of stones disturbed by something—or someone. Her fingers traced the edges of faint imprints in the sand. "Footprints," she murmured. Her eyes followed the path leading east. "Jeron's?"

Mishka straightened. "Finally," she hissed.

The team surged forward, hope flickering ever so slightly as they followed Aldin's discovery. The prints meandered toward a rocky slope, where shadows gathered thick and dark beneath crumbling boulders.

Silas crouched beside the tracks, his hand brushing lightly against the loose earth. He adjusted his scanner, highlighting the thermal remnants of a recent passage. "They're fresh."

Mishka grinned, her fingers tightening on her blaster. "Gotcha, you sneaky bastard."

Ridley's eyes narrowed, scanning the ridge ahead. "No more mistakes. No more chances. We take him down."

As they crept closer, a low, guttural growl rumbled from the shadows. A hunched, feral shape lurched into view, its eyes reflecting the pale starlight.

"Wait!" Silas hissed, raising a hand to halt the others.

The shape shifted, revealing not Jeron, but a ragged coyote with patchy fur and sharp, hungry eyes. It snarled once, then slunk away into the night, leaving only silence in its wake.

Mishka swore under her breath, her excitement collapsing

into disappointment. "Seriously?" She kicked a stone hard enough to send it tumbling into the ravine.

Ridley clenched her fists, fury rippling beneath her calm exterior. "He's mocking us. Leading us in circles."

Aldin sighed, her shoulders sagging. "This isn't working. We're chasing shadows."

"We need a new strategy," Silas muttered in frustration.

The weight of defeat pressed heavy on their shoulders as they sped back to their ship. The hatch opened with a soft hiss, and the team shuffled inside, their faces drawn with fatigue and simmering anger.

Once inside, Silas activated the navigation display, his eyes fixed on the map projected before him. Red markers dotted the valley, each one a dead end.

Ridley paced the room like a restless predator. "He's using the terrain against us." She stopped, her eyes burning. "And we're stumbling around blind."

Mishka crossed her arms, leaning against the bulkhead. "So what do we do? Sit and wait for him to strike?"

"We think like him," Silas said, his voice cold and deliberate. "He's not running without a purpose. He's got a plan, and it's tied to the organism. He's scouting. Preparing."

"For what?" Aldin whispered.

"For the same thing that destroyed Terran," Silas replied grimly. "But this time, he wants us to watch."

The silence that followed rang with an unspoken scream of impending doom.

For a long time, the hum of the ship's systems filled the chamber with a steady, monotonous drone that amplified the silence stretching between them. Silas's gaze remained locked on the projection of the valley. His jaw tightened as he marked another dead-end on the map with a flick of his finger. Mishka sighed heavily, her frustration palpable, while

Ridley stood with her arms crossed, tapping her fingers against her elbow in irritation.

Aldin suddenly lifted her head, a spark igniting behind her eyes as a thought took shape. She stood, brushing a lock of dark hair behind her ear.

"We're going about this all wrong," she said.

Mishka's eyes flicked toward her. "Enlighten us, then?"

"We've been focused entirely on Jeron," Aldin began, stepping closer to the console. "Trying to predict his movements, track his trails—but we're not thinking about the bigger picture."

Silas turned to face her fully, interest piqued. "Go on."

Aldin pointed to the digital map. "When the organism was released here in this region, there were survivors, people who played a direct role in stopping the spread of the infection. We know Jeron's obsessed with finishing what his uncle started, and he'll be sure to seek them out. And if they pose a threat to his plan…"

Mishka narrowed her eyes, catching on. "You think he's targeting them?"

"Yes," Aldin said, her voice gaining momentum. "He'll want to study their tactics, their weaknesses. He's probably already researching them. If we monitor those same people, we'll find him. He won't be able to resist getting close enough to watch."

Ridley nodded slowly, the logic settling in. "It's a smart play. He's egotistical. He wants to be seen, to toy with his prey."

Silas folded his arms, processing the idea. "Who are these people? How do we find them?"

Aldin swiped her hand across the display, accessing a new data stream. "We have the records from the planetary surveillance scans. Cross-reference them with public security footage and communications logs. We'll search for names associated with the event reports from the last outbreak. Police, civilians—anyone who made an impact."

She paused, scrolling through the list that appeared. One name glowed on the screen: William Patterson.

Ridley leaned closer. "Who's that?"

"A former police officer," Aldin explained. "He was instrumental in coordinating the defense against the infected animals. He fought alongside someone named Guerera, a soldier who helped neutralize the swarm. They were right at the heart of it."

Mishka raised an eyebrow. "If Jeron's interested in anyone, it'll be them."

"We'll start with Patterson," Silas agreed. "Set up a tracking algorithm. Monitor his movements, his home, his work—anything that might draw Jeron out."

Aldin nodded, her fingers flying across the interface as she initiated the search. "It'll take some time to build the network. We'll need to integrate with local systems without tripping their primitive security protocols."

"Do it," Silas said. "We're running out of time."

As Aldin worked, Ridley spoke, her voice lower, more thoughtful. "Do you think Patterson knows what's coming next?"

Silas's expression darkened. "Not yet."

"Then we'll be there when he finds out," Mishka muttered, her eyes hard.

The soft glow of the screen reflected on their tense faces as the search took shape. Outside, the desert stretched endlessly under a sky heavy with secrets, the darkness waiting for the chaos that Jeron would soon unleash.

Chapter 23

Jeron stood unnervingly still in the dim alleyway, his body almost too rigid, his breaths too measured—like he was conserving energy for something bigger. Rodrigo noticed it first, how Jeron never shifted his weight from foot to foot or fidgeted like the rest of them did when waiting. He just *was*, motionless in the shadows, his yellow eyes gleaming faintly in the dim light spilling from the street.

It was something he did often, something that unnerved Luis and Rodrigo even if they wouldn't admit it. His senses stretched farther than theirs, taking in vibrations, electrical currents, and the subtle hum of life itself. The neon flickers of a distant liquor store sign cast erratic flashes across his sharp features.

"You ever blink, man?" Luis muttered, rubbing at his arm as if a chill had settled there.

Jeron's head tilted slightly, the motion eerily smooth, his gaze locking onto Luis with unsettling intensity. "Why waste energy on unnecessary actions?" he replied flatly.

Luis scoffed, shaking his head. "Creepy as hell, bro."

Rodrigo ignored the exchange, exhaling through his nose as he kept watch on the street. "Enough messing around. We doing this or what?"

Jeron finally moved, stepping forward with calculated precision. "Yes. But not with reckless impatience." He turned his gaze to Rodrigo and Luis, his tone calm, assured. "The window is short. When we move, we move without hesitation. No second-guessing."

Luis gave Rodrigo a wary glance but nodded. "Yeah, yeah. Just don't stare at me like that while we're doing it."

Jeron blinked, slow and deliberate this time, as if mimicking human behavior just to unnerve Luis further. Then, without another word, he turned his attention back to his tablet, his fingers flicking across the screen in rapid, purposeful movements.

"This is the best chance we have," Jeron said, his voice smooth but carrying an unnatural precision, as if each word had been calculated before it left his lips. "We take the truck tonight. No risks, no loose ends."

Luis shifted uncomfortably, watching Jeron with narrowed eyes. "You keep saying 'no risks' like stealing a goddamn truck is easy."

Jeron's head turned in a single fluid motion, his gaze locking onto Luis in a way that made the man's skin crawl. "It is," Jeron answered. "For those with a plan."

Rodrigo, leaning against the brick wall, flicked a cigarette between his fingers before tucking it behind his ear. "And I'm guessing you got one?"

Jeron tapped the tablet again, bringing up grainy security footage of a fenced-in lot filled with transport vehicles. At least three of the trucks bore the insignia of *Aegis Logistics*, one of the companies contracted by Ames Research Facility.

"This company moves classified cargo between research sites. Their drivers have clearance." Jeron's lips curled upward slightly, "Once we have the truck, we have our way in."

Luis rubbed the back of his neck. "And how exactly do we get past the security?"

Jeron's head tilted again, almost birdlike. "Who said anything about going past it?"

Rodrigo and Luis exchanged a wary glance.

"The driver of Truck 417," Jeron continued, "Conner Reed. Human male. Predictable. Every night at exactly 10:45, he stops at a diner off the highway. Leaves the truck running. Sits at the counter, orders black coffee, eggs over easy, and a slice of pie. In that order. Every time." Jeron tapped the screen again, playing a time-stamped clip showing Conner stepping inside the diner.

Luis gave a low whistle. "Damn. You really thought this through."

Jeron didn't blink. "I do not leave things to chance."

Rodrigo pushed off the wall, cracking his knuckles. "Alright. Let's get ourselves a truck."

***

The stolen sedan rolled up to the diner with its headlights off, blending into the long shadows of the parking lot. Jeron sat unnervingly still in the backseat, his long fingers resting lightly on his knees. Luis, behind the wheel, glanced at him through the rearview mirror. "You sure about this? We don't even have a look—"

The grainy security footage showed Conner Reed's truck pulling into the diner parking lot. Right on time. The man didn't turn off the engine, as was his routine, but before stepping out, he took a moment to scroll through his dashboard screen. The wait felt endless, but Jeron didn't shift, didn't exhale impatiently—he just *watched*.

The moment he disappeared inside the diner, Jeron's fingers twitched just the slightest in anticipation. Through the windshield, they could see Conner Reed hunched over the counter inside, sipping from his coffee cup halfway through his routine meal.

Jeron's arm shot out, pointing toward the truck parked just a few yards away. "Now."

Rodrigo didn't hesitate. He slipped out of the car, moving low and quick toward the truck, hugging the shadows. Jeron followed, his movement eerily silent, his posture too smooth, too precise—like he had studied how humans walked rather than having grown up doing it.

They crossed the lot quickly but without rushing, blending into the late-night desert quiet. Jeron reached the truck first, running his palm lightly over the door handle before gripping it. The motion was small, but Rodrigo swore he saw Jeron's fingers twitch oddly, almost as if sensing the vibrations in the metal.

Jeron yanked the door open and slid into the driver's seat in one fluid motion, his eyes scanning every control, every flickering light on the dashboard. Rodrigo jumped into the passenger side, scanning the lot as Jeron's hands hovered over the controls.

Gently, Jeron pressed his fingers against the truck's ignition panel. His skin hummed against the surface, and the vehicle stuttered to life with a low, mechanical purr.

Rodrigo's head snapped up. "How the hell—"

Jeron smirked. "Human security systems are primitive."

Rodrigo stared at him, then at the truck's dashboard, then back at Jeron.

Then, Jeron reached beneath the dashboard, his fingers moving with uncanny certainty. There was a faint *snap*, followed by the release of a small hidden panel. A red light blinked inside.

"What you call a tracking device," Jeron murmured. He plucked the tiny transmitter free and crushed it between his fingers, letting the pieces scatter onto the floor. "Ames would've known the moment we moved it."

Rodrigo exhaled slowly.

Luis's voice crackled over the radio. "We good?"

Jeron lifted the receiver, speaking in a voice completely devoid of concern. "We are leaving."

Luis peeled out of the lot just as Jeron and Rodrigo guided the truck onto the highway. Behind them, Conner Reed still sat at the diner counter, blissfully unaware that his night had just taken a very bad turn.

Jeron eased the truck out of the lot with eerie smoothness, maneuvering with a precision that made Rodrigo's stomach twist. No wasted motion, no second glances—like he had already calculated the entire route in his head.

Inside the diner, Conner's head lifted slightly as the faint rumble of his engine reached him through the glass. He turned, confusion knitting his brows, before realization struck.

Rodrigo glanced back just in time to see the man bolt toward the door, hands flying for his pockets—probably reaching for a phone.

"Floor it," Rodrigo snapped.

Jeron's fingers twitched again, and the truck *lurched*, the wheels kicking up gravel as they peeled onto the highway. The motion finally forced something human out of him—a grunt of effort, his posture stiffening for the briefest of moments before returning to that unnatural stillness.

Rodrigo chuckled, heart still hammering from the near miss. "Guess we're really doing this."

Jeron didn't respond. His focus was already ahead—on

what came next. On Ashton. On the organism.

This was just the beginning.

The drive to the hideout was quiet, save for the occasional check-in over the radio. Jeron sat in the passenger seat of the truck, his gaze locked on the road ahead, his fingers tapping an irregular rhythm against his thigh—almost like a silent countdown. Rodrigo kept stealing glances at him, unnerved.

Luis followed in the car, keeping enough distance to avoid suspicion.

Finally, they reached the abandoned warehouse. The massive metal doors yawned open as they pulled inside, the truck's headlights illuminating the dust-covered floor.

Jeron stepped out first, rolling his shoulders as if shaking off the weight of the night. He turned to Rodrigo and Luis. "This truck is our key. Tomorrow, you drive it to Ames. Retrieve the cargo. Do not draw attention." His voice was steady, but something in his expression darkened.

Rodrigo swallowed hard. "Right. No problem."

Luis turned to Jeron. "And what about you?"

Jeron's gaze flickered, something unreadable behind his eyes. "I have… other matters to attend to."

Rodrigo and Luis exchanged a glance, but neither dared to ask questions.

Jeron took a slow step back, disappearing into the shadows of the warehouse as Luis and Rodrigo climbed back into the truck.

The next phase was in motion.

And Jeron was already thinking ten steps ahead.

Chapter 24

The stolen box truck bounced along the rough road leading to the Ames Research Facility, its headlights cutting erratically through the darkness. The low hum of the engine filled the cab's cramped interior, but the silence between Rodrigo and Luis was thick with tension. Luis gripped the wheel, his knuckles white, eyes darting between the road and the rearview mirror. Rodrigo sat next to him, his fingers tapping nervously against his knee.

"Man, I don't know about this," Luis muttered, breaking the silence. He had been quiet for most of the nine-hour trek. "This shit doesn't sit right with me. NASA? Really? This is too big. Too much heat."

Rodrigo narrowed his eyes. "What the hell are you talking about? We're in, Luis. We get the shipment, we get out. Simple as that."

"I'm telling you, I don't like it." Luis's fingers tightened on the steering wheel. "I don't know who the hell these fuckers Vogel and Kafka are, but they don't feel right. What if we're walking into a trap?"

Rodrigo shifted in his seat, his eyes locking with Luis's for a second. "You wanna back out now? After all this?"

Luis's jaw clenched, but his voice was shaky. "I'm not saying I want to back out. But we're talking about NASA, man. We're talking about shit that's way over our heads. What if we get caught? What if this whole thing blows up in our faces?"

Rodrigo's fingers curled into a fist. "You think this is the first time we've done something like this? No, we follow through, Luis. We've come too far to bail now. You pull this kind of job, there's no turning back."

Luis's eyes flickered to the side, his gaze lost in the dark stretch of road ahead. "I'm just saying… we don't know what we're moving. What if it's some dangerous-ass shit? I've just got a bad feeling, man."

Rodrigo gritted his teeth, his patience wearing thin. "You think I don't feel it too? But backing out now doesn't change anything. We're already in deep. What's the point of looking over our shoulder the whole way? Either we finish this, or we end up as part of the problem."

Luis let out a short laugh, but it sounded forced. "Yeah, well, I didn't think I'd be moving crates for NASA when I started out in this game. I thought we were just gonna hit some warehouses, grab some cash, and get out."

"Times change, Luis," Rodrigo snapped. "And we change with them. You want to bail now, that's your choice, but I'm not going down that road. Not without the score. Not without the money. We're going through with it."

There was a long pause. The only sound was the soft hum of the engine. Luis's grip on the wheel relaxed, but his shoulders remained tense.

Finally, he spoke, his voice quieter. "I just don't want this to end badly, Rodrigo. For all of us."

Rodrigo leaned back against the van's interior, his mind racing. He didn't blame Luis for being hesitant. Hell, he was nervous too. But this was it. There was no turning back.

"We're fine," Rodrigo said, his voice steel-hard. "We do this clean. No mistakes. Now, just focus. We're almost there."

Luis exhaled sharply, his eyes narrowing in determination. "Yeah. Almost there."

Rodrigo's eyes flicked back to the road ahead, the headlights illuminating the darkened NASA facility in the distance. His gut twisted, but he pushed the feeling aside. It had to be paranoia. It had to be.

He turned to Luis. "Just drive."

Luis didn't say another word, his foot pressing harder on the accelerator as the van sped up toward the looming gates. The night swallowed them whole as they approached the checkpoint.

The truck slowed as they approached the security checkpoint. A uniformed guard stepped forward, his face impassive as he scanned the ID hanging from Luis's vest.

"ID and work order," the guard said.

Luis handed them over smoothly. "Late-night transfer. Last-minute request. You know how it is—bureaucratic bullshit."

The guard flicked on his flashlight, scanning the papers. His frown deepened.

Luis stiffened.

The guard flipped through the documents, brows furrowing deeper. "I don't have this in the system."

Rodrigo's fingers curled into fists.

"Maybe check again," Luis said, keeping his tone easy. "This came straight from upper management. You really wanna be the one to hold up their shipment?"

The guard hesitated, debating his next move.

A voice cut through the moment like a razor. "Is there a problem?"

Luis turned, his stomach twisting as a tall and imposing man stepped into view, his expression calm but commanding. Beside him, a woman adjusted the glasses on her nose, fixing the guard with a withering stare. Both of them were adorned with white lab coats they wore under their robes of authority.

The entire energy of the checkpoint shifted.

The guard straightened. "Sir, this transfer isn't logged in the system. I was just about to—"

Vogel didn't let him finish. He smiled, but it didn't reach his eyes. "That's because it's classified. And I doubt you've high enough clearance to be asking questions."

The guard stiffened.

Kafka stepped forward, her arms crossed defiantly. "Do you really think we'd be standing here if this wasn't legitimate?" Her tone dripped with disdain. "I suggest you let these men do their jobs. Now."

Luis saw the moment the power struggle collapsed. The guard gritted his teeth, clearly unhappy but unwilling to push back against someone outranking him.

"Fine," the guard muttered, handing the ID back to Luis. "Move along."

Luis grinned. "Will do, boss."

Rodrigo exhaled slowly as the gate buzzed open, the van rolling forward into the facility.

"That was too close," Luis muttered softly.

The loading dock was eerily silent, the fluorescent lights cold and sterile against the polished concrete.

Rodrigo's eyes locked onto the massive containment unit in the center of the bay.

It was big, nearly the size of a coffin, with thick reinforced plating. Frost curled around the biohazard symbols lining its surface, and vents along the sides hissed softly, keeping its contents frozen.

And it wasn't alone.

Nearby, several smaller containment units sat stacked neatly, each humming with a low vibration—whatever was inside them was alive, but sleeping.

Luis's unease deepened. He let out a whistle, running a hand over one of the crates. "This some real Area 51 shit, man."

"Shut up and load it," Rodrigo muttered, already moving toward the nearest pallet jack.

They worked quickly, securing the massive crate onto the jack and rolling it toward the truck. The wheels squeaked against the concrete, the sound too loud in the cavernous bay.

As they neared the loading doors, Kafka appeared again, her hands clasped behind her back.

Rodrigo's stomach clenched.

"You have exactly two minutes before the next scheduled patrol comes through," she said evenly. "I suggest you finish loading."

Luis didn't need to be told twice. He and Rodrigo hauled the heavy container up into the truck, before securing the smaller ones.

Rodrigo turned to Vogel, who stood by the dock entrance, watching everything with a serpentine calmness.

"What the hell are we moving?" Rodrigo asked, keeping his voice low.

Vogel's lips curled into something that wasn't quite a smile.

"You don't want to know."

Rodrigo's jaw tightened. He was right.

The last crate was strapped in.

Kafka checked her watch. "Time's up. Go."

Rodrigo jumped into the passenger's seat as Luis hit the

gas, rolling smoothly back toward the checkpoint.

Everything was fine.

Until it wasn't.

As they neared the exit gate, the same security guard from earlier stepped forward, holding up his hand.

Rodrigo's pulse kicked up.

The guard turned to his partner, speaking quietly. Then, he raised his radio—

"Wait—"

Before he could finish, Vogel appeared again, moving with an eerie calm.

"Problem?" he asked smoothly.

The guard hesitated. "Sir, I was just—"

Vogel tilted his head, and something about the way he did it made Rodrigo's skin crawl.

"You're wasting time," Vogel said, his voice almost bored. "Do you think I would personally oversee an operation if it wasn't cleared?"

The guard swallowed, his hand tightening around the radio.

Rodrigo could see the fight happening inside him—protocol versus self-preservation.

Then, Vogel smiled.

It wasn't friendly. It wasn't kind.

It was a promise.

A warning.

The guard lowered the radio.

"Understood, sir," he said stiffly, stepping back. "Proceed."

Rodrigo let out a slow breath as the gate buzzed open, the van rolling through into the night.

Rodrigo tapped on the dash, smirking. "Told you. Like taking candy from a baby!"

Luis didn't answer. His mind flicked to the containment

units in the back, fear creeping along the edges of his mind. He imagined something shifting inside them, something horrible and dangerous. A deep chill ran through him.

Chapter 25

Rodrigo wiped a sweaty palm down his jeans as he stepped out of the van, his boots crunching against the cracked pavement of the Disneyland parking lot. The night air was thick, humid, and wrong—like the city itself was holding its breath.

He exhaled slowly, his fingers unconsciously tightening around the handle of his pistol tucked into his waistband.

They shouldn't be here.

Not like this.

Luis leaned against the hood of the truck, arms crossed, a cigarette dangling from his lips. "I don't like this, man." His voice was low, sharp. "We jacked NASA. Now we're making some back-alley drop with some crazy motherfucker?"

Benny let out a nervous laugh from the side. "Shit, you already played FedEx for this dude once. Now, you call us in here to play U-Haul with you too?"

Rodrigo didn't laugh.

Chuy, who had been quiet, rubbed at his temple like he had a migraine. "I been thinkin'… we already knew this dude was bad news. First time we met him, he was out there in the mountains, runnin' from those other weirdos like he stole something." He nodded toward the sealed crates in the back of the truck. "Now we're out here stealing shit for him?"

Rodrigo knew what they were thinking.

They were thinking the same thing he was.

How the hell did we get this deep?

A soft clap echoed from the darkness.

They all turned at once.

Jeron stepped forward from the shadows, his presence as unnerving as ever. He didn't wear the cloak this time—he didn't need to. There was something inhuman about the way he carried himself, like he was always a step ahead, like he saw five moves down the board while everyone else was still figuring out the rules.

Rodrigo swallowed hard.

He didn't like how calm Jeron looked. Like he already knew what they were about to say.

Luis took the cigarette from his mouth and flicked it onto the pavement. "We gotta talk."

Jeron's lips curled slightly, but it wasn't a smile. "I assumed as much."

Rodrigo squared his shoulders, forcing himself to meet Jeron's gaze. "Look, we played along. We got your shit, risking our necks at that NASA place." He jerked a thumb toward the truck. "But none of us signed up for whatever this is."

Jeron tilted his head slightly. "And what, exactly, do you think this is?"

Benny let out a dry chuckle, "Ain't normal, that's for damn sure."

Chuy scoffed. "We ain't no mercenaries. We ain't soldiers. We're not tryna end up in some sci-fi horror movie, man."

Rodrigo nodded. "So, if this is where we shake hands and go separate ways, now's the time."

Silence.

A long, dragging silence.

Jeron sighed, shaking his head as if they were a bunch of slow students in his classroom. "It's fascinating," he mused. "You've all killed before. You've stolen. You've run drugs, moved weapons, terrorized people in your own city. And yet, here you are—scared."

Rodrigo clenched his jaw.

Jeron took a step closer, his dark eyes unreadable. "You're already mine. Every one of you." His voice wasn't raised, but it sank into them, like a hook slipping into flesh.

Benny muttered, "Man, fuck that."

Jeron's head snapped toward Benny so fast it was unnatural. His lips parted slightly. "Say that again."

Benny's mouth clamped shut.

Rodrigo felt it before he even saw Jeron move—the air shifting, the way his gut twisted.

Jeron was suddenly right in front of Benny, moving faster than a normal man should. He didn't touch him, didn't even raise a hand—he just stared.

And Benny collapsed to his knees, hands gripping his head like it was about to split open.

A strangled scream tore from his throat.

Rodrigo lunged forward, but before he could reach him, Jeron turned his gaze toward him—and Rodrigo felt it.

A pressure.

Like a thousand invisible hands were crushing his skull from the inside.

The world warped, his vision darkening at the edges, every sound muffling, like he was sinking into deep water.

And then it was gone.

Benny gasped for air, falling forward onto his hands. Rodrigo stumbled back, his pulse roaring in his ears.

Luis and Chuy had their guns drawn—but it wouldn't matter.

They all knew it wouldn't matter.

Jeron smiled.

"Do not confuse me with the people you're used to dealing with." His voice was still calm, but there was a razor edge beneath it. "I do not give second chances. And I do not tolerate… disobedience."

Rodrigo wiped at his mouth, still feeling like something had crawled into his head and left scars. He glared at Jeron, hating him, hating that they were trapped now.

Jeron sighed again, as if bored with their resistance. "Let's be clear—you are not free men anymore. You are tools. You will do as I say. Because if you don't…"

His expression darkened.

"…I will kill every single one of you."

A chill ran through Rodrigo's spine.

Jeron turned to him, his face as unreadable as ever. "So, Rodrigo… are you ready to accept your place in this?"

Rodrigo gritted his teeth. He had no choice.

"…Yeah."

Jeron's smirk returned. "Good." He turned toward the truck, placing a hand against its side. "Unload the cargo. We have work to do."

Rodrigo glanced at the others. Benny's face was pale, his breathing ragged. Luis looked furious, his hand still gripping his pistol like he wanted to use it. Chuy wouldn't even meet Rodrigo's eyes.

This wasn't a deal anymore.

This was survival.

Rodrigo rolled his shoulders and motioned for them to move. "Let's get this done."

They had no way out now.

Chapter 26

Rodrigo clenched the wheel of the truck as he pulled into the nearly abandoned Disneyland parking lot and rumbled to a stop near a dimly lit employee entrance, his stomach twisting into knots. This was a mistake. They should have walked away when they had the chance, but now? Now they were in too deep.

His crew stood in tense silence against the cargo van parked next to him. Luis drummed his fingers against hood of the vehicle nervously, his eyes scanning the darkened lot. Benny checked his gun, even though they weren't supposed to need it tonight. Chuy muttered under his breath, maybe a prayer, maybe a curse—Rodrigo couldn't tell anymore. Rico stood motionless, his expression unreadable, but Rodrigo could feel his unease.

The park had been closed for over an hour, but a few workers still lingered, finishing maintenance and security rounds. Rodrigo hated that. Fewer people meant fewer eyes, but it also meant if something went wrong, there'd be no one to help.

The back doors of the truck suddenly swung open, and Jeron appeared before them without a word.

Rodrigo stiffened. Every time he saw the bastard, it was like his body knew before his brain did—some primal instinct screaming at him to run. But there was nowhere to run now.

Jeron's cold gaze swept over the containment units stacked neatly in the back. The cargo they had risked their necks to steal.

"Good," Jeron murmured. He turned toward them, his presence heavy and suffocating. "Now, let's move. We don't have all night."

Rodrigo exhaled sharply. "So… what exactly are we doing with this shit?"

Jeron's smile was slow, sharp as a knife. "We're preparing a demonstration."

Luis scoffed. "Man, that don't answer shit."

Jeron's eyes flickered toward him. Luis tensed, gripping his gun tighter. But Jeron only chuckled. "You don't need to understand. You just need to do as I say."

Rodrigo felt every nerve in his body scream in protest. But he knew what Jeron could do. He had seen it firsthand. If they stepped out of line, they wouldn't live to regret it.

He gritted his teeth and nodded. "Fine. Let's just get this over with."

They moved like ghosts through the park with the aid of an anti-gravity cart Jeron had crafted, rolling the crates along hidden maintenance paths beneath the watchful glow of dimmed floodlights. Rodrigo hated every second of it. The eerie silence, the flickering lights, the way the park felt different without the laughter of kids or the chatter of tourists.

Disneyland wasn't supposed to be quiet.

Luis walked beside him, pushing one of the heavier carts. "I don't like this, bro. This shit feels cursed."

Rodrigo didn't answer. He didn't have to.

Ahead of them, Jeron led the way, his cloak barely rustling as he navigated through Employee Only corridors like he'd worked here his whole life.

They passed an empty parade float, its smiling cartoon figures grinning hollowly in the darkness. The animatronics in the distance twitched, their motions stuck in eerie loops. The place was wrong.

Rodrigo looked over his shoulder. No guards. No workers. They were deep enough into the park now that no one would stop them.

Finally, they reached the first drop-off point—The Haunted Mansion.

Jeron turned to them. "Set two containment units inside."

Rodrigo frowned. "What's in these things?"

Jeron's expression didn't change. "That is not your concern."

Luis didn't move. "I ain't rollin' no damn mystery boxes into a haunted house, man."

Jeron's gaze darkened.

Rodrigo knew what was coming before it happened—knew it the second Jeron turned his full attention on Luis.

Luis suddenly gasped, his knees buckling as he grabbed his head. His breath hitched in sharp, pained gulps. "What the—fuck—"

Rodrigo grabbed his friend's arm, but the moment he touched him, a wave of nausea slammed into his own skull.

His vision blurred. His ears rang.

Then, just as suddenly as it started, it stopped.

Rodrigo stumbled back, clutching his temples. Luis sagged forward, panting.

Jeron stood completely still. Unbothered. Unmoving.

His voice was like a blade cutting through the silence.

"Put the units inside."

Rodrigo swallowed the bile rising in his throat and motioned for his crew to move.

Once completed, the next drop was Tomorrowland Theater.

Rodrigo's hands shook as he helped Chuy push one of the final crates inside. The others unloaded the rest, stacking them exactly where Jeron instructed.

The place was dead silent—except for the faint beeping from the containment units.

Rodrigo exhaled shakily, wiping sweat from his brow. "This it?"

Jeron nodded. "Almost."

Rodrigo narrowed his eyes. "And when it's done? When whatever-the-fuck this is happens?"

Jeron smiled. "Then you'll witness something magnificent."

Rodrigo didn't want to witness anything. He wanted out.

But there was no out.

Jeron turned away, pressing a few buttons on his wrist device. The containment units hummed in response.

Rodrigo stared at them, his stomach twisting.

Whatever was in those things... they weren't supposed to be here.

Neither were they.

And soon?

This place would never be the same again.

Chapter 27

Silas gripped the ship's controls tightly, eyes fixed on the digital map overlay that illuminated their departure from the Coachella Valley. The ship glided through the night sky like a ghost.

In the seat next to him, Mishka scoured over a pulsing radar screen, each faint signature reflecting Jeron's erratic movement. "His trail's gotten weaker, but it's heading toward the core of this... Anaheim place," she murmured, squinting as she read the labels on the foreign maps. "He's taken refuge in some kind of gathering site for humans."

Silas furrowed his brow, peering closer at the maps displaying peculiar attractions and structures with names that seemed absurd to them. "Disneyland?" he muttered, tapping the name. "According to the data, it's some kind of amusement zone. If Jeron is using it to hide in plain sight, it's a bold move."

A sense of foreboding gripped them all as he initiated the ship's descent and steered toward a secluded area bordered by dense greenery at the park's edge, each of them recalling the perilous moment when they had first entered this world. "We'll keep to the shadows and do this quietly," he ordered, voice low. "This isn't just about finding him—he's got something big planned, and we need to uncover it without raising alarm."

They touched down silently, the cloaking field blending the ship into the backdrop of trees. The crew equipped themselves with the spectral modifiers to conceal their presence. The strange place hummed with a low, ambient noise that was almost calming, yet an undercurrent of something sinister hung in the air, sending tension through the team.

"Alright," Silas said. "We split up. We're looking for any signs of tech that doesn't belong here—energy traces, communication devices, anything that stands out. Jeron will be hiding near areas with plenty of cover, and from what we've gathered, he's using some kind of containment units. Report in if you find anything unusual."

They dispersed, each moving along winding pathways lined with structures resembling artificial landscapes and castles. As Silas crept along a dimly lit corridor that bordered an area marked "Adventureland," he observed the unnatural terrain, dotted with odd plants and artificial sounds of wildlife. The faint hum of the scanner picked up subtle readings from various places, but it was clear these were normal to the strange environment. Still, he continued on cautiously, scanning everything within range.

In his earpiece, Ridley's voice came through. "Silas, picking up electromagnetic interference around the structure marked as… 'Tomorrowland.' Some foreign tech in play here, likely Jeron's attempt to mask his equipment."

Silas adjusted his grip on his scanner. "Good work. Proceed with caution. We'll regroup at the ship when we're finished."

Continuing along, he rounded a corner and entered a

deserted area, his scanner emitting a faint chime. A hidden signal was close, fluctuating as he moved toward a large, dark building with an ominous facade, its entrance eerily marked with fake graves and statues. The sign above read "Haunted Mansion".

He crouched low, the scanner indicating an elevated energy source concealed just beyond the building's walls. His gaze flickered over the entry points, mentally mapping potential escape routes as he moved closer. The signal pulsed stronger—there was no doubt Jeron was nearby.

"Mishka, I'm at the Haunted Mansion," he whispered into his earpiece. "Strong energy signals here. Jeron's set up something in or around this building."

A soft crackle echoed back, Mishka's voice taut with apprehension. "Understood. Proceeding to your location now."

As he edged closer to one of the doors, a faint shimmer caught his eye—a cloaked device wedged into the masonry, barely visible unless one looked closely. Silas scanned it swiftly, logging its data and sending it to the ship's central system. The readings confirmed his suspicions; Jeron's containment devices were primed and ready. They didn't have much time.

In his earpiece, Ridley's voice broke through again. "Silas, I found an open panel in Tomorrowland—contains high-level tech camouflaged as 'park infrastructure.' Whatever Jeron's doing, he's hidden units throughout the entire area. This isn't just a hideout—it's a staging ground."

Silas clenched his jaw, forcing himself to remain calm. "Good find, Ridley. Clear out and head back. Mishka, let's regroup and make an extraction plan. If Jeron's in here, he's preparing for something catastrophic."

With every step, Silas's dread grew. He inched toward the

building's side entrance, slipping into a dim hallway that twisted and turned like a maze, decorated with garish, dusty relics that seemed to mock his purpose. He could feel Jeron's twisted sense of humor in the setting.

"Just outside your entry point now, Silas," Mishka stated through her comm. "I'll cover your exit."

As Silas neared the containment area, his skin prickled, the dark hall stretching into what looked like a large room lined with strange, grinning effigies and a ceiling painted with faded stars. Just beyond, he spotted a faint glimmer of the containment field around one of Jeron's prized subjects.

"Going in," he whispered. He darted into the room, quickly assessing the alien containment unit. Inside, a figure moved, eyes locked on him, muscles twitching as though it sensed freedom was close. The creature stared back at him through the containment's glass, its teeth bared in a silent, taunting grin.

Before he could move, the creature growled again, louder this time. From deeper within the building, another growl responded, reverberating through the walls. Silas's blood chilled. The containment units weren't idle; they were active, and the creatures were waiting.

"Mishka, Ridley—get back to the ship now," he ordered, his voice strained. "We'll regroup and take Jeron down at first light. Don't let anything catch your trail."

With one last glance at the creature snarling in its containment, Silas ducked back into the hallway, weaving through the corridors and back to the edge of the building.

"We know where he is," he muttered, adrenaline flooding his veins. "And if we don't act fast, he's going to unleash something far worse than we imagined."

***

* * *

Jeron moved through Disneyland like a shadow, his steps silent against the carefully maintained pavement. The park was long closed, the last of the guests having shuffled out hours ago, leaving only a skeleton crew of overnight workers tending to maintenance and security rounds. He had timed everything perfectly—his masterpiece was already in place. Now, he just needed to confirm that nothing was amiss before the performance began.

He tapped the small device on his wrist, and a faint ping resonated in his ear. A grid of the park's layout materialized on the screen, twelve glowing markers blinking steadily at their designated locations. The containment units were secure.

Still, he needed to see them for himself.

Jeron's path took him through an employee-only access gate, slipping through unnoticed as a janitor wheeled his cart toward a break area, too preoccupied with his phone to glance up. The air inside the service corridors was cool and sterile, the hum of unseen machinery vibrating beneath the floors.

Jeron moved quickly. First stop: The Haunted Mansion.

He entered through a back door, weaving through the dim corridors of the attraction. Cobwebbed chandeliers cast eerie flickers across the walls, and animatronic ghosts loomed from darkened corners, frozen in their lifeless dance until the ride powered back on.

Jeron knelt by the first containment unit, concealed beneath a false gravestone in the graveyard scene. He pulled up his wrist device, scanning the module's status. Power levels steady. Release mechanisms functional. Perfect.

He repeated the process through the rest of the mansion, tracing his fingers over the smooth metal of each container, whispering to them like a father soothing his restless children. They were his now, each one containing a gift for this world.

Satisfied, he moved on.

Next stop: Tomorrowland Theater.

Jeron's boots barely made a sound as he navigated the futuristic, metallic pathways of Tomorrowland. The park's vision of the future was optimistic, a shining beacon of humanity's potential. It would be poetic to watch it all crumble.

He reached the closed theater, where several smaller containment units were embedded into the walls and beneath the seating area. A single tap on his wrist device pulled up their readings—all functional, all ready.

He allowed himself a rare smile.

With the final checks complete, Jeron made his way to a hidden access room, where he could oversee the park's security feeds. The monitors cast a dim glow over the control panel, showing the empty walkways and the silent attractions.

His wrist device synced with the system, pulling up his customized interface. One by one, each containment unit appeared on his screen, waiting for his command.

He leaned back against the chair, fingers hovering over the activation sequence. He could unleash hell right now if he wanted to. But no… not yet. The timing had to be perfect.

His eyes flickered toward the corner of the room displaying his greatest creation—the monstrous fusion of man, beast, and nightmare. The containment field pulsed softly, its energy barely holding the thing in place. Even in sleep, it radiated hunger.

Jeron activated the viewport, watching with fascination as the beast inside twitched. Its form was obscured by shadows, but he could see the gleam of its red eyes, the slow, controlled rise and fall of its grotesque chest. Even in its suspended state, it radiated power.

Jeron smiled.

"It's almost time," he whispered, his voice barely audible over the soft hum of the machines around him.

Then, he powered down the screen, blending back into the darkness of the park, a ghost among ghosts.

When morning came, Disneyland would open its gates as if nothing had happened. Families would flood inside, blissfully unaware that their fantasy was about to become a nightmare.

Chapter 28

Gia stood in front of her bedroom mirror, holding two dresses against her body, each getting its turn in the spotlight. "What screams 'cute but chill' without being 'try-hard because Danny's gonna be there'?"

Behind her, Marco leaned against the doorframe, munching on a piece of toast. "I'd say both scream 'I spent an hour picking this because Danny's gonna be there.'"

Gia whipped around, her hairbrush already in hand. "Do you *mind*?"

Marco darted out of the room, laughing as he disappeared down the hall. "I'm just saying, red's more your 'I-like-you' vibe. Blue's too friend-zone-y."

Gia groaned, dropping the hairbrush onto her dresser. Her brother wasn't wrong, but she hated that he had a sixth sense for all her crush-related dilemmas. Picking up the red dress, she held it up again, sighing. "Today's the day," she whispered to herself. "No chickening out. I'll tell him how I feel."

She grabbed her phone and fired off a message to her group chat with Mia and Aiden.

Gia: Emergency. Red or blue dress? Danny's gonna be

there. Help.

Mia: Red. Duh. You look like a total Disney princess in that one.

Aiden: Why are you asking me? I'm a guy.

Mia: BECAUSE she needs opinions. Don't make me kick you out of this chat.

Aiden: Red. Guys like red. Happy now?

Mia: See? Told you.

Gia tossed her phone on the bed and pulled on the red dress, checking herself in the mirror one last time. It was perfect—cute without trying too hard. She slipped on her sparkly Mickey Mouse ears, stuffed a small notebook into her bag for backup, and headed downstairs.

Her mom was in the kitchen pouring coffee, humming to herself. Marco sat at the counter, still working on his toast, now covered in an obscene amount of peanut butter.

"Don't you have anything better to do than bug me all morning?" Gia asked, grabbing an apple from the fruit bowl.

"Nope," Marco replied with a mouthful of peanut butter. "Also, good call on the red. Danny's totally gonna notice."

Before Gia could fire back, she felt a sharp sting on her forearm. She flinched, letting out a startled yelp as the apple fell to the floor.

"What the—" She looked down to see a tiny bee flying lazily away.

"Oh no, are you okay?" her mom asked, rushing over with a damp towel.

Gia pressed the towel against the growing welt on her arm, wincing. "Seriously? A bee sting? Today?"

Marco smirked. "Maybe it's a sign. You know, like, life's gonna sting a little, but it's sweet in the end."

Gia rolled her eyes. "You've been spending way too much time on those motivational TikToks."

Her mom chuckled, handing her a tube of cream. "Rub this on before you leave, sweetheart. And take an antihistamine just in case."

As Gia smeared the cream on her arm, a small shiver ran up her spine, a strange unease she couldn't quite shake. She glanced out the window at the sunny morning, the bee already forgotten.

"Great start to the day," she muttered.

"Hey," Marco said, grabbing his backpack, "if you survive the bee sting, maybe confessing to Danny won't be so hard after all."

Gia pointed her apple at him like a weapon. "Out. Now."

He grinned and darted out of the room, leaving her alone with her mom, who patted her on the shoulder. "You'll be fine, honey. It's just a bee sting. And Danny would be lucky to have a girl like you."

Gia smiled weakly. "Thanks, Mom."

As she slung her bag over her shoulder and headed for the door, her mom called after her, "Have fun! And remember, it's Disney—magic happens there!"

Gia forced a laugh but couldn't shake the lingering discomfort as she climbed into the car. The tiny, throbbing sting on her arm pulsed faintly, a small but persistent reminder.

"It's nothing," she whispered to herself. "Just nerves."

But as she pulled away from the house, the morning sunlight glinting on the horizon, she couldn't help but glance at her arm again, the faint ache somehow feeling heavier than it should.

****

The sun had barely started to rise when the Palm Desert High seniors started trickling into the school parking lot, filling the early morning air with chatter and laughter. The day was finally here—their senior trip to Disneyland. After months of late nights, cramming sessions, and senior stress, this was the day they could let loose.

Aiden was the first to burst out of his mom's car, nearly leaving his bag behind in his excitement. He jogged over to the group forming by the school bus and grinned wide, slinging an arm around Danny, who had been yawning.

"Danny-boy, wake up!" Aiden said, shaking him by the shoulders. "We're going to the happiest place on Earth! No sleeping allowed today."

Danny rolled his eyes, giving Aiden a playful shove. "Yeah, yeah. Tell that to the three hours of sleep I got last night. You know how hard it is to sleep when this guy won't stop blowing up our group chat?"

"I was hyping us up!" Aiden shot back with a grin.

Gia and Mia joined them a moment later and Gia immediately held out her phone, pulling the others into a group selfie.

"Everyone smile like it's the best day of our lives!" she said, aiming for the perfect shot.

Mia raised an eyebrow but smiled anyway, though her look of bemusement wasn't lost on Danny. "You act like we're not going to see each other every day this summer," she teased, stepping back from the group as Gia reviewed the selfie with a critical eye.

"Just humor me, alright?" Gia said with a shrug. "I need to make some memories I can actually frame and look back on after college starts."

"Can you believe it, guys? Disneyland. Today. Us. Finally!" Aiden exclaimed, his face lit up with an infectious grin. He was the charismatic one, always pushing the group into wild ideas and daring schemes.

Beside him, Gia rolled her eyes, though her smile gave her away. "You're acting like you haven't been there a thousand times already, Aiden."

"Yeah, but this time, it's different! Last big hurrah, remember? After this, it's college, and we're all gonna go off and forget about each other," Aiden said dramatically, flinging an arm around Mia and Danny.

Mia shrugged him off, laughing. "Trust me, Aiden, we're not gonna forget you. Unfortunately."

Danny pulled his Palm Desert High cap lower over his eyes, a grin peeking through. "Let's just get to the rides. I don't wanna waste a second once we're there."

As the bus pulled into the parking lot, the group scrambled toward it. The past year's stress, the looming uncertainty of the future—all faded in the face of a day meant for laughter and memories.

The adults began herding them onto the bus, each chaperone doing their best to keep the energy level contained. Mr. Fernandez, the overly enthusiastic AP History teacher, tried to get them organized as he stood by the bus door, checking them in.

"Let's go, let's go! I don't want anyone left behind," he said, glancing down at the list. "Hey, Aiden, you remembered sunscreen, right?"

Aiden waved him off with a laugh. "Relax, Mr. F—I'll be fine. Worst-case, I'll come back with a free tan."

"Oh no, you won't," Ms. Katz, the strict-but-caring chemistry teacher, cut in, handing him a mini bottle. "Apply this now, mister. I don't want to deal with any lobster faces by the time we're back tonight."

The students shuffled onto the bus, and within minutes, they were on the road, bouncing with excitement. Aiden led the charge, of course, plugging his phone into a portable speaker and immediately blasting their "Senior Trip" playlist.

"Alright, party bus!" Aiden yelled, and the bus exploded in cheers and laughter.

Mia, who'd snagged a window seat, watched the desert scenery flash by, letting the noise around her settle into background excitement. Beside her, Danny and Gia argued over the music choices.

"Aiden, you had your turn—now it's ours!" Gia called out.

"But my playlist is the best," Aiden shot back. "It's scientifically designed to get you hyped."

"I'll show you hyped," Danny muttered, grabbing the aux cord. A brief tug-of-war ensued, with Ms. Katz eventually stepping in, confiscating the speaker with an eye-roll and a little smirk.

"We'll need to save some energy for the rides," she said, silencing Aiden's protests. "Remember, this is an all-day thing."

On the way, they joked about which rides they'd tackle first, what snacks they'd eat, and which of them would chicken out on the roller coasters. They'd been through everything together: heartbreaks, betrayals, endless nights studying, and reckless nights sneaking out. Today, they were here to forget it all.

As they rolled closer to Anaheim, a collective murmur of excitement began to spread through the bus, with everyone pointing out the first hints of rollercoasters and towers peeking over the tree-line.

"Hey, there it is!" Aiden exclaimed, pressing his face against the window. The first glimpse of Disneyland's gates sparked a new wave of chatter.

Mr. Fernandez turned in his seat at the front, clapping his hands to get their attention. "Alright, listen up! Once we get there, stay with your chaperone group and be at the meeting spot by 8:30 tonight. Got it?"

A scattered chorus of "Yes, Mr. Fernandez!" echoed back, not that anyone seemed to be listening too closely. They were already halfway out of their seats as the bus pulled to a stop.

As they spilled out into the parking lot, Ms. Katz made her rounds, reminding each group about safety, while Mr. Fernandez did a final headcount.

"Have fun, and remember to call if you need anything!" he called as they moved toward the entrance.

As they walked toward the park's entrance, the anticipation had reached a fever pitch. Aiden was already talking about which ride they'd hit first, while Gia had pulled out her phone, determined to get at least one more group selfie in front of the gates.

The park stretched before them like a world all its own, and as they handed in their tickets and walked through the entrance, everything seemed to sparkle with magic, promising to make their day unforgettable.

Chapter 29

William awoke with a jolt to find Kate's face inches from his own, staring at him with a sternness that seemed comically out of place against the sparkling tiara perched on her head and the ruffled pink Princess Aurora dress she wore. Her brows knitted together, and her lips pressed into a serious line.

"It's 'bout time you're awake, Mister," she said, her voice taking on an exaggerated tone of authority.

William rubbed his eyes and let out a long yawn. "What time is it?" he muttered, sitting up just enough to squint at the window, where the faintest glimmer of dawn seeped through the blinds.

"Six o'clock," Kate replied briskly, her little hands on her hips. "And you need to get up."

He sighed, sinking back into the pillow, a faint smile tugging at his mouth. The bed felt far too comfortable to abandon just yet.

"Oh no, you don't!" Kate scolded, poking him in the shoulder. "You promised."

At that, he bolted upright, trying to shake off the grogginess. "Alright, alright, I'm up!"

Melinda appeared in the doorway, dressed in khaki shorts and a white blouse, her arms crossed but her expression amused. "I thought I told you not to wake him up, young lady?"

Kate looked indignant. "I didn't! I was super quiet. He woke up all by himself, I swear!"

Melinda raised an eyebrow but smiled. "Even so, give him a chance to get up and get ready. Why don't you go see if Tommy needs help with the cooler?"

Kate huffed but finally relented, pointing a tiny finger at William as she hopped down from the bed. "No dilly-dallying, got it?"

William smirked, failing to stifle a laugh at her unyielding seriousness. "Where did you even hear that phrase?"

Kate shrugged casually, her dress rustling as she moved. "I dunno, but it means don't waste time."

As soon as she had stomped out of the room, William and Melinda burst into quiet laughter, their amusement softened by the early morning light.

"She's going to be a handful," Melinda sighed, still chuckling.

"Just like her mother," he teased, pulling her close. They shared a long, warm kiss, that thawed the last remnants of sleep from his bones.

"Are we sure it's not too soon to do something like this?" Melinda asked as she pulled away.

William shook his head gently. "No. I think we need it, Melinda. Maybe it'll help things feel a little... normal again."

She gave him a hopeful smile. "Let's hope so. Now, you'd better get a move on before our little drama queen storms back in here."

Minutes later, William was dressed and found his way into the living room, where chaos was unfolding. Tommy struggled under the weight of the cooler, visibly straining as he tried to make it to the door, while Kate had piled herself with bags, wobbling as she dragged them along, her determination outweighing her balance.

"Looks like I got here just in time," William said, grinning.

Melinda walked in, a steaming cup of coffee in hand. "I thought I told you two to wait for your dad?" she said, eyebrows raised.

William waved it off, taking the coffee from her gratefully. "I'll take it with me and drink it in the car." He bent to pick up the cooler, only to pause as he felt a sharp twinge in his knee.

"Is it bothering you again?" Melinda asked with a look of concern crossing her face.

He nodded, grimacing slightly as he stretched his leg out. "Yeah, not used to all this running around." He offered her a reassuring smile. "Just grab me a few pain pills, and I'll be fine."

Moments later, Melinda returned with the pills and a glass of water. "Just… take it easy today. No crazy rides, alright?"

William nodded in agreement as he swallowed the pills. After loading the last of their things into the SUV, he felt a slight tug of nostalgia as he looked at his kids through the rearview mirror, bright-eyed and chattering.

Melinda turned to him. "Guerera's still planning to meet us there, right?"

"Yeah," William replied, starting the car. "I texted her last night."

"Who's Guerera?" Kate asked, her eyes wide with curiosity.

"She's the one who helped your dad beat the bad guys," Melinda explained.

Kate gasped. "So, she's like a superhero!"

William chuckled. "You could say that. Plus, she's bringing a friend for you two. Her name's Ashley."

"Great," Tommy groaned, flopping against the window, clearly unimpressed. "Just what we need—another girl."

Kate grinned. "Now there'll be more girls than boys!"

William caught Tommy's sulking reflection in the mirror and smirked. "Guess we'll have to stick together, bud. Looks like we're outnumbered."

With one last glance at his family, he backed the SUV out of the driveway. For the first time in a long time, they felt like a family on the verge of something special.

***

The first thing William noticed as they approached the gates of Disneyland was the noise—an endless, pulsing hum of voices, laughter, and distant music, all blending into a surreal kind of harmony. It was the sound of pure, unfiltered joy, something that felt almost foreign after everything they'd been through. But today was different. Today was about pretending things were normal.

Two and a half hours of bumper-to-bumper traffic, restless kids, and a near-miss with a minivan full of tourists had finally led them here—to the glossy, too-perfect façade of "The Happiest Place on Earth."

William let out a slow breath, trying to convince himself he felt the same excitement as the people around him. His family, at least, had no trouble slipping into the moment. Kate bolted ahead, her tiny feet barely touching the pavement as she spotted him—the legend, the icon, the reason little kids lost their minds: Mickey Mouse.

Before William could blink, she had latched onto the poor guy's leg like an octopus, her arms squeezing with the kind of unwavering devotion usually reserved for saints and fairy tale princesses. Mickey, ever the professional, patted her head in exaggerated delight. To her, it was a silent performance of pure magic.

Tommy, on the other hand, held back, his hands in his pockets, while rocking on his heels like he wasn't impressed. But William caught that quick glance at Mickey's oversized gloves, and the way Tommy's fingers twitched like he wanted to reach out. The kid was holding onto some crazy idea of being too old for all this, but it was slipping.

Mickey must've sensed it too because he extended his hand in a grand, sweeping motion. Tommy hesitated, then, finally, extended his own hand for a shake. Mickey gave it an over-the-top waggle, making Tommy's lips twitch in what he clearly didn't want to be a smile. William smirked. The last thing his son wanted was to be caught enjoying himself. *He's trying to grow up too fast*, he thought bitterly. But, with everything that'd happened recently, could he really blame him?

As he scanned the crowd, he spotted Guerera and Ashley standing off to the side. Ashley clung tightly to Guerera's leg, peeking sheepishly out from behind her, her blue princess dress sparkling in the bright sunlight.

William waved emphatically in their direction, both to get their attention, and to embarrass Tommy. The cringing look on Tommy's face suggested it had worked perfectly. Melinda chuckled and shook her head, giving William a wide smile as they walked across the lot—something that had been in short supply these last few months.

Once William and Melinda had each given Guerera a fierce hug, each one filled with a love and friendship born in tragedy, William presented the rest of his family. "Guerera," he said with a warm smile, "let me introduce you to the rest of our crew."

Tommy stiffened as William ruffled his hair. "This here is my son, Tommy."

"Dad," Tommy groaned, stepping out of reach and fixing his hair like the world was watching.

Guerera chuckled, giving Tommy an approving nod. "You look just like your old man."

Tommy scowled. "I don't know if that's a good thing, or a bad thing?"

William laughed. "I'm choosing to take it as one."

Then he gestured toward Kate, who was now staring up at Guerera with an expression of pure awe. "And, this our daughter, Kate."

"Daddy says you're a superhero," Kate announced, matter-of-fact as anything.

Guerera snorted. "That so?"

Ashley, still half-hiding, perked up. "You should've seen her! She wore this whole space suit and was blasting fire everywhere! She saved us from the whole nasty swarm!"

William gave a knowing look. "Sounds pretty superhero-y to me."

Guerera rolled her eyes, waving them off as her face began to flush ever so slightly. "Alright, alright, enough with the superhero talk. We're here to have fun."

Ashley glanced at Kate's dress, her fingers fidgeting at the tulle of her own. "I like your dress," she whispered.

Kate grinned. "Thanks! Yours too! I almost picked Aurora, but I decided on Cinderella instead."

Ashley nodded solemnly. "Aurora's great, but Cinderella never gives up. My mom used to say that."

A flicker of something deep and painful passed behind Guerera's eyes. It was gone in an instant, masked by a quick swipe of her hand over Ashley's head, messing up her carefully combed hair.

"See? Told you guys they'd hit it off," William said, watching as the two little girls linked hands and started skipping ahead.

Tommy groaned beside him. "Dad, if they start talking about tiaras, I'm gonna be sick."

William threw an arm around his son's shoulder, guiding him forward with a smirk. "Too bad, kid. We're in the thick of it now. There's nowhere to run. Nowhere to hide."

As they moved toward the entrance, something cold snaked down William's spine. It was irrational—maybe just an old habit, the side effect of spending too long in situations where things always went sideways. But as the music swelled and the crowd buzzed around them, a feeling settled deep in his bones.

Like something was waiting.

Then the moment passed, swallowed by the laughter around him, the light of the sun bouncing off Cinderella's castle in the distance, and the promise of happiness this little paradise extended.

Today was for them—a chance to get back to normal.

And he was going to hold onto that for as long as he could.

Chapter 30

Jeron lurked in the shadows, his eyes focused on the beast as it stood eerily still. This was the first successful link with the Alpha, and Ashton would be thrilled. Satisfied, he pressed the device embedded at the nape of his neck, disappearing from view. With a flicker of a grin, Jeron dashed forward, sending a quick encrypted update to Ashton. Despite the primitive technology of this world, the device he'd appropriated had proven remarkably effective.

He scaled the Haunted Mansion's stone wall with silent precision, slipping through a concealed side entrance he'd scouted days before. Out of all the attractions, this one was his favorite—a playground of twisted illusions, hinting at dark forces that lingered just beneath the surface. It was perfect.

In one of the alcoves, hidden among the faux crypts and tombstones, lay his cache. Jeron retrieved a large, heavy case and ducked behind a towering oak, working swiftly as the energy in his spectrum modifier waned, flickering dangerously close to failure. He couldn't afford detection—not when he was mere moments from unleashing Ashton's creation on this unsuspecting world.

The case clicked open, revealing a small display screen and a compact, retractable keyboard. The array of twelve units pulsed on the screen, each status bar at full capacity, ready for release. Jeron's fingers flew over the keyboard, initiating a countdown. Soon, each containment unit would disgorge a terror that would render this "Happiest Place on Earth" into a nightmare Ashton himself would relish. The bitter irony made Jeron chuckle, his pulse quickening as he imagined the horror that would ripple through this place.

With the case repacked, Jeron slunk out of the shadows, weaving through the park's winding pathways until he reached the rear door of the Tomorrowland Theater. He needed to check the Alpha's link one last time before the countdown hit zero. As he slipped inside, the spectrum modifier emitted a weak, final beep before dying completely. He'd have to move fast.

He secured the access center door, striding to the far corner where an invisible containment chamber now shimmered into view. Jeron set the case down and activated the display. The screen showed a steady beep from within the chamber; the special organism was stable, thriving even. The neuro-image panel displayed the brain activity of the "host"—a masterpiece Ashton had cultivated from the limited resources on this world. Jeron leaned closer to the viewing panel, his breath catching at the beast's grotesque brilliance.

The creature, a primate base twisted beyond recognition, was astonishingly massive. Ashton had incorporated macabre enhancements—tentacles cascading from its shoulders, a human face grafted grotesquely onto its torso, eyes filled with a seething hatred. The human mouth spat soundless curses at Jeron. Smiling, Jeron tilted his head. "Not yet, big guy. Your moment's coming. Trust me—you'll get your revenge."

The beast went still, a devious smile stretching across both its faces.

As the countdown ticked down, Jeron's anxiety grew. Each passing second edged him closer to the culmination of their plan, and his heart thrummed with eager anticipation. The containment units scattered across the amusement park were synced, ready to release their "guests." He could hardly wait for the screams to echo through the air as Ashton's creations tore through this foolishly cheerful world.

Finally, the timer hit zero. Jeron's eyes gleamed as each unit blinked on-screen, their doors releasing a horde of ravenous, undead monstrosities. He looked back to the containment chamber, watching the beast—Clause, as Ashton had dubbed him—react to the live footage fed directly to his mind. The creature's eyes flared with an intelligence and fury that sent a thrill through Jeron. He pressed the release button, and with a monstrous roar, Clause exploded from the chamber. The grotesque fusion of gorilla and human glared down at Jeron, a hunger blazing in its eyes, before uttering one word: "Guerera."

Clause didn't wait for permission. He lunged for the door, tearing it off its hinges, then burst into the hallway, his hulking form vanishing down the corridor with a speed that belied his size. Jeron barely had time to settle in before he heard the first bloodcurdling screams echo through the theater. They rose in a crescendo, then fell silent, one by one. Jeron watched the footage, savoring the thrill as panic spread and chaos unfurled in every corner of the park.

Satisfied, he switched the screen view, tapping into the camera embedded in Clause's forehead. Now he would have a front-row seat to the carnage as they unleashed a new age of fear and destruction upon this world—a world that would soon come to know him as its God.

Chapter 31

Brandon Martinez had worked at Disneyland for almost six years. He'd seen it all—entitled guests, screaming children, drunken tourists who somehow snuck alcohol past security. But nothing in his life had prepared him for *this*.

The night had started like any other. He was stationed in the projection booth of the abandoned Tomorrowland Theater, a relic of past attractions that had been repurposed for storage. His shift was almost over when the power flickered. A deep, resonating *thud* echoed through the building, followed by a guttural, inhuman roar that sent an icy spike of terror through his spine.

His radio crackled. "What the hell was that?" a voice on the other end asked.

Brandon grabbed his flashlight and moved cautiously toward the service corridor, his heart hammering against his ribs. Maybe one of the animatronics malfunctioned? Maybe some idiot tried sneaking in to vandalize the place? He reached the door and hesitated. A deep, primal instinct told him not to open it.

Then came the screams. Bloodcurdling and raw, just beyond the wall, they echoed down the hallways meant only for cast members. Brandon staggered back as the metal door in front of him suddenly *buckled* outward, denting with a force so violent that dust rained from the ceiling.

His brain screamed at him, *Run!*

After a moment of shock, his legs finally obeyed, carrying him down the dimly lit hallway toward the emergency exit. The radios were going crazy now—panicked voices overlapping, security calling for backup, desperate cries for help.

Brandon burst into the backstage area and sprinted toward Main Street, his breath coming in ragged gasps. A horrified shriek rang out to his left. He turned just in time to see a maintenance worker—Jerry, a guy he knew from breakroom poker games—get *ripped* off his feet by something massive, something that moved like a nightmare given flesh.

Brandon barely had time to register the grotesque fusion of muscle and metal, of human and beast. It stood at least eight feet tall, its hunched frame rippling with unnatural power. A gorilla's body, thick with sinewy strength, but with something worse attached—twisting tentacles sprouting from its shoulders, each one writhing like a nest of vipers. And in the center of its massive chest, staring straight at Brandon with unmistakable rage, was a *human head*.

Its clawed hands closed around Jerry's torso. There was a sickening *crunch* as bones shattered, and Jerry's screams turned into a gurgling wheeze. Then, just as quickly, the beast hurled what was left of him into a nearby popcorn stand, sending kernels and blood flying into the air.

Brandon *bolted*, running faster than he ever had in his life. The park was *bedlam*. People stampeded through the streets, trampling over fallen bodies. The cheerful lights of the attractions flickered ominously against the carnage, turning Disneyland into a twisted parody of itself.

* * *

***

The scent of popcorn and churros lingered in the air, mixing with the artificial fog that curled through the Haunted Mansion's waiting area. Eric had worked at Disneyland for three years, and though he was used to the eerie décor, but tonight something felt... off.

It started with the alarms. First, a blip—an error message flashing across his security tablet. Then, the doors to the ride malfunctioned, sealing shut on their own. Eric was about to call maintenance when the power flickered, the overhead lights stuttering as if the whole system was on the verge of collapse.

Then the screaming started.

But these weren't the delighted shrieks of guests enjoying a jump scare—no, these were raw, panicked cries, the kind that sent ice through Eric's veins. He stepped out from the control room, peering into the dim corridors of the attraction. Shadows stretched unnaturally long, and the normally campy, automated ghosts seemed distorted, their flickering forms trapped in stuttering animations.

A guttural, unnatural growl echoed through the hallway, so deep it vibrated in Eric's chest. He took a hesitant step forward, his flashlight beam barely cutting through the fog. His radio crackled to life, as a garbled voice cut through.

"… Please… help me…"

The signal cut out.

Eric's stomach twisted. He turned the corner, stepping into the grand ballroom scene, but what he saw wasn't an illusion.

The body of one of the custodians lay sprawled across the floor, his spine bent at an impossible angle, eyes wide and empty. Blood soaked the polished wood, pooling beneath a set of heavy footprints too large to be human. Eric's breath caught in his throat. The air smelled of iron and something worse—like decay, like something that had crawled out of a grave and never left.

A shadow loomed in the corridor ahead, impossibly large. Eric's pulse hammered as he ducked behind an overturned bench.

It stepped into the dim light of the attraction, and Eric had to shove a fist against his mouth to keep from screaming. The thing was a nightmare—a grotesque fusion of gorilla and man, its hulking body stitched together from something unholy. Its arms were unnaturally long, roped with thick muscle, and from its shoulders, a grotesque cluster of writhing tentacles flexed and curled, tasting the air. But the worst part was its face.

Not the gorilla's.

The human one.

It's half-rotted lips curled into something resembling a sneer, his milky eyes sweeping the room like a predator assessing its territory.

Eric's fingers clenched around his radio, but he didn't dare move, didn't dare breathe. Maybe if he stayed still, it wouldn't see him. Maybe—

The beast sniffed the air, searching, then turned its head and looked right at him.

Eric ran as fast as he could, crashing through the ballroom doors and sprinting through the mansion's maintenance corridors, his only thought: *Get out. Get out. Get out.* Behind him, the beast roared, the sound shaking the walls.

A loud crash behind him signaled that the creature was after him, and it was gaining.

Eric flew down the hall, his legs burning as his breath came in ragged gasps. The emergency exit was just ahead.

His only escape.

The beast roared again and the ground trembled as a massive hand swiped at his back, missing him by inches.

Desperately, Eric lunged for the door and shoved it open. He was inches away from safety when a tentacle lashed out, wrapping around his ankle.

A scream flew from his mouth as the beast yanked him back with monstrous force, sending Eric sprawling onto the floor. His head hit the ground with a hard crack. Instantly, his vision blurred as a wave of pain radiating through his skull.

Eric blinked, his vision swimming as the creature loomed over him. His grotesque face was twisted into something between curiosity and amusement.

"No," Eric pleaded weakly as the massive hand of the beast curled into a fist.

And then, with resounding force, it came down.

The last thing Eric saw was his own blood splattering across the walls of the Haunted Mansion.

Chapter 32

Their first stop, much to Tommy's chagrin, was Sleeping Beauty's Castle. Though he complained about the *princess stuff*, William caught him sneaking curious glances at the towering, fairy-tale architecture. The turrets glowed in the morning sun, the pastel pink stone seeming almost unreal against the bright blue sky.

Inside, the dimly lit hallways shimmered with brilliant mosaics, each tile catching the light as they moved past. The air was thick with magic, the scent of polished stone and something faintly floral. Kate and Ashley ran ahead, pressing their hands against the cool glass of the animated storybook windows, watching as the illustrations flickered to life.

Guerera and Melinda followed behind, both of them smiling as they watched the kids in their element. Ashley turned to Tommy with an eager grin. "Come on! This is so cool!"

Tommy crossed his arms, trying to look unimpressed. "Yeah. Super exciting."

Melinda smirked, nudging William. "I swear, he gets that from you."

William chuckled but turned just in time to see Tommy

freeze in place. The sinister green mist of Maleficent's magic curled up the walls, casting eerie shadows that danced like living creatures. Then, in a flash, the dragon appeared.

Tommy's eyes widened.

William leaned down. "Still not cool?" he teased.

Tommy scoffed but didn't look away from the dragon. "It's… *okay*, I guess."

Guerera raised an eyebrow at William and smirked. "I bet if it *breathed* fire, he'd be a little more impressed."

"Yeah," Tommy muttered, "now *that* would be cool."

Their next stop was the *Mad Tea Party*. Though Tommy rolled his eyes as Kate and Ashley squealed in excitement, he still climbed into a giant pink teacup beside his dad. Guerera took a blue cup with Ashley, while Melinda chose a purple one, giving Kate the honor of controlling the spin.

As the ride began, the cups twirled gently, the soft sound of clinking teapots and whimsical music filling the air. But Tommy had other ideas.

"Let's go *faster*," he challenged, gripping the center wheel.

William grinned. "You're on."

They threw their weight into the spin, and suddenly, their teacup became a *blur*. Kate and Ashley shrieked with laughter, Melinda's giggles turning into gasps as she tried to steady herself. Guerera, always up for a challenge, spun hers just as wildly, and the two competing teacups became a battle of centrifugal force.

By the time they stumbled off the ride, they were breathless and disoriented.

Melinda crouched down low, placing a hand to her forehead.

"Mommy, you looked like you were gonna throw up!" Kate teased.

Melinda groaned. "I *felt* like I was gonna throw up.

Actually, I still do."

Tommy grinned triumphantly. "That was *awesome*."

As their stomachs settled, they made their way to *Mr. Toad's Wild Ride*, an attraction Tommy had been eyeing with a mix of excitement and suspicion.

"You sure about this?" William asked, noticing his son's hesitance.

Tommy squared his shoulders. "I *guess*."

They climbed into the old-fashioned motorcar, and as soon as the ride jolted to life, they were off, barreling down cobblestone streets, crashing through a tavern door, and nearly flattening a group of frantic townsfolk. The car twisted and turned wildly, the old-school cutout animations adding to the chaos.

"Watch out!" Ashley shrieked as they swerved past a line of runaway barrels.

"Where's the *brake*?!" Guerera shouted as the ride veered dangerously close to a suit of armor swinging a sword.

"It's *Mr. Toad*! He doesn't *use* brakes!" Kate laughed, gripping the side of the car.

They crashed through a final set of doors and the ride coming to an abrupt end. Tommy sat frozen for a second before he turned to William, his face flushed with thrill.

"That. Was. Awesome!"

William laughed, ruffling his son's hair. "Told you Disneyland was worth it."

As they climbed out of the cars, Guerera adjusted her jacket, shaking her head. "That was more intense than I thought. Who designed this thing?"

Ashley beamed. "Some guy who really wanted to scare people!"

Melinda chuckled, draping an arm around Kate's shoulders. "Well, next time you're driving, sweetheart."

Kate grinned. "Deal."

As they made their way toward their next adventure, William took a deep breath, feeling the warmth of the moment settle over him. Just for today, they had nothing to worry about. No battles, no nightmares—just a perfect day, wrapped in laughter and spinning teacups.

Eager to try something bigger, they headed toward the Matterhorn Bobsleds, but the line snaked endlessly in front of them, dimming Tommy's excitement. Not wanting to waste too much time, they turned and set off for Critter Country, hoping for a shorter wait.

Finally, they arrived at Splash Mountain, and Tommy's face lit up. When they were told that the girls weren't tall enough to ride, he smirked as Melinda and Guerera led Kate and Ashley off toward the nearby Winnie the Pooh attraction, giving him a moment alone with his dad in the line for the first time all day.

He gave an exaggerated sigh, folding his arms with satisfaction. "Finally."

William chuckled. "So, it's been that bad, huh?"

Tommy's expression softened. "Not bad, just... different. With you working again, we don't hang out like we used to. I miss it, you know?"

William pulled him close, feeling a pang as he remembered their quieter days, just the two of them exploring and making each other laugh. "I know, bud. I miss it too," he admitted quietly, squeezing his shoulder. "But sometimes we have to make hard choices. This was just something I had to do."

Tommy shrugged, looking off as they inched forward in line. "Yeah, I get it," he mumbled. "Doesn't mean I have to like it."

They moved closer to the loading zone, and William inexplicably felt his heartbeat quicken, his arm tightening protectively around Tommy's shoulders as they climbed into the log. The darkening skies and whisper of an evening breeze made the cheerful music and singing animatronics somehow seem ominous. He tried to shake the feeling, but the unease lingered. A gentle mist rose from the water as their log began to glide forward, the cheerful animal figurines beckoning them deeper into the ride's cavernous heart.

As the log crept up the first incline, they passed from daylight into shadows, with the air turning damp and cool. Tommy's voice broke the silence. "This is way higher than I thought," he muttered, hands clenched around the safety bar as they reached the top. They both held their breath, staring down the steep drop that lay ahead. Just as the log tipped over the edge, William heard a whisper of movement below, sending a chill skittering up his spine. They plunged downward, adrenaline and laughter mixing, but William's thoughts lingered on the shadow he thought he saw at the base of the hill.

As they glided toward the next section, William spotted a man far below, gazing up intently, his face partially obscured by shadows. Recognition hit like a bolt of lightning—it was the same man from the police station. But then, just as quickly as he'd appeared, a crowd shifted in front of him, and the man vanished. William's grip tightened on the bar, his instincts screaming that something was wrong.

"Dad? What's wrong?" Tommy asked, catching the unease on his father's face.

"Nothing," William lied, forcing a smile. "Let's just enjoy the ride."

They passed into the underground section, where eerie, glowing lights illuminated a world of strange, dancing creatures. It was almost pitch black, save for faint flickers of colored light. Beneath the hum of cheerful music, a low, droning buzz filled the air.

Then William felt it—a feather-light touch skittering up the back of his neck.

His entire body went rigid. His breath hitched as his hand shot up, swatting violently at the unseen sensation.

Not again. Not here.

"Keep your eyes open, Tommy," he whispered, his voice raw, strained.

Tommy frowned, leaning forward. "What? Why? Dad, what's going on?"

William's throat tightened. He could barely hear his son's voice over the pounding in his ears, the way his pulse surged as the dark cavern seemed to shrink around him. His vision blurred at the edges, the glowing figures along the ride warping, twisting—they weren't decorations anymore. They were staring at him. Watching. Waiting.

He blinked hard, forcing himself back to reality, but his body didn't listen. The air was thick, suffocating, pressing against him. The scent of sweat, dirt, rotting flesh.

This isn't real. It's not the valley.

But it was.

It was the Coachella Valley all over again. The endless swarms, the razor-sharp bites, the choking cloud of wings that swallowed the sky. The screams of people who never made it out—those trapped, torn apart by the relentless tide of black wings and gnashing teeth.

He saw them. The bodies. The ones they couldn't save.

His breath came in short, sharp gasps. His grip tightened on the safety bar, his knuckles white. His stomach churned as his mind dragged him back to that night, back to the stench of blood and decay, to the sound of flesh peeling away as hundreds of tiny legs burrowed, dug, feasted.

His own skin had crawled just like this.

"Dad?" Tommy's voice cut through the haze, sharp and scared.

William jerked, inhaling sharply as the tunnel closed in.

Then the first scream tore through the air.

A woman yelped ahead, "Ouch!" The cry echoed through the cavern, followed almost instantly by frantic rustling and panicked gasps. William snapped back to the present just as chaos erupted around them.

The buzzing swelled to a roar.

A horrible, all-too-familiar sensation surged over him— tiny legs crawling, biting, stinging.

"No," he breathed, his chest constricting as if something were burrowing into him all over again.

The others in their log flailed and swatted, their terrified movements mirroring the panic that had haunted his nightmares for months.

It was happening again.

The darkness came alive with writhing, invisible bodies. A swarm, unseen but merciless, sank its teeth into any exposed flesh it could find.

"Protect your face!" William bellowed, throwing an arm over Tommy as his son cried out in pain. The past and the present overlapped, fusing into a horrific déjà vu. He was back in the valley, trying to fight them off, while those things chewed through people like they were nothing but meat.

He lashed out blindly, his arms shaking and smacking away phantom creatures that may or may not have been real. The log lurched forward, dragging them deeper into the tunnel. His pulse raced as the panic choked him, but he couldn't let it control him.

Not this time.

Tommy was shaking, his face buried against William's side. The buzzing was everywhere, seeping into his bones.

William gritted his teeth, focusing.

And then the log burst out of the tunnel, sending blinding daylight pouring over them like a cleansing flood.

The buzzing stopped immediately as the swarm lifted, vanishing into the sky.

For a long moment, no one moved. William's breaths were ragged, sharp, his hands still raised like he was ready to fight off another wave. His entire body shook with the effort to stay present, to keep himself from slipping back into that nightmare.

Tommy stirred against him. Alive. Unharmed. Safe.

William forced himself to blink, to let go of the suffocating weight pressing on his chest. He slowly lifted his trembling hands—there was nothing there. No bugs. No blood.

But when he looked at Tommy's scratched, welted arms, he felt like he was still drowning in the past.

At the front of the log, a couple of young women had started crying, clutching at each other as they stared up, watching the ominous cloud of insects hover far above them. They hung in the air like a sinister shroud, blackening the sky, waiting.

As they approached the final drop, the ride jolted to a pause at the top. The surrounding silence was broken only by a single scream, piercing and shrill, from the front of the log. William looked forward in horror as he saw a dark figure standing on the ledge beside the water channel—a figure whose eyes gleamed with a sickening, familiar malice. The figure lunged, a flash of movement in the corner of his eye, and the log careened down the hill as cries of horror replaced what would usually be gleeful shouts.

Water splashed high, drenching them, but as the ride drifted to a stop, William's heart nearly stopped at the sight below. The water had turned red, thickening and swirling around the base of the log. He looked up in horror to see one of the girls from the front slumped lifelessly against the side, her neck marred by a savage wound, blood streaming down and pooling in the water. He barely had time to take in the horrifying sight before he grabbed Tommy's hand.

"Come on! We're getting out of here. Now."

Ignoring the attendants shouting for them to stay seated, he pulled Tommy out of the log. People in the crowd were screaming, their panicked cries filling the air, but William had eyes only on the steps that would lead them away from the ride. But as they reached the top, he stopped dead.

There, at the bottom of the stairs, was the man again, the one from the police station, his face twisted into a cruel smile that sent chills down William's spine. Their eyes met for a fleeting moment, and then, as if a shadow had swallowed him whole, the man disappeared.

Tommy's voice, thick with fear, pulled him back to the moment. "Dad… it's happening again, isn't it?"

William forced himself to stay calm, gripping his son's shoulder protectively. His phone was already in his hand, dialing Dr. Leonard as they stumbled toward the edge of the frenzied mob. The roar of some distant creature echoed across the park, sending a ripple of terror through the crowd as William's call connected.

"Dr. Leonard, it's William. We've got a problem. It's happening again."

Chapter 33

The memories resurfaced in Patrick's mind immediately, the pain sharp and unrelenting, tearing through him as though everything had only happened moments ago. Samuel—his closest friend, his trusted partner—gone, because Patrick had put him in the line of fire. Even though he knew there was no way he could have foreseen the brutal apocalypse that had engulfed them, a wave of guilt threatened to drown him. The vivid memory of Samuel's last moments clawed at him.

He took a steadying breath and forced himself to focus, his voice a barely controlled tremor. "Are you certain?" he asked, bracing himself for the answer he already knew.

"Yes, I'm certain," William replied in a strained and worried tone. "And I think Ashton's involved again. It has his fingerprints all over it."

Patrick's mind sharpened as his eyes narrowed, a flicker of intensity in his gaze. "You've seen him?" his voice was tinged with urgency, a hint of disbelief creeping in.

"Not directly. But someone's been tailing me—a shadow, always a step behind. They're connected, Patrick; I can feel it."

Patrick let out a deep breath, his mind racing as he

weighed his options. "All right, what do you need?"

"First, I'm at Disneyland with my family. I need you to call park management. Get them to evacuate the entire place, quietly and quickly. And then do everything you can to find Ashton. Track him down. This ends now."

Patrick's stomach twisted, knowing the herculean task that lay ahead. "I'll make the call to the park and hope I can persuade them to shut it down. As for Ashton…he went dark before the FBI raid. No labs, no trace. He's buried himself deep."

William's tone darkened. "Ashton won't have gone far; he needs the tech. He's relying on lab access to fuel this madness."

"Understood," Patrick replied, steel in his voice.

The call ended, leaving Patrick staring at his phone, his fingers poised over the keyboard as he searched for the Disneyland contact information. His heart hammered as he pushed through layers of automated responses, finally reaching Karen Teplar, Vice President of Disneyland Park. Her voice betrayed a crack of tension as she picked up. "This is Karen."

Patrick replied, "Mrs. Teplar, This is Dr. Leonard from NASA's research facility. I have an urgent matter to discuss with you."

"Dr. Leonard, what can I help you with?"

Patrick's tone was swift and urgent. "You need to evacuate the park immediately."

"Excuse me?" Karen replied in disbelief.

"Mrs. Teplar, there's no time for explanations. I'm sure you're aware of the incident that just occurred at the park only moments ago?"

"Yes… but that poor girl died from an animal attack. That hardly warrants evacuating fifty thousand people."

Patrick's voice dropped to a dire whisper, each word crisp and laced with urgency. "Mrs. Teplar, this wasn't an ordinary animal attack. I've witnessed firsthand the destructive potential of what's brewing, and I assure you, if we don't contain it now, California itself could be engulfed in days. This isn't a risk worth taking."

She hesitated. "How could you possibly know that?"

He clenched his fist, feeling the ache in his chest and seeing the faces of those lost. "Because I watched it rip through Coachella Valley, tearing lives apart in hours. We barely stopped it last time."

Karen's silence was tense, her breath shallow on the line. Then, after a pause, she muttered, "I'll...do what I can."

The call disconnected, and Patrick sat in a moment of silence, weighing the looming shadow that was sure to come. He ran a hand over his face, forcing his mind to steady as he assessed his next move. They'd bought a narrow window of time, but Patrick knew better than to waste it.

Without hesitation, he pressed another button, patching through to the control room. Justin answered on the first ring, alert and ready.

"Dr. Leonard? What's the situation?"

Patrick's voice was low and fierce. "Justin, I need every file we have on the Ames Research Facility. Building plans, blueprints—current and historical. Find it and get it to me immediately."

"I'm on it," Justin replied.

"Good," Patrick replied, his tone grimmer than ever. "There's no time to waste."

***

Karen sat motionless after hanging up with Dr. Leonard, a

heavy weight pressing on her chest. The logic was clear: the shareholders would raise hell if she shut down the park, and a premature evacuation could cost Disneyland upwards of three million dollars. But her conscience wouldn't let her forget the girl who had just died in broad daylight, nor the chaos that had swept through Coachella Valley not too long ago. That disaster had left California reeling, and if even a fraction of that terror had resurfaced here, the loss of human life would be unthinkable. Worse yet, if it came out that she had the chance to prevent it and didn't, it wouldn't just ruin the company—it would ruin her.

Taking a deep breath, Karen picked up the phone and dialed Victor's number. He answered immediately. "Mr. Frankle? I need you to evacuate the park. Now."

Victor's hesitation was immediate. "Karen, I understand what happened at Splash Mountain was tragic, but you realize evacuating will take every resource we have? You want us to pull the plug on fifty thousand people?"

Karen's grip tightened around the phone. "I don't care if you have to deploy every single staff member on hand—get everyone out of this park now!"

Without waiting for his response, she hung up, letting out a shaky breath. "Well, fuck me," she muttered, rubbing her temples, "here goes everything."

Chapter 34

Melinda and Guerera climbed into the middle seat of the ride car, while Kate and Ashley darted to the front, bursting with excitement. As the girls' laughter rang out, Melinda and Guerera shared a smile, feeling an unexpected warmth in the midst of all the darkness they'd been through. For a moment, the horrors they'd survived seemed far away, like some half-forgotten nightmare.

"I'm so glad they're having fun," Melinda murmured.

"Me too," Guerera replied, her gaze lingering on Ashley. "I wasn't sure how she'd handle it after… everything. Since it's just us and my aunt, she's been so quiet."

Melinda nodded, glancing at Kate, who was giggling with her new friend. "Kate's been the same way—withdrawn, distant. This is the first time in a while I've seen her truly happy."

"Yeah, you wouldn't know by looking at them now," Guerera chuckled.

The ride started with a gentle jolt, taking them through slow, winding turns beneath colorful scenes of playful animatronics. Kate and Ashley erupted into giggles when a robotic Pooh attempted to wrestle a honey pot off his head.

Watching her daughter laugh so freely, Melinda felt a lump rise in her throat. For so long, she'd feared she might never hear that sound again. Happiness had felt like a distant memory, something slowly fading out of reach. But here, even for just a few minutes, she felt a glimmer of hope.

When the ride stopped, the girls jumped out, brimming with excitement. "What's next, Mommy?" Kate asked, her eyes wide with anticipation.

Melinda glanced around. "Let's wait here for your dad and Tommy, and then we'll decide."

Ashley tugged at Guerera's sleeve, motioning for her to bend down so she could whisper something. As Ashley spoke, Guerera's eyes softened, filling with tears before she nodded and embraced the little girl. Ashley's face lit up, giving Guerera one last squeeze before looking back at Melinda with a proud smile. Guerera met Melinda's questioning gaze and mouthed, 'I'll tell you later.'

Just then, William and Tommy came running over, breathless and disheveled. Melinda's heart sank as she noticed the cut on Tommy's cheek and the angry red welts dotting his arm. "Tommy, what happened?" she asked, reaching for him instinctively.

"He scratched his cheek on the seat," William answered quickly.

Melinda looked at him, her eyes searching for something. "How did that happen?" Her voice trembled as she sensed he wasn't telling her everything.

Tommy's voice broke through, barely a whisper. "I was trying to get away from a swarm of bugs."

Melinda felt her throat tighten. She shot William a pleading look, silently begging him to tell her that this wasn't what she feared. But then Ashley's soft, quivering voice filled the silence, "The monsters are back... aren't they?"

Before William could answer, a low, rumbling growl echoed from behind them. Everyone froze, slowly turning to see a black-and-white spotted dog standing just twenty yards away. Its mouth was smeared with blood, and a horrifying patch of skin was missing from its face, exposing bone.

"Don't move," William whispered, his gaze locked on the dog. The crowd around them reacted in shock, screams tearing through the air as people pushed and scrambled to flee. The undead creature remained unnervingly still, its eyes fixed on William as if it recognized him. Then he saw why. Standing behind the dog, near the entrance to the Hungry Bear Restaurant, was the familiar figure of his stalker, watching him with a sinister smile.

***

Silas leaned forward as a loud, tinny voice blared from the park's central speakers, cutting through the evening's lull. The announcement was fast, garbled, but unmistakably urgent. Red lights flashed over various attractions below, signaling a fast-growing emergency.

Mishka's voice was tense as she stared at the monitor. "Something's triggered their alarm systems." She ran her hand over a dim screen displaying heat signatures. One stood out—a concentrated group at an area marked Splash Mountain.

"They're reacting to something. Whatever Jeron had planned, it looks like its started." Ridley said as she adjusted the video feed, catching glimpses of a terrified crowd running frantically in every direction.

As Silas observed the nightmare unfolding at the park, he recalled their world's ruin only a short time ago. He grimaced, shaking off the image, then pointed to a moving cluster near Splash Mountain. "There. A family's caught up in the middle of it, and there's a male figure with them who's biometrics match the tracking readings we have for William Patterson."

"Izzit's there," Aldin said sadly. "Whatever she's become, we can't leave her behind to be twisted any further."

Silas activated the ship's descent controls, adjusting to keep the cloak secure, and murmured, "Everyone, ready to intervene on my command. Mishka, keep track of Jeron's movements and flag anything suspicious."

The cloaked ship moved swiftly, hovering just above the chaos below. Ridley scanned the feed for an opening. "There's a break near the edge of the main path. We'll land close to their position, close enough to cut through."

Mishka threw a last glance at the screens and glanced at Silas. "If we're lucky, we'll get to them before Jeron strikes."

Just before setting down, Silas turned to his crew, his eyes filled with hard determination. "Get ready to move."

Silas signaled to the crew as the rear hatch of their ship hissed open, the air rushing in with a biting chill. One by one, they dropped silently from the cloaked vessel, their boots landing soundlessly on the ground. Each activated their individual cloaking devices, their forms shimmering into near invisibility.

Silas motioned for his team to stay close as they slipped into the chaos erupting across the park. The crowd had devolved into a panicked stampede, throngs of people screaming and shoving as they scrambled away from something near Splash Mountain. Through the visor of his cloaking field, Silas could see the erratic heat signatures of terrified humans fleeing in every direction, their voices merging into a cacophony of confusion and terror.

Ahead of him, Ridley tapped her wrist controls, her voice a

sharp whisper over the comm. "Got an abnormal heat signature—it's small, close to the humans Jeron's targeting. Confirming now."

"It's Izzit," Aldin murmured once more. "I'm sure of it. She's moving toward them."

Silas's jaw tightened. "Then we're on borrowed time. Split up, converge on their location."

The team scattered, maneuvering carefully through the frantic crowd. Their movements were swift and precise, threading between fleeing parkgoers without drawing attention.

Near the center of the chaos, William and his family stood frozen, their faces pale as they confronted something out of a nightmare.

It was indeed Izzit, or rather, what was left of her.

Her small frame had been grotesquely twisted, her fur patchy and clinging to sinewy muscle that glistened in the dim light. Her jaws hung at an unnatural angle, dark drool spilling onto the pavement, and her once-bright eyes were now clouded, gleaming with a feral hunger.

***

William's breath hitched. The image hit him like a freight train, dredging up memories he had tried to bury. His vision blurred, the world around him fading as the nightmare clawed its way into his mind.

He wasn't at Disneyland anymore. He was back in Coachella, staring down the undead animals that had charged at him the first time this madness had erupted. He could still hear the inhuman growls echoing in his ears. His hands trembled as the phantom scent of blood and decay filled his nose.

"William?" Melinda's voice broke through the fog, distant and faint.

His daughter clung to his leg, shaking him slightly. "Daddy? What's wrong?"

William blinked hard, forcing himself back to the present. He moved instinctively, shielding his family with his body as he locked eyes with the horror standing just feet away.

"Stay behind me," he rasped, his voice unsteady.

***

Silas and the crew materialized around the scene, their cloaking devices disengaging as they moved into position.

"It's her," Aldin sobbed, her voice cracking as she stepped forward. The sight of Izzit brought a wave of tears crashing over her.

Izzit let out a low, guttural growl, her clouded eyes locking onto William. Then, with a sudden, unnatural burst of speed fueled by hunger, she lunged.

"Move!" Silas shouted.

In a blur, Silas intercepted Izzit, slamming a long, pulsing rod into her side. It emitted a sharp burst of energy, throwing her back with a yelp that echoed unnervingly across the chaos.

"What the—?" William staggered, his voice faltering as he stared at Silas, who was now fully visible.

Silas raised a hand in a placating gesture. "Stay calm. We're here to help." His voice was steady but tinged with an unearthly cadence of someone not of this world.

"Get everyone back," he said urgently to William. "I'll handle this."

Izzit recovered, snarling as her body contorted unnaturally, readying for another attack. Her gaze briefly flickered to Silas, and something shifted. For a fleeting moment, the monstrous snarl softened, replaced by a faint glimmer of recognition.

But the moment was gone in an instant. Izzit lunged again, this time with a ferocity that shattered any hope of the creature she once was.

Silas stepped forward, his weapon blazing. The shot hit Izzit squarely in the head, the force dropping her mid-air. She hit the ground with a whimper, her body twitching once before going still.

William's group stood frozen, their faces pale and etched with horror. "Who... who are you?" William's voice was a hoarse whisper, his eyes darting between the strange beings before him.

Silas straightened, his expression somber. "I'm from a world that fell to this same plague. We failed to save our home," he said, his gaze locking with William's. "I'm here to make sure that doesn't happen to yours."

William stared at him, his mind reeling. As he looked back at Izzit's lifeless form, the weight of what lay ahead pressed down on him like a storm cloud threatening to burst.

Chapter 35

As William and his group stood there in shock, they saw three women, or at least he thought they were women—because, just like his mystery stalker, something was different about them—rushing toward him.

Aldin yelled out, "Izzit! No!" and slid next to the downed creature, crying as she picked up the dead thing and held it close to her. She turned to one of the other women, "Why would he do this?"

"Because he's evil, just like his uncle," Ridley replied.

"We don't have time for this," Mishka said impatiently.

"She's right," Silas answered as he turned back toward the rear of the attraction. "We need to get out of here immediately. Everyone, follow me!"

"What's going on here, William?" Melinda pleaded.

"I have no idea," William replied, "but I think we need to do what he says."

As if to emphasize the point, a flurry of screams rose in all directions. William turned around quickly and watched as panic threatened to turn into a full-fledged stampede.

The large man called out to his entourage as they made their way into the wooded area surrounding the park,

"Mishka, you and Ridley take up the rear. Aldin, stay with the women and children."

Before they went any further, William grabbed Silas's arm, "You know what's going on here, don't you? How it's started again?"

"Call me Silas," the man said. "And yes, I know how it started again, and who started it. But if we don't move fast, it'll be too late to stop it."

"I'm scared, G," Ashley said as they started running.

Guerera replied, "Me too, baby girl, but we'll be okay. I promise."

She stopped for a second and picked up Ashley, holding her as if she were one of the heavy military packs she had grown accustomed to carrying.

William followed suit and hoisted Kate up into his arms as their pace quickened through the brush.

Silas stopped suddenly as a mangled coyote sprang from between the trees. It gave out a grizzly yell from its broken jaw as if it was alerting the rest of the undead nearby. Then it charged.

Silas shot it quickly in the head, dropping it before it could get close. But the damage had already been done, as a flurry of howls rose all around them.

They picked up their pace, hurrying through the trees around the edge of the park, toward a clearing next to Frontierland, separated by the Disneyland Railroad. One of the steam engines, pulling six passenger cars, sat unmoving on the tracks while screams of terror and death flew from the passengers within. Behind them, on the tracks, another train continued its predetermined path, unaware of the disaster up ahead. Unable to stop, whether because of natural or unnatural causes, the second train plowed into the back of the first with enough force to dislodge both from the tracks. A loud screech of metal against metal ripped through the air before it was replaced with a loud explosion.

"My god!" William exclaimed.

"This wasn't your god's doing, William," Silas said as he directed the group toward the middle of the clearing.

The howls of the dead closed in on them from behind and William turned around to see Mishka and Ridley fending off a small horde with a flurry of blaster shots. Somehow, the horror movie they were trapped in had evolved into science-fiction, complete with laser guns and aliens. Their old reality was gone, never to return.

Silas turned his arm as he ran and pressed a couple of keys on a small pad attached to his wrist. A second later, a loud mechanical sigh filled the air in front of them as the hydraulics of the cargo ship opened up the rear door.

Silas quickly ushered everyone inside as a pack of undead creatures rushed toward them. He fired a flurry of blaster shots, dropping a couple of the beasts before the rear door closed.

Outside, they heard a flurry of pounding and clawing at the ship as the remaining animals tried to force their way inside.

"Don't worry," Silas said. "There's no way they can get inside."

Ridley replied, "Yeah, but all the creatures here can see the ship even when it's hidden."

"Without recalibrating the spectrum modifier to account for the varying range of ocular sensitivities, which would make us completely visible to everyone for a short time, there's no way to avoid it. Eventually, the hunger should take over and they'll move on."

"What do we do in the meantime?" Mishka asked.

Silas replied, "For now, we make our guests comfortable.

Then we come up with a plan to stop this, once and for all."

"Before we discuss anything," William said, "you should start by explaining who you are, and how I'm sitting here in a goddamn spaceship!"

"Fair enough," Silas replied. "To give you the condensed version, we are from a planet called Terran on the other side of the galaxy. Our world fell victim to the same deadly organism that crashed on your planet a short time ago. Now, we're here to stop it from spreading further."

"So, you're real-life aliens?" Kate asked abruptly.

"That's not very polite," Melinda scolded.

Silas smiled, "I'm not sure what you mean by the term alien? I guess, in terms of being foreign to this world, then yes. Although it appears our two worlds are very much alike."

"I don't understand?" Guerera said. "Why would you come across the galaxy to help us when your own world was under attack?"

"Because our world didn't survive," Aldin said as her eyes misted over.

"We barely made it out alive, before the planet exploded," Mishka said.

"Exploded?" Tommy exclaimed.

Silas sensed the group's immediate fear and said, "Our world was constructed a million years ago by a group of advanced beings using a series of nuclear power stations as its core. Not knowing their true names, we simply called them the Architects. This technology allowed Terran to flourish and grow at an astounding rate. Unfortunately, it ultimately became our doom. The beasts ran rampant through a number of scientific facilities that resulted in a series of great explosions that set off a chain of events leading to a planet-wide nuclear meltdown."

The group sat there, stunned.

Silas continued, "From the data I was able to collect in a short time here, your planet isn't constructed in the same way."

"So, instead of your planet exploding," Mishka said, "the beasts will just turn it into a barren wasteland."

"We won't let that happen," William said.

"We might not be able to stop it," Mishka said.

Guerera held Ashley tight, trying to keep her from crying, "We did it once, and we'll do it again."

"Speaking of which," Aldin said, "how did you stop it before?"

William replied, "Our scientists discovered that one of the organisms was controlling them all, so we found that one and blew it up."

"That's it!" Aldin said. "It's like a hive mind, with a queen controlling the rest of the horde."

"That's exactly what our scientists believed. Turns out she was right."

"But how do we find out where the queen is now?" Ridley asked.

Silas replied, "I think I have an idea where to look. We find Jeron, we find the queen."

"I'm guessing this Jeron guy is the one who's been following me?" William said.

"It seems so. Although I can't figure out why?"

"Who is he?"

"We thought he was our friend," Ridley stated, "until he betrayed us. Although, given that his uncle was insane, it makes sense."

"Regardless," Silas said, "we're running out of time. Ridley, you and Aldin stay here with the women and children. William and I will try to find Jeron before it's too late."

"I don't have a weapon," William said.

Silas picked up a blaster rifle from their cache and tossed it to him. "Will that do?"

William held the rifle in his hands, gauging the weight, and was surprised at how light it was. He grinned, "Yeah, it'll work."

Silas turned to Ridley, "Once we're gone, close the door and don't open it for anyone."

As the rear door began to rise, Melinda held William tight, tears streaming down her cheeks, while his kids clamped on from the side. "Please, don't die," she said.

William kissed her forehead softly, "Not planning on it." He looked at Guerera and nodded, "You keep them safe."

"What she said. Don't die," she replied.

William chuckled nervously as he and Silas exited the rear door. Luckily, the animals had indeed given up their attempt to infiltrate the ship and had gone to seek other victims. A chorus of howls could be heard wafting through the air in all directions. Then, above them all, a loud, powerful roar sounded that sent a cold chill through their souls.

Chapter 36

The warehouse's single overhead light flickered, casting long, jagged shadows across the floor as Ashton Brown leaned over a makeshift table strewn with documents, satellite images, and intercepted memos from NASA's Near-Earth Object (NEO) program. His eyes, dark as obsidian, moved with deliberate precision over every piece of paper, each detail a thread weaving into a sinister tapestry of ambition. Across from him, Darcy watched in silence, her arms folded tight to her chest, her sharp features illuminated by the ghostly glow of a nearby screen.

"Darcy," Ashton finally spoke, his voice a rasp of smoke and command. He didn't look up from the file he was marking with his signature red pen—a thick circle around Dr. Leonard's name. "You understand what's required of you?"

She didn't hesitate. "Get close to Leonard," she said, her tone smooth, almost playful. "Close enough that he can't breathe without me knowing."

A thin smile pulled at Ashton's mouth. "Closer," he murmured. He snapped the file shut and slid it across the table toward her. "You'll be the air he breathes, the whisper in his ear, the answer to his doubts. The man is meticulous, driven by his intellect, but all men—" he finally lifted his gaze, cold and calculating, "—all men have cracks. He's no different. Exploit his weaknesses, fill the empty spaces with exactly what he thinks he's been missing."

Darcy traced her finger along Leonard's photograph, memorizing the lines of his face, the guarded weariness in his eyes. "He's brilliant, but I've read his psych profile. He's lonely. Overworked. A man searching for meaning in the vastness of space." She chuckled softly, a note of cruelty in her voice. "Perfect prey."

Ashton nodded approvingly. "It's not just his trust we need. Leonard is the gateway. When something otherworldly happens—and it *will* happen—it's his team that will be at the forefront of discovery. His lab where it will be analyzed. His mind that will shape its fate." He leaned in, the table creaking beneath his weight as he lowered his voice. "And we will control it all through him."

Darcy arched a brow, the corners of her mouth twitching with amusement. "When do I begin?"

"Now." Ashton's eyes gleamed. "The NEO program is accelerating their tracking. They've already picked up fragments from the outer belt. Leonard's team is prepped for recovery. You'll be placed as a late addition—an eager, wide-eyed researcher, hungry to learn from the best."

"And when he asks about my background?"

A smile curled Ashton's lips. "Give him a story. Something tragic, but noble. A father lost to disease, a passion for discovery that burns like justice in your soul. Make it convincing, but never perfect. Real lies," he said darkly, "are messy."

Darcy smirked. "And how long before I move?"

"You'll wait," Ashton said sharply. "Leonard's no fool. Trust comes slowly with him. He'll test you. Probe for cracks.

But in time, he'll bring you into the fold. He's starving for connection, and you'll be the perfect feast."

She tilted her head, her eyes gleaming with dangerous amusement. "And when he realizes he's been played?"

Ashton waved the thought away like smoke. "By then, we'll have what we need. He'll be irrelevant—another relic in the shadow of progress."

For a moment, silence reigned between them. Darcy held his gaze, then gave a slow, deliberate nod. "He won't see me coming."

Ashton's expression darkened with pride. "I chose you for this because you're ruthless. Because you're smart. And because you're *mine*."

Darcy's smirk widened. "Of course, Daddy. I'll make you proud."

The light flickered again, and in that brief, stuttering moment, the world seemed to hold its breath.

***

Patrick poured through the documents that Justin had sent him until his eyes started getting blurry and his head hurt. He knew something was there, he just hadn't found it yet. "Dammit!" he cursed at the screen. "Where the fuck are you, Ashton?"

"It'll take months to go through all of these documents! Jesus, Justin, where did you find all of this?" He didn't have days, let alone months.

Then luck finally patted him on the shoulder and he came across an old newspaper article dated, September 9th, 1942, describing an explosion at one of the main labs that resulted in a large section of the facility being demolished. The cause of the accident wasn't disclosed, and rebuilding efforts were implemented immediately, but it led Patrick suddenly to the possibility he was looking for.

Patrick quickly pulled up the original blueprints for the facility and compared them with the most recent ones on file. It took him a few minutes, but then he spotted the inconsistency. A whole section of the lab lay hidden, apparently deemed unsafe structurally, and covered up when the new construction began. Either that or the government was hiding something? Whatever the case, he was convinced that Ashton had exploited this to his advantage. *God knows what he's doing in there?*

He called his assistant and told her to cancel his appointments. Then he called the hangar and told them to ready his plane. He was going hunting.

As he walked toward the elevator that would take him to the main floor, he tried to connect all the dots to form a more substantial theory, only to realize all he had was a hunch. Albeit a strong one, but still a hunch, nevertheless. He needed to get a little more insight before he started this on his own. Hopefully, William was in a position where he could talk for a moment?

To his surprise, William answered the phone almost immediately. "William! Thank God you're okay."

"Things are starting to escalate here pretty fast," William replied. "Did you find something?"

"I think so. I compared two sets of blueprints, one from 1942 and one from recent, and there seems to be a discrepancy. I think Ashton found a sealed-off section of the facility and transformed it into some kind of personal lab. The problem is that I don't know how to go about investigating this without alerting him?"

"Is there anyone there you can trust?"

Patrick thought about it for a moment. He hadn't had a lot

of close contact with most of the staff there, but there was one person he knew he could trust. "My nephew is a systems analyst there. I helped get him the job. If there's anyone there I can trust, it's him."

"Good. Talk to him first and find out if he's seen or heard anything unusual without mentioning Ashton."

"Makes sense."

"And I would alert the military again and let them know the situation."

Patrick cringed, knowing full well how *that* conversation would go, but said, "Will do. Be safe out there."

"Planning on it."

After hanging up his phone, Patrick searched through his contacts until he found James Anderson. He took a deep breath before he dialed the Sergeant.

He was almost relieved when the call went unanswered for a couple of rings, until the man's gruff voice then sounded through the speaker, "Anderson here."

"Sergeant Anderson, this is Doctor Leonard."

"I know who the fuck this is," Anderson replied. "I can read my god-damned phone. What I want to know is why the hell you're calling me in the middle of a fucking Saturday afternoon when I'm trying to enjoy a little R & R? And it better not be what I think it is."

Patrick hesitated for a brief second, "Unfortunately, Sargent, I'm afraid that's exactly why I called. It's happening again."

The sergeant was silent for a second before he said, "Well, fuck me! ... Okay, let's have it."

Patrick quickly gave Sergeant Anderson the details about their newest nightmare and made his way through the hangar urgently, his shoulder bag slamming against his side as he moved in a kind of trot-lope-jog, knowing time was running short. After boarding the plane, he pulled out his laptop and immediately pulled up the two sets of blueprints so he could study them in further detail on the way to the facility. The plane exited the hangar and taxied to the runway.

As the plane lurched upward, before leveling off at thirty-one thousand feet, he heard a voice behind him that sent a chill through his bones. "Hello, Patrick," Darcy said in an icy tone.

Chapter 37

The alarm blared through the park with an unrelenting wail, sharp and merciless, driving into the skull like a blade. Words followed—calm, collected, and entirely futile—urging orderly evacuation. But the crowd had already shattered into a storm of panic.

A crush of bodies surged in all directions, a human tide smashing and trampling anything in its path. Feet pounded the pavement, grinding fallen belongings—and fallen people—underfoot. The screams came in layers: terror, pain,, agonizing death, and somewhere beneath it all, a low, guttural sound that grew louder.

It wasn't human.

The buzzing started low, like a hum deep in the bones, a sound that climbed inside the skull and vibrated. Then it grew. A tempest of wings and mandibles—a black mass seething with evil—blotted out the sun in a swirling, writhing swarm. It moved like a living thing, undulating and pulsing with a hunger that was endless.

Silas grabbed William's arm. "Move!"

They sprinted, weaving through the chaotic flood of people. The swarm swept down in a dark wave, smothering screams as it descended. Shadows flickered over the pavement, blotting out patches of sunlight, and the sound—the relentless drone—was like the grinding of a thousand teeth.

"Where is he?" William shouted, shouldering his way through the crush of bodies.

"I tracked him to the far side of the park," Silas yelled back, his face grim. "But his signal went dark."

William's gut tightened. "He knew you were tracking him?"

"Maybe. Or maybe his equipment failed." Silas didn't slow his pace. "His tech runs on systems you can't imagine."

William gripped the blaster rifle Silas had handed him, its weight reassuring in his hands. He had fallen in love with the alien weapon the moment he pulled the trigger. The first time he used it, a German Shepherd—its split jaw hanging grotesquely by a ribbon of muscle—had charged him. A quick squeeze, and the beast crumpled in a heap of smoking flesh.

The rifle hummed now, alive in his grip, as they pushed through the frenzied crowd. Silas's eyes swept the park, sharp and calculating, while the swarm tore into the people around them.

A group of teens, some in yellow *Palm Desert High* T-shirts, screamed as they were caught in the chaos. Their laughter from earlier was now twisted into desperate cries. One boy stumbled, grabbing at his hair. "It's fake, right? A prank?"

"No!" a girl shrieked.

She clawed at her scalp as tiny black shapes scuttled over her head, their legs tangling in her curls. She let out a scream—a sound that came from the depths of human terror—as the bugs swarmed her ears, her mouth, her eyes.

"Get them off me!" she howled.

The insects burrowed in deeper. Her hands shook violently as she scraped at her own flesh, nails raking bloody grooves across her temples.

Danny watched, paralyzed, his stomach clenching with a cold that rooted him to the spot. When the first beetle disappeared into her open mouth, he finally moved, slapping at her head. For every bug he crushed, a dozen more surged forward, relentless.

"They're in my ears!" she choked, her voice tearing itself apart. "*Help me!*"

Danny tried. God, he tried, but her eyes—her pleading, terrified eyes—locked onto his. *Don't leave me*, they begged.

"I'm sorry." His voice cracked.

Aiden yanked him backward. "We have to go!"

Danny turned away.

"Run!"

They bolted into the crowd, Gia's screams chasing after them, rising, rising—until they stopped.

William's stomach lurched as he pushed forward, the swarm a tempest above him. Gial stumbled into his path, her hair alive with crawling things. He saw them—flies, beetles, bees—all pouring into her ears, her nose. Her mouth opened in a silent scream before a ball of insects plunged inside.

William had seen death before—too much of it—but this was different. This wasn't death by gunfire or disease. This was *alive*.

The girl in front of him staggered, her red dress soaked in a darker shade of crimson. Her hair writhed like a living thing as insects crawled and burrowed through it, their tiny bodies squirming under the surface of her scalp like maggots in fresh meat. Her mouth opened wide, a desperate scream tearing free—and that was when the swarm struck.

A seething ball of flies and bees surged forward, a single,

unified entity with a malevolent will. They rocketed into her open mouth, a grotesque stream of wriggling bodies. She gagged, her eyes rolling back, her fingers twitching as she clawed at her throat.

She fell hard, convulsing, her body thrashing like a hooked fish. Her eyes, bloodshot and bulging, locked on William—pleading, begging, full of the agony of someone who *knows* they are about to die.

"God forgive me," he whispered, the words sticking in his throat like a bitter stone.

He raised his weapon.

The shot cracked through the air. Her body jerked once, and then she stilled.

For a heartbeat, there was silence.

Then the insects spilled out.

They writhed from her mouth, poured from her ears, oozed from every wound like black ichor. They gathered on her chest, their legs clicking, their wings vibrating. They paused, collectively, a single, pulsating mass that seemed almost to *breathe*.

And then, impossibly, they *looked* at him.

William felt it—felt the weight of their gaze, the impossible sentience behind the swarm. His skin crawled, his soul recoiled.

The insects shifted, pulling upward, a churning spiral of black bodies against the darkening sky. They twisted and coiled in an unnatural sync until they came together to form a shape.

The face took form in the writhing, buzzing cloud: hollow eyes, a cruel grin.

William's breath caught. *No... that's not possible.*

He knew the face smiling back at him.

Chapter 38

Sgt. Anderson leaned back in his chair, his gaze sharp as he heard the heavy footsteps outside his office a moment before the sharp wrap on his door. "Enter," he barked.

The door opened, and Sgt. Reece Conner and Lt. Darren Macin strode in. Both men carried themselves with a grim authority earned from more firefights than they cared to count. Conner was tall and sinewy, with a keen gaze that picked apart a room before he ever crossed the threshold. He had a reputation for speed and precision that had earned him the nickname "Razor." Macin, on the other hand, was all hard muscle and silence, with a single faded scar bisecting his brow, a souvenir from a mission no one dared ask about.

Anderson motioned for them to sit, but neither moved. They weren't the sitting type, so he got right to the point.

"You're both aware of the zombie animal apocalypse that hit recently," Anderson began, his voice even but tense. "Looks like we're about to deal with Round Two."

Conner folded his arms, expression unchanging. "Thought we put that mess to bed."

"Everyone did. Until we got a report yesterday from Disneyland—wildlife and insects acting...unnatural, just like before. Problem is, it's worse this time. This isn't random—it's targeted. Swarms, hive mind coordination, you name it."

Macin's mouth curled in distaste. "Aimed attacks? That's calculated. These things adapting?"

"Seems like it," Anderson said, eyebrows knitting. "And we're not taking any chances. I called Bravo and Delta squads in, but I need you two to spearhead this. One with Bravo, one with Delta. I need your experience to guide them through this, because God knows the last thing we need is more casualties."

"Disneyland," Macin muttered, running a hand over the scar on his forehead, as if the memory itself was enough to make it itch. "Crowded as it gets."

Anderson nodded, grim. "You'll be facing civilians packed in like sardines. No backup from outside forces until we secure the area. I need calm, calculated responses, and I need those squads kept under control. They're good soldiers, but they haven't seen what you've seen."

Conner's expression finally shifted to something that almost resembled a smile. "I'll take Bravo. I know Fisher. He won't like orders, but he'll follow when the heat's on."

Macin gave a small nod, indicating Delta would be his. "Delta's rough around the edges, but they'll manage."

Anderson's gaze lingered on each of them, more weight in his eyes than he usually let show. "If there's any chance to stop this, it's going to be you two leading them through it. Get in there, get our people out, and end this—preferably without the media plastering it all over the evening news."

Conner's face hardened, his cold blue eyes meeting Anderson's. "Understood, Sarge. We'll end it."

Macin gave a simple nod, more gesture than words, but Anderson could see the grim determination in his set jaw.

"Good," Anderson said, the briefest flicker of relief

crossing his face. "Get yourselves prepped. Vipers are on standby, but we're on a countdown. Civilians are already in danger, and I want this stopped. Now."

With a curt nod, Conner turned, and Macin followed, both slipping out of the office like shadows. There was no need for further words—just the weight of their mission and the adrenaline already beginning to surge.

***

The command blasted through the speakers, "Bravo and Delta squads, report to Sargent Anderson's office A.S.A.P."

Immediately, Fisher felt a twinge in his gut. Something was up, and he had the horrible notion he knew what it was. A demon in the back of his mind whispered, "It's happening again." The lighting in the mess hall suddenly took on an ominous tone as he looked at Jackson sitting across the table from him with the same nervous look in his eyes.

"Okay, you heard the command," Fisher said as he stood up from the table and grabbed his food try, which had been hardly touched. Jackson took a quick bite of his greasy burger before depositing his tray in the bin right after.

Amidst a wave of groans, the rest of Bravo Squad begrudgingly followed suit, with Delta squad right behind.

"I hope this isn't what I think it is," Jackson said to Fisher as they walked across the field toward the Sargent's office.

"Whatever it is," Fisher replied, "we'll deal with it like we always do."

"Kick the shit out of it and make it our bitch?"

"Exactly!"

"Still hope it's not what I think it is."

"Yeah, me too."

Fisher cut the conversation short to avoid any unnecessary

questions from the rest of the squad. Except for him and Jackson, the rest had either recently been promoted or transferred from other bases to replace their fallen comrades. It was still a hard pill to swallow. And the reality was that he didn't know enough about them to trust them with his life yet. Delta squad was even more of a challenge. In their minds, each one of them thought they were better than the Bravos. Their egos spoke volumes just by the way they glared at him constantly.

He sighed. The one thing they all had in common though, was that they had lost someone close to them recently. Hopefully, that would be enough to bring them together for whatever fucked-up mess they were being thrown into. *Shit's about to get real again,* he thought.

"Come in!" the Sargent's voice bellowed after Fisher knocked on the door.

It was only after both squads had piled into the office that Fisher noticed the two men standing next to the Sargent, one on each side of him. He recognized the insignia of the Raiders immediately—a white skull set inside a red diamond, with five stars surrounding it. A title that was only given to the best of the best. Judging from the battle-worn hard exterior that the men presented, each with prominent scars that descended across their face and down their necks, these were probably the toughest bad-asses that Fisher had ever seen, and that included Sargent Anderson.

Both men stood unmoving, with an ice-cold stare as the Sargent began speaking, "Most of you were here when the world went to shit not too long ago and saw first-hand the beginning of a god-damn animal apocalypse. Luckily, we stopped that disaster before it could spread any further. Problem was, it didn't stop it for good.

Fisher spoke up, "Are you saying that it's started again,

Sargent?"

"That's exactly what I'm saying, Corporal."

"Well, shit!"

"My thoughts exactly. We don't know how or why it started again, and to be honest, I really don't give a fuck. I just want it stopped. This time I'm sending two squads in, along with a couple of the world's best soldiers. One will accompany Bravo Squad and the other Delta Squad."

Andrew Benton, a short, stocky guy, puffed out his chest to make himself appear taller than he actually was, said, "No offense, Sargent, but is it really necessary to have these guys babysitting?"

Anderson glared at him, "I've already underestimated this threat once and we lost a lot of good men. I'm not about to make that mistake again. Now, if you want to question my direction, Corporal Benton, I'm sure I can find someone else a little more cooperative to lead your squad."

Benton shrank back down, "That won't be necessary, Sargent."

Anderson replied, "Good," then he turned toward Fisher. "Since you've had the most contact with these god-forsaken things, why don't you inform the rest of the group what they're up against?"

"There are two types of threats," Fisher said. "The zombified animals and the insects. The animals you kill just like any of the fucking zombie movie you've ever seen. Shoot the bastards in the head and they stay dead. The insects are another story. The only success we had was with the flamethrower."

Anderson interjected, "According to the scientists that were there the first time, the key is to find what's controlling them. They figured out it was some kind of hive mind or some shit like that. All I know is that we blew the fuck out of that swarm and all the infected animals went down."

"Where's the threat this time, Sargent?"

"Disneyland, of all fucking places. So much for the 'Happiest Place on Earth' shit."

Fisher's heart dropped instantly, "Guerera's there with Ashley! She was meeting Patterson and his family!"

For a brief second, a twinge of emotion fluttered into the Sargent's eyes before he squelched it down. "Then I suggest you get your asses there A.S.A.P. and finish this once and for all! Two Vipers are waiting on standby. You have ten minutes."

As the two squads quickly filed out of the office, Anderson called out to Fisher, "Bring her back alive."

Fisher replied, "I will, Sarge."

***

Fisher felt a surge of adrenaline, fueled by the urgency of the situation, and the impending danger one of his closest friends was facing on her own, as he climbed inside the chopper.

"Guerera's one tough senorita," Jackson said as he sat down next to him. "I'm sure her and Ashley are just fine."

"I wish I shared your optimism," Fisher replied.

The helicopter lurched upward as the rest of Bravo Squad settled in. A short distance away, the second Viper lifted off, carrying Delta Squad on board.

While the flight would only take a couple of hours, for Fisher it might as well have been on the other side of the world. Guerera was in danger, and he needed to be there. Now!

"Are you gonna be a problem?" a voice spoke.

Fisher glanced up to see the Raider seated in front of him, watching him coldly.

"Are you talking to me?" Fisher replied.

Instead of answering the question, the man said, "Just remember, our orders are simple: we stop this threat. That's it. Anything else jeopardizes the mission."

"You got a name?" Fisher asked.

The man smiled, "Just call me Sam."

"Okay, Sam. I don't care what you've done in the past, or who you've had to kill to get to where you are right now, but I tell you what? You follow your orders, and I'll follow mine."

Sam smiled at Fisher, "Fair enough. Just don't get in my way, Corporal."

That last part was said with a sneer, telling Fisher all he needed to know about the guy. *What a prick!*

He looked around the cabin at the rest of his squad, hoping they were ready for the nightmare, knowing some of them wouldn't make it out alive.

Chapter 39

The sound of her voice sent a chill through Patrick. It shouldn't have. If it became a physical confrontation, he could overpower her easily enough. But something in the back of his mind told him to be careful. She was working for Ashton, and that meant he had to be ready for anything.

His fear proved true when Darcy walked past him with a gun in her hand and sat in the opposing seat, keeping the weapon trained on him like she was the villain in a suspense thriller.

He had to measure his words carefully, "Is that necessary?"

She looked down at the gun and smiled, "Just a little insurance in case you try something stupid."

"We're forty-thousand feet in the air! What could I possibly do?"

Darcy tilted her head a little to the side, pretending to be contemplating the situation, "Well, you are going after my dad, after all. So, I'm not putting anything past you."

The lightbulb went on. The situation just became even more dangerous. *That's why she's working with Ashton! She's his kid. How did I miss that?*

"Ding, ding, ding, we have a winner!" she chuckled. "I thought you were smarter than that, Dr. Leonard? He's been playing you for a long time and you had no clue."

As Patrick sat there regarding the girl across from him, posing to be the hardened criminal she wasn't, he could feel the vein in his forehead starting to bulge. He didn't deny that her relationship with Ashton had caught him off-guard, but by implying that Ashton had been playing him and he hadn't known it, she was questioning his intelligence. And that pissed him off. *Keep it together, Patrick,* He thought. *You're not helping anyone if you get yourself killed.*

"I admit I didn't realize what Ashton's plans were, or what his ultimate goal was," he said, "but we were friends. Had been for a long time. He had always been ambitious. I thought that was just one of his colorful personality traits?"

"See, that's what did you in," Darcy replied. "He was never your friend. You were just a means to an end. That's all."

"And what exactly is his end-game, Darcy?"

She laughed, "You think I'm stupid? Why would I tell you?"

"People are dying! Isn't that a good enough reason?"

"Sacrifices always have to be made in the name of science. Consider their deaths contributions to the evolution of the planet toward a savage new world, where only the strongest and most ruthless survive."

"Let me guess...Ashton's going to be king of this new world?"

"Something like that."

"And, what if I try to stop him?"

Darcy gripped the gun a little tighter and centered it on Patrick, "I guess I'd have to put a bullet in your brain then, wouldn't I?"

"What happened to you, Darcy? You were such a sweet young girl when I hired you. Always upbeat and eager to learn."

"It's called acting, Dick-wad. You know, for a smart guy, you're really pretty dumb."

"So, what happens now?"

"Oh, you'll see. Daddy's got something special planned for you."

Patrick was running out of time and options. He tried hard to disguise his anxiety as his mind raced. If their course was still set for Ames they'd be there soon and he'd find himself at Ashton's mercy for God-knows-what kind of torture he had planned? If they were taking him somewhere else then he had no clue. Either way, he felt like he was doomed. His only choice was to disarm Darcy and force the pilot to land.

He slowly made a move to stand up.

"Where do you think you're going?" Darcy spat.

"I need to go to the bathroom," Patrick replied.

"Tough shit! Sit your ass back down!"

For a brief second, he thought his little disarming attempt was going to be easy, but her demeanor changed his plans quickly. He feared he was going to have to try something drastic. Hopefully, he was up to the task.

"I'm serious," he pleaded. "I'm about to have an accident here."

"You can piss yourself for all I care. Just keep your ass in that seat."

He pretended to squirm in agony for a few moments, contorting his face into that of a child who had to pee badly and couldn't hold it.

"Oh, for fuck's sake!" Darcy exclaimed. Then she sighed in resignation, "This is giving me a headache! Make it quick, you son-of-a-bitch."

As Patrick stood up from his seat, the plane suddenly hit a patch of turbulence and lurched up and down violently, jostling him back and forth. He reached out to grab onto the edge of the table and his momentum propelled him forward, throwing him right into Darcy. The decision was made before he could even comprehend what was happening, a split-second moment born out of desperation and fear, and he immediately tried to wrestle the gun from her.

Even though he outweighed her by nearly a hundred pounds, she was fast and agile, allowing her to spin away from his initial grasp. Desperately, he reached forward, grabbed a handful of her hair, and yanked hard, sending a loud howl flying from her mouth.

The maneuver was enough to allow him to grab onto her hand that clutched the chamber of the gun. She tried feebly to wrestle away from him, but this time his strength proved too much. Then, as he reached with his other hand to pry her fingers from the weapon, a shot rang out. A second later, the plane began a sharp dive downward.

Chapter 40

The door to the rear of the ship closed with a thud, and instantly the same feeling of dread overcame Melinda that she had experienced under nearly identical circumstances only a short time ago. He had left her then to go save the world, filling her with a real fear that she'd never see him again. This time, that fear was amplified a hundred-fold.

Guerera saw the worry in Melinda's eyes and put her arm around her shoulder, "He's going to be fine. If anyone can save us, it's your husband."

Melinda wanted to believe her; wanted more than anything else in the world to have the unwavering faith she desperately needed so she could be strong for her family.

Then Kate said, "Yeah, mom, dad's one tough son-of-a-bitch!"

Melinda's eyes grew wide, "Kate! Where did you hear that?"

Kate shrugged, "I don't know? Somewhere. It's true, though."

Melinda chuckled as she bent down and scooped Kate up in her arms, "You're right, sweetie. Your dad is one tough son-of-a-bitch."

Aldin spoke up, "What does tough son-of-a-bitch mean?"

Guerera replied, "It means he's a bad-ass, tough motherfucker who can handle himself."

Mishka thought about it for a second and said, "Then Silas is also one tough son-of-a-bitch."

"And a bad-ass, tough motherfucker who can also handle himself," Ripley added.

Ripley looked at Mishka, "I would also say that you're a bad-ass motherfucker too."

Mishka said, "Why, thank you. And I would say that you're a bad-ass motherfucker as well."

"What about me?" Aldin asked.

Ripley put her arm around Aldin's shoulder and leaned in to kiss her softly, "To me, you're the baddest motherfucker of them all."

Guerera looked at the trio of alien saviors standing in front of her, beaming with a sense of pride at their newly expanded vocabulary, and chuckled silently. *They have no idea what those words mean.*

Aldin stepped forward and took Tommy's hand, "Let's see if we can get those wounds of yours healed?"

***

Tommy looked around the ship wide-eyed as Aldin led him toward the front. "Wow! I can't believe I'm actually in a real-life spaceship!"

Aldin grinned, "Yeah, I guess it would be pretty special for you. Me? I guess I've been around technology like this my whole life, so it doesn't get as exciting anymore. Although, this was the first time I've ever gone through hyper-space."

Tommy suddenly remembered the whole reason they were there was that their planet blew up. With his head slunk low, he said, "I'm sorry about your planet."

Aldin stifled back a tear. She didn't have time to mourn again. There would be time for that later, after they put this threat to rest once and for all. *If we live that long,* she thought bitterly.

"It's okay," she finally said as she stopped at a small medical station near the edge of the locker area. She pulled a small bottle from one of the drawers beneath a stainless countertop. "Close your eyes," she instructed right before she spraying some kind of solution onto his face, focusing on the cut running across his cheek.

Tommy let out a slight gasp as the solution hit his face. It didn't burn so much as it tingled while he felt the skin on his face tighten. The sensation only lasted a few seconds and then was gone, replaced by a cool, gentle, soothing feeling.

"You can open your eyes," Aldin said.

Tommy tentatively reached his hand up and touched the side of his face. He was shocked to find his wounds completely healed. "Wow!" he exclaimed. "It's like magic!"

"I don't know the term 'magic', but it's just an advanced bio-chemical antigen, coupled with a local anesthesia and antihistamine, designed to accelerate your body's natural healing properties."

Tommy just stared at her blankly.

"It's science," she said with a slight smile.

Her smile quickly faded when she heard the first few pings on the roof of the ship, like rain sprinkling down on a tin roof. She cocked her head to one side to listen more closely as the sound grew gradually in intensity until it became a tempest.

"It sounds like it's raining," Tommy said.

"I don't think so," Aldin replied. "The sound isn't as consistent as it should be."

Mishka ran past her toward the front of the ship as the others joined Aldin and Tommy.

"What are you doing?" Ridley asked.

When Mishka turned briefly around to answer, she realized for a brief second just how alone she was. Ridley was holding Aldin tight, while the humans did the same to their own. She had no one.

She brushed it aside like she always did and pressed the button to open the front viewport on the ship. Seconds later, the horror was revealed. Millions of insects scurried back and forth on the glass and across the hull of the ship, trying to get at them.

Ashley screamed. And as Guerera sought to calm her down, the gigantic swarm suddenly let out a collective, manic screech. The mass skittered across the glass frantically until it started to form a pattern. Guerera cried out as the pattern settled into a form that resembled her worst nightmare. "No! It can't be!" she cried as she looked at Clause's grinning face made up of a million tiny, squirming insects.

The face opened its mouth in a roar before the image dispersed and the insects renewed their attack on the ship with increased vigor.

"They can't get in here, can they?" Melinda asked.

Mishka replied confidently, "The ship is designed to be airtight. There's no way they can get in."

A gasp escaped her lips, though, when the front glass began to crack under the insect assault.

"We have to get out of here!" Guerera said.

Ashley held onto her tight, crying desperately, "We can't go out there! The monsters are out there!"

Guerera lifted her head and looked at her sternly, "If we stay in here any longer, the insects will get inside and there won't be anywhere to run. Do you understand?"

Ashley nodded her head sadly.

"She's right," Ridley said. "We're going to have to get out of here. Everyone, grab one of the blaster rifles."

When Tommy reached for one of the weapons, Melinda gave him a questioning eye for a second and then nodded slightly.

"The lever on the side of the rifle changes the focus of the laser. The wide setting is best for the insects," Mishka said.

As the group adjusted their weapons, Aldin rushed around frantically, grabbing numerous weapons and supplies and throwing them into a large pack. "What about the transports?" she asked.

Ridley said, "Aldin, get the children into the main transport. The other two will ride with me and Mishka."

Melinda held onto her kids tightly, while Guerera clenched onto Ashley.

"You're not going to separate us!" Guerera said.

"It's the only way," Ridley said, "and we're running out of time."

Ashley refused to let go of Guerera's leg, but when a large crash hit the glass once more, she screamed and Guerera knew she had no choice. She looked at the little girl, who in every sense of the word had become her daughter, "We're running out of time, Ash. You're gonna have to go in the transport with the others."

"But, I'm scared, G," Ashley pleaded.

"I know, sweetie. Me too. But we're gonna get through this. Okay?"

With tears streaming down her face, Ashley nodded.

Guerera rushed Ashley over to the transport. "If anything happens to her..." she said to Aldin as she hoisted Ashley into the vehicle.

"I'll protect her with my life," Aldin said as she turned the transport on.

"You better," Guerera replied.

As Ridley and Mishka jumped onto the gyro-cycles, Melinda quickly ushered Tommy and Kate to the transport. Ashley clung to Kate, each girl seeking comfort from the other amidst a clamor of tears.

A loud crash, and the swarm zoomed into the ship. They only had seconds to act.

Aldin quickly pushed a button on the console of the transport and the rear hatch began to open. As she sped forward to escape the horror, Guerera jumped on the back of Mishka's cycle, while Melinda hopped onto Ridley's.

When they burst out into the open, the madness surrounding them was unparalleled. People were running and screaming everywhere. Undead animals with broken bodies ravaged through the crowd of people as they sought a fleeting escape. Those that weren't mauled by the savage beasts were trampled underfoot, where they died in the throes of fear and disbelief.

Aldin steered the transport desperately through the crowd around the outskirts of King Arthur's Carousel, toward Sleeping Beauty's Castle. She chanced a glance and was relieved to see Ridley and Mishka right beside them.

As they neared the centerpiece of the theme park, a figure emerged from the side of the building. The beast stood before them—an abomination that betrayed all the laws of nature—and roared. It stood fully upright, easily measuring over six feet tall, and weighing at least four-hundred and fifty pounds. Then the Clause head embedded in its chest yelled a single word, "Guerera!"

The octopus tentacles dangling from its shoulders came to life and reached forward as it sprang toward them.

"No! It can't be!" Guerera cried.

Chapter 41

The plane rocketed downward at five hundred miles an hour, heading for a deadly collision with the earth below. The inertia of the dive slammed Patrick downward into the closest seat, while Darcey was flown across the cabin and disappeared.

Patrick only had seconds to act. He pulled himself toward the cockpit, using anything he could grab as a handhold. His muscles strained with each movement as he scrapped forward. He barely dodged a service cart that had dislodged itself as it shot toward him, twisting his body in ways it had never been twisted before to avoid a collision.

When he finally reached the opening to the cockpit, he instantly knew why they were plummeting to their deaths. The bullet hole in the interior wall of the plane right behind the pilot's seat was a precursor to the nightmare he entered when he pulled himself fully into the cockpit. The pilot, a man Patrick had never seen before, lay sprawled across the cockpit, dead from the bullet wound that had sent his heart exploding from his chest onto the plane's windshield.

Patrick desperately pulled himself over the dead man's body, smearing blood in a wide streak across his chest, and quickly grabbed the yoke, pulling back with all his might. Slowly, the plane started to level off.

After he had gotten the plane somewhat stabilized, he pushed the pilot's body off to the side and jumped into the pilot's seat. He had no idea what to do next, but he had a strong feeling that he wasn't going to survive, whatever it was.

He pulled his phone out and called William. No answer. He could only imagine what kind of horror they were facing on the ground. Quickly, he sent a text detailing the information he had found on Ashton and the hidden section of the lab. At least if he didn't survive, then William would have enough to make Ashton pay.

He sent the text and then reached for the radio, hoping to reach someone at the nearest control tower who could help him land the plane safely. *There's something I never thought I'd have to do,* he thought grimly.

Then he heard her voice again, but, unlike before, it sounded strained and desperate, "Get your hand away from the fucking radio!"

Patrick froze for a second, and then slowly turned in his seat to see Darcey standing in the doorway to the cockpit. She had recovered the gun and held it pointed at him, albeit with a shaky hand. A large gash stretched across her forehead and was bleeding profusely, sending a river of blood down the left side of her face. She was bent over slightly, holding her left arm tightly against her stomach, which indicated that she had either broken her arm, or had some internal injury and she was trying to compress the pain.

"Are you going to do this now?" Patrick said. "If we don't land this plane, then we're going to die."

"You just don't get it, you stupid fuck! This is bigger than both of us. My father deserves his moment of glory, and I won't let you ruin it for him."

"You're just as insane as he is!"

"I guess you're entitled to your own opinion. I'd prefer to say we're committed to our cause."

"Committed is an interesting word to use, considering that's what both of you should be. Tossed into the looney bin and the key thrown away. That's what they should do."

Darcey's eyes grew dangerous. "Out of the seat, now!" she demanded.

Patrick started to argue, but held it back. He knew what was about to happen. His only choice was to fight and hope for the best.

But Darcey was ready for his attack. As he stood from the seat, she slid over to her left behind the pilot's seat. When Patrick lunged for her, she quickly fired. The bullet hit him in the stomach and he fell to the floor at her feet.

She stepped over him as he feebly tried to grab for her in his last death throes. "Goodbye, Patrick," she said as she sat down in the pilot's seat and began flipping a number switches like she had done so many times before. She grabbed the radio and switched the frequency before speaking. "Genesis One, do you read me?"

A moment later, Ashton's voice spoke through the speaker, "This is Genesis One. Go ahead."

"The crisis has been averted. Dr. Leonard will no longer bother you, Daddy."

"Fantastic! Proceed to the rendezvous point. You've done great, sweetie! I'm so proud of you."

Patrick gasped his last breath, listening to the madman and his daughter revel in their perverted glory, knowing that he had failed to stop their madness.

Chapter 42

They had just passed Anaheim Hills when the pilot of the Viper spoke through their headsets, "Get ready, ladies. We'll be touching down in ten."

"Where are we landing?" Fisher asked.

The pilot replied, "Park management said they'd clear a set of parking lots on the West side of the park for us. Let's hope they come through. Otherwise, I'm going to have to drop your asses out the side and put this beast down somewhere else."

Jackson tried to think of a smartass remark but came up blank. He looked at Fisher and saw the same concern in his eyes. They were heading into the belly of the beast again, even while nightmares still haunted their dreams of the horrors they had faced the first time. There was no telling what they were going to face now. Still, they were prepared to face whatever the fuck Hell could throw at them to save one of their own. If she was still alive.

A few minutes later, they were approaching the Santa Ana River when the sky suddenly grew darker. Fisher and Jackson immediately grew concerned. They had seen this story play out before.

"What's going on?" Fisher asked.

"Relax, soldier," Sam said smugly. "Nothing to wet your pants over. I'm sure it's just some cloud cover."

A series of 'pings' pelted the helicopter, like shots from a BB gun hitting a tin can. "What the fuck!?" came the pilot's voice through their headsets.

"Still think it's nothing?" Fisher asked when he saw the slightest hint of uncertainty in Sam's eye.

Sam was just about to snap back when the Viper was slammed with a barrage of what sounded like shots from a howitzer. His eyes grew wide when he looked over and saw the other chopper, flying a hundred yards alongside and slightly ahead of them, suddenly engulfed in a dark mass.

"Get us out of here now!" Fisher yelled through the comm.

As their helicopter began to abruptly descend, rocking back and forth violently, they watched in horror as the Viper carrying Delta Squad began to spin out of control. Then it plummeted downward in a deadly spiral. The cries of Delta Squad echoed through the comms before they were suddenly silenced when the chopper hit the ground and was engulfed in a giant fireball.

While Bravo Squad watched their comrades die a fiery death, their helicopter shot forward as fast as it could, aiming for their original destination, the pilot fighting against the insect swarm that was quickly overtaking the chopper. A minute later, Disneyland came into view, looking like anything but the happy place it was designed to be. Smoke rose in columns from several fires throughout the five-hundred acres that encompassed the park, and Fisher could imagine the screams of terror in his mind from those down on the ground, running in fear from the monsters that he knew all too well.

The insects swarmed their way into the cabin, mercilessly

attacking the soldiers. As they were waving their arms around to swat away at the pests, one of the newest members of Bravo Squad, a young man they called 'Little Ricky', forgot to remove his finger from the trigger of his M16 and sent a burst of machine-gun fire ricocheting through the cabin.

Before anyone could react to the gunfire, the Viper plummeted downward at a rapid speed. Instead of a safe landing outside the theme park, they were heading for a crash landing in the middle of 'It's a Small World'.

"Hold on!" the pilot shouted moments before impact.

The front of the right skid caught the edge of one of the castle's turrets overlooking the lazy river, sending an avalanche of rock and debris tumbling to the ground below. The impact was enough to slow the Viper just enough to avoid an explosion, but the pitch of the chopper was too extreme, causing the mast to snap off when the rotors hit the ground, sending metal shrapnel flying in all directions.

Finally, the hulking mass of twisted metal settled to the ground with a loud thud that shook the earth beneath them. Amidst a cloud of dust and smoke, Fisher shook his head and looked grimly around the cabin to check on the status of his Squad. Two of his soldiers were missing. Little Ricky, and another newbie simply named Tom, were nowhere to be seen. His best guess was that they fell out of the side of the chopper as it was descending. *With any luck, they're still alive,* he thought briefly. But he knew luck wasn't exactly on their side at the moment.

Sam had been thrown to the floor of the cabin during the impact and was slowly struggling to his knees. He had a large gash across his forehead but seemed stable.

Jackson, on the other hand, didn't look so good. He was still sitting on his seat with his body hunched over. His breathing was shallow and strained.

Fisher lifted Jackson's head and his heart dropped. He quickly pressed his hands over the bullet wound in his stomach, but even as he tried to staunch the flow of blood, a river of red liquid streamed through his fingers.

Jackson looked at him through eyes that were distant and weak, "I don't feel so good, Fish."

Chapter 43

The swarm of insects morphing into Clause's image was one of the most terrifying things William had ever seen, and recently he had seen a lot of scary shit. Luckily, it had only stayed a few seconds before it dispersed. Still, the picture was there, ingrained in his brain, and he couldn't unsee it.

They pushed through a flurry of animal attacks, at times bracing themselves against a throng of people to prevent from being thrown to the ground and trampled to death.

After a long struggle, they made their way past Pixie Hollow and the Matterhorn Bobsleds toward Tomorrowland. As soon as the coast was clear, they stopped to catch their breaths for a minute. "Okay, where to now?" William asked.

"I'm not completely sure?" Silas replied. "The signal went dark in this area."

William thought, *If I was an alien stranded on a strange planet hellbent on bringing about an apocalypse, where would I hide?*

They were standing directly in front of the Star Wars Launch Bay exhibit. He stared at the structure for a minute, recalling childhood memories of the first time he had seen the movie. A story about a group of heroes fighting to save everything they hold dear from the clutches of evil. A New

263

Hope. We could certainly use a little of that right now.

For a moment, he thought it would be a perfect spot for Jeron to hide out in, even if it was a bit cliché, until Silas spoke up, "I think I have a good idea where he's hiding."

William followed his gaze toward the entrance to the Tomorrowland Theater, where he saw a line of rotted-flesh beasts—at least twenty of them—standing like sentries guarding the castle gate to keep the usurpers at bay, each one snarling through blood-soaked teeth as black ichor dripped to the ground.

"Any ideas?" William asked.

Silas replied, "Hit them hard, and hit them fast!"

"I like it!"

Both men drew their blasters and aimed at the unholy beasts. After firing a barrage of shots and dropping a few of the creatures, they were shocked to see the remaining ones still guarding the entrance instead of attacking. Then they heard the sound. Like the roar of a tornado off in the distance that got louder as it grew closer.

"Whatever that is, we won't survive out here in the open like this," William said.

"Then we have no choice," Silas replied.

Both men looked at each other before they gathered themselves and charged at the wall of monsters, firing their blasters in a desperate attempt to kill as many of the beasts as they could before they reached the door. An unholy symphony of howls rose from the creatures that chilled them to the bone.

They were twenty yards from the entrance, with a dozen of the maddened creatures still standing between them, when the tempest arrived overhead, heralded by the death-trumpet of a murder of crows, swooping down on them with hunger in their eyes. Those with broken wings were carried by others and were dropped on William and Silas like bombs dropped from a Boeing B-17, while the rest zoomed down like torpedoes. Unsettling cries flew from their beaks as they attacked.

William turned around just as one of the undead birds landed on his shoulder and tore a large piece of flesh from his ear, ripping the bottom lobe off. He cried out as he swatted the thing away, feeling its twisted talons rip another section of flesh from his shoulder as it fell to the ground. He immediately blasted it into a mound of feathers and guts.

Silas wasn't faring any better. One of the birds had its talons gripped around his right leg as it buried its beak into his thigh, while he fended off another trying to peck his eyes out. He cried out as he took the butt of his blaster and pummeled the thing in the head until it was dead.

"We've got to get inside!" William cried.

With a wild spray of blaster fire coming from both men's guns, they staggered forward as best as they could, concentrating mainly on the undead that still blocked the entrance. It was only when they had closed the distance between them and the entrance to a few feet that the animals attacked, converging on them with savage abandon.

They had managed to take down a few more of the animals—leaving five remaining—but they were now also facing the deadly bird attack from above. Talons raked across both men's bodies as they desperately fought the beasts on both fronts. One caught Silas on the forehead and pulled back across the top of his skull, while a German Shepherd with one eye missing and a big hole in its chest clamped its jaws on his left leg. Silas brought his blaster around and killed the mangled dog, for good this time.

This is it, William thought as he found himself trapped between a Pit Bull loping on three legs and a mangled coyote with half of its face missing. *There's no escaping it. We're going to die here.*

All hope seemed lost as the creatures closed in, until William found himself back-to-back with Silas, ready to make his last stand. "Goodbye, friend," he said. "It was a pleasure to meet you."

"The feeling is mutual," Silas replied.

Both men gave out a loud yell of defiance toward the beasts as they readied themselves for their final act of bravery.

A barrage of machine-gun fire erupted around them suddenly, followed by a familiar voice shouting, "Get down!"

Both men dropped to the ground and watched as the ground quickly became littered with the dead. A rainfall of blackbirds dropped to the concrete amidst a chorus of thuds and splats, and the remaining sentries were dispatched in a matter of seconds.

As unconsciousness threatened to overtake William, he watched through blurry eyes as Fisher walked toward him, "It's about time," he said weakly.

Chapter 44

Jeron could hardly contain himself as he watched the whirling transport fall from the sky and be engulfed in a fiery explosion upon impact with the ground below. The optical link, coupled with the neural transmitter embedded at the base of the Clause monster's brain was working perfectly. Not only did it allow him to watch his greatest achievement unfold with unabashed glee, but he could also alert the beast in real-time of incoming threats. Through his telepathic link with the rest of the horde, Clause could then dispatch the creatures wherever needed.

Once both of the air transports were destroyed, he scrolled through his video feeds, tuning into the different frequencies of the various creatures, until he found what he'd been looking for. The ship! And that meant they were there.

He typed a few lines of code on the keyboard that would relay the images from the insects to Clause. When the insects finally broke through the front glass, bringing into view the occupants of the craft, he could almost feel Clause's anger seeping through psychically.

Jeron switched the feed to the camera on Clause's forehead so he could get a first-person view of the action. His pulse raced as he watched the beast storm through the crowd of people like a war machine. He took a special delight in watching Clause grab a young man who was scrambling to get away, wrapping his tentacles around each arm, then grabbing each leg in his strong hands, before pulling the man apart. The scream that issued from the man was music to Jeron's ears. "Magnificent!"

The Clause-beast let out a mighty roar as it raced toward the ship fervently. Jeron knew it had only one thing on its mind. Revenge. *Go forward, you wondrous creation, and claim that which is yours.*

***

As Clause turned the corner, he saw them. They were fleeing the ship, desperate to escape the swarming insects, oblivious to the far worse fate awaiting them. He stopped for a moment, letting the hatred flood his veins, feeding the inferno within him. His massive arms tensed, claws flexing, and his feet slammed against the ground, shaking the earth in defiance. The thick tentacles writhing from his shoulders coiled and twisted, eager to wrap around Guerera's throat and crush the life from her.

"Guerera!" he roared, his voice billowed with rage. Then he attacked.

He surged forward, his powerful legs propelling him with terrifying speed. The larger vehicle swerved left, skirting past him, but he ignored it—his focus locked onto one of the cycles. Guerera clung tightly to the rider in front of her, her wide eyes brimming with shock and terror. The sight was intoxicating. He would savor her agony.

He was so caught up in the thought of her cruel death, that he didn't realize until it was too late that she had whipped a blaster around and focused it at him. Then pain flared across his body. A volley of blaster shots struck him, most deflecting harmlessly off his thick hide. But one burned too close to his chest, making him falter for a split second. Before he could recover, another shot ripped through the middle of the tentacle on his left side. A searing pain lanced through him, and he roared in fury.

A snarl ripped from his gorilla-like maw as he lunged, his bulk slamming into the back of the cycle just as it veered sharply to evade him. Though it wasn't a direct hit, the sheer force was enough to send the two women hurtling from the bike. They crashed hard into the dirt. Clause landed in front of her in a crouch, his eyes locked onto his prey.

He was nearly upon her when agony ignited at the base of his skull. A firestorm of pain exploded in his head, white-hot and blinding. His vision warped, filled with images that weren't his own—black wings beating against the night, beaks tearing into flesh. He saw two men, struggling beneath a swarm of shrieking birds. Soldiers joined the fight, and then —him. The man he despised almost as much as Guerera.

Clause's muscles tensed, fighting against the command clawing through his mind, but the pain only grew sharper, unbearable. He had no choice. A guttural, primal growl rumbled in his chest as he bent low, his massive jaw opening in a deafening, rage-filled roar at Guerera. His glare burned into her, promising the hunt wasn't over.

Then, with a final snarl of defiance, he turned and bounded away.

***

An alarm on Jeron's console began flashing, indicating an

issue outside the structure. He quickly changed the feed to see what had triggered the alarm at the front entrance. He mouthed a silent curse when he saw Silas and William approaching. *How could they possibly know where I am?* Almost immediately the answer came to him. Silas had placed a tracker on him somehow. *No matter. I'll show them who's in control here!*

Another search through the feed brought the black avians into view. A quick series of commands sent to Clause brought the creatures together and sent them rocketing toward the two men. *There's no way you're getting through that!*

His thoughts nearly proved correct. Their deaths were all but assured until two soldiers suddenly appeared with their weapons blasting wildly. As he watched the remaining animals guarding the structure fall, he was forced to call Clause back. The beast wouldn't like it. *Oh well. He'll get over it. This is more important than his silly vendetta.*

Jeron was so absorbed in watching the events play out on the screen, switching back and forth between different feeds, that he failed to notice the man enter the data room until he was standing right in front of him. The name tag on the gangly boy's shirt read 'Paul'.

"What are you doing in here?" Paul said. "We need to get out of here now!"

"Calm yourself, Paul," Jeron said. "Why not just relax and enjoy these last few moments of your life while you can?"

Paul stared at him with a questioning look, "What are you talking about?"

Then he saw the console beside Jeron with the video feed playing out in real-time. "What the hell is that?"

Jeron glanced over at the screen for a brief second and then back at Paul, beaming with pride. "That's the beginning of the end, my friend. Isn't it beautiful?"

"You're insane! There's nothing beautiful about people dying!"

"That's a matter of perspective?"

"Who are you?" Paul asked nervously.

Instead of answering him, Jeron replied, "While I've thoroughly enjoyed our little interaction here, I have more pressing matters to attend to."

He quickly brought his blaster up and pointed it at the boy. "Goodbye, Paul."

The shot hit Paul in the chest and dropped him to the floor before he had a chance to react.

Chapter 45

It was the most frightening sound Guerera had ever heard, and when she turned to see the source, she nearly had a heart attack. The beast with Clause's head embedded into its chest was an abomination that even Hell would've spit back out. The tentacles wriggling from its shoulders dripped with oily, black mucus as they reached forward. The gorilla head, the one that was supposed to be there, roared in defiance. Then it charged.

Guerera quickly looked at Aldin in the transport beside her, "Get them out of here, now!"

She watched as Aldin spun the transport around the perimeter of the area, steering clear of the beast. Her heart dropped when she saw Ashley's wounded face looking back at her, almost accusing her of breaking a promise she shouldn't have made.

Ridley and Melinda circled the left side of the courtyard, blasting away at the beast to distract it long enough for the transport to escape. As soon as the vehicle was far enough away, Mishka sped her cycle around to the right, following Ridley's example. Most of the shots just bounced off harmlessly, and the beast moved too fast to get a clear shot.

One of the shots, though, hit one of the tentacles, slicing it in half so that it was little more than a wriggling stump oozing out black blood onto the pavement.

The beast spun around as it leaped forward, hitting Mishka's cycle in the rear with just enough force to send both women skidding to the ground. As Guerera struggled to her knees, the creature raced forward. The gorilla mouth opened wide in a loud roar, raining black ooze and spittle over her, while Clause sneered victoriously. He was inches from ending her life when a pained look overcame both faces and he stopped. A second later, he turned and bounded away.

Melinda immediately jumped off the back as Ridley brought her cycle around and skidded to a stop right in front of Mishka and Guerera. "Are you okay?" she asked while giving Guerera a hand up.

Guerera brushed herself off as she stood up, "Yeah, just a bit shaken up."

"Did I just see what I think I saw?"

Guerera shuddered as she nodded.

"But, that's impossible! He's dead."

"We were taught at an early age that nothing is impossible," Mishka said. "Given that Jensen was a profound genius, even if he was completely insane, he pushed the theories of science beyond their limits, and it looks like he passed on his knowledge to his nephew."

"Who apparently is working with Ashton Brown," Melinda added.

"Then he needs to be stopped, once and for all," Guerera said.

"You want to go after the beast?" Mishka said.

Guerera had gotten past her initial shock at seeing the Clause-thing and was now seething with renewed hatred. "We killed him once, we can do it again."

"You really are a bad-ass motherfucker," Mishka said.

"Okay, let's not say that anymore," Guerera said.

A small frown crossed Mishka's lips, but she refrained from speaking. She was beginning to like this human, mainly because she reminded her so much of herself.

Then they all had the same thought at the same moment. Aldin!

Ridley tried to reach her through the communicator but got no response. "I'm sure they're fine," she said after a long pause, trying to convince herself just as much as the rest of the group.

"We're going to have to split up," Guerera said. "Mishka and I will go after Clause, while you two find Aldin and the kids."

"Nice of you to volunteer me," Mishka said.

Guerera replied, "It's the logical choice."

Mishka cocked her head to one side for a brief second, as if considering Guerera's response. "You're right,' she said a moment later.

Both women jumped up and climbed back on the cycle, ready to take off on their pursuit to stop the Clause-thing when they found themselves surrounded by a ring of undead animals waiting to attack.

***

Aldin raced the transport around the monster, swerving through a sea of screaming people. She breathed a little easier when they had gotten far enough away that the creature didn't pose an immediate threat. But they were far from being safe.

Tommy tried his best to remain strong, while the girls screamed hysterically, calling out for the women that were supposed to protect them. "It's okay, girls," Aldin said in a feeble attempt to calm them down. "Everyone's going to be fine. We'll all get through this and you'll see them again. Soon, I promise."

An undead coyote suddenly leaped onto the front of the transport, snarling at them through a broken face, its fur matted and bloody.

"Get down!" Aldin yelled as she brought her blaster up and shot the animal in the head. Instead of falling to the ground, it dropped flat and remained on the hood of the transport, attached to the metal by the stickiness of the blood and mucus covering its body. It became an unholy hood ornament that served as a statement of the world they lived in now. It also made it hard for her to see.

After a harrowing few minutes, she found herself in a small cul-de-sac, sandwiched between the Royal Hall and the Royal Theatre, with the only way out the same way she came in.

Aldin zig-zagged her way around several carcasses while she tried to turn around in the small space. The transport bounced and rocked as it climbed over the bloody remains of mutilated animals. Just as she was about to complete her turn, a large shape blurred into view from the corner of her eye, racing towards them with a terrifying speed. The sickening crunch of bone and the sharp scent of fear filled the air as she barely registered the sight of a huge, misshapen white horse before the collision. A high-pitched squeal, filled with rage and power, ripped through the air as the massive animal hurtled towards them, its hooves drumming the earth.

"Hold on!" she shouted.

Then the beast hit the transport with enough force that it sent the vehicle rolling.

Chapter 46

Rodrigo's lungs burned as he sprinted through the chaos, his boots slamming against the pavement. Screams filled the night, blending with the guttural growls of creatures that shouldn't exist. Disneyland, once a place of childhood wonder, had become a graveyard of horror.

Behind him, Benny's desperate cries were suddenly cut short—a sickening crunch replacing them.

Rodrigo didn't dare look back.

"They're on us!" Luis roared, panting, his voice ragged.

Rodrigo gritted his teeth. Jeron had set them up.

He had promised them power, protection—a future. Instead, he had thrown them into a massacre. The creatures weren't just attacking park-goers—they were hunting, and they knew exactly who their prey was.

Ahead, the neon lights of Tomorrowland flickered, casting a hellish glow over the panicked crowd. Smoke curled from overturned food stands, blood streaked the pavement. Bodies —mangled, chewed, half-eaten—littered the ground.

Rodrigo turned toward a side path. "Through here!"

The others followed, darting down a service alley behind the rides. The air was thick with the stench of burning plastic and coppery blood. Luis was limping, a deep gash running down his calf, but he still clutched his gun tightly, his eyes wild with fear.

A horrible, inhuman screech cut through the night, and Rodrigo's stomach dropped.

They weren't alone.

A blur of fur and sinew barreled out of the shadows.

A coyote, or what used to be one. Its tan coat was patchy and slick with decay, its ribcage exposed through gaping holes where muscle should have been. One of its ears was missing, and its jaw hung unnaturally slack, revealing jagged, rotting teeth. Its milky, dead eyes locked onto them, dripping thick, black fluid.

Luis barely had time to scream before it lunged.

Rodrigo raised his gun— too late.

The coyote's teeth clamped onto Luis's throat, dragging him to the ground.

"Luis!" Chuy fired wildly, bullets ripping into the creature's side—but it didn't let go.

Luis's screams gargled with blood, his fingers clawing at the pavement as the coyote ripped deeper.

Hector grabbed Chuy. "We gotta move!"

"We can't leave him!" Chuy shouted.

Rodrigo didn't hesitate. He aimed at Luis and pulled the trigger.

The gunshot echoed and Luis's body slumped.

The coyote jerked its head back, gnawing hungrily at the fresh corpse.

Rodrigo turned away. They didn't have time to grieve. Instead, they ran.

One by one, the trio burst back into the main thoroughfare, barely dodging the trampling crowd. Chuy wiped the sweat from his face with a bloodstained hand, panting. "Tell me you got a plan, Rodri!"

Rodrigo wasn't listening. His eyes flicked across the carnage, searching for any way out.

And then a series of piercing howls split the air nearby.

Rodrigo turned, his heart dropping into his stomach.

Another pack of coyotes, their flesh hanging in strips from their bones, eyes clouded with death, teeth dripping with black ichor, stalked forward, their movements eerily synchronized.

The lead coyote let out a broken, guttural growl—and lunged.

Rodrigo barely had time to shove Hector aside before the creature slammed into him, teeth snapping inches from his throat. They hit the ground hard, the animal's fetid breath hot against his face.

Chuy emptied his clip into its skull. The coyote howled, convulsed and then went still.

Rodrigo shoved the body off him, his ribs aching. He spotted a door at the rear of a nearby building. "Back door! NOW!"

They ran, crashing through the door into a small storage room filled with crates and boxes stack haphazardly with assorted maintenance equipment. They quickly pushed through the mountain of gear, only to find a metal door blocking their path into the rest of the building.

Hector turned back when he heard the unholy growls behind them, horror dawning in his face. The coyotes were scratching and clawing at the door, and would be inside any second.

"Fuck, fuck, fuck—"

Rodrigo spotted a fire extinguisher, grabbed it, and slammed it against the door's handle.

Nothing.

Chuy and Hecter joined in, kicking the door with everything they had.

The coyotes pushed through the door, knocking over shelves, claws scraping against tile.

Rodrigo swung again. This time, the lock snapped.

"GO!"

As they burst through the door into the small souvenir shop on the other side, one of the beasts pounced, its claws raking down Rodrigo's back and sending him crashing to the floor. The rest of the pack were on him in an instant. His gargled cries echoed through the small space before they were violently silenced.

Hector slammed the door shut behind them. Immediately, they began stacking everything possible to form a barrier between them and the undead.

Panting, hands shaking, Chuy turned to Hector.

Only the two of them remained.

Hector leaned against the wall, bleeding from his ribs. "What now?"

Chuy wiped the sweat from his brow, looking through the window out at the burning skyline of Disneyland.

Their gang was gone.

Everyone else was dead.

Only he and Hector were left.

Chuy's grip tightened around his gun.

"Now?" He glanced at Hector, his expression cold.

"Now we survive."

Chapter 47

After the first strafe of machine-gun fire decimated the aerial attack from the demon birds, Fisher and Sam brought their guns around to take out the rest of the undead. As they ran closer, both Marines drew out their M9 Berettas and focused on the animals that were closest to the two men.

When Fisher saw William go down amidst a sea of rotted flesh, he yelled fiercely and charged forward, shooting anything that moved. He was not going to let William die.

A crazed Husky darted at him from the side. Fisher saw the creature just in time to dive sideways, but he landed right next to one of the fallen birds that refused to die. It shot its beak deep into his arm, causing him to drop his gun. Immediately, he reached over with his other hand, grabbed the bird's head in his hand, and squeezed hard. Blood and brains oozed between his fingers, followed by a loud 'pop'. He threw the dead bird away in disgust and quickly grabbed his gun as he jumped back up to his feet.

After downing the last of the canines, Sam turned to see a trio of maddened felines leap toward him hissing and screaming. He batted one of them away with a strong forearm swing, and kicked another one in the stomach, launching it high in the air like he was a punter in an apocalyptical football game. But the third one got through and clamped onto his back, sinking its claws deep. He cried out as the deadly daggers pierced into his skin. Then he felt sharp teeth rip into the back of his shoulder. Desperately, he reached back with his other arm to remove the animal.

"Hold still!" Fisher yelled to him as he rushed over to help.

Sam replied, "Get this fucking thing off me!"

Fisher tried to grab the feline by the scruff of its neck, but as the animal squirmed under his grasp, a large patch of fur and flesh broke off in his hand. He brought his gun up and pointed it at the side of the animal's head, hoping he wasn't about to put a bullet into Sam's back instead. He breathed a sigh of relief after he fired and saw that the bullet had gone through the skull of the feline without injuring the Marine.

After he had pried the dead cat from Sam's back, Fisher rushed over to William. The man was wounded in numerous spots, but he was still alive.

"It's about time," William said weakly.

Fisher smiled, "Better late than never," as he helped William to his feet. "Who's your friend here?"

"Fisher, this is Silas. He's... not from around here."

Silas nodded to Fisher from his position on his knees as he lifted his right leg and plucked the dead blackbird from his thigh that was still dangling there.

"Thanks for helping, friend," Silas said.

"I'm just glad we got here in time," Fisher replied.

"Time is a fleeting thing," Silas said. "Something we're almost out of."

"He's right," William said. "We need to get inside that building right away and stop the person behind this."

"The Tomorrowland Theater?"

"And if we don't hurry, there won't be a tomorrow."

As they started toward the building, William stumbled and nearly fell until Fisher grabbed his arm and held him up.

"Are you sure you can make it?" Fisher asked him. "Maybe you should wait outside and let me and Sam catch this guy, whoever he is?"

William shook his head, "No, I'll be alright. There's too much at stake for me to stay behind."

Silas removed a small aerosol bottle from his robe and sprayed a fine mist on William's leg. A few seconds later, his wound had closed. "How does it feel?" Silas asked.

William put pressure on his leg and was shocked when he hardly felt anything at all. He looked at Silas, amazed.

"It didn't heal it completely," Silas said, "it just accelerated the process. It still going to take a little bit of time for it to completely heal."

"Well, whatever it did, I'll take it," William said.

Fisher took a good look at Silas for the first time, "Not from around here, huh?"

"It's a long story," William said. "I'll fill you in when this is over."

Silas proceeded to cover most of the men's wounds with his 'magic' solution until the liquid was finally used up. "That's all I have," he said. "I won't be able to help any further."

"Then, I suggest we don't get hurt again," Fisher said.

"That's easier said than done," William said.

A thunderous roar nearby suddenly interrupted their discussion. The four men turned and saw the abomination standing forty yards away, seething. A swath of black oily mucus striped his left side, starting at the base of the severed tentacle and running down his furry leg. Even from there, they could smell the acrid decay emanating from the beast.

"What the fuck is that?" Sam exclaimed.

"Something that shouldn't exist," Silas replied.

Then Fisher realized the face in the creature's chest belonged to someone that shouldn't be alive anymore. "That's impossible! We killed him!"

"Obviously, you didn't do a very good job," Sam said.

Fisher bit his tongue. Instead of answering with a smart-ass comment, he just said, "He used to be one of us."

"This shit-stain used to be a Marine?"

Fisher nodded. "Yeah, until he betrayed us."

That got Sam's blood boiling. In his mind, there wasn't anything worse than a Marine that turned his back on his fellow soldiers. "Then let's put this motherfucker down once and for all!"

All four men turned and let loose on the beast, a barrage of machine-gun and blaster fire raining down. But the creature was too fast, moving at an incredible speed to dodge the attack. And those few shots that did connect had no effect, penetrating flesh that was already dead.

"Aim for the head!" William shouted.

As the Clause-thing leaped toward them, Fisher took his Baretta out again and fired a clean shot that hit the gorilla head right between the eyes. The head went limp atop the creature's shoulders, but that didn't stop it from charging. Then he saw Clause sneering at him. *It's Clause that's controlling the monster!*

Before he could get off another shot, he found himself fending off a swarm of insects. As he struggled to keep the insects at bay, he suddenly felt a tentacle wrap around his chest and squeeze hard. He turned his head toward the other three men, his face wracked with pain as blood started to bubble from his lips. "Get inside!" he cried.

William cried out, "No!" as he watched the beast grab Fisher's head in both hands and squeeze. His skull caved in like it was a rotten pumpkin gone soft after Halloween.

The Clause-thing threw the body aside and stood there triumphant as a large swarm of insects flew toward the remaining men. In a matter of seconds, they were overrun.

Chapter 48

Mishka raced her cycle toward the ring of dead animals surrounding them, firing her blaster with reckless abandon, while Guerera held onto her waist with one arm and followed suit. Together, they blasted a path big enough to squeeze through without getting ripped apart. When a large bobcat suddenly leaped out at them, Guerera's foot nearly got lodged inside its skull as she kicked it aside. It landed in a heap on the pavement, the hunger finally gone from its eyes.

"I like you, Guerera," Mishka said, "You're one badass motherfucker."

Guerera replied, "I thought we agreed not to say that anymore?" Then she tightened her grip around Mishka's waist slightly and smiled to herself. *You're pretty badass yourself,* she thought.

Guerera turned her head to see Ridley and Melinda skirting through the rest of the horde until they made it out into the main thoroughfare. *Please, find them safe.*

The ground was littered with bodies as they wove their way forward until they found themselves at the foot of the Matterhorn Bobsleds unsure of which direction to go. When Guerera looked to her left and saw the bent chunk of metal that was once a Marine helicopter laying off in the distance atop the castle of 'It's a Small World' she immediately thought of Fisher. Fear and panic flooded through her, and every instinct told her to rush to try to save her friend. Then she saw the insect swarm overhead, speeding in the opposite direction, and she knew they had to follow it.

As they raced toward the Disneyland Monorail, Guerera's mind instantly flashed back to her first real encounter with the undead, when a woman had jumped in front of their Humvee only to be decapitated in front of her eyes a second later. That scene replayed itself in real-time as a young boy, who couldn't've been more than eight, ran toward them crying and screaming. This time it was a black Rottweiler the size of a small bear that pounced on the child. She closed her eyes tight to avoid having the image burned into her skull, even though she could hear his dying screams.

Mishka kicked the cycle into overdrive and made a sharp right as she continued to follow the path of the swarm. They heard a flurry of gunshots in the distance and shot forward, circling around the Star Wars Launch Bay only to hear the weapons silenced a moment later. The swarm had disappeared from view, leaving both women guessing as to the magnitude of horror they were rushing into.

They arrived just in time to see William and Silas, along with another man, enter the Tomorrowland Theater while fending off the insect swarm. The Clause-thing threw a mangled body to the ground before it gave pursuit, and Guerera knew instantly who it was.

Mishka threw the cycle to the ground as Guerera leaped off the back and ran toward Fisher's crumpled body. She said a silent 'Goodbye' to her fallen friend before she rushed in after the beast.

* * *

***

Melinda almost didn't see the overturned transport in a little alcove as they started to turn toward Main Street. "There!" she shouted, pointing desperately toward the vehicle while saying a silent prayer that her kids were alright.

Ridley quickly spun the cycle around and headed toward the transport only to find her path suddenly blocked by the hindquarters of a charging white Clydesdale that was storming toward the downed transport.

Melinda fired a quick shot into the raging horse. It wasn't enough to bring it down, but it did serve to get its attention. A second later, it turned around and reared up on its hind legs, screeching loudly, before it charged toward them.

"Oh, shit!" Melinda said.

Both women jumped off the cycle and dodged out of the way just as the rotted-flesh horse slammed into the machine, leaving it an un-usable chunk of twisted metal.

When the horse reared up again, they both fired desperately at the beast's head, hoping for a miracle. One of the shots connected, hitting it in the eye and burning a hole into its skull before it thudded to the ground with enough force to shake the ground beneath them.

Immediately, Melinda and Ridley raced to the downed transport, each one praying to a different god that they were still alive. When they got there, they were shocked to find the transport empty.

***

Even though the transport's safety field had been implemented properly, preventing serious injury, the jolt from the impact with the equine was still enough to daze

Aldin's senses for a moment. It took her a moment to realize they were upside down, and that the beast was gearing up for another charge.

She craned her neck around and was relieved to see that the kids were, mostly, unhurt, even if they were crying hysterically. But she knew they wouldn't last much longer in their present circumstances. "You need to be quiet. We have to get out of here," she whispered urgently.

When the animal struck the transport a second time, it sent it spinning like a top, causing it to skip across the pavement until it came to rest near a small line of trees that served as a border to Frontierland. Quickly, she pushed the button on the control panel, hoping it was still functional. For a brief second, nothing happened. Then, slowly, the rear hatch began to open. "Go, now!" she urged.

It was a tight squeeze, but eventually, they were all free of the vehicle and inched their way quickly among the trees seconds before the animal slammed into it again. When they were out of sight from the beast, they stood up and ran.

The closest place of shelter was a little Mexican restaurant nearby, Rancho del Zocale Restaurante, but as they ran toward it, they were nearly trampled by a large group of park employees, all dressed in various costumes, who, instead of trying to save the terrified park guests like they were trained to do in an emergency, had all said 'fuck it, I'm saving my own ass!', and raced toward the same building.

Aldin smelled it a moment before the group ran inside, a strong methane-type of smell coming from the building. She knew little about this world yet, but she knew something bad was about to happen. Immediately, she turned her back to the building and shielded the kids a second before the structure exploded.

The force of the explosion sent them crashing to the

ground amidst a shower of debris. She cried out as she felt something sharp impale itself in her side. Immediately, a river of blood began to flow. As her sight became blurry and she felt herself slipping into unconsciousness, her only thought was that she had failed to keep her promise. She knew the children would be dead soon, and it would be her fault.

***

They heard the explosion nearby and felt the earth shake beneath their feet as they sifted through the trees in a desperate search for Aldin and the children. They could barely make out a series of tracks through the dirt, but as they followed them, the smoke from several fires throughout the park continued to make visibility difficult. It was only when they nearly fell over the mound of bodies that they realized it was Aldin lying on top of the children, protecting them like a mother bear would protect her cubs. But, none of them were moving.

Ridley quickly slid to her knees. "Aldin! Wake up!" she cried desperately. Then she saw the metal rod sticking out of her side and a surge of panic flew through her. There was so much blood!

She quickly felt for a pulse, not finding any sign of life initially. But then she felt it, faint, but it was there. Ridley jumped to her feet and began running back toward the trees. "Don't move her!" she shouted to Melinda.

"I'm stuck, Mommy," Melinda heard Kate mumble beneath Aldin's body.

Melinda's lips quivered as she spoke, "It's okay, sweetie. Just don't try to move."

"But she weighs a ton. I can't breathe."

"Aldin's hurt, baby. We can't move her until Ridley comes back with something to help."

Melinda saw the top of Tommy's head peeking out from under Aldin's shoulder and grew worried when she saw a puddle of blood nearby. She didn't know if it was his or Aldin's. "Tommy? Are you okay?"

For a second, he didn't respond. Then she saw his head nod slightly. "I don't know if you heard what I told Kate, but don't try to move. Aldin's been injured."

Another slight nod told her that he understood.

That just left Ashley. Her black hair blended in with the black dirt and black smoke, making it hard to distinguish her head from Aldin's arm that lay draped over her face.

"Ashley?" Melinda called softly. "Are you okay?"

No response.

She tried again, this time a little louder, "Ashley?"

Still nothing.

Against her better judgment, and Ridley's order not to move her, Melinda lifted Aldin's arm and slid Ashley's unmoving body out from under her. Even under the obscure lighting, her skin gave off a blueish hue. She wasn't breathing.

Melinda immediately began trying whatever she could to revive the girl, but nothing worked. "No!" she cried. "Wake up, Ashley! Please, wake up!"

"What's going on?" Ridley asked as she rushed back to them carrying a small silver box. "I thought I said not to move Aldin?"

Melinda turned to her with tears streaming down her face, "She's not breathing."

For a brief second, Ridley was torn. Save the woman she loved, or save the little girl she had just met? She knew what Aldin would do. She turned toward the little girl, "Move away. Let me see what I can do."

Ridley opened the box and withdrew a small vial containing a silver liquid. After unstopping it, she propped Ashley's lips open and poured a few drops of the liquid into her mouth.

"Now what?" Melinda asked.

"Now, we wait."

Both women watched nervously as the color began to come back into Ashley's face. Then a deep gasp sounded from her before she opened her eyes. "She saved us," she said weakly before she closed her eyes again.

As soon as she saw that Ashley was going to be okay, Ridley moved quickly over to Aldin. She removed a small aerosol from the case and shook it vigorously for a few seconds. She looked at Melinda, "On the count of three, pull the rod from her side."

Melinda looked at her nervously and nodded as she grabbed the piece of metal with both hands.

"One, two, three."

Melinda yanked hard, pulling the rod from Aldin's side. Immediately, Ridley sprayed the wound with the aerosol. An initial surge of new blood streamed out, free from the barrier that the rod had presented. Then, a second later, the wound began to close.

"Help me roll her over," Ridley said tensely. Melinda could hear the fear in her voice. It was a feeling she had grown accustomed to recently.

Ridley shook the last few drops of silver liquid into Aldin's mouth, praying desperately that she wasn't too late.

Moments passed with no sign of life. Tears began streaming down Ridley's face as she placed her head on Aldin's chest. "Please, don't leave me," she cried softly.

Tommy and Kate scooted over to their mom, both kids

crying. Melinda held them tight as they watched Ridley mourn for her fallen lover.

Chapter 49

The three men raced for the entrance to the theater in a desperate attempt to escape the monstrosity chasing them. Once inside, they quickly looked for a way to block the door, but found none. They only had seconds before the beast would be on them.

Hiding around a corner, the men crouched behind a large column, waiting. "What now?" William asked.

Silas replied, "Logic suggests that Jeron would be hiding somewhere he had access to network capabilities."

"We'll need to split up," Sam said. "We can cover more ground."

Before anyone could object, the Clause-thing burst through the doors.

Sam turned to William and handed him a pair of grenades, "Find this son-of-a-bitch and blast him to oblivion."

"What are you going to do?" William asked.

"I'm going to buy you guys some time."

Firing a barrage of shots toward the creature as he jumped from his hiding place, Sam started running toward the rear of the theater. "Hey, fuck-face! Eat this!" he yelled before he slammed through another door.

When Clause hesitated for a second, they thought his plan had failed. Then he let out a loud roar and charged after the marine.

They waited a few seconds to make sure the coast was clear before they went in search of Jeron. "Contrary to what our friend suggested," William said, "Given the shit we're facing, I think we should stay together."

Silas replied, "I agree. Separating right now would put us both at risk."

As if we aren't at enough risk already? William thought.

Their first thought was that there would be a control room located somewhere behind the main stage. As they approached a door leading to the back, Silas stopped. "Be alert," he whispered. "Jeron is sure to have additional resources protecting him."

William didn't like the sound of that. *Additional resources?* He was scared to think of the possibilities.

The door led to a long hallway that made a sharp turn to the left forty yards ahead. Several rooms dotted each side with signs above the doorways indicating they were dressing rooms for the various acts that had played out on the stage. Their only occupants were the costumes and set dressings from the magical stories they once told.

As they continued, a 'chattering' noise began echoing through the hall coming from around the corner. Both men held their weapons ready as they approached the bend. They thought they had seen everything in this nightmare world, but they weren't prepared for what lay ahead of them. The hall was choked with spiderwebs, spanning from floor to ceiling. A large mass of arachnids writhed and undulated together as one creature in the middle of the silken entanglement, while thousands of others, an assortment of species with some as big as a man's hand, skittered along the perimeter back and forth, acting as lookouts.

"Holy shit!" William exclaimed, realizing too late that he should've kept silent. Immediately, a collective hiss filled the hallway as the large mass charged toward the men.

"Go back!" he shouted as they ran away from the skittering monstrosity.

When they turned the corner, they found their way blocked by an advancing horde of undead. A score of mangled dogs and cats shifted and loped on broken bodies toward them. As they stood for a second, contemplating a way out, the spider-mass came into view. They were blocked in.

William looked at Silas, "Get ready."

He held the grenades, one in each hand, and pulled the pins out with his teeth, spitting the metal rings on the floor as Silas watched curiously. Then he waited for a few seconds as the two threats converged on them from each side. When they were close enough, he threw the grenades away from him, each one landing squarely in the middle of its target. "Get down!" he yelled as he threw himself at Silas with enough force to propel them through the door of the dressing room behind them.

***

Jeron felt the ground shake a second before he heard the explosion and immediately switched the feed so he could look through the beast's eyes once more. He was disappointed when he found that the primate head had become lifeless, forcing him to switch to Clause to get a first-person view. He had started to sense the resistance in Clause's brain to the influence of the behavioral chip he had installed, something he hadn't counted on. It didn't happen when he was looking through the eyes of the other creatures, only through Clause's eyes himself. *It must be the direct connection to his optic nerve that's causing the conflict.* In the future, he would try to limit this direct contact, at least until he could bring him in and have Ashton do a little fine-tuning.

He watched intensely as the beast sped through the building, bounding after a man wearing a green uniform. When the man exited through a door and the beast followed, Jeron suddenly realized that he was leading Clause away from this building, making him vulnerable. His only hope was the arachnids, although he feared the explosion was directed toward them.

He looked down at Paul's body lying on the floor and suddenly wished he hadn't killed the man. The likelihood of Silas and the human finding him was slim, even so, if he had something to bargain with just in case, he'd feel a lot better about the current situation.

His only choice was to bring the beast back to him.

***

The noise from the blast left a loud ringing in both men's ears as they struggled to their knees. "Are you okay?" William asked Silas.

Silas nodded, taking a moment to catch his breath.

After a minute, they both inched their way toward the doorway. Holding their weapons tight, they jumped into the hall, standing back-to-back, ready to fire at anything that moved. To their relief, only a handful of spiders skittered across the floor toward them, remnants of the unholy mass still trying to carry out their last command. With a series of loud stomps, the men squashed them underfoot.

As they looked around, they realized they had another

problem. The hallway was blocked with rubble in both directions. "I guess I didn't think that through very well," William said.

Silas chuckled, "You did well, my friend. There was no other choice."

"Yeah, but how do we get out of here?"

Silas looked around for a moment and then went back into the dressing room. He set the stream of his blaster to a very fine beam and aimed at the left wall. Holding his hand on the trigger, he worked the stream like a laser, cutting a hole in the wall big enough for them to step through.

"Impressive," William said.

"It's effective, but it takes a lot of energy. One more use and it'll be rendered useless."

"Then switch and use mine. At least then we'll have a few shots left afterward for whatever we meet next."

Silas nodded, and they exchanged weapons. They stepped through the opening into the adjacent dressing room and he repeated the process. This time, the opening led to the hallway the spider-mass had guarded. Although the thick tangle of webs was still present, the creatures that had created it were gone.

The webbing was thinnest at the base of the wall, giving them just enough room to crawl slowly underneath the obstacle without getting completely tangled up. It was still a struggle to push forward, the thick silky strands sticking to parts of their bodies that shouldn't have been touched, but finally, they cleared the web of horrors and found themselves standing outside a room with a placard above the doorway that read 'Authorized Personnel Only'. That the door had been wrenched off its hinges told them they were at the right place. There was only one thing that could've done that.

William crouched down and slowly leaned forward to get

a glimpse inside the room. While he couldn't see far enough inside to tell if Jeron was there, the dead body of one of the park employees laying near the doorway suggested so. He listened closely for signs of life inside and thought he heard a voice mumbling to himself, but he couldn't be sure. He said a small prayer for the boy before he retreated.

"I think he's still in there," William whispered to Silas.

Silas replied, "Let me go in first. I know him best. Maybe I can persuade him to give up this madness?"

William knew better. There was no reasoning with the insane, a lesson he had learned too late. But he agreed to let Silas go first. "Just be ready."

"I'll do what I must," Silas replied.

I don't doubt that my friend, William thought.

They slowly worked their way into the data center, stepping carefully over the body, until they spotted Jeron hunkered down in the corner in front of a portable workstation, typing fervently at a small keyboard. He was so distracted by the screen in front of him, that he didn't notice the two men sneaking up on him until it was too late.

"Take your hands off the keyboard, Jeron," Silas said.

Jeron was stunned as he looked up and found himself staring into the barrel of Silas' blaster. "Silas!" he stammered. "I'm so glad you're here. You're just in time to help me stop this."

"Don't lie to me, Jeron. We know you're the one behind everything."

"You have it all wrong, Silas. I swear."

"Then what about the dead body on the floor?" William asked.

Jeron craned his neck to the side, glancing at Paul's body. "He was already here?" he suggested.

William and Silas frowned at him.

"Okay, you win," Jeron said. "Yes, it was me. I set this whole cyclone of destruction in motion. Isn't it beautiful?"

"Why?" Silas asked.

"For my uncle, for science, for the natural order of things. And why should you care? You're not part of this world, and you never will be. In fact, for you, my friend, it'll all be over in a matter of minutes."

When Jeron made a move toward the keyboard, William blasted the workstation, sending a shower of sparks into the air. A crackling and hissing followed, signaling the death of the machine.

"Do you know what you've just done?" Jeron exclaimed.

"I put an end to your insane plan," William replied.

"No. You just released the beast from my command. Now no one will be able to stop it."

"We'll see about that."

Anger quickly turned to rage on Jeron's face and he reached for the blaster perched atop his knees. But before he could get a shot off, Silas put a blaster hole through his chest.

"I told you I would do what was necessary," Silas said.

Chapter 50

Guerera ran toward Fisher's body as she watched the Clause-thing enter the theater. For a brief second, she thought she might be able to revive him, but his skull was crushed beyond recognition. She tried to stifle her cries but couldn't. Fisher was the closest thing to a brother she had ever had.

Mishka came up behind her and put her hand on Guerera's shoulder. "He meant a lot to you, didn't he?"

Guerera nodded slowly as she fought to gain control of herself.

"Then let's honor his death by destroying the beast and stopping this madness," Mishka said as she squeezed Guerera's shoulder. "Just know that I am here for you, Guerera, for anything you need."

Guerera reached up and grabbed Mishka's hand, squeezing it tight for a second as she looked up at Mishka and immediately got lost in her eyes. She quickly shook the feeling from her mind and jumped up, wiping her eyes with the back of her hands. "Before we go after Clause, I want to check out the downed helicopter back there."

"Whatever you want," Mishka said before she turned and walked back to the cycle.

Guerera watched her walk away, thinking that she might've found something special in this savage apocalypse.

***

Silas pressed the back of his neck to activate his communicator, "Mishka, are you there?"

Mishka answered a moment later, "I'm here, Silas."

"We found Jeron. It appears he was using a behavioral modification program linked directly to the beast through a cerebral chip. The controls are destroyed."

"And what about Jeron?"

"He's dead."

"Good. He got what he deserved, just like his uncle."

Silas was silent for a moment, turning away from Jeron's dead eyes staring up at him. "Where are you now?"

Mishka replied, "We're at the downed human flying transport."

"The beast was last seen heading toward the attraction located behind the theater complex. We believe he's the one controlling all the other creatures."

Mishka simply replied, "On our way," and cut the transmission off.

After the communication went silent, Silas gathered Jeron's broken device, while William grabbed Jeron's blaster.

"What are you going to do with that?" William asked.

Silas replied, "We can't leave it for anyone to find. I'll destroy it after all of this is over."

William stepped out into the hall, looking both ways, before motioning to Silas that the coast was clear. Then they ran as fast as they could toward the rear of the building, shooting anything that had more than two legs and moved.

As they exited the building, they heard a roar coming from

inside Space Mountain, the sound drowning out all the other sounds of a world gone mad around them—people screaming, the undead howling, explosions tearing through the park—none were as chilling, as Clause seemed to be channeling his inner gorilla and exerted a cry that shouldn't be possible from a human mouth. But Clause wasn't human anymore.

Chaos was everywhere as they raced toward the park's fabled attraction. The smoke in the air became thicker with every passing second, working in connection with the undead all around them to choke the remaining life from their bodies.

They wound their way up the stairs at a frantic pace, intent on stopping the beast, until they reached the top platform that led to the main attraction. Immediately across from them, near the far edge, Clause stood there holding Sam's limp body. One arm was clenched around his leg, the other on his arm, while his remaining tentacle wrapped tightly around his throat. He smiled at William and Silas, a wicked grin that stretched across his whole face, and then he pulled in each direction at once, yanking the arm, leg, and head from Sam's body simultaneously. The bloody stump and appendages landed on the ground near them with a wet splat.

***

"Silas, are you there?" Mishka said through her communicator.

She began to worry when the other end was silent for a moment, but then Silas spoke up, "Yes, I'm here."

"Do you see the beast?"

"I'm looking right at him."

"Where are you?"

"We're at the top of the ride called Space Mountain."

Mishka looked at Guerera, "We'll never make it up there in time."

"Leave that to me," Guerera replied as she slid from the back of the cycle and unslung the rocket launcher from over her shoulder. She knew she only had one shot at this as she quickly loaded the SMAW.

She yelled at the top of her lungs, "Clause! I'm here if you want me!"

At first, nothing. Then a chorus of howls went up in all directions, followed by the tempest of buzzing in her ears closing in on them. She stood there still and focused, using every ounce of military training to remain fixed on her objective: kill the monster, once and for all.

Mishka stood next to her firing at the animals that rushed at them from every angle. "This beast needs to show itself, soon, or we're going to be overrun!"

Then Guerera saw him. With a powerful leap, it jumped from the roof of the attraction, landed halfway down on the side of the structure, and then leaped off once more to land on the pavement with a resounding force that shook the ground. The look in his eyes was more than hatred, holding a deep level of animal savagery inside, reflecting how much the animal had taken hold of Clause's soul. He gave out a loud roar once more and leaped toward her.

Guerera saw a blur of shapes rushing toward her on her periphery, then felt the first stings and bites from the insects as the swarm reached them. Still, she held firm, refusing to even flinch. She would die if she needed to, as long as she took Clause with her.

In a matter of seconds, Clause had closed the gap between them. Guerera's finger stiffened around the trigger of the heavy weapon perched on her shoulder. *Come on, you bastard. One more second. Just a little closer.*

Her eyes became blurry, both from the smoke and ash clotting the sky and the intense pain of the insect assault. Still, she resisted the attack, fighting with every ounce of strength she had. And then she pulled the trigger and let the rocket fly.

She watched as Clause tried to leap out of the way at the last moment, but the rocket caught him squarely in the chest, exploding his hell-spawned body into a million tiny fragments.

Immediately, the insect attack stopped, as the whole swarm plummeted to the ground, landing amidst the rest of the fallen animals. It was over.

Guerera dropped the SMAW to the ground and turned toward Mishka, "I don't feel so good."

Mishka held her tight as she kneeled down, cradling her in her arms. She brushed Guerera's hair from her forehead and kissed her lips gently, "You really are one bad-ass motherfucker."

Guerera returned the kiss and smiled weakly, "You got that right."

Then she closed her eyes.

Chapter 51

As Ridley lay bent over Aldin's body, with tears streaming down her face, she suddenly heard a tremendous explosion nearby, seconds before the air went still. She looked up and saw all around them that the animals were still, nothing more than rotting corpses dotting the landscape in all directions. Somehow, it was over, yet with Aldin gone, the thrill of victory was meaningless. She felt empty.

"Are the younglings safe?" she suddenly heard Aldin sputter.

Ridley looked down at Aldin and immediately began to cry even harder. Then she pulled back and punched Aldin lightly in the shoulder, "Don't you ever do that to me again!"

"Ow!" Aldin said, rubbing her shoulder with her other hand. Then she tried to sit up and immediately regretted it when a sharp pain wracked through her side.

"Don't try to get up," Ridley said.

"What happened?"

"You saved us from the monsters," Ashley said.

She saw Melinda sitting across from her with the three children holding onto her tightly.

"Thank you," Melinda said.

Aldin craned her neck around as best as she could and was confused when she saw the dead animals scattered around. "Is it over?"

Ridley nodded, "I think so."

"Ridley? Are you there?" Mishka's voice said through her communicator.

Ridley pressed the back of her neck and replied, "I'm here, Mishka."

"I need your help. Guerera is injured."

"Where are you?"

"We're in front of the attraction called Space Mountain. She was directly attacked by the swarm."

Ridley looked at Aldin, "Guerera needs my help. She was attacked by the swarm of insects and is in bad shape."

"Go," Aldin said. "You saved me, now go save her. It's what you do."

Ridley looked torn for a second. Then Melinda said, "We'll be fine. I'll keep an eye on her."

Ridley gave Aldin a quick kiss and sped away on her cycle a second later.

***

"Stay with me, Guerera. Help is coming," Mishka said.

Guerera's face had turned a pale shade of yellow, with patches of deep red, and her breathing was short and raspy, as the various venom and toxins worked their way through her system. Numerous boils had surfaced on her face and arms.

Guerera struggled to speak, "If I don't make it, take care of Ashley for me."

Mishka's lips quivered as she watched Guerera suffer in her arms, "Don't talk like that. Help is on the way. We'll make you good as new. You'll see."

"I like you, Mishka. You're okay in my book."

Guerera's eyes suddenly opened wide as she struggled to breathe, the fear of death close and real.

"Stay with me, Guerera! You're not getting away from me that easy!" Mishka bent down and placed her mouth over Guerera's, desperate to breathe life back into her.

Ridley brought her cycle to a screeching halt in front of them and jumped off. She rushed forward, carrying the emergency kit she had secured from the transport. She threw the box to the ground next to them and pulled out a large strange-looking inhaler with two cylinders secured to the top, one filled with a purple liquid and the other a silver swirling gas.

After jamming the end of the apparatus between Guerera's lips, she pressed a button on the side and watched anxiously as the gas mixed with the liquid before escaping into Guerera's mouth. Then they waited.

Moments later, William and Silas came rushing excitedly from the entrance to Space Mountain, cheering and waving toward them. Their expressions immediately turned grim when they saw Guerera lying lifelessly in Mishka's lap.

"Is she—?" William began to ask, but not finding the courage to finish his question.

Ridley looked at him solemnly, "I've done everything I can right now. We just have to wait and hope for the best. She took in an enormous amount of toxins all at once. Luckily, she's strong."

"I've never seen anyone so brave," Mishka said softly.

"You have no idea," William said. "This woman will go to hell and back for those she loves."

Mishka brushed her fingers through Guerera's hair as feelings she hadn't felt before surged through her. She was beginning to understand the bond that Ridley and Aldin shared, and hoped she'd have the chance to experience the same.

They all watched anxiously as Guerera's breathing slowly steadied and the color returned to her skin. A moment later, her eyes fluttered open.

Guerera looked up at Mishka and smiled weakly, once again getting lost in her eyes. This time, she surrendered and let herself be drawn in and felt her soul floating in a sea of tranquility. "Is it over?" she asked softly.

"Yes, my love," Mishka replied. "It's over."

Guerera smiled again. Before, any mention of that word would've sent her scurrying for cover. This time was different. She didn't know why. She didn't care. It just felt right.

After a few minutes, she found the strength to sit up. Her skin burned and itched all over her body, but she was alive and that's what mattered. She would heal soon enough.

As Mishka helped Guerera stand, Ridley asked, "Can you walk? We need to get back to Aldin. She was injured protecting the younglings and I need to check on her."

Guerera nodded as Mishka helped her take a couple of staggering steps before her footing steadied and she was able to move on her own. Even so, Mishka kept an arm around her waist for good measure.

Chapter 52

Although the smell of rotted flesh baking in the sweltering California heat burned their nostrils, causing each of them to force down the urge to vomit, while the thick ash and smoke hanging in the air stung their eyes, they found a little solace in the fact that darkness had overtaken the daylight as they trekked back toward the cargo ship. At least they wouldn't have to see the carnage first-hand.

Melinda held onto William's hand tightly, afraid to let go. She had almost lost him twice now in a matter of weeks. She vowed not to let him go again. "I'm glad you're okay," she said quietly.

"Yeah," Tommy said as he walked alongside. "I'm glad you didn't die. That would've meant I'd have to take care of everyone. I'm not quite ready for that."

William chuckled, "Don't worry, I'm not planning on going anywhere for a while."

"Good," Kate said. "Cause Tommy's not 'bout to be the boss of me."

Then William grew somber and said softly to Melinda, "Fisher's dead."

Melinda was shocked, "What? How?"

"Clause, or the creature that Clause had become, killed him when he and another Marine saved Silas and me outside the theater."

Guerera was walking with Mishka and Ashley beside them and said sadly, "Jackson's dead too."

Mishka wrapped her arm around Guerera's waist and held her tight, hoping to comfort her. When she felt Guerera lean into her, she felt a warmness flow through her that she hadn't felt before.

"When did this happen?" Melinda asked.

Guerera just shrugged. "It's kind of a work in progress, I guess," she said with a sheepish smile on her face.

As they approached the ship, Silas pressed a button on his wrist and the rear hatch opened up. The group ushered in slowly, not caring if any outsiders saw them. It wasn't lost on any of them how up close and personal death had walked amongst them, and how miraculous it was that they were still alive.

A collective sigh echoed through the cabin as each one collapsed onto the floor in an exhausted heap. No one spoke for a long time. Even Kate, who was normally a chatterbox, kept quiet as she sought comfort in the arms of her mother.

"What now?" Guerera finally asked.

"I guess we find a place to settle in and then try to assimilate into this world as best as we can," Silas said.

"I think I can help with that," William said. "We have a rental property in North Indio that is vacant at the moment. It's nothing fancy, but it's a place you could call home for now, if you want?"

Home. Aldin cringed at the mention of the word. She supposed that she would forever be haunted by the memories of her planet and all the souls that were lost. But maybe, with time, the pain would lessen somewhat and she would feel like she deserved to live once again.

Silas took a moment to survey the rest of his group and then said, "We would be honored."

William dug into his front pants pocket, suddenly remembering that his phone had been buzzing incessantly while they were fighting for their lives and he hadn't been able to answer it. His heart dropped as he read the text from Patrick, then he showed the screen to Silas, "It looks like this isn't over yet."

chapter 53

Hector leaned against the stolen van, pressing a trembling hand to his side where the claws of one of the undead beasts had torn through his flesh. Warm blood seeped between his fingers, sticky and thick, but he barely felt the pain anymore. His gaze swept over the wreckage of Disneyland—what was left of it. Flames flickered in the distance, casting eerie shadows over the twisted remains of the park. The air reeked of charred wood, burned flesh, and something worse— something foul and unnatural. The battlefield had no victors. Only survivors.

His stomach twisted as flashes of the past few hours flooded his mind—Luis's body crumpling to the ground, Benny's screams as something dragged him into the dark, Rico firing wildly before the swarm overtook him. The sound of their voices still rang in his ears, ghostly echoes that refused to fade. They never stood a chance. None of them did.

Chuy sat on the hood of the van, his usual cocky grin wiped clean from his face. He rolled an unlit cigarette between his fingers, his faraway stare fixed on nothing. The silence between them stretched, heavy with everything they'd lost.

"Shit," Chuy muttered, shaking his head. "This ain't what we signed up for, man."

Hector exhaled sharply, dragging a hand through his blood-matted hair. "Yeah? What the hell did we sign up for, then?"

Chuy scoffed, tapping the cigarette against his knee. "Survival. Ain't that what Jeron promised?" He spat onto the cracked pavement, his voice laced with bitterness. "Motherfucker lied."

Hector let out a hollow laugh. "Doesn't matter now. Jeron's probably dead." But even as he said it, unease coiled in his gut. Dead or not, Jeron wasn't the real problem. He was just a pawn in whatever twisted game they'd been caught in. And if Jeron was gone, that meant someone else was still out there, pulling the strings.

Before he could dwell on it, a voice cut through the night.

"What did you just say?"

Hector snapped to attention, his pulse spiking. Instinct took over, his hand reaching for a weapon that wasn't there.

A group of figures emerged from the shadows, limping, bloodied, but standing. They were hardened survivors, like him, but there was something different about them—something that sent a chill through his bones.

At the front was a tall man with sharp blue eyes and a cop's stance, his hand hovering near his hip, ready to draw. Beside him, a woman moved with the rigid discipline of a soldier, her gaze raking over them like she was sizing them up for a fight.

But it was the ones behind them that set Hector on edge.

Tall. Sharp-eyed. Moving with an eerie calm that didn't belong in a war zone. They weren't soldiers. They weren't cops. They weren't like anyone Hector had ever seen—except for Jeron.

And at the center of them stood the tallest one, his piercing green eyes locking onto Hector like a predator scenting blood.

"You mentioned Jeron," Silas said, his voice measured but laced with quiet menace. "Tell me what you know."

Hector's gut twisted. He exchanged a glance with Chuy before folding his arms. "Who the hell are you?"

The cop-looking guy stepped forward. "William Patterson. La Quinta Police Department." His tone was all business. "And I don't like it when people dodge questions."

Hector scoffed. "La Quinta? Man, you a little far from your turf."

William's jaw tightened. "After what I just went through tonight, you don't wanna push me."

Silas stepped closer. His presence alone made Hector's skin crawl. "Jeron is indeed dead," he said, voice cold as steel. "But he wasn't working alone."

Hector hesitated, flashes of memory surfacing—the crates, the quiet way Vogel and Kafka had pulled strings at AMES, how security barely blinked as they let them through.

"Two people," he admitted finally. "Scientists, I think. A man and a woman. Vogel and Kafka."

William and Silas exchanged a dark glance.

"And where did you take the cargo?" Silas pressed.

Hector exhaled. "Here. Disneyland. After hours. Behind the Haunted Mansion."

Guerera cursed under her breath.

Chuy let out a bitter laugh. "And then shit goes sideways, Jeron gets wasted, and we get left for dead."

Silas's expression darkened. "And you didn't think to ask what was in those crates?"

Hector snorted. "I ain't stupid. I knew it was bad. But

when you're getting paid, and when a guy like Jeron tells you not to ask questions?" He shrugged. "You don't ask questions."

William stepped closer, his gaze sharp. "And now you know exactly what you helped bring here."

Hector held his stare. He didn't flinch. "Yeah. But this shit ain't all on us. He forced us to do it."

Silas frowned. "What do you mean?"

Chuy spoke up. "He did this Jedi mind trick shit and nearly made Hector's head explode if he didn't follow orders."

William shot Silas a look—one of wary understanding. Then, for the first time, he really saw the gemstone embedded in Silas's forehead, the full scope of what kind of man he was standing beside.

Silas sighed, his expression unreadable. "My best guess? Jeron created a Neural Oscillation Disruptor. Similar to the Psycho-Kinetic Modulator embedded in my forehead to amplify my own abilities, but designed to target the thought-waves of a nearby target and subjugate them."

Silence. Everyone just stared.

Aldin crossed her arms. "He means it was a weapon that attacked a person's brain through imperceptible sound waves."

Hector shook his head, his voice quiet but firm. "Look, whatever it was, it nearly killed me. Like I said, we had no choice. Either I did what he said, or my brain turned to mush inside my skull."

William studied him carefully, weighing his words. He knew one thing for certain—Ashton Brown was still out there. And until they found him, this nightmare was far from over.

"I need you to tell me everything you know, from the

beginning. Every single detail."

Hector hesitated, defiance flickering in his tired eyes. "Look, man, I just wanna go home. I didn't ask for this shit."

William's stare was unyielding. "Tell me what you know, and maybe you can go free."

With a heavy sigh, Hector began to recount everything—Jeron on the ridge, the loading dock at AMES, the containment units, and then how it all went to hell.

"Besides Vogel and Kafka, did you have contact with anyone else?" William asked.

Hector shook his head. "No, it was just Jeron and those two. But I got the feeling someone else was pulling the strings. Didn't even dream of asking. I knew better."

Chuy let out a slow, wary breath. "That's all we know, man. You got what you wanted. We done?"

William studied them, then gave a reluctant nod. "Yeah. You're done."

Hector exhaled in relief—until William added something that made his stomach twist.

"But if you think of anything else, you contact the La Quinta Police Department. Because until we put this nightmare to rest... there's always a chance it's still out there."

Chapter 54

Ashton felt like a proud father as he leaned forward, his eyes glued to the screen. The flickering feed displayed his creation's viewpoint, watching through Clause's monstrous eyes as he wrapped his massive, sinewy fingers around the Marine's throat. The soldier's boots kicked and scraped against the ground, his muffled screams turning into sickening, wet gasps. The beast's grip tightened. Bones snapped like dry twigs. Then, silence.

A wicked smile crept across Ashton's face. Clause had just taken another life. The masterpiece was performing exactly as he had envisioned—feral, unrelenting, unstoppable. The lifeless body crumpled to the ground, landing with a sickening *thud*. Blood pooled beneath it, soaking into the cracks of the pavement like ink bleeding through paper. Clause's chest heaved with primal fury, his grotesque frame trembling with unbridled rage.

"Magnificent," Ashton murmured, his fingers twitching against the desk.

His exhilaration only grew as he watched Clause charge after the three men fleeing into a nearby building. He could practically taste their fear, the delicious panic that sent them scurrying like vermin. He leaned in closer, anticipating the carnage that would soon unfold.

But then something shifted. Instead of destroying them all, Clause was chasing just one of them , while the others disappeared into the building. Ashton's smirk faltered.

"What are you doing?" he hissed under his breath.

Clause lumbered after the lone Marine, following him up stairwell after stairwell, hallway after hallway, a relentless force of nature that could not be stopped. But something was wrong. The Marine wasn't just running—he was *leading* Clause, keeping just enough distance to lure him further into the labyrinth.

Ashton's fingers tightened into fists. *Intelligence never was one of your strong suits, was it, Clause?*

Then—*static.*

The screen flickered once. Then twice. And then, nothing. A blank, black void where his masterpiece once was.

Ashton's breath caught. His fingers flew over the controls, trying to re-establish the feed. He switched to different camera angles, rewired the signal manually, bypassed the encryption sequences—*nothing.*

"No, no, no," he muttered, his calm exterior cracking. His jaw clenched, the vein in his temple throbbing as his pulse quickened.

He snatched his phone and called Jeron. Straight to voicemail. His lips curled back in fury.

"Damn it, Jeron, answer me!"

Only silence.

Then, an insidious thought slithered into his mind. One he didn't want to entertain. *What if… they've destroyed the Queen yet again?*

The possibility sent his thoughts spiraling. If the Queen was dead—if those same insufferable fools who stopped the first outbreak had managed to do it again—everything was undone. The cycle, the infection, the transformation—it would all be for nothing.

His heartbeat thundered in his ears. He needed a failsafe. He needed a solution.

His grip on the phone tightened as he pivoted sharply.

"Kafka! Vogel!" His voice lashed through the control room like a whip.

The two scientists practically ran to his workstation, their lab coats swaying with the force of their movement. They knew better than to keep him waiting, especially when his temper was razor-thin.

Ashton's eyes were wild, gleaming with something dark and feverish. "Start the Andromeda program."

The room fell into a stunned silence.

Kafka's lips parted slightly, her throat tightening. "Are you sure you want to do this?" she asked cautiously.

Ashton's gaze snapped to her like a predator locking onto prey. "We have no other choice."

"But sir," Vogel interjected, adjusting his glasses with shaky fingers. "There's no turning back once the process has begun. If we initiate Andromeda now, we—"

"I *know* the consequences, Vogel," Ashton snapped, his patience shredding. "Do it. *Now!*"

The two scientists exchanged uneasy glances, but neither dared argue. With stiff nods, they turned and hurried toward the lab's main terminal.

Ashton exhaled sharply, trying to rein in his frustration as he pulled out his phone once more. This time, Darcy answered immediately.

"We've begun preparations to implement the Andromeda program," he informed her.

A sharp intake of breath on the other end. Then a pause.

"Isn't there another way?" Her voice was softer than usual, laced with something dangerously close to doubt.

Ashton's grip on the phone tightened. "I'm afraid not," he said, forcing his voice back to its calculated coldness. "Somehow, our plan has failed *yet again*, and I suspect the same group of idiots is responsible. Although it's a setback, this will assure our ultimate success."

Darcy didn't respond immediately. He could hear her breathing, steady but hesitant.

Finally, she exhaled. "…I won't let you down, Daddy."

"I know you won't," Ashton said, his lips curling into a smirk.

He ended the call and turned back to the screen, watching as Kafka and Vogel entered the final authorization codes.

On the monitor before him, the words blinked in large, crimson letters: ANDROMEDA PROGRAM INITIALIZED.

A slow grin spread across Ashton's face. The game wasn't over. Not yet. The virus had evolved once before, and now, with the Andromeda Initiative in motion, it was about to take its final, most *glorious* step forward.

And when the world realized what was coming for them, it would already be too late.

Chapter 55

William stared at the blank wall in front of him for a long moment. *I'm missing something. I know it!*

Silas stood beside him, silent as he watched the man work through the problem in his mind. Alongside them, a dozen officers, led by an FBI agent named Mack—an older man with a long scar down the side of his cheek—stood ready. Nearby, a small group of NASA officials watched anxiously, some nervous, while others were visibly impatient.

"Come on, William," Mack said. "I've given you the benefit of the doubt because of our history together. But enough is enough. If we don't come up with something soon, I'll be forced to call off this wild goose chase."

The officials close-by nodded their agreement, giving William a collective stare.

William shrugged off their contempt and focused on the task at hand. He had to find the way in. *It's here somewhere!*

He turned and walked back toward the elevator, retracing the steps that Ashton would've certainly taken to get there. Then something caught his eye. It was the tiniest of details, but it was there—a small smudge mark at the base of the light sconce hanging directly across the large, vacant wall.

After studying the fixture for a moment, he found a small cover that slid over to reveal a keyhole. He fished a small knife from his pocket and opened up the screwdriver blade.

"What in the blazes do you think you're doing?" one of the officials exclaimed. The man was tall and thin, with a whisper of a face.

"I'm doing my job," William said, as he began to unscrew the bolts holding the fixture to the wall.

"Listen, I don't care who you are or what kind of outrageous accusations you've made, but this is a government facility, and as acting Deputy Director, I will not have you—"

William ignored the man and continued disassembling the light fixture. As he pulled it away from the wall, he saw that there were two sets of wires attached. He ignored the common and black wires and concentrated on the loom of wires entwined around them. After ripping the pigtail out of the socket attached to the hidden lock, he twisted various ones together to try to 'hot-wire' them. A few seconds later, he heard a low rumble before the wall behind him opened up.

"Well, I'll be damned," Mack said, while the NASA officials stood there with looks of disbelief and embarrassment on their faces.

William walked to the front of the group of officers with a sly, smug on his face. "Don't get cocky," Mack said.

"You should know better than to doubt me, Mack," William replied.

Mack chuckled, "Fair enough."

Both men pulled their guns out and advanced slowly down the long hallway, with the rest of the officers following close behind in a S.W.A.T. formation. The group of officials hung back near the secret entrance, waiting apprehensively.

After finding the side rooms empty of anything other than computer equipment, they made their way to the end of the hall, where they were met with an impenetrable solid door and a security panel on the wall next to it.

"He's in there," William said. "I can feel it."

He turned to Mack, "What do you think? Can we blow it?"

Mack studied the panel for a moment. "I don't think so. It would likely make the door completely inoperable. Not only that, but it could bring the whole place down around us."

William's desperation was becoming visible as he stood there searching his brain for a solution. He was too close to fail now.

He turned to Silas with a questioning look in his eyes.

Silas nodded and walked up to the panel. He placed his hand on the panel and closed his eyes. The yellow gem in his forehead began to glow for a second and then faded. He opened his eyes and withdrew a small gadget from his pocket that at first resembled a cell phone. When the screen lit up, he pressed a series of commands, and an array of metal prongs extended from the top. After pressing the prongs into the bottom of the security panel, a soft click was heard a second before the door opened.

Mack looked at Silas for a second and then over at William, "Do I even want to know?"

"Probably not," William replied.

The heavy steel doors groaned as they slid open, revealing the cold sterility of Ashton's hidden laboratory. William and Silas stepped inside cautiously, weapons drawn, scanning the dimly lit room for any sign of movement. The air was thick with the scent of antiseptic and old machinery, but beneath it, there was something else—a faint, almost organic musk, like something had been living in the shadows for far too long.

Rows of cylindrical containment chambers lined the far

wall, their surfaces coated in frost, illuminated only by the dull red glow of flickering status lights. Most were empty, their glass panels shattered or dark. But one remained intact.

The hissing of relief valves and the whining of gears straining created a foreboding atmosphere as they entered the mad scientist's lab. The air was thick and stale, with a distinct chemical smell that assaulted their nostrils. Then, motion sensors brought the room to life as a series of bright lights switched on throughout the large expanse, illuminating the horrors within and bringing a collective gasp from the lips of everyone there.

The perimeter of the lab was filled with partially dissected carcasses splayed out on tables—an assortment of domestic and wild animals, each with rotted flesh that had disintegrated away from the bone. A series of shelves nearby held numerous glass jars filled with appendages floating in a thick, viscous liquid. But what really made their skin crawl was the head-less body lying on another table. Numerous bullet holes riddled the man's chest, and William immediately knew he was looking at Clause's remains.

How in the hell did he bring this bastard back to life? And then put his head in the middle of a fucking gorilla? William thought. Then he glanced at Silas, who was studying each subject carefully. He thought about the spaceship that had brought him and his group from a distant galaxy to this planet. All the technological wonders that William had seen were mere commonplace in their world. He supposed it wasn't out of the realm of possibility that they had discovered a way to cheat death. Or at least those among them that were morally corrupt had.

One of the officers called out, "You might want to check this out, Mack."

Mack stepped away from the glass jars he was examining

and walked toward the center of the lab, with William close behind. Their horror was amplified exponentially when they saw the large tubular units spread out across the main area, each one containing a human body in a state of suspended animation.

"Oh my god!" William exclaimed as he rushed over to one of the units trembling. "That's Captain Harrison! What the fuck was he planning on doing with these people?"

At the same moment, the Deputy Director let out a loud gasp as he joined the rest of the group near the front of the closest containment unit. "Ashton! Why?"

Inside it, Ashton Brown stood motionless. Preserved like a fossil in an amber tomb, his lifeless gaze was frozen in time, a man who had built an empire of nightmares and then chosen to become one with them.

Suspended in cryogenic stasis, his face was eerily serene, as if he were merely sleeping through the apocalypse he tried to create. His body was hooked up to a complex web of cables and intravenous lines, feeding him something William had no interest in identifying. The chamber's monitor pulsed steadily, reading out vital signs that were far too strong for a man who should be as good as dead.

"I guess instead of getting caught," Mack said, "he figured he'd off himself. Better to end it yourself than have someone else pull the trigger, I reckon. At least it's over now. He can't hurt anyone else."

As the words left Mack's mouth, William had a little stab of doubt stinging at the back corner of his mind. *I hope you're right.*

Silas, meanwhile, was focused on the data terminal beside the chamber, scrolling through lines of encrypted code. Then he froze. His fingers hovered over the keyboard.

"William," he murmured. "There's something else here."

William moved beside him, peering at the screen. The files labeled ANDROMEDA INITIATIVE sent a chill through him, but that wasn't what had caught Silas's attention.

A heartbeat monitor was blinking on-screen.

Not Ashton's.

Something else.

A secondary containment unit was still active.

Before either of them could react, the lights flickered. A shrill beep rang from the console, and for a brief moment, the system's status readout changed.

Then, as quickly as it appeared, the system rebooted, the screen went dark, then power to the whole lab went dead. Sparks flew from various pieces of equipment as a self-destruct sequence spread through the system.

Mack frowned. "What the hell was that?"

"It appears as though Ashton had set up a self-destruct sequence to be activated upon his capture," Silas replied.

William shook his head. "Whatever it was, I don't like it."

Something gnawed at the back of his mind, a whisper of doubt too quiet to ignore.

And beneath their feet, in the hidden sublevel that none of them knew existed, a machine stirred to life.

A containment pod hissed open, releasing a cloud of frigid vapor.

Inside, something moved.

A figure—tall, emaciated, yet unmistakably familiar—lifted its head.

The resemblance to Ashton was there, but twisted. His features were grotesquely warped, stretched too tight over elongated limbs, as if his body had been forced to evolve into something beyond human.

And his eyes burned with something far older.

As the entity stepped forward, a soft, synthetic voice

echoed through the chamber, a pre-recorded message meant for one person alone.

"Andromeda Initiative activated.

"Subject awakening.

"The next phase begins."

It smiled.

And in its mind, Ashton's consciousness stirred.

The End

Hellish Preview

Hellish
Book One:
Tortured Souls

By Scott Dokey

Chapter 1

The first one he beheaded was Gadreel.

Belial followed him down to the east bank of the Euphrates, where the current flowed swift and strong. The water was dark and dirty, filled with rotting plants and animals, the whole scene reeking of death and decay. It was a fitting place to find the answers he so desperately sought. If any of his brothers or sisters knew Lucifer's plan, it would be him.

"Gadreel!" he called out as he approached the water's edge. His armor was dented and splattered with blood, not his blood, though. He didn't know whose blood it was. It had dried on his breastplate, staining his armor like a gruesome celestial painting.

Dressed as a commoner, Gadreel's face was that of a man who had lost everything. His skin was pale and withered, as if his will to live had been sucked from him, causing him to shrivel up. He turned to face his brother, a tattered turban covering his head, shocked to hear his name called, and even more shocked to see Belial there. It didn't surprise him to see the angry look on his face, though, and he knew he had to tread carefully. "Belial! I'm surprised to see you. What can I do for you, Brother?"

"You can disperse with the pleasantries, Gadreel. I want answers, and I want them now."

Gadreel measured his words slowly, "I'm afraid I'm at a loss here, Belial. What answers are you looking for?"

Belial's eyes glowed bright red, and his nostrils flared like an angered bull. "Don't play games with me, Gadreel!"

Gadreel didn't know exactly what Belial was talking about, but he had a good guess. "I'm not sure what you believe to know, Brother, but something has clouded your judgment. You're not thinking straight."

"Don't you dare tell me how to think!"

"What I mean is simply that what happened, happened. There's no changing the past. It can't be un-done."

"But I can make those that failed pay!"

"It's not a simple question of failure versus success. We fought long and hard, but in the end, we weren't strong enough."

"That's a lie! We should've crushed them. Our forces were more than enough to win."

"But they weren't, and we didn't."

Belial's smile grew like a crescent moon, and in the light of his eyes all that shone was madness. "It was you! You're the one who betrayed us! I should've known all along you'd be the one to sell us out to earn Father's good grace."

"That's not true, Belial. I was simply stating that we underestimated our opponent and overestimated ourselves. We all paid the price for our short-sightedness. Myself included."

"Liar!" Belial shouted. "You were against our plan from the beginning."

"And yet I fought with you. Why would I stand with you if I were against you? Listen to yourself, Belial. You're not making sense."

His words fell on deaf ears, as Belial's sword was already in his hands. The blood on the blade reeked of violence and stank of death.

Gadreel had one chance left to diffuse the situation. In a last-ditch effort, he turned his back on Belial and walked away. "I won't argue with you anymore, Brother. I've made my peace with Father's decision. I suggest you do the same."

He had hoped those last words would be enough to steel his brother's temper and give him the chance to flee. He should've known better. In Belial's ears, they were simply an arrangement of words, inconsequential sounds without meaning.

"How dare you turn your back on me, coward! Turn and face me!"

"I will not fight you, Belial."

"Then you will die like the traitor you are!"

Belial's blade hissed as it cut through the air, a diagonal slash that would've split Gadreel in two if he hadn't rolled out of the way at the last minute. While he was lucky enough to dodge the first attack, he wasn't fast enough to evade the second.

Belial recovered quickly and spun to his left as he brought his blade around. His eyes narrowed and his lips twisted into a sneer. His blade glinted in the flickering light, its edge sharp as razors as it raked across Gadreel's back, sending him crashing to the ground in agony.

Belial grabbed Gadreel's hair and yanked his head back. "I'm going to give you one last chance, Gadreel. Admit to your deceit and I may let you live."

Gadreel knew what was coming. He saw the look in Belial's eyes; the bloodlust that had taken over. It wouldn't matter what he said at this point. Belial had already made his mind up. And if that was the case, he would die admitting his mistake and hope that his ultimate act of repentance would carry with him to the afterlife.

Gadreel summoned up his last ounce of strength, blood spraying from his mouth as he spoke, "The only thing I will admit to, Brother, is that I made the mistake of following you and Lucifer into battle, and I pray to our Father for his mercy and forgiveness."

Belial's eyes were raging infernos as he brought his sword around in a great arc, which bit through the flesh of Gadreel's neck and sliced his head off.

After Gadreel's body hit the ground with a wet thud, Belial reached down and picked up the severed head of his fallen brother, holding it in front of his face. The look of a man filled with remorse flashed over him for a quick moment as he realized what he had done.

Quickly, though, the eyes of a cold-blooded killer returned to reclaim their ocular residence. "Look what you made me do, Brother! It didn't have to come to this. All you had to do was tell me what I needed to know. But, no, you couldn't do that!"

He pulled his arm back and hurled the bloody head into the churning waters of the river. It splashed and sank, leaving a trail of crimson foam. The rest of the corpse he abandoned on the parched earth to rot and feed the swarming flies—a deserving fate for a coward.

Then he went in search of the others.

Uzziel was the next victim of Belial's wrath. He sat at the foot of the Great Pyramid, gazing at the starry sky with a heavy heart. Sand and dust carried the pungent scent of the ancient lands, of hidden secrets and distant fires, of life and death in endless cycles. He wished he could touch the bright lights that danced above him, and feel their warmth chase away his inner darkness. But before he could reach out, Belial appeared and ended his life in a brutal way, just like he did to his brother.

And after that, Arioch. His siblings had vanished to the edges of the earth, hiding from his fury. But Belial was unstoppable in his hunt, consumed by his need for the truth. He caught up with her after centuries of searching. She had tucked herself deep under the ground, in a bleak cave that no human could ever stumble upon. Belial was not human, though, and he faced her with his eyes ignited like hellfire. When she failed to satisfy his twisted logic, he ended her in a snap.

Haurus had fled to the open water, working as a deckhand on a merchant ship that navigated the Red Sea. He wished to forget the nightmares of the fall. Unfortunately, Belial found him waiting at the port in Elim, where the ship moored. Haurus cried for his life, trying to persuade Belial that he was not the traitor he accused. But Belial had grown deaf to the desperate pleadings of his people long ago. He snuffed him out swiftly.

There were many more after that, with each one ending as the first, leaving Belial more and more desperate for the truth. He was consumed by a burning thirst for answers that nothing could quench. He tried to wring out the secrets from his kin that he knew they were hiding, but they only gave him silence and defiance. He finally surrendered to the cruel reality that he would never know the answers he sought, no matter how much agony he unleashed on his brethren.

As he perched on the summit of the Andes, the highest and most majestic mountain range in the world, he gazed at the crimson snow that stained the pristine white landscape. Another angel had fallen by his hand, another life snuffed out in his quest for the truth.

But then, a sudden revelation struck him like a bolt of lightning. He had been chasing shadows all along, blind to the real answer that lay before him! *It was Lucifer's fault! It had always been Lucifer's fault. He's the one I need to go after!*

And so, he got to work on a plan that would be both his revenge and salvation!

Chapter 2

Phlegethos had no stars to brighten its black sky, only the flickering light of fire that burst out of cracks in the rocky terrain. The air was filled with the roar of flames and the smell of sulfur. The earth shook constantly, as if a giant beast was stirring beneath the surface. Far away, molten lava poured down from jagged mountains, creating dazzling firefalls that devoured everything in their path. This was a realm of fire and fear, where no one could escape the wrath of the inferno, and Belial was both its master and slave.

After a millennium of solitude, he still couldn't forget the bitter taste of defeat, the humiliation of losing a battle he should've won. The images of his enemies' triumph haunted his every waking moment, fueling his fury to a boiling point. He had abandoned his throne of Abriymoch and stormed out to find his allies, determined to make them pay for their failure and extract the truth from their broken bodies.

He had not realized the terrible price of his quest—the infernal bond that chained his soul to his hellish domain. As he wandered the world in search of answers, he felt his vitality draining away. His last fight in the Andes had pushed him to the brink of exhaustion, reducing him to a shadow of his former self. Then, in his darkest hour, he finally understood the truth. With a new resolve, he made his way back to Phlegethos, where he could recover and plot his next move.

The ashen road stretched out before Belial, a winding ribbon of gray that seemed to go on forever. The air was hot and dry, and the only sound was the crunch of Belial's footsteps on the ash.

Belial was deep in thought, lost in his own world, that he didn't notice the figure lurking in the shadows. The figure raised a dagger and hurled it at Belial, striking him in the chest with a loud thwack, causing him to stagger backward.

Belial looked down at the silver dagger protruding from his chest, and his eyes widened in pain. He turned to face his attacker, and saw the hatred in his daughter's eyes.

"Fierna," he said, "what are you doing?"

Fierna's eyes were cold and hard. "I'm doing what I have to do," she said.

"I'm your father," he said. "How could you do this to me?"

"I'm not doing this to you," she said. "I'm doing this for you. You need to be stopped."

Belial reached out to her, but she backed away. "Please," he said. "Don't do this."

"I'm sorry," she said. "But I have to."

She pulled a second dagger from her belt, and Belial closed his eyes, waiting for the inevitable. But the blow never came. Instead, he heard her footsteps walking away. He opened his eyes and saw her disappearing back into the shadows.

Belial slowly pulled the dagger out of his chest. He was wounded, but he was alive. He knew that he had to find Fierna and stop her before she ruined everything. He had to make her understand.

Belial started walking down the ashen road, following the

path that Fierna had taken. He didn't know where she was going, but he had a good idea. He walked for hours, following her trail until he came to the entrance to Naome's Tomb. It was a place both of them frequented when they felt lost, unable to determine their next direction.

The mouth of the tomb beckoned to Belial like a lost friend, and he felt a sliver of sorrow course through him as he walked toward the entrance. Naome had been the only one who understood his torment as he struggled to accept what Fate had thrown at him. Sadly, their daughter didn't share the same understanding.

Belial walked up to the door of the sepulcher and laid his hand on the handle. A soft click resounded, and he pushed it open. An acrid stench greeted him as walked down a long hallway to find Fierna on her knees in front of a large sarcophagus.

She heard his soft footsteps approaching and turned to him. "Father," she said. "What are you doing here?"

"I think we need to talk," Belial said. "I want you to understand where I'm coming from."

Fierna looked at her father for a long time, her eyes studying him coldly. Then she finally softened, allowing him a moment to talk to her as father to daughter, instead of an adversary.

"I know that I haven't been a good father," he said. "I've made mistakes, and I've hurt you. But I want you to know that I love you."

"Then why are you trying to leave me?"

Belial searched his mind for a moment, trying to find the right words to say. How could he tell her he longed to go home again, to be where he truly belonged instead of this hellish landscape? Finally, he just said, "I need to go home."

"This is your home, Father."

"No, this place is a prison. I don't belong here."

"Get over yourself, already," Fierna shot back. "With all the shit you've done in the past, Hell is exactly where you belong."

Belial seethed. "Do not pretend to know me, Fierna, or to understand the reason behind my actions."

"Besides the fact that you're an ego-maniac who couldn't handle losing? Did I get it right?"

Belial's eyes flashed with fury as he drew his sword. "You would do well to remember your place, Daughter!" he roared.

Fierna leaped to her feet, her hair erupting into a living mass of fiery tendrils that hissed and spat molten lava. "You're one to talk!" she cried as she hurled a silver dagger at her father's throat.

Belial parried the dagger with his sword, but the force of the blow knocked him off balance. Fierna took advantage of his momentary weakness and lunged at him, her tendrils of flame wrapping around his body in a burning embrace.

Belial struggled to break free, but Fierna's grip was too strong. He could feel the heat of her flames searing his skin, and he knew that if he didn't do something soon, he would be consumed.

With a roar of rage, Belial drove his sword into the ground, using the hilt to pry Fierna's fiery tentacles off his body. As soon as he was free, he lashed out with his sword, slicing through the tentacles and sending them writhing to the ground.

Fierna staggered back, her eyes wide with pain. "You've gone too far this time, Father," she said, her voice trembling with anger.

Belial ignored her. He turned and looked at the stone coffin that had been cracked open by his sword. Inside, the body of his beloved wife lay, her skin as pale as marble and her eyes closed in eternal sleep.

Belial's heart sank. He had lost control in his rage, and now he had defiled the resting place of the only woman he had loved. He fell to his knees, his head in his hands.

"I'm so sorry," he whispered. "I never meant for this to happen."

Fierna stood over him, her eyes filled with hatred. "You're a monster," she said. "I never want to see you again."

And with that, she turned and walked away, leaving Belial alone.

Belial sat there for a long time, staring at the damage he'd done. He had desecrated Naome's tomb, and for that, he could never forgive himself. He felt lost and alone.

Suddenly, there was a gentle touch on his shoulder. He looked up and saw the spirit of his wife standing before him, her dark hair cascading around her shoulders, and a bright smile on her lips.

Belial's eyes widened in surprise. "Naome?" he whispered. For a long moment, he just stared at her, his heart pounding in his chest.

Soft tears gathered in his eyes as his head dropped to his chest. "Please forgive me, my love. Once again, I let my anger control me."

Naome replied, "I'm not the one you should be asking for forgiveness, Belial."

"She'll never understand me like you do."

"She's more like you than you think. She'll come around."

Belial sighed. "I'm not so sure. You know me better than even myself. What should I do?"

Naome reached out and ran her hand softly against his cheek. "You already know the answer to that. Follow your heart."

"Even if that means leaving you?"

"You know, more than anyone else, that you can never truly leave me. I'll always and forever be a part of you."

Belial reached up and clasped his hand over hers, feeling her soft touch for what he knew would be the last time. "I love you," he said.

"I love you too," she said. And with that, she kissed him gently on the forehead and disappeared.

Belial sat there for a long time. He felt a sense of peace that he hadn't felt in a long time. He knew that he would never be truly alone again, as long as she was with him.

Chapter 3

Abriymoch stood on the rim of a massive volcano that dominated the landscape. It was a dark and twisted structure of basalt, obsidian, and crystal. This was Belial's place of power, where he ruled over his land cruelly but justly. It was here that he felt the strongest, and as he stood on the balcony that jutted from the throne room, looking into the depths of the flowing lava far below, he began to formulate his plan, knowing that prolonged absence from his domain would weaken him, and could ultimately lead to his demise. He quickly shook that thought from his mind. Death was not an option.

As his mind raced, he paced back and forth on the balcony until frustration began to burn like a fire in his chest. Belial roared out in aggravation, slamming his fist against the wall, sending a crack racing through the stone.

Suddenly, there was a flash of light, and a figure appeared in the doorway. A young woman, dressed in black, with long fiery red hair and intense green eyes, stared at him cooly.

Belial turned to face her. "You're either extremely brave or incredibly foolish. Who are you to enter my fortress uninvited?" he asked threateningly.

"Someone who can help you. I'm Circe," the woman said. "I've seen many things in my lifetime; the rise and fall of empires; the birth and death of gods. And I've seen the end of the world."

Belial's eyes widened. "You know about the end of the world?" he asked.

"Yes," Circe replied. "I know all about it. Granted, it's only one possibility, but it's a strong one, guaranteed to succeed if you play your cards right."

Belial was intrigued. "Tell me everything."

Neither of them noticed Fierna watching from the shadows seething with fury.

***

The parched and fissured land of the Shattered Abyss stretched out before them, a vast wasteland of cracked earth and jagged rocks. The only sound, apart from them, was the wind whistling through the empty spaces, and the only movement was the occasional cloud of dust kicked up by that wind.

Circe led Belial across the barren landscape, her boots crunching on the broken ground. Finally, in the distance, a sinister vortex whirled. As they neared the tempest, the surrounding air grew thick with smoke and dust, and the sound of it was like the roar of a thousand demons. Circe walked with Belial towards the vortex, her eyes fixed on the swirling darkness.

Above them, the sky split open. A dazzling web of lightning bolts snaked down, striking all around them. The ground shook and trembled beneath their feet, while the smell of sulfur overwhelmed their nostrils.

As they reached the eye of the vortex, the shadows

swallowed them whole, and they were plunged into darkness. A moment later, they emerged in a hidden cavern deep inside a colossal mountain.

The cavern was lit by a single torch, which cast flickering shadows on the walls. A massive cauldron dominated the cavern, its surface covered in dark bubbles.

Circe's fingers trembled as she clutched the four tiny vials, each containing a unique shade of liquid. Belial's eyes burned with fascination as he watched her carefully pour them into the cauldron. The concoction swirled around and then suddenly erupted in an intense burst of light. The cavern glowed with an eerie brilliance; its walls illuminated in an ominous red hue. Everywhere around them, the darkness seemed to vanish, consumed by the enchanting yet sinister luminescence.

Belial grew cautious. "Why are you helping me?"

Circe looked at him, "Let's just say I've been waiting for a long time to see the world above die."

He studied the witch standing before him, judging her intent, then watched as she pulled a silver dagger from her belt and sliced it across her palm, sending a stream of blood pouring out that splashed into the cauldron, mingling its essence with the bubbling liquid.

Raising her arms above her head, Circe began to chant. Her voice, low and guttural, echoed off the walls of the cavern. The flames in the cauldron grew higher and brighter, and the shadows seemed to dance around them.

Belial felt a strange tingling sensation all over his body. He looked down at his hands, and he saw that they were glowing with a faint blue light. He closed his eyes and concentrated, and he felt a surge of power flow through him. He opened his eyes, and he saw that the cauldron was now filled with a swirling vortex of light.

Circe stopped chanting, and the light from the cauldron began to fade. The shadows in the cavern retreated, and the flames in the cauldron died down. Then Circe was gone, and he was alone in the cavern, standing in front of the cauldron.

He reached out to the cauldron. The surface was cool to the touch, and it felt smooth and polished. He looked down into the cauldron, and saw four vials filled with a swirling silver liquid.

Belial picked up the vials and held them in his hand, watching the liquid dance inside each one as if alive. He thanked Circe silently and smiled, knowing that he was now one step closer to achieving his destiny.

***

There was a distinct spring in his step when Belial returned to Abriymoch, and immediately made his way downward toward it deepest level. He had hope again. Something he thought was forever dead. Now that he had a plan, one so intricate in its design that it was nearly foolproof, there was no way he could lose.

The asylum was a maze of cells, corridors, and torture chambers, where the inmates were subjected to endless agony and madness. Located deep in the bowels of the stronghold, the screams of the damned echoed through the halls, mingling with the laughter of Belial's twisted servants. It was here that Belial kept his most prized possessions: the souls of the most dangerous criminals. The asylum was his place of horror and madness.

Belial walked eagerly into the main office of the sanatorium and pressed a button on the desk that sent a loud buzz resounding through the room. "Nazur, can you come here, please?"

A nasally voice with a thick German accent responded immediately. "Right away, Sire!"

A minute later, a short and skinny creature with a bulbous head and long, jutting nose rushed in. He held a clipboard in one hand, cradling it like it was a prized treasure. "You wanted to see me, Sire?"

Belial unrolled a scroll and placed it on a table nearby. The papyrus contained an intricate drawing of an assortment of complex apparatus, all wired together into a morbid closed-circuit television system. "I need this built as soon as possible."

Nazur studied the plans intensely, scribbling notes onto his clipboard at a fevered pace. After a few minutes, he pulled back. "This is quite an interesting display, Sire. May I ask its purpose?"

Belial replied, "Just tell me whether you can build it or not?"

Nazur looked over his notes carefully, flipping pages back and forth. "Of course, Sire. Who do you want to use as a power supply?"

Belial thought for a long moment. He had a few in mind, but hadn't quite decided yet. He needed someone who embodied evil; someone strong and ruthless. "Elizabeth Bathory," he finally said.

Nazur nodded. "A wise choice, Sire. She should work perfectly."

"I don't want a maybe, Nazur!" Belial snapped. "This must succeed!"

Nazur cringed, "My apologies, Sire. It was merely a slip of the tongue. I assure you everything will work perfectly."

"Good. Then I suggest you get to work."

"Of course, Sire. We'll get started immediately."

Belial's eyes followed Nazur's departing figure, then

darted around the room eagerly, envisioning the events that would soon unfold to make his scheme a reality. A wicked grin stretched across his face. Everything was falling into place.

346

Chapter 4

The dirty tile floor of the neglected classroom was stained with muddy footprints and dried spills. A trash can next to the desk at the back of the room was overflowing with crumpled papers, empty bottles, and rotten food. And a musty smell like dirty mop water hung in the air. Maybe that's why Michael was drawn to this place. It felt like home; a place he belonged—neglected and forgotten. Unfortunately, the meetings also pulled a sense of shame and vulnerability from him he didn't enjoy facing. And, God knows, he didn't like talking in front of other people.

Michael perched on one of the chairs that were arranged in a circle in the middle of the room, feeling exposed and vulnerable. His beat-up leather jacket and ripped jeans blended in with the worn and stained outfits of the others. His knee bounced up and down as he fidgeted with his fingers, picking at the loose skin around his nails—both, habits he had developed over the years to cope with his anxiety. His dark hair was disheveled, and his eyes held a haunted presence in them, as if he had seen things no one should ever see.

As he looked around at the group, he saw himself in the

reflection of those seated near him. Everyone wore the same cursed and tortured look on their faces. No one wanted to be there, yet all of them knew they needed to be. For some of them, it was the only thing keeping them alive.

The silence was broken by the sound of heels clattering on the floor behind them as Dr. Madison finally walked in. She removed her jacket and laid it across the top of the chair at the head of the group before sitting down. She took a moment to remove a writing pad and pen from her purse and then adjusted her glasses, which reflected her sharp eyes.

The girl sitting next to Michael muttered, "It's about fucking time."

Michael gave a soft chuckle. Lexi's dark demeanor matched the black clothes and make-up she wore perfectly. She wasn't afraid to say what was on her mind, and she didn't care who heard it.

If Dr. Madison heard her, she ignored it and started the meeting right off, "Thank you, everyone, for coming out tonight."

A chorus of mumbles rose from a few of those gathered, but most remained quiet.

"Now, who would like to start things off?" the Doctor continued.

Nearly everyone slunk down in their seats like they were back in school trying to avoid being called on by the teacher.

Then the unthinkable happened. She looked straight at Michael and said the words he dreaded to hear. "What about you, Michael? Would you like to share with the group?"

For a brief second, Michael considered running from the room in fear, but then thought better of it. "Not really," he replied.

A frown covered Dr. Madison's face. "We've talked about this, Michael. You can't heal until you open yourself up and confront your fears."

Michael sighed and resigned himself to his fate, "Okay, fine. My name is Michael, and I'm an addict."

The rest of the group responded in unison, "Hello, Michael."

He took a deep breath. "Not sure what to say since most of you know me, except that every day is a struggle. Has been for a long time."

Various members of the group nodded their heads and murmured words of agreement, both offering their support to each other and revealing their own inner demons.

"How about if you share some of those struggles?" Dr. Madison prodded. "Maybe a few of us can relate?"

Michael hesitated, picking at his fingers again as his knee bounced up and down with greater velocity. Then he finally continued, "I guess it was a few years ago. I don't remember the exact moment, but I know the nightmares started and I couldn't shut them out. They were relentless, attacking me every night until I couldn't take it anymore! I became desperate and realized the only way to quiet them was through drugs and alcohol. Even then, though, I could still feel them, waiting for me in the back of my mind."

Michael paused for a few seconds, trying to find the nerve to continue.

"It's okay, Michael. You're with friends here. Take all the time you need."

He looked around the room. Each one's expression cried out that they understood all too well. The air grew thick with sorrow and hopelessness. He was all too familiar with the well of tears reflected in their eyes. "Eventually, my drug use grew heavier until I found myself in the hospital one day nearly dead. That's when I got clean. At least the first time, anyway."

Michael closed his eyes as he recalled the events of that day. He could still feel the desperation that had surged through him as he rushed into the bathroom and slammed the door. The needle glistened as it slowly pushed into his vein. Seconds later, euphoria flooded through him, vanquishing his darkness. He could breathe again.

The next thing he remembered was being rushed into the hospital on a gurney. As his body convulsed violently, he was dimly aware of the dead man walking behind the group of emergency personnel attending to him. Blood flowed from a bullet hole in his forehead as he reached out to Michael, desperate for help.

Dr. Madison's voice suddenly brought him back to the present. "You're not alone, Michael," she said. "I think it's safe to say that everyone here has had a setback or two in their recovery. The important part is that we keep pushing forward."

A few members of the group murmured their agreement, giving Michael the strength to keep going. "It worked for a while. I stayed clean for nearly six months. The nightmares disappeared, and I finally felt like I had control of my life again. I should've known it wouldn't last."

"And why do you say that?"

"Because, when it happened again, it was worse than before. It felt like my skull was on fucking fire twenty-four-seven, and nothing I did could stop it. I finally tried to end it all myself. If it wasn't for my girlfriend, I wouldn't be here today."

Dr. Madison grew quiet for a moment as she looked at the broken man sitting before them. "I'm sorry, Michael. But I'm glad you're here."

"I wish I could say the same thing," Michael replied.

Dr. Madison looked around the group. "Who else is glad

that Michael's here with us today?"

Everyone raised their hand except for Lexi. She jumped to her feet and jabbed a finger at Michael, her expression full of hatred. "What gives you the right to be here, you fucking bastard? You use your 'bad dreams' as an excuse, but the real problem is that you're weak and pathetic. Too weak to even fucking kill yourself the right way!"

Michael looked at Lexi speechless, while Dr. Madison rose from her chair.

"Lexi!" Dr. Madison snapped. "That's no way to talk to Michael. It's not his fault he has no idea what's going on here."

Dr. Madison turned to Michael. Her head shook back and forth vigorously for a few seconds, until the flesh from her face loosened and fell to the floor, revealing a demonic visage underneath. Her red skin glistened with fresh blood, her eyes were black ink wells of the darkest evil, and a wide mouth full of razor-sharp teeth smiled at him. "It's time for you to see what real Hell feels like, Michael!"

Michael screamed as he turned and ran for the door, nearly falling over the chair. The otherworldly snarls and growls behind him told him she wasn't the only Hell-spawned nightmare after him. He heard the other demons behind him scream as they parted ways with their human forms, becoming monsters.

He dashed for his car with a surge of panic, feeling the wind whip his face as he ran faster than he ever thought possible. His heart thudded in his chest and his lungs gasped for air. He was twenty yards from escape, when demonic Lexi flung herself from the second-floor window and landed on the roof of his car, denting it with a loud crunch and sending shards of glass flying.

Michael's only hope for escape now lived in the dense

forest surrounding the small, secluded church. Immediately, he changed course and sped forward, hoping to find sanctuary among the trees.

He sprinted through the hellish woods, feeling the razor-sharp claws of branches and vines slicing his skin and splashing his blood on the dark soil. He could hear the demonic hissing and growling of his hunters behind him, closing in on him like a tornado. Suddenly, a monstrous root burst from the ground and ensnared his ankles, hurling him to the forest floor. He barely had time to scream before he was devoured by the beasts. The claws of the demons ripped into Michael's flesh, spilling his blood in a gruesome display.

As Michael cried out, a bright light exploded from him. Angry cries and torturous shrieks flew from the demon's mouths as the light engulfed them. Once it had subsided, he stood up and looked around to find all the members of the group lying on the ground dead, each one back in their original form with their eyes burned out. He dropped to his knees alone and afraid, his soul crying out to be saved from his nightmare.

Dr. Madison's voice suddenly snapped Michael back to reality. "Who else is glad that Michael is here with us today?"

Michael looked around the room in a panic. Everything was back to normal. The demons were gone, their unholy visages replaced by the original group members. Dr. Madison was back to her normal business-like self. Even the musty smell of the classroom returned.

He felt a sudden and intense burning on his right hand. When he looked down, he was shocked to see blood gushing from a deep and jagged wound that slashed the back of his hand, soaking his skin and splattering on the floor. He felt a surge of fear and pain, and without thinking, he leaped from his chair and bolted from the room, his face contorted in horror.

Michael rushed down the hall toward the small bathroom at the end and burst through the door. Blood turned the white porcelain of the sink a bright shade of red for a moment before the water from the faucet washed it down the drain.

As he ran the cut under the water, he looked at his reflection in the mirror. For a split second, the scene changed, and he saw the bodies on the ground again, smoke rising in a steady stream from the earth surrounding them, their hollow eyes screaming at him, asking him why? Then the reflection returned to normal.

Michael clung to the sink's edge, his chest heaving as he wept bitterly. He felt a surge of despair wash over him, drowning him in sorrow. As the darkness flooded over him, he wondered how long before it consumed it completely?

Author Bio

Scott Dokey is a creative force whose storytelling spans across writing, filmmaking, and visual art, delivering haunting, immersive experiences. Growing up in the shadow of Notre Dame's Golden Dome, Scott discovered early on the magic of turning a blank page into a captivating work of art. This love for creation only grew, leading him to explore writing and filmmaking, with a special focus on horror and the supernatural. His novels, including the Savage Apocalypse series, and the acclaimed *Hellish* series (*Tortured Souls, The Chosen, Unholy Religion,* and *Vizibir*), have cemented his place as a master of dark, psychological terror, where human fears are confronted with unrelenting force.

Scott's career isn't just about writing; he's an award-winning screenwriter who has produced and directed several short films, along with a no-budget feature that showcases his resourcefulness and vision. His dedication to the indie film scene is highlighted by his previous role as president of Mid-America Filmmakers, where he helped foster new talent and bold ideas. As with his novels, his films create unsettling atmospheres where the supernatural meets real-world anxieties.

Now living in Southern California with his wife, Jennifer, and their daughter, Kaylee, Scott enjoys the extreme contrasts of desert life—the blistering 120° summers balanced by the bliss of an 85° winter. His life and work continue to push the boundaries of what horror can achieve across multiple mediums. For more about Scott's creative journey, you can visit his website at www.scottdokey.com.

www.ingramcontent.com/pod-product-compliance
Lightning Source LLC
Chambersburg PA
CBHW031203310726
48969CB00001B/200